Readers love
the Long Con Adventures
by AMY LANE

The Mastermind

"This story is a prime example of a highly
complicated long con complete with a family of the
heart, a reunion of two souls destined to be together
forever, and Revenge with a capital R."
—Rainbow Book Review

"This new series is going to be wonderful… I'm
already jonesing for the next."
—Paranormal Romance Guild

The Muscle

"This is an exciting novel, both for its terrific
adventure and the romantic love story."
—Love Bytes

By Amy Lane

Published by DREAMSPINNER PRESS
www.dreamspinnerpress.com

By Amy Lane (cont.)

Published by DREAMSPINNER PRESS
www.dreamspinnerpress.com

The Driver

AMY LANE

DREAMSPINNER
PRESS

Published by
DREAMSPINNER PRESS

5032 Capital Circle SW, Suite 2, PMB# 279,
Tallahassee, FL 32305-7886 USA
www.dreamspinnerpress.com

This is a work of fiction. Names, characters, places, and incidents either
are the product of author imagination or are used fictitiously, and any
resemblance to actual persons, living or dead, business establishments,
events, or locales is entirely coincidental.

The Driver
© 2022 Amy Lane

Cover Art
© 2022 L.C. Chase
http://www.lcchase.com
Cover content is for illustrative purposes only and any person depicted
on the cover is a model.

Mass Market Paperback ISBN: 978-1-64108-261-7
Trade Paperback ISBN: 978-1-64405-987-6
Digital ISBN: 978-1-64405-986-9
Mass Market Paperback published May 2022
v. 1.0

Printed in the United States of America
∞
This paper meets the requirements of
ANSI/NISO Z39.48-1992 (Permanence of Paper).

So my husband picked me up from the airport after a trip to St. Louis, and all I could talk about was how insane the drivers were there and how happy I was to get back to where stoplights are more than hints, scents in the air, and the merest whispers of suggestions. Also, I was super happy to see my husband. So here's to all the people who obey the traffic rules so the Chuck's of this world can drive right by us to save the day. And here's to Mate, who keeps picking me up from the airport and listening to me talk about goofy things. Also Mary, the kids, the dogs, the cats, the friends, the colleagues, the people who listen to me ramble…. All of you make writing possible.

Growin' Up for Good Luck Chuck

Ten Years Ago

"CHARLIE. I'M sorry, Charlie, I didn't have anyone else to tell!"

Charles Calder—also known as Chuck—gasped in dismay and opened the door to his dorm room to let Maggie Siddons in.

She looked terrible.

Maggie had been Chuck's college try at heterosexuality in his freshmen year. The sex had been unremarkable—but not regrettable. She and Chuck had become each other's plus-ones during visits home and at fraternity mixers. For Chuck, Maggie had been an easy way to not have to tell his parents that he was gay, although Chuck's parents seemed to be happily oblivious and not particularly interested in his love life. For Maggie, Chuck had been an easy way to not have to answer any questions about why she wasn't seeing anybody right now.

But Maggie—who had pale bronze skin, charming cheekbones, and spiral ringlets that all added up to her being one of the prettiest, most popular girls at their small midwestern university—didn't look pretty and adorable right now.

That pale bronze skin was showing purple, and it was swollen under her eyes and along her jaw. Her eye itself was showing brick red, and she had a split over her eyebrow that would scar. Her body—tight and athletic—wasn't moving too well, and Chuck tried to still the hammering of his heart as he took her in.

"Maggie, oh dear God!"

She threw herself into his arms and began to sob.

It took her half an hour to get the story out—but Chuck had it figured out long before she did. She'd been seen flirting with some dork named Kyle. Jock, not dumb but lazy. At first, Chuck thought Maggie would see through the guy and his pathetic, "Help me, Maggie, only you can tutor me out of obscurity!" schtick, but everybody had their blind spot. Chuck's mother's blind spot was his father's infidelity, and his father's blind spot was the contempt his children held for him because of it. Maggie's blind spot was apparently blond, entitled Kyle Miller, and while Chuck hadn't liked the guy, it wasn't like he could just beat the crap out of Miller because Chuck had a bad feeling about him.

Well, apparently Chuck needed to trust his bad feelings more, because Maggie had said stop when Miller said go, and Miller said, "Fuck me, you dumb bitch," and Maggie had barely gotten away.

Chuck looked at his friend, who had cheerfully bared her soul to him from the beginning of their doomed relationship, and who'd forgiven him for not being that into girls. At that moment, Chuck decided that Kyle Miller was going to be the one who wished he'd gotten away.

"Charlie, you can't hurt him," Maggie hiccupped. "He'll kill you. He and all his dumb jock assholes will kill you. You know it. Their fathers will get them off because they have money and—"

"Oh, darlin'," Chuck said. "It's not like I'm all that breakable, right?" He was, in fact, decked. He loved physical exercise as much as he loved studying. Didn't particularly have any ambition, and there wasn't a competitive bone in his body, but he did love doing things simply for the sake of doing them—like a zillion bench presses until his muscles ached, and then a zillion more. It wasn't as much fun as a blow job, no, but there was still a certain visceral satisfaction to be had.

But even Chuck knew you couldn't face off with an entire football team for visceral satisfaction.

But that didn't mean he didn't have a plan.

It involved some sodium bicarbonate and some vinegar and then one extra ingredient of a slightly more incendiary nature.

All he needed to do was cut class one day, sneak into Kyle's room in the frat house, and put everything in cups that he placed upside down in Kyle's toilet tank. Everything would be fine… until Kyle flushed.

Then—God willing—the toilet would explode.

Hopefully all over Kyle, the giant piece of shit, because look what he'd done to Maggie!

Chuck planned it carefully. He didn't want Kyle to *die*, but he did hope he'd be hurt. And embarrassed. And made small. Because Maggie was a force larger than life, and that's what Kyle had done to her.

It was bad enough that they couldn't even report him to campus police for fear of reprisals from Kyle's father, who was a state senator and on the board of trustees for the college—but now Maggie was afraid to cross campus by herself, and had taken to sleeping in Chuck's room at night. Chuck didn't begrudge her one second of safety, but he did (as he told his blowjob buddy) sort of miss having his own room.

He had also put a plan of reprisal and humiliation into play, as he attempted to tell his blowjob buddy right after he'd set it up.

His blowjob buddy might have had more to say about the matter—questions about what he'd done, perhaps—but Chuck had been mid-blowjob at the time. Dan Torres was the local ROTC instructor and on-campus Army recruiter, and while he was very *in* the closet, he was also very *out*-spoken about his appreciation of Chuck's skills.

Lucky for both of them, Dan had a small office in the back of the physical fitness offices, with a door that locked and a television mounted on the far wall that they turned on to mask their noises.

So Dan was not exactly *quiet* about Chuck's plan for revenge on Kyle Miller, but he wasn't exactly articulate, either.

"You… oh God… you… you… *holy fucking God! You blew up his toilet?*"

Chuck pulled back far enough to wipe his mouth off on his shoulder. "Yeah—that's what I was trying to tell you. How did you know?"

Suddenly Dan was tucking himself into his pants and reaching for the remote control. "Chuck—man—look! You *blew up his fucking toilet!*"

Chuck gave a little whimper of dissatisfaction—it had been his turn for the blowjob next, and he was *hard*, dammit! He'd been concentrating on the blowjob, and the TV was white noise in the background. What was the big deal now?

Then he registered Dan's horrified fascination and turned to look at the screen.

There stood the hated jock frat house, Sigma Eta Phi… except it was bursting out at the seams—literally. It sat crooked on its foundations, the windows broken from the strain, and a sort of pink foam was oozing out of one window. There were ambulances, firetrucks, and one very dazed-looking Kyle Miller being taken away from the scene with his clothing in tatters and what looked to be second-degree burns on his ass.

Chuck sucked air in through his teeth. "Wow. That did *not* turn out like I thought it would."

Dan turned to him in disbelief. "Chuck, seriously? Are you kidding me? You destroyed the frat house! You could have killed somebody! Do you know how bad this is?"

"Well, it says no fatalities, so, uhm, not as bad as it could be?" He gave a mean chuckle. "Think Miller's balls got a little crispy? Think it'll keep him from beating on the next girl who says no?"

Dan bent his head and massaged the back of his neck. "Chuck, you have got to fucking disappear, man. I mean, off the map. Canada or something. They are going to put you in *prison* for this much collateral damage."

Chuck was going to ask Dan how he knew Chuck would go to prison, when the reporter said, "Police are looking for this man in connection to what appears to be a horrible prank gone wrong." The picture they flashed was from Chuck's freshman year in high school, when he was all ears, teeth, and elbows, so not even his mother would recognize him, but still.

Chuck sucked air through his teeth. "You know, I'm telling you right now, prison does *not* work for me."

Dan gave a persecuted groan and tilted his head back so he now addressed the heavens. "How about the Iraqi desert, Chuck? How's that work for you? Because

I could get you to boot camp in a week. All you gotta do is pack up and lay low."

Chuck thought about it. "Yeah, can I blow shit up there?" His stomach was pretty tingly from seeing his handiwork on television. He wondered what it would be like to see that in person.

Dan gave him a long-suffering look. "Yeah, Chuck. I've got a buddy who recruits for the army. I'm pretty sure we can find a spot in munitions and transport for you in Iraq."

Chuck grinned at him. "Righteous! Want me to finish that blowjob now?" He shuddered. "I gotta tell you, I might go off in my pants just from the buzz of blowing up the frat house. That is some *hot* shit right there."

Dan—who wasn't a bad-looking guy, with dark hair and hazel eyes and a sort of wistful smile one didn't usually associate with the military—stared at Chuck in disbelief.

Chuck grinned easily, hoping for the best.

Dan shrugged and looked at the television, then looked at his watch, then looked at the pillow on the ground by his feet, and then looked at Chuck's grinning face again.

He undid the button on his khakis.

"Fan*tastic*!" Chuck said, sinking to his knees with all the enthusiasm of a kid with an ice cream.

Or a Good Luck Chuck getting himself some *luck.*

Three years and two months later

THE BAR in Cleveland was tacky—worn veneer, uncomfortable wooden booths, mashed red-felt carpet, vinyl stools that were held together with duct tape and ass juice, and shutters over the windows that stayed closed even in the middle of the day.

Which was good, because Chuck needed to drink and think and the reminder of time passing was only going to stress him out.

Iraq had been fun. Now, most people didn't see it that way, but Chuck had been put in charge of munitions and had put that two-quarters of a chemical engineering degree to good use. He'd also learned to drive pretty much everything—truck, Jeep, tank, motorcycle, small plane—to the point that if anybody had to transport a fuckton of something that would go boom if it got shaken or stirred, Chuck was the guy to call. He'd almost re-upped, because it felt like he had found his calling, but there was that whole following-orders thing.

Chuck really sucked at it.

He took all his tests and did all his drills and shot endless rounds into the desert target range, and he was pretty fucking good at all of it. But when his CO told him to stand up straighter, he put his hands in his pockets and slouched. He probably would have spent his entire stint in the brig, but dammit, people kept needing his skill set.

All his CO's hated him like poison—including the guy who had been assigned when he'd gotten his papers asking if he'd wanted to re-up. Nope—with this guy, Chuck would spend all his time in the brig. It had definitely been time to clear out.

Unfortunately, he'd been sleeping off his jetlag in a shitty hotel in Cleveland when he'd gotten word that his parents, who'd told him he could live at home for a month or two while he got his civilian legs back underneath him and found a job, had been killed in a car accident.

He'd arrived at the old homestead in time for the funeral after-party—and to see his sister get the thirty-day notice of foreclosure on his parents' home.

Daphne was living there too, waiting for her divorce to come through and trying to raise her infant son, Dougie, on her own. Chuck, jetlagged and sad, had walked into the house and been confronted by his sister, grief-stricken and desperate, falling apart in front of his parents' entire neighborhood association, while their older brother, Kevin, told her to suck it up and learn how to work for a living.

Chuck was pretty sure he hadn't broken Kevin's jaw, but that was only because he pulled the punch at the last second.

He wouldn't exactly say he'd *matured* in the desert, but being in charge of all that firepower had made him cognizant of how to use power so one did not blow up one's teammates. That restraint had bled into other areas of his life, and he was reasonably grateful it had saved his brother's life that morning.

Or at least his jaw.

After Kevin had gotten up and stormed out, Chuck and Daphne had had a long conversation about how much she needed to keep the house afloat, and how much their parents' insurance was, and what her living expenses had been to date.

Chuck had hugged her and left—mostly because there were mutters among the neighborhood mourners and extended family about calling the cops. But before he'd left, he'd promised her that he'd find a way to drum up the money.

He didn't have a plan. He didn't have any resources. All he had was a hotel room with pretty much everything he possessed in the world and this bar right here, which served him a beer once every forty-five minutes, the perfect interval in which to help him think.

After a couple of hours, the one thing—one thing—he knew beyond all certainty, was that the only way to get enough money to keep Daphne and her kid from getting evicted from their parents' house was probably illegal.

He closed his eyes on that thought and massaged the back of his neck, much like Dan Torres had done the day Chuck blew up the frat-house toilets.

The bartender shoved another beer at him, and Chuck blinked at it. "Thanks," he said, meeting the guy's eyes for the first time.

Ooh—not bad. A little older, thirties maybe, and a little paunchy, but he had a good-natured face. The kind of face you could trust, really.

"You thought it up yet?" the guy said, friendly-like.

"Thought what up?"

"That thing you been thinkin' since you got here."

Chuck grunted. "Not so much. World's oldest dilemma. How do you get money quick without ending up in prison even quicker."

The guy gave a brief nod. "See those guys over there?"

Chuck looked over his shoulder to where a bunch of guys who practically had Criminal spray-painted across their black windbreakers sat, huddled over a table with intense, angry faces.

"Yeah. They got money?"

Guy shook his head. "No. They got a plan, though—and they're short a driver. You know how to drive?"

Chuck made a low rumbling sound that passed for a chuckle. "Little bit."

Guy nodded. "Thought so. You may want to hit them up."

Chuck wasn't stupid. He knew that if someone needed a driver for something, it was usually an illegal sort of something. And he'd learned his lesson from blowing up those toilets. If you were going to do something that could get you removed from the entire free world for a while, it was a good idea to get your sex in *now*, while you could.

"You sure I can't hit you up instead?" he asked the bartender appraisingly.

The bartender gave him a heavy-lidded smile. "I get off in an hour," he said, voice low. "They got three days before they do their thing."

Chuck grinned. "Perfect," he said. "I'll be back here to walk you out in an hour."

And then he turned to where the "criminals" all sat, arguing with each other. He pulled up a cheap wooden chair and straddled it, leaning on the back, amused when all the guys in black windbreakers and balaclavas turned toward him in a panic.

"No worries, guys," he drawled. "Word on the street is, you fellas need some transportation. Believe it or not, this is your lucky day."

Four years later

TEXAS—CHUCK had lived there as a kid, but it seemed hotter and sweatier now.

God, the worst thing about hanging out with criminals wasn't the dishonesty—although that seemed inherent in the breed, at least in the bank robbers Chuck seemed to end up with. But he'd sort of taken it upon himself to steer them toward honesty, at least as thieves. It just made everything so much less bloody by the end.

He thought he'd been doing an okay job of being an ethical thief until the quiet corner of the garage where Carmichael Carmody was giving *Chuck* the blowjob for once, was suddenly not so quiet.

The corner itself—a sort of makeshift office with barriers to make a cubicle and a door, as well as a couple of fans—was in the back of the garage itself, and anybody entering, either from the bay door or the smaller door to the side of the shop, could be heard before they were seen. And that was exactly why Chuck and Carmichael were in that little corner.

Besides the fact that they were in Texas—and not the gay-friendly part of Texas—and what they were doing could probably get the shit beat out of them, Carmichael had a wife and three kids whom he adored, mostly, but he'd admitted shyly to Chuck that the only way he'd fathered three kids was to think about NASCAR racers in the nude. Chuck had been exchanging blowjobs with him ever since—it felt like a service to the needy, really, and Carmichael certainly was sweet and appreciative.

Of course the rest of Carmichael's family was so awful, living in the closet was practically a relief for the poor guy. Besides his brothers and their friends being a part of the he-man-gaybie-haters club, they were also bank robbers.

Dumb ones.

Chuck had been drafted from another group—he had a reputation by now, after eluding the police a couple of times and helping plan a few jobs that otherwise might have gotten sticky. He wouldn't have gone in with them—he didn't like Wilber Forth, Klamath Jones, or Angus and Scooter Carmody at all, not from the first moment Wilber had grabbed his arm with fingers trying to bruise and practically told him he'd be

driving for them because that was his job, wasn't it?
No, Chuck hadn't liked getting treated like a piece of
meat—but as he'd been about to pound Wilber into a
mound of plasma, he'd seen Carmichael in the corner
of the bar, shying away from the forward waitress and
looking miserable as fuck.

"Who's that?" he asked, interrupting Wilber's dia-
tribe about why Chuck absolutely had to work for him.

"That's Car-Car." Wilber had laughed rudely.
"He's gonna tune your ride, man, but he doesn't have
the nerves for anything else."

And that had decided Chuck, really. This kid needed a Chuck in his life—even if it was just to give him a
reason to come out of the closet and pay his wife alimo-
ny from anywhere but Erstwhile, Texas.

Of course, the more Chuck had gotten sucked into
Carmichael's life, the more he realized that Car-Car
couldn't desert his wife or his kids, and getting on a
plane out of Texas would leave him without a support
system—or a pot to piss in, because his shop was mort-
gaged to the hilt as it was.

The kid was well and truly trapped, Chuck figured.
The best he could do was give him a little bit of kindness and some happy moments, and maybe a few more
years of not getting the shit kicked out of him because
he turned those big brown eyes on the wrong guy.

That was what they were doing in the back of the
closed garage, the night breeze coming in through a
skylight overhead, Carmichael's mouth sweet and hard,
exactly the way Chuck liked it. Nothing like a good-
luck blowjob to make sure a job came off right.

Right then, Wilber and Klamath came barging in.

"Sh!" Klamath whispered. "You're going to get us
caught!"

"No," Wilber said, laughing rudely, "I'm gonna get those Carmody kids caught. You and me, I'm gonna get off scot-free!"

With that, he snagged a set of keys from a pegboard by the door and moved to the car, a basic model SUV, a little scuffed and very unremarkable, the kind of thing a soccer mom would haul her kids in. Chuck and Carmichael had long since pulled up Chuck's pants and dropped down behind the counter of the office. But even from their precarious hiding place, they could still hear Wilber and Klamath talking.

"What are you doing there?" Klamath asked urgently.

"Sabotaging the gas line," Wilber told him. "It'll take a while. We'll get there okay, but while Chuck's got it in idle, the car'll just die. Then you and me can take off in the burner car we've got parked around back, and everyone else'll get caught."

"Man, why would they give us all the cash?" Klamath demanded. "Your plan don't make no sense at all."

Wilber sucked in a breath. "Well, I guess it'll make sense if they're dead, won't it?"

Chuck met Carmichael's eyes under the counter, and he read the dreadful truth there.

Carmichael couldn't tell his brothers about this. He absolutely couldn't. Besides wanting to know what he was doing when Wilber and Klamath were sabotaging the car, they would flat out not believe him. Carmichael hadn't wanted to be in on the job in the first place. It was a big bank in a sizable town, and they were robbing it the day after paychecks went out, when there would be plenty of cash in the drawer. If Carmichael mentioned this to his brothers, they'd believe Wilber over Carmichael, and he'd be dead.

If he didn't mention it, he'd be there for the robbery, and Klamath and Wilber would shoot him.

If he survived the robbery, he'd be in prison, which might possibly be the safest option. But prison in Texas was no picnic.

Chuck couldn't help it. He looked Carmichael in the eyes and said, "Don't worry. I've got a plan."

Well, his plan had worked—and it hadn't. At the end of it, he'd driven off with the money from the job while Carmichael, Scooter, and Angus went to prison, and Klamath and Wilber went to big holes in the ground.

Chuck's plan had involved contacting someone he knew in the sheriff's department and making sure Carmichael and his brothers knew to lie down on the ground the minute they heard the bullhorn.

A sniper got Klamath and Wilber after Chuck had helped them load their car. And while Chuck didn't exactly mourn them, he'd abandoned Carmichael to prison, which hadn't set right with him. It didn't matter that he'd taken the money and invested it. When Carmichael got out in two years, he'd have enough money to set his wife and kids up right and still get the hell out of Dodge and live a good life. But so, sadly, would his brothers. And it had meant leaving a friend behind.

He'd run the plan by Carmichael that morning, before Carmichael's brothers swung by to pick him up. The kid hadn't hesitated. He'd told Chuck prison was better than death, so Chuck had done the deed with Carmichael's blessing. But God, it had hurt. Chuck had admitted—to himself, if not to Carmichael—that it would have hurt a lot worse if Carmichael hadn't gotten out of there alive.

A tough decision, and an opportunity to get out of the life he'd accidentally fallen into.

Chuck lived simply, for the most part. He liked high-rise apartments but didn't mind if they were small and simply furnished. He liked fast cars, but Carmichael had taught him enough about cars to know fast wasn't always expensive. And he liked his clothes comfortable and not flashy. With a little bit of education on the stock market and some good investments, he managed to quadruple the money he got from the bank job and set the brothers up with bank accounts full of untraceably laundered cash.

Carmichael had written him a carefully worded letter, saying that his wife and kids lived in a house now, instead of an apartment, and that she had promised to be faithful to him while he was in jail.

Well, Carmichael had always wanted to do right by her, Chuck figured regretfully. He wished the guy well—he'd done his part and more than.

Of course, Angus and Scooter hadn't written him a damned thing after he'd sent them their account numbers and information. He wasn't sure if they were too dumb to realize how lucky they'd been to get out of that bullshit alive, or if he was going to have to live his life looking over his shoulder once they got out of prison. But that would be a while. They were in for five-to-ten because, unlike their brother, it had *not* been their first offense.

Eighteen Months Later

GOD, CHICAGO was ice fucking cold in the winter. But it was still better than Texas.

He'd told himself that he'd left Texas because he didn't want the po-po to connect him to the bank job gone wrong. His sheriff buddy had wanted Wilber and Klamath and hadn't cared so much about the bank-insured money Chuck had gotten away with, but still—he wasn't the only deputy near Erstwhile who'd be on the lookout. So, no Texas for Chuck. Sure. That was it. He was afraid he might get busted.

It was a lie he told himself to avoid thinking about the brown of Car-Car's eyes as he'd turned and given Chuck a last forlorn wave before marching off to the bank—and to prison.

But Chuck had sworn off bank jobs—no more of that noise. He'd made his nut with investments, and could probably live comfortably off his portfolio as long as he didn't go too hog wild, but he hated being bored. So he enrolled in school again, figuring maybe he'd finish up his degree, or maybe learn something else. He *had* a job, he figured, but learning things like art history and regular history and economics, well, *that* could be a fine hobby.

And it turned out there were enough dumb criminals in Chicago for him to never be bored.

Which was how he'd met Josh Salinger.

He'd been intent on mischief—not the criminal kind, nothing that would hurt anybody, but he needed to inflict a little bit of karmic revenge on a douchebag. He figured that along with transportation and munitions, karmic revenge had become sort of his calling, and it was sure calling his name now.

He entered the parking garage casually, even though he'd planned for this. Went to the fourth floor, where he knew the asshole kept his Porsche, ignoring the cute kid in the elevator with him. Chuck wasn't trading blowjobs or anything else these days, and the kid in the elevator—brown eyes, dark brown hair, neat as a pixie and twice as tight—was depressingly young. Besides, Chuck had some payback in mind this time, and a kid holding what looked like a grocery bag in his hands was not on his list.

The elevator door opened, and Chuck strode over to the Porsche in its customary spot, little radio fob in his hand. The fob was something he'd developed in the military—an electronic master key allowing him to pilot any of the vehicles in the auto bay. When he'd started driving for bank robbers, he'd teamed up with an electronics whiz and a dedicated car thief to come up with a handheld version of his own.

The fob worked, but he knew that car-alarm companies were constantly trying to find new cryptocodes to keep car thieves out. He kept in contact with Teeter the electronics whiz and Skinny the car thief, though—they'd been so excited about the concept he'd come up with, they'd kept him eyeball-deep in prototypes ever since.

This one didn't let him down. In fact it hadn't let him down the last six times he'd tried it on this car.

The car beeped as he disabled the alarm, and he gave a sigh of relief, sliding into the Porsche and stretching luxuriously before looking around.

Oops! There was a new security camera on the visor, and another one located behind the pressure plate on the steering wheel, and—oh, hey—he felt carefully and located the dye pack under the seat, ready to blast him when he moved the seat back.

Pity.

The douche-nugget who owned the champagne-colored ode to ridiculous spending was about five six, and Chuck was six three. Ah well, no luxury ride today.

He was so involved with figuring out how to maneuver with his knees up to his chin, that the opening of the passenger door almost caused his heart to jump out of his chest.

"Dye pack under the driver's seat?" The pretty boy with the dark hair and eyes stuck his head inside. "Here, get out of the seat and I can disable it for you. You weren't planning on stealing it, right? Just relocating it in the parking garage, like you've done for the last two weeks?"

Chuck stared at the kid. "Well, uhm, yeah."

"I heard Gaetz talking, you know. Asshole's been whining about his precious gross car since you started doing it to him. Revenge, right?"

Chuck opened his mouth, then closed it while those doll-bright eyes stared at him and the kid waited patiently for his response.

"Not for me," he finally croaked.

"Yeah, I know. For Professor Ledbetter, right? I sit in the back row during class, but I was there that day."

Chuck tried to swallow his anger and couldn't. "It was a shitty way to be outed," he said, referring to the day Toby Gaetz had looked at the grade on his latest paper and sneered, "A D-? I don't think so. My dad is on the board of trustees, you know, and he doesn't like faggots."

Chuck had been appalled—and the gentle sixty-ish Dr. Ledbetter had been almost in tears. Chuck had stalked out of the classroom hell-bent on finding a way to torment Gaetz for being an asshole, and this kid….

Chuck frowned, remembering that this kid, wearing an adorable little fedora and a leather jacket that made him look like a combination of Frank Sinatra and Fred Astaire, went to talk to the professor earnestly as everybody left.

"I told him my father was Felix Salinger," the kid said, "and he really hated bigots. Don't you remember? Torrance Grayson ran that series on homophobia in academia the next week?"

Chuck sucked in a breath, stunned. "You did that?" he asked.

"Well, Torrance Grayson did that," he answered, referring to the beautiful, openly gay anchor for the Salinger News Network, Chicago's answer to CNN. "But yeah, my dad told Gaetz's dad that if anything bad happened to Ledbetter because of his son's nasty mouth, they'd kill, fry, and eat the current board of directors for the university, and they'd do it live on the air." The kid gave a sweet smile. "My dad is pretty much the greatest guy on the planet. Gaetz may not be so loud now, but he's still spewing bile about Ledbetter—or he was, until his precious Porsche started disappearing. I heartily approve. In fact, I've got a wrinkle, but I need you to get up so I can disconnect the dye pack first, okay?"

Numb, Chuck finally managed to get out of the vehicle, and he stood back, watching as the kid produced a tiny tool kit from the sleeve of his natty black leather jacket.

It took him less than a minute, and he was humming the whole time. When he'd finished, he gestured for Chuck to get in and then ran around the front of the vehicle and got into the passenger's seat. As Chuck put his seat belt on, he watched the kid do the same.

"Didn't you have groceries?" he asked.

"Hm? Oh yeah, they're in the back. Don't worry about them. Hey, my last class of the day is over. How about yours?"

Chuck nodded. "Yeah, nothing but weekend. Why?"

"Well, I happen to know they're about to put new cameras in the parking garage. The only reason you've gotten away with this so far is that the old ones were disabled about a month ago while they fixed the system. Anyway, this is your last day to do this, and Gaetz is about to be locked in the bathroom for—" His pocket buzzed, and he pulled his phone out of his impossibly tight black jeans before reading the text and smiling. "—three, four hours. How do you feel about taking this thing for a spin?"

Chuck grinned at him. "Kid, what's your name?"

"Josh. Josh Salinger."

Chuck put out his hand. "Chuck Calder."

They shook hands. "Once around the city, Jeeves, and then we can go for pizza."

They bullshitted on the drive around the city, talked about the class and cars and ex-boyfriends. Chuck might have let some of his more colorful past exploits escape, but it was so easy to talk to this kid who harbored no judgments. When the gas gauge showed nearly empty, Chuck returned the car to the parking garage—in a totally different place, of course—and he and Josh got out of the Porsche. Then Chuck followed Josh to his own vehicle, a roadster as natty as his outfit.

"Nice," Chuck said. "I've got a Chevy myself."

Josh grinned. "Parked here, or did you take the L?"

"I've got an apartment in the suburbs. I take the train in."

"Well, I'm driving back to the suburbs after I pick my friend up from in front of the campus."

Chuck eyed the interior of the roadster skeptically. "Will your friend fit?"

"He crawls through ventilation shafts as a hobby. The back seat will be fine."

Chuck laughed and let any hope of getting into Josh's pants fade into the wind. That was fine, though. He'd had plenty of lovers, but he'd never had a friend he could talk with about art history, philosophy, and car theft. Josh was the little brother he never knew he needed.

As Josh pulled the roadster out of the parking garage, Chuck realized Josh had forgotten the little plastic bag of groceries he'd had in his fist when he'd gotten into the Porsche. It wasn't until three weeks later, when he heard Gaetz complaining about how somebody had left a bag of rotting fish in the center console and the car was practically undrivable now that he knew what Josh had done.

By then, Chuck realized that he might never sleep with Josh Salinger... but he would surely die for him.

Pale Faces

LUCIUS BROADSTONE didn't like hospitals, but he supposed nobody really did. The only people who had good memories of a hospital were those who'd had children, and usually those memories got much better once the parents brought the baby home. Lucius had spent too many hours in hospitals—as a kid, getting bones set, or as an adult, watching his mother die. And he couldn't forget all those silent hours with his brother, because neither of them had words to cheer the other up after a lifetime spent learning to be quiet in the most brutal of ways.

But like the hospital or not, Lucius had been called into the chemo ward in one to do business, and while he hated the venue, he was appreciative of the time these people were giving him when they so obviously had other things to deal with.

The boy in the hospital bed looked pale, young, and ill; there was no other way to put it. Josh Salinger had been diagnosed with leukemia earlier that summer, and while Lucius understood the prognosis was hopeful, the boy—who was scarcely twenty-one as Lucius understood it—was going to have some hard weeks ahead of him.

Unfortunately, Josh and his family were the very people he had to ask a favor of, when they had already done more for him than he probably deserved.

"You brought me flowers?" Josh said, brown eyes lighting up in amusement. "That's amazing! We're not even dating. We're not even *going* to date, and you brought me flowers. I may never date again."

The wraith-thin young man sitting on the bed next to Josh—Josh's best friend since they were practically in diapers, Lucius gathered—took the flowers and breathed in lightly.

"You'll never date again anyway because you're stupid and you got sick. And you have no sense of smell right now, so I'm claiming the flowers because I *have* a boyfriend, and I need to brag about that."

"Grace, give me those." A brawny arm belonging to a red-headed drawling cowboy swept out, snagging the flowers before Grace—whose real name was Dylan—could object. "Thank you, Lucius. I'll put these in water and we can *all* enjoy them."

Lucius gazed helplessly at Charles Calder and tried not to whimper. God, it was so unfair. Long rangy body, brawny arms and a chest as wide as a barn, and that didn't even touch on the auburn hair and green eyes, or the lantern jaw and the lean mouth. Chuck Calder was every rich boy's dream of a bad boy with a killer smile.

And God help him, Lucius wanted him. So bad. It wasn't even fair. But besides the occasional flirty wink and some really enjoyable banter, nothing about Charles screamed "serious." And as the CEO of a company struggling not to go under and of some other enterprises of questionable legality, perhaps, but great importance to the people those enterprises served—Lucius could not afford to be anything but serious.

He didn't have *time* to go around sweeping charming Charles Calder off his feet, dammit! But Charles didn't seem to need any time to do the same thing to Lucius. Oh no. That happened for Charles as easily as *breathing.*

Speaking of… breathe in, breathe out. Remember: manners and appearance.

"Thank you, Charles," Lucius said with a little nod of his head. "That's nice of you."

"Well, they're keeping me around for my charm and good looks. Figure I've got to deliver." Charles followed that up with a wink, even as he was setting the flowers on the counter by the sink. Josh had been having a hard time keeping food down with the chemo—he'd gotten dangerously dehydrated with his last dose, so they were keeping him in for observation after this treatment. Lucius could tell that his family and friends had tried to make this room home for him. A colorful throw on the bed, some stuffed animals that had obviously been provided by Grace, and flowers, lots of them, brightened the place up for what was probably only a two-day stay.

But Josh's parents could probably have afforded the entire wing of the hospital to themselves, if they'd wanted it. Looking at the faces of the boy's mother and the man Josh called Uncle Danny, though, Lucius thought that his parents would probably have given all of their fortune if only Josh would get well.

"I was hoping to find Felix around," Lucius said, trying not to sound censorious. Felix Salinger, Josh's father, owned the local network news station and was purported to be one of the richest and most powerful men in Chicago. The perception around town was that Felix held the purse strings and controlled the direction the family took. Lucius, though, had seen the family—and he used the term loosely, because Charles Calder and the other people in the Salinger orbit did not appear to be related by blood—working together in something that could be best described as syzygy as opposed to patriarchy. So perhaps presenting his case to Julia Dormer-Salinger, Felix's ex-wife, and Benjamin "Danny" Morgan, his current lover, would hold some weight.

"I'm afraid Felix had to be at the office today," Julia said, understanding in her porcelain-blue eyes. "We're trying to balance ourselves so there's somebody here should Josh need us, and I'm afraid Felix drew the short straw today."

Josh mock-coughed. "Babysitting. Babysitting."

And Dylan "Grace" Li was having none of it. "Yes, we're babysitting you. If you hate it, get better."

Josh narrowed his eyes. "I liked you better when you told the rest of us to fuck off. Can we go back to doing that?"

"No, because I like being grown-up enough to lord it over you. Get a job, find a boyfriend, and stop wasting our time in the cancer center. I'm getting bored."

"Piss off. I'm enjoying the rest."

"Then you take what you can get. Now, you're the one who said to listen to the man, so shut up and listen."

Lucius smiled at them, enjoying their banter, and then he noticed their hands clenched tightly, and he realized Josh was in a great deal of pain.

He sucked in a breath and adjusted to the idea that his usual smooth boardroom theatrics weren't necessary here; in light of the circumstances, they'd be downright rude. Without another word, he pulled a stool up behind him and scooted closer to the bed, addressing Benjamin Morgan and Julia Dormer-Salinger across the bed, Josh in the center of the it, and Grace perched on the edge.

Charles Calder, he noticed, was leaning against the doorframe slightly behind the bed, almost as though he was a security guard or hired muscle, which didn't surprise Lucius at all. The last time he'd seen Charles Calder, the man had kissed him senseless, disrupted a formal gala, and dismantled an explosive device all in the same evening. Something told Lucius *that* Mr. Calder would be all ears for whatever the rest of the group was planning.

"So," he said into what was obviously a waiting silence. "When we first met, I was trying to track down stolen tech that was bleeding my company dry."

"Did you find the internal source that was providing information to Sergei Kadjic?" Benjamin Morgan asked.

Lucius nodded. "Yes. It was much easier once the distributor was taken care of. We just looked for an employee looking jumpy as fuck and trying to find a buyer for his information. Done. The guy is in custody, and he's looking at five-to-ten, and my company is running slightly better," he said. But while he kept his voice smooth, it was the "slightly" that bothered the hell out of him.

That wasn't lost on the other people in the room.

"Slightly?" Josh said. "Did you hear that, Uncle Danny? He said after all we went through to get rid of Sergei Kadjic, his company is running 'slightly' better."

"I did hear it, dear boy. I am, in fact, overwhelmed by Mr. Broadstone's praise. What about you, Julia? Are you swoony yet?"

Julia Dormer-Salinger, an impeccably beautiful woman with blond hair swept up off her nape, a charming summer frock in white, and a thin cardigan in pale pink to ward off the hospital chill, fanned her face in an imaginary hot flash.

"Almost, Danny. I may need ice."

Lucius contained a smile, but he was the only one. Josh, Grace, and even Charles Calder all let out smirks. Charles may have even given a soft snort. These people surely did enjoy keeping each other amused.

He thought of Josh and Dylan's clenched hands and decided he'd better kick things in gear.

"My tech is still leaking, but that's not the worst part," he said bluntly. "The worst part is *how* it's leaking and what's being taken with it. Thomas Daren, the guy who was handing off projects to Kadjic right and left, did so one project at a time. He'd smuggle the information out in a thumb drive, or later on, a small chip. Old-school stuff. But what's happening now isn't a project or a discrete unit of things. It's random. Someone will buy up stock before I was about to, or one of my supply chains will be disrupted but not another. It's like somebody is getting random bites of information from my computer servers and using it to sabotage me. But that's not the worst part either."

"Really?" Julia said, sounding fully concerned. "Because that's pretty frightening. Someone with a purpose is easy to find, Mr. Broadstone. Somebody with a random vendetta is much harder to track down."

"I know it," Lucius said grimly. "I've reorganized my office twice and replaced all of my hard drives at the administration level. Each time the disruptions stopped for about a week, and then they'd start up again. It's like somebody is gathering data from the ether, and we just can't figure out where to plug the leak."

"But you said that's not the worst thing," Josh Salinger said, his voice hoarse. Lucius took a deep breath and tried not to look at the young man's pale face. God, he didn't want to be here, distracting this nice family from taking care of someone they were obviously devoted to. Trying desperately not to think about his own younger brother.

"No," Lucius said. "The worst thing is Caraway House."

"Is that like Cassowary House, with shitty Australian birds?" Grace asked randomly.

"Uncle Danny thought it was a place for drunk poets," Josh said, smiling through cracked lips.

Benjamin "Danny" Morgan shrugged. "There are worse charities," he said, smiling fondly at both of them before turning fox-clever eyes on Lucius. "But that's not what Caraway House is, am I right?"

Earlier that summer, Danny and Felix had researched Lucius with a thoroughness that should have made them enemies. And it might have, but the first thing they'd offered Lucius was help to keep Caraway House afloat, which was one of the reasons Lucius was trusting them now.

"Sadly no," Lucius confirmed, and in spite of how hard everybody was working not to make this place too serious, his own expression grew grave. "Caraway House is a shelter for abused women and their children. It is, by necessity, off the radar. Ex-boyfriends, ex-husbands, stalkers—there are a lot of people who would like to know where Caraway House is and how to get access to it. I've got three different locations, one in Peoria, the city proper, one in Chicago, and one on the far corner of the campus that houses Broadstone Industries. By any sort of road, the two buildings are a good four or five miles apart. I doubt if anybody working at the tech campus knows about Caraway House, and I've worked hard to keep it that way."

"You've had problems there?" Julia asked, concerned.

"I have security," Lucius said. "But we've been fending off cyberattacks at least once every other night for the last week. The Broadstone campus facility is for women whose husbands have resources. I know the common assumption is that domestic abuse is a problem of poverty, and to a certain extent, that's very, very true. But it's also a problem of power, and often the rich and powerful men who abuse their wives don't have anybody richer or more powerful to deny them. Caraway House is meant to be the protective arms that give women a chance to get on their feet and take back their lives. Only we can't do that if we're afraid to let them past the gates in case somebody's abuser is lying in wait and our security let them through."

"Darling!" Julia Dormer-Salinger's voice was almost... panicked. And while Lucius knew Danny Morgan was her husband's lover—fiancé, in fact, if what the papers said held water—Lucius was not surprised when Danny's hand, nimble and quick, closed over hers. Danny, who was perhaps two or so inches taller than Julia, leaned over and kissed her temple. "We'll protect them, sweetheart," he said softly. "That's why we're us." When he spoke next, it was to Lucius. "Do you think the attacks on Caraway House have anything to do with your other cyber leaks?"

Lucius ran a shaking hand over his face. "I'm thinking yes, but I only have a gut feeling to go with that. I... I've been chasing my tail here," he admitted. "First, there was the stolen projects. Then there was finding my tech was being sold to a mobster, and in the background, this was going on. But it wasn't critical until this last week, when Caraway House was hacked repeatedly. I am so scared. Those women put their faith in me, you understand?" The only reason he hadn't dismantled his father's tech company from the ground up, by hand, was because it funded this endeavor. The irony of that man's legacy going to fund a safety net for women like Lucius's mother was the savage nectar that kept Lucius from simply throwing it to the wolves.

"Of course we do," Danny said, and then to Lucius's surprise, he turned to the sick young man in the bed. "Josh, we're a go with this one, right?"

"Absolutely, Uncle Danny," Josh said through a gruff throat. Then he yawned. "But if you're going to plan, make it quick. I'm afraid I'm not going to be awake for long."

"Moron," Grace said. "You're going to fall asleep, and they're going to leave me with you and go plan, and then when you wake up, I'll brief you. Who do you think you are, cancer boy? Super Josh?"

Josh chuckled rustily. "If only," he murmured and then closed his eyes.

Lucius looked at him in dismay. Was that it? Was that the end of his audience?

"Good idea, Grace," Charles Calder said softly. "Do you mind sitting with him? Danny, Julia, and I can take Mr. Broadstone to the cafeteria. I'm *dying* for a soft serve. How about you?"

"Milkshake," Grace said. "Lots of whipped cream." And then he curled up on his side next to Josh and pulled out his phone before looking over his shoulder. "Now all of you go away and let him nap." His imperious tone softened when he looked at Julia and Danny. "This is my job. It's why you bring me. So I can make him smile. Go do important things, okay?"

Julia bent down, squeezed Grace's shoulder and kissed his temple, her eyes red-rimmed and bright. "You *are* important, Dylan. Thank you. You make this entire ordeal better." She straightened and traced a fingertip under each eye, fixing her makeup. "Shall we go?" she said. "Danny, I'm afraid you're buying the soft serve. Grace just lifted my wallet out of my purse, and I'm too fond of him right now to ask for it back."

Grace smiled at her and slid the wallet under his cheek. Lucius did a slow blink, not understanding this family in the least, before Charles slid open the door of the room and gestured them all out like the gentleman Lucius was almost sure he was not.

They reached the end of the corridor, and Julia said, completely composed, "I'll be just a moment. I'm going to use the ladies' room."

She disappeared into the alcove with the restrooms, and Danny said, "I'll wait for her here, gentlemen. If you two wish to go on to the cafeteria, we'll be there shortly." They continued out of the chemo ward, and Lucius had time to note the plants and skylights in the one-story building that was set slightly apart from the rest of the hospital.

"Why do they do that?" he murmured to himself. "Not put it in the main building?"

"Probably to help keep it isolated from the germs in the rest of the hospital," Charles answered, startling

Lucius. The taller man had kept pace with him so easily, Lucius had almost forgotten he was there.

Almost.

They stepped outside to where the late August humidity smacked them in the face, only alleviated a little by a stiff wind coming off the lake. Many of the hospitals in Chicago were clustered in this area, which had always surprised Lucius a little. Didn't people get sick in other parts of the city?

Still, it didn't stop him from turning his face to the wind and taking a deep breath as they walked down the sidewalk joining the rest of the hospital campus.

"It's rough in there," Charles said quietly, plainly noticing Lucius gulping air. "It's especially hard seeing Josh there. Kid's sort of a powerhouse. Reminds all of us why it's not great to get cocky."

Lucius eyed his companion with fascination. "A powerhouse at what?" he asked delicately. He knew— sort of. He'd seen Josh Salinger at work, herding an eclectic group of people who only fit in at cocktail parties if they were running a scam. A couple of them were college-aged, like Josh and Grace, but not all. Lucius had met Interpol agents, insurance investigators, and mercenaries in the Salinger den, and a couple of months earlier, the entire collective had helped him stop his company from hemorrhaging developing technology at a fatal rate.

When he'd realized that Caraway House was under siege, they'd been the first people he'd thought of. But he hadn't counted on the heart of the operation being so ill.

"At everything, I guess," Charles said meditatively. They approached the main lobby of the hospital, where the cafeteria sat on the ground floor, next to an in-house Starbucks, and Charles took a couple of quick steps to open the door for him.

The gesture was so natural, so smooth, Lucius was halfway over the threshold before he realized that it was a power move—or a seduction move. And when Charles put light fingertips on the small of Lucius's back, he was reminded of the kiss.

It hadn't been real; at least thinking back on it, Lucius assumed it hadn't been. But at the time, when Charles had been running into a gala at the Art Institute and Lucius had inconveniently recognized him, it had *felt* real. Charles had been strong and commanding, which were usually the things Lucius prided himself on, and after a few brief, memorable moments of being manhandled in the shadows, Lucius had found himself barely standing while Charles wiped Lucius's mouth with careful thumbs and told him to stay there until Charles came back out again.

Lucius had no idea how many moments had passed before he saw Josh's friend Grace, dressed completely in black, but still recognizable by his almost complete invisibility, getting ready to climb up to the roof to intercept Lucius's stolen tech. That was when he'd realized that Charles had been getting him out of the way.

On the one hand, Lucius had been relieved. The group of people he'd put his trust in, in spite of the fact that they'd had no reason to help *him*, were coming through. His company provided for a lot of families, and it funded his charitable endeavors, and he really hadn't wanted to face letting all those people down.

But on the other, that kiss had been nothing but a smoke screen, and since it took a good twenty minutes for Lucius's heart rate to return to normal, well, he was a little embarrassed.

He'd had a healthy sex life. He'd been kissed a lot. He was even, he'd thought, considered something of a player. But that lanky cowboy had put on a monkey suit and kissed Lucius until his brain fell out, and Lucius didn't know how to even *talk* to him anymore.

For a man who had inherited a not-quite Fortune 500 company before he'd turned thirty, it was a little demoralizing.

"Mostly," Charles said now, jerking Lucius back to the moment, "Josh is sort of the heart of the group. He's really good at bringing people together."

Lucius shoved the kiss back into the box it had popped out from and tried to think like an adult. "Will you all be able to help me, do you think?" He grimaced. "God, I hate to even ask. He's practically a baby, and he's sick, and his parents are obviously worried stupid, and—"

"And the reason we all love that kid is that he wants us to put our individual talents into helping people, and we hadn't really thought of that before. So don't worry. We may be worried about our friend, but if the whole Robin Hood thing is important, well then…." He shrugged, and Lucius was left to draw his own conclusions.

"Then the team has to function without him?" he hazarded, knowing it was a hard thought to have.

"At least for now," Charles said staunchly. "And here we are at the world's best cafeteria, bar none." He smiled toothily, and Lucius tried not to roll his eyes.

Failed.

"What makes it the world's best cafeteria?" he asked.

"Why, Margie here," Chuck said, smiling pleasantly as he walked up to the counter, complete with plastic partition, behind which stood a stout middle-aged woman in full food-service regalia of apron, gloves, hairnet, and mask. "Margie, how you doin', beautiful?"

"Better now that you're here, Chuck," Margie said back. Her lined face softened, and even behind the mask, she looked almost girlish. "How's your friend?"

Charles kept his smile, but his eyes grew a little sad, and Lucius realized that the charming flirtation he'd formed with this woman held a core of sincerity in it. He remembered hospitals when his brother had been ill, and how cold and lonely they'd been. Charles Calder had managed to find humanity in the middle of that coldness, and Lucius was in awe.

"He's sleeping," Charles told her. "Doing a lot of that these days, but the doctors say if he can get past this rough spot, he should be on the way to mending."

"Any word on the bone marrow transplant?" Margie asked, and as she spoke, Lucius noted she was dishing up a plate of chicken-fried steak, gravy, mashed potatoes, and buttered vegetables—extra steak, extra gravy. She put it up on top of the glass partition for Charles to take, not minding the tray or the usual process to go through the register in the least.

"We've got a some ideas," Charles said. "And aren't you a dear to remember. Now you need to let me pay for this, Margie darlin', and my friend here too." He turned to Lucius. "They've got a turkey sandwich here that Margie makes fresh. It's good shit, hoss, I'm not gonna lie."

"A turkey sandwich sounds perfect," Lucius told Margie.

"Let me guess," she said, holding up a plastic-gloved hand. "No mayonnaise, no cheese, just turkey, lettuce, and wheat, am I right?"

"Pickles and tomatoes?" Lucius told her, a little embarrassed.

Margie looked at Charles. "See? What did I tell you, Chuck. I can spot 'em a mile away."

Charles grinned. "And so you have—a man on a diet. You're a wonder." He turned all those white teeth to Lucius, as though inviting him to join in on the joke.

"I put on weight like you wouldn't believe," he said sheepishly, and Charles laughed.

"It's 'cause you're a guy in a suit, Mr. Broadstone. Not enough elliptical machines in the world to burn off chicken-fried steak when you're a guy in a suit."

It was on the tip of Lucius's tongue to ask Charles what *he* did for a living when Margie produced his sandwich, with fat slices of dill pickle and what looked like freshly carved slices of turkey.

In fact, it looked as good as any deli in New York, and he smiled gratefully at Margie.

"That looks delicious, even if it's not steak," he said, and Margie's smile made her eyes practically disappear.

"It's on the house, Chuck," she said. "For both of you. Don't forget your water and fruit now. You know it keeps you healthy."

"Aw, Margie," Charles said, and to Lucius's surprise, he actually blushed. "Thank you, darlin'. Now I told Grace I was going to bring him back a milkshake, so when we're done—"

"Triple-thick strawberry with lots of cream," she said. Her voice dropped. "Are your friend's parents coming in too?"

Chuck looked behind him, biting his lip. "They should be here in a few," he said softly. "Just Julia and Danny today."

Margie nodded. "I'll make 'em something special," she told him, and Chuck thanked her again, grabbed himself a water and an apple, and led the way to one of the tables in the corner, facing the window and giving them a view outside.

"Wow," Lucius said quietly as Charles started tucking into his food. "That's some four-star treatment."

Charles gave him a faint smile. "Yeah, well, we were here on a shitty day for Margie. Her son had gotten arrested for stealing from his job as a restaurant manager. She was so distraught, and she'd been so kind to all of us when we'd been losing our minds about Josh. The boy said he was innocent, so we did some digging around and figured out it was the district manager above Cory who'd been doing the stealing. We nailed the district guy, but the kid still lost his job. Julia gave him a job organizing the soup kitchen for one of her downtown charities, and he's apparently doing a bang-up job of it. He's sent Julia more than one thank-you card, and she tells Margie what a great kid she has all the time." Charles shrugged. "You don't want to kick kindness in the teeth like that, you know?"

Lucius regarded him curiously. He wondered who had done the chatting up. Charles, who seemed to get along with everybody? Or Danny, who had a way of making people trust him? Certainly not the aloof odd duck who was Josh's best friend or the lion-blond Felix Salinger, who intimidated the crap out of people.

Charles caught his gaze—and the pause that came with it. "What? What is that look? What are you thinking?" He punctuated the question with a hearty bite of chicken-fried steak, and Lucius tried not to look yearningly at it. He remembered eating it at his grandmother's table in Atlanta when he'd been a child, and it had been the one meal he'd requested for his birthday every year until she'd passed.

"You and your crew are just… fascinating," he said, taking a sip of the water he'd grabbed at Margie's urging.

Charles snorted. "What's so fascinating? We're just a bunch of people who like crime, that's all."

Lucius snorted. "Yes, Charles. You like crime. That's why two law enforcement officers were standing in a parking garage watching you disarm a bomb on the night of the gala. And not an arrest in sight." Ah, back to that night, the night of the infamous kiss. When Lucius had left the gala because after a single glance around, he'd realized that not a soul there would hold as much interest for him as the cowboy who'd kissed him senseless and then run away. A cell phone alert that his car alarm had gone off had given him a convenient excuse.

It turned out that Charles and his friends had been the reason the alarm had gone off. Apprehending bad guys was a risky business, and Lucius had the bill for the broken light to prove it. But worse than the damage to his car had been the group of tense-faced people surrounding a van because two of their own had been in it. Underneath the van, in his shirtsleeves, with his tuxedo coat on the ground holding bomb parts, Charles Calder had been very competently working to make sure nobody got blown up.

"Well," Charles said now, a glint in his eye, "I worked munitions in the military. Who else was going to disarm the bomb?"

"Charles…." Lucius shook his head, because he had nowhere to start with this man.

"Chuck," his companion said, giving a disarming smile. "Good Luck Chuck. Charles is a rich guy, and I've never been him."

Lucius's mouth went sideways, and his eyes lost focus. That smile. It was taking the starch from his sails and the strength from his bones. "Chuck," he agreed, unable to keep that bit of formality between them.

"So, you ever go by anything besides 'Lucius'? Cause that's the name of a bad guy in pop culture, you know."

Lucius had been ten when that franchise had been made into a movie, and he could do nothing but shake his head. "Yes," he said grimly, "I know."

"So, like, Lucy?"

"No."

"Shush?"

"No."

"Your middle name?"

"Is Walter."

Chuck put his hand over his mouth. "That's appalling."

Lucius shut his eyes. "I know."

"That's like child abuse."

"It was my father's name." God rot his soul.

"You hate him, right?" Chuck asked anxiously, like this was Lucius's only recourse.

"More than words can ever allow," Lucius admitted.

"Good," Chuck said, as though every boy was perfectly entitled to hate his father. "Then we've got something to work with. Okay—let's try out other names. How about Scott? Scotty? Scotland?"

"No." But Lucius could feel a smile tugging at the corners of his lips. Oh, he would have given a lot of money to have been Scott in high school and college.

"No what?" Julia asked, coming in behind Lucius and almost scaring him silly.

"We're trying out new names for him," Chuck said. "Margie's got something special for you, by the way."

"She's so kind," Julia told him. "Danny, would you want to—?"

"Of course." Danny was already on his way, and Lucius noticed, for the first time, that while he was wearing khaki slacks and a neatly pressed polo shirt in blue, he didn't look particularly comfortable in them. He wondered what Benjamin Morgan wore on an ordinary day.

Julia slid into the booth across from Lucius and next to Chuck. "So, what new names have we tried?"

"Scott," Chuck said. "No go."

"Mm." Julia regarded Lucius playfully through porcelain-blue eyes, with only a hint of red to betray that she'd been crying in the bathroom. "Something upscale and, I beg your pardon, rich and white."

Lucius grimaced. "If I have to play to type."

"Well, you do try to make the best of your type," she said. "How about Bryce?"

"Bryce?" Chuck asked, smiling a little.

"Well, yes. I always thought that if I had another child, I should name him Bryce."

"Why didn't you have other children?" Lucius asked curiously. Both Julia and Charles froze.

"What?" Lucius asked. "What did I miss?"

"That entire episode of *Good Morning Chicago*, in which Julia's ex-husband came out and admitted he'd been in love with Benjamin Daniel Morgan for his entire life?" Chuck asked, as though Lucius were dense.

"Well, I saw that," Lucius said. "But doesn't that mean…. Didn't you ever…?"

But Julia's eyes were faraway, and there was a look of profound epiphany on her face.

"Julia, darling," Danny said, coming behind her with a tray loaded with food. "I have your salad here, and a half a sandwich, and I need you to eat every last bit."

"Of course," Julia said, smiling at him with her eyes bright. "I wouldn't dream of disappointing Margie."

Danny looked at her questioningly, and he and Chuck exchanged looks. Danny shook his head, and Chuck backed off, and they both turned to Lucius.

Lucius, who had become wholly entrenched in the nonverbal sparring and the Dormer-Salinger-Morgan family history, was suddenly reminded that he had a reason to be there.

"So," Danny said, his eyes sharp, "what you need from us is twofold. You need our tech experts to find the hole in your firewall and figure out how bits and pieces of your tech keep leaking out."

"Yes," Lucius said, "and I'd love a name to give to the authorities, as well as some evidence to prosecute."

"Good. We have two people who can investigate your tech and your facilities. One of them works for an insurance company, on the up-and-up, but I think he'd be happy to lend himself to a good cause. I assume they need to be on-site?"

Lucius nodded, then looked anxiously around him. "Yes. I know that's difficult right now."

"Well, it does cut into our numbers a little," Danny said with a shrug, as though the boy he considered a son was not in this very facility. "But working the job from here will give Josh something to occupy himself with, and it will give the others a chance to get out of Chicago and do something with themselves while he recovers."

"Others?" Chuck asked, and it was clear he was awaiting orders.

"Yes. I think you and Hunter need to go over security, and Molly should work from the inside. We need to see what kinds of security breaches Mr. Broadstone is experiencing and then have Molly question the women—delicately, perhaps undercover—to see if any of their abusers would have the knowledge, skills, or connections to break into Caraway House in that manner."

"What about Grace?" Chuck asked, grimacing. "I mean, I think he and Hunter will do okay apart, but—"

"We'll leave that for Grace and Josh to decide," Julia said, biting her lip. "I think Grace would probably prefer to stay here, if you don't need his skills."

"And you'll be bringing Soderburgh to help with the investigation of the company proper, along with Stirling," Danny added.

"Carl?" Chuck said, brightening visibly.

"Well, since his day job is as an insurance investigator, he can help us look legit. And when we find whoever is breaking into Lucius's company, Carl can give us ways to make the charges stick without revealing ourselves."

"Transport?" Chuck asked. "That's a lot of folks to haul three or four hours down the interstate."

"Plane," Lucius and Julia said at the same time.

"It's how I travel to Chicago and back," Lucius said, a little embarrassed. "Commuter plane."

"Mm, yes," Julia agreed coolly. "Felix has one as well. And a pilot."

"Hunter and I both can fly," Chuck said, and Lucius stared at him. Everything. Could he really do everything?

Julia and Danny's expressions were more along the lines of wonder. "Really?" Julia said, a genuine smile lighting up her classically elegant features. "You have a pilot's license?"

Chuck gave a grin and an insouciant shrug. "I did, yes. Probably still current. Military, ma'am. I worked transport and munitions. Took the classes 'cause they got me a promotion. Kept the license because who wouldn't, am I right?"

"It would be very helpful in your line of work," Danny said, and Chuck's wink at him was sly, as though the two of them knew things that the rest of the world didn't.

Lucius cleared his throat grumpily. He hated feeling as though he had nothing to offer, and these people were quickly taking over the operation.

"Well, I will need to fly back tomorrow. How quickly can you all be ready?"

"Did you bring building schematics and a security outline?" Danny asked, all business.

"Yes, but—"

"Well then, bring them by the house this evening. You're free to stay for dinner. Everybody will be thrilled to have a new playmate. During dessert, we'll spend some time planning and refining, and we can leave in the morning. You, of course, are free to fly home in your own plane, as long as you make your airstrip available to us." Danny frowned. "Would you object to having a couple of vehicles ready at the airstrip? That way the team can split up immediately and go to their separate venues. If Stirling and Carl are going under-cover as investigators, and Chuck, Hunter, and Molly are covering Caraway House, we're going to need to keep everybody's identities separate."

Lucius was suddenly on point to help make this operation go again. "I can help supply everybody with transportation and IDs," he said readily. "And room and board, albeit as part of the covers."

"Perfect," Chuck said, grinning. "We can start planning tonight!"

Just like that, Lucius realized he'd done it. He'd come to ask for help and a plan for helping to protect his company and the women who looked to him for care, and these people had done it. They'd jumped into the breach.

It wasn't until his throat thickened that he realized how worried he'd been and how alone he'd felt. All of that weight, pressing on his shoulders; he'd been lifting it since he'd inherited the company two years ago and his father had loaded rock after rock on his back, even from the grave.

Finally—*finally*—Lucius felt like he had someone to help with the heavy lifting.

Outside Your Lane

CHUCK LIKED driving, so he usually took it upon himself to be the chauffeur when the family was going somewhere. He and Hunter shared the duty when they were both in the car, but Chuck had become very familiar with the route from the Salinger mansion in Glencoe to the hospital in Chicago.

Given how much he missed Josh's sharp banter during the rides, he really wished he hadn't had to make this trip quite so often.

But this trip home was actually sort of exciting, because they had a job, and the one thing that had united everybody under Josh was love of the job.

Danny, who was seated in the back so Julia could have the front, spoke up. "We should tell Hunter as soon as we get home. That way, he can drive to the hospital to see Grace and pick up whatever he needs from his apartment."

Chuck and Julia both *hmm*d in agreement, and Danny added, "And I should have asked—Chuck, was there anything *you* needed?"

When Chuck and Josh had met, Chuck had been renting an apartment in an outlying suburb—not a great part of town. He hadn't minded. He helped his elderly neighbors with their groceries, and they, in turn, gave him the sort of benevolent protection that elders can give to a person. He was keeping someone's nana safe—he got to be hands-off. But Danny had been leasing an apartment in downtown Chicago that he'd only used a couple of times a year during the years he and Felix had been broken up. Once they were reunited, he still had a five-year lease and an empty apartment. While Chuck—and his cat—were happy to move into the mansion in Glencoe when the Salingers offered, Danny had also given him the keys—and carte blanche to decorate—the downtown apartment as well.

Chuck had been grateful. He had money—he had been carefully investing his bank-heist money and had now accrued a stack of it, collecting interest—but having the apartment in Chicago afforded him some privacy, while the room in Glencoe gave him family. Hunter did much the same thing, and Chuck had to jump on the commuter bandwagon—it really was the best of both worlds.

"I've got most of what I need at the big house," he told Danny, touched that the man would think about him. "I've got a couple of suits if I need them, and most of my working clothes are there." He flashed Julia a quick smile while keeping his attention on the road. "If Lucius wants me to wear anything flashier, he'll need to provide it himself."

Danny's chuckle was low and a little bit dirty. "I don't think he'd mind, if you must know the truth. I'm not sure what went on between you two the night of the gala, Chuck, but that man was *very* taken with you today."

Julia made a sound too delicate to be a snort. "Danny, you know perfectly well what went on at the gala. Grace was practically screaming it over the coms!"

Another one of those dirty chuckles. "Oh yes, I remember now. 'Stop it, Chuck! You're making babies on the lawn! Get your tongue out of his mouth! I'm gonna throw up!' Or, you know, something along those lines."

Chuck's hair may have turned from fiery red as a kid to a rather rich dark auburn now, but that didn't mean his cheeks couldn't show the same fire.

"It was a *distraction*," he said, emphasizing the word. "We didn't want him crashing the gala. We hadn't informed him of what we were doing!"

Now both of them snorted.

"What?" he demanded, knowing he sounded defensive but unable to stop himself. "It was a *kiss*!"

"Yes," Julia agreed. "And it's one that had high color on Mr. Broadstone's face all during lunch. So even if it was an average, everyday kiss to *you*, you may want to be gentle with Mr. Broadstone's feelings, yes?"

Chuck took a deep breath, suitably chastened, and then compelled by the honesty that had dogged him all his life, he said, "It was, in fact, a *very good* kiss." It was a tough admission to make. After Car-Car, he'd sort of sworn off men. Poor Car-Car. Chuck hoped he'd done right by the guy, but he'd driven off with the money and left him to go to *prison*. Even if it had been Car's best option at the time, it still felt wrong.

"And now you have a chance to follow it up," Julia said. While Chuck would normally have very gently told her that he was too old to need a mother, well, Josh's pale face, his ragged breathing and chapped lips, were haunting him as they were probably haunting everybody in the car. If Julia felt better exercising her "momness" on Chuck, he would gladly offer his love life on the altar as a sacrifice.

"Maybe Lucius doesn't really *need* a Chuck in his life," he said, keeping his voice gentle. "Have you thought of that? I have. He lives in Springfield/ Peoria, I live in Chicago. He owns a company, and I help break the law. He's skilled in business, and my specialties are munitions and transpo. It's not exactly a match made in heaven, you guys. He's in the lime-light, and it would be really great if I was never recog-nized, you feel me?"

"Those are obstacles, dear boy," Danny said, and Chuck did appreciate how he tried to "dad" him like Julia tried to "mom" him, when they were both in "big brother/big sister" territory at the most. "My entire life with Felix is as a pseudonym, and my day job has me flouting a professorship I never really earned. But that doesn't mean it's a lie."

A corner of Chuck's mouth lifted unbidden. "Yes, but Danny, you and Felix are extraordinary."

"Well, so are you and Lucius. I mean, you have to admit, one doesn't always find a Lucius Broadstone helming an aspiring tech company, does one?"

Chuck took a moment to think about that. They'd met Lucius when he and his perfidious head of securi-ty had broken into Grace's hotel room, trying to locate some of Lucius's stolen tech. They'd stumbled into a much bigger problem—including the fact that Lucius's head of security was corrupt, and carried a gun, which Lucius did not know. Instead of demanding that Josh's crew turn over all their evidence regarding Lucius to Lucius alone, he'd simply asked to be a part of their operation and kept in the loop. He'd done well, making himself useful when asked and keeping quiet when things happened that he shouldn't have had a thing to do with.

Chuck approved, mostly. Much like he approved of Lucius's priorities—the company was important because of the people it fed and housed. His security was important not because of pride, but because of safety.

And Chuck very much approved of giving battered women and children a sanctuary. The fact that Lucius did too—no matter what his motivation—made him an even tastier dish.

And he *was* a dish. On paper, his features were very standard white-male-businessman. Brown hair, hazel eyes, skin that probably needed a base-tan not to turn pink in the summer. He was a few inches shorter than Chuck and twenty to thirty pounds lighter—he looked very dapper and trim in a well-cut suit.

And there was something about his eyes. They were set close enough to almost cross, and it made him look a tad out of his element, even though he seemed very shrewd. His lips as well, which weren't too lean and not too pouty either. Even his chin, which had the trace of a cleft before it squared off. It all added up to more than average.

Together they added up to very, very… watchable.

Above-average in the watchability department.

In fact, he was sort of damned cute.

"Trust me, Danny," Chuck said, shaking the idea that Luscious, erm, *Lucius* Broadstone would be interested in a getaway driver without an actual college degree to his name. "He may think I'm meat on the hoof, but he's not gonna take me out to dinner anytime soon."

Danny let out a little grunt of disapproval. "I think you do yourself a serious disservice, Chuck. And perhaps Mr. Broadstone as well. Do you really think he's that shallow?"

Chuck thought about it as he deftly maneuvered the SUV through traffic. He and Hunter timed this trip in a mildly friendly competition, and Chuck's times were almost always two to five minutes quicker than Hunter's. He didn't want to lose his crown.

"Shallow, no," he concluded. While in company Lucius seemed polite, kind, and even self-effacing. When he'd realized his head of security was corrupt, he'd immediately joined forces with Josh's crew, apologizing profusely for the damage Jenkins had caused. And Chuck had to admit, Caraway House alone showed the guy had some depth.

"What, then?" Julia asked curiously.

"I think he has better things to do," Chuck said, feeling a little ping in his chest. "I'm not a serious guy here. You all know that. No ambition, no aspirations to go straight. For the first time in my life, I *like* what I'm doing, and I could do it for a *very* long time. But Lucius is on paper, and he's doing shit that's real. He doesn't need a Chuck in his life. Why would he?" Chuck shook his head, trying not to sound wistful. "Flirting's fine with that one. Besides, we got shit to sort."

"Mm…." It may have only been a syllable or a sibilant or whatever, but Chuck could swear Danny was saying volumes.

"Mm-hmm." And Julia said a dissertation back. The problem with working with two people who'd been on the game for more than twenty years was that they could practically read each other's minds.

"What's that supposed to mean?" Chuck asked, diving for a spot and getting cut off by a beat-up Toyota going about ten miles below the speed limit.

Goddammit, if he didn't beat Hunter's last time, he was gonna be *pissed.*

"It means, dear boy, that you very possibly have uttered famous last words. But we'll have to see what the next to last words are to know for sure, won't we, pet?"

"We will," Julia said, sounding happy and full of herself. Chuck wanted to send a quick glance her way, but he couldn't because he had to—*yes!* Take that, you brown crapbag of a car! He left the Toyota to eat his dust and tried to figure out why Julia seemed so much *lighter* today. She still carried worry and sadness like a cloak, but there was a sort of transcendent brilliance glowing off her. Under normal circumstances, he would have chalked it up to her being Julia Dormer-Salinger, a woman who'd grown up being abused by her father until she'd sought help from two con men who were trying to fleece him. Danny and Felix had abandoned their original plan and focused on getting Julia out of her father's grasp.

The marriage to Felix was supposed to have been a sham—a way to cover for the fact that she was pregnant by a virtual stranger and to give Danny and Felix some security when they'd been living off the grift in Europe together for probably too long. But Julia had given birth to Josh, and from what Chuck could see, the three of them had become a very effective parenting team.

And Josh had grown up in a grifter's paradise and seemed determined to keep up the game.

Julia Dormer-Salinger was an incredibly strong woman, but she was also smarter than Chuck could ever lay claim to, and while she preferred to let Felix be the front man for the cable network company they'd inherited from her monstrous father, Chuck had seen them working together and knew that they would have accomplished nothing without Julia.

He also knew that while Danny and Felix knew excellent forgers—the traditional degrees on the walls of their offices proved that—Julia's paperwork was bona fide, and it was from Vassar.

If she was thinking about something that made her happier, eased some of her worry, and let some of her luminosity shine through, Chuck was 100 percent behind it, no matter what it was.

Chuck saw another hole, this one in the commuter lane where everyone was going wazoo miles an hour, and dove for it, slowing down enough so he didn't have to brake once they were in.

Next to him, he heard Julia make a very small noise through her nose.

"Problem?" he asked, hoping there wasn't one. He was going ninety, and the little app on his phone said all the cops were somewhere closer to the city proper on the other side of the freeway. Ten miles to the offramp; nothing but net.

"No, darling," Julia said, her voice not tense in the least. "I was merely thinking about how kind of you it was to make this ride like a roller coaster. It certainly does keep my mind from my troubles."

Chuck preened. "Thank you, ma'am. It is literally my pleasure."

Danny grunted behind them. "I'm so glad," he said. "We live for your pleasure. Just remember, you can't lord your best time over Hunter's head if we're all dead."

Oh.

A little sheepishly Chuck took his foot enough off the gas pedal to not feel obligated to finger the tailpipe in front of them.

"Good point," he said, and then into the silence, he added, "So about this job—any ideas?"

"Yes," Danny said decisively. "I think we're going to need to ask a bit more of Lucius. I think Stirling needs to go undercover as an employee, not security. And Soderburgh as well. And you need to be a handyman or something. Something the women will trust."

"Self-defense teacher," Julia said ruminatively. "And not just physical. I can give you some tips to deal with the psychological warfare of being in an abusive home."

"That is *awesome!*" Chuck said, perking up. "I would *love* to do that!" It was the one thing he'd always regretted with Car-Car, not being able to give the boy any pointers on how to keep himself safe in prison or from his brothers. He'd offered—he really had—but Car-Car had been proud, insistent that he was a man and could stand up for himself.

Well, yeah—but not when the odds were two to one. Or worse.

"Should Molly teach self-defense too?" he asked. "They'd trust her more."

"Yes," Julia said thoughtfully, "but she's so young. I know that will count against her, because women really *do* take these things into consideration. I wish we could send Phyllis in as a counselor." Phyllis was their housekeeper, and one sharp cookie—but Chuck didn't think they could function without her. "Or—"

"Or Molly could come in as a woman escaping an abusive relationship," Danny said impatiently, and Julia sucked in a breath.

"That would be brilliant," she said, sounding surprised she hadn't thought of it herself. Molly was one of Josh's friends—and one of the members of Josh's original college and high school crew. She was an amazing actor—and a truly gifted con artist. "Of course, I'm too well known these days to do it or I'd suggest myself." Julia's voice lowered sadly, and Chuck didn't have to ask why.

He swallowed against a sudden lump in his throat. "Well, darlin', you do have other things on your mind these days."

"Yes, and Molly would probably love to throw herself into a part like this. Well then, you, Molly, and I shall have a little breakout session today after we finalize the plan." She raised her voice a tad so she could address Danny. "And I have something I need to run by you and Felix—don't let me forget."

"Of course, lovely," Danny said. "Confab in the bedroom after the kids go to sleep. You bring your pajamas, I'll bring popcorn, Felix can bring the boardgames."

Julia's throaty laughter was a cool balm on this scorching day.

CHUCK WASN'T sure how the tradition had started—the big meal in the dining room followed by Conspiracy 101 in the den—but he liked it. Tonight he sat next to Hunter and gave him the news that he'd probably have to leave Grace in town while they went to Peoria to help Lucius.

Hunter took it with a grimace. Grace seemed as independent as an alley cat, but Chuck suspected that even alley cats needed a place to curl up and be safe, and Hunter was Grace's.

"Josh staying overnight again?" he asked quietly.

"Yeah."

"Rough on him." And that, from Hunter, was practically a treatise on his feelings.

"Grace or Josh?" Chuck asked.

"Both." Hunter took a big breath. "Used to be jealous, ya know?"

Chuck had never thought about it. Josh and Grace were too much like conjoined twins. If one of them didn't tell the other to fuck off at least once an hour, something was seriously wrong with the world. That was the love language of college-aged boys, right there.

"Of them?" he said, to make sure.

"Not that way." Hunter took a bite of casserole and closed his eyes. He and Chuck worked out together a lot, because they were both security people—eating something that contained sour cream, mayonnaise, cheese and chicken was practically health food.

"What way, then?" Chuck wondered at the thing in him that let him speak like Hunter, with lean, brief sentences, and then patter with Lucius and Danny and Julia. Did being born the middle child in an average neighborhood give him magic chameleon skills? If so, it was probably the nicest thing his parents had ever done for him.

"I have to share him," Hunter said simply. "But Grace is high maintenance. So I'm not sharing *Grace* with Josh. I'm sharing his maintenance."

Chuck almost spit out his casserole. "That's a brilliant way to look at it," he said, cackling. Unbidden came that moment with Julia and Danny in the car. Another three-way friendship. "I'm more of a herd animal. I wander around with my herd, take lovers on the side."

Hunter paused eating and turned his head, eyeing Chuck like he'd study a particularly difficult tactical challenge. "Why don't you take lovers *from* the herd?" he asked.

Chuck thought depressingly of Car-Car.

"'Cause I'm a criminal," he said before taking a bite and chewing thoughtfully. "And most of my guys tend to be on the sweet and narrow, if you know what I mean."

Hunter let out an unlikely snort. "Chuck, I'm not sure what makes you think you can't be a sweet guy and a criminal, but I think you've crossed that line."

Chuck wasn't sure where the wounded feeling came from. Hunter was trying to be nice. But still, it almost felt like a betrayal of their brotherhood of muscle, arms, and transport.

"You take that back," he muttered.

As though to prove that Hunter had lightened up a little since he and Grace had gotten together, he had the nerve to guffaw. But something on Chuck's face must have hit him right, because he got his laughter under control, and after looking around the table to see that everybody was listening to Danny give a chirpy, cheerful version of Josh and Grace playing videogames in the hospital that day, he lowered his head and spoke softly.

"Chuck, we all have skeletons. We all have scars from the life that brought us here. Everybody who has sat at this table has, at some point, chosen their personal agenda above the law. And those of us who have done it long enough, have seen it go bad. But that's anybody.

Lucius is a rich guy, and as far as I can see, those people have more blood on their hands than most mercenaries. If he's managed to keep his conscience clean, well, that'll be a first."

Chuck regarded him carefully. "Felix is a rich guy," he said.

"Yeah, but Felix grifted Julia's father's company and money away by learning how to do his job on the frickin' fly and hiding Danny from him for ten years. He and Julia were super smart—con-man smart—and quintupled old Hiram Dormer's fortune in their first two years. They throw their money around because the fortune was never as important to them as the game, even when the game was legit. The fact that the game now is to help people just makes it that much more exciting for them."

Chuck thought of some of the stories he'd heard bandied around by the three of them. "Don't kid yourself, Hunter. The game was *always* to help people."

Hunter glanced away for a moment, and Chuck caught a truly soft look on his face. "Grace started stealing stuff so he could drive the mean girls apeshit," he said, a note of pride in his voice. "Josh started helping him so he wouldn't get caught."

Chuck held a hand to his heart, and he was mostly sincere when he gave a mock sniff and said, "Kids. Ah."

Hunter burst out laughing and then threw a roll at him, and table time was on. Before Chuck could get sucked into a conversation about dream jobs—jobs for revenge or justice that were on his wish list—Phyllis disappeared to answer the door and came back with Lucius Broadstone.

He stood at the head of the table, encouraging people not to rush their dinner on account of him, and

Chuck noticed a little tic in the corner of his mouth. It wasn't fear, especially of public speaking.

But… there it was again, complete with a dash of eyes to the right, and Chuck's heart—already softened by the discussion of Josh and Grace, his little brothers, as it were—melted right through the floor.

It was *shyness*. Oh dear Lord, Lucius Broadstone, billionaire playboy, was *shy*. Suddenly Chuck's doubts about him and Lucius became immaterial. He couldn't let the boy stand there and blush.

"By all means sit down," Danny was saying. "We'll be finishing up in a bit. Feel free to nosh a little yourself if you like."

"Got an open seat right here," Chuck said, patting the one next to him. Normally Grace or Josh would have sat there; the table felt a bit empty without the two of them, that was for sure. "Come sit, have a sampling of Phyllis's famous comfort casserole, and we'll go downstairs and have dessert in a bit."

"Casserole? In the summer?" Lucius asked, and while the question may have been snooty, he was moving toward the high-backed ash-wood chair next to Chuck, so that was okay.

"We've been eating comfort food for the last six weeks or so," Molly said from the other side of the empty chair. "Not great for the waistline, but awesome for the boobs!"

Lucius laughed, giving her a charming smile, which she returned. Molly Christopher was a tall young woman, with long sunset-colored ringlets—some of them dyed rainbow colors—stunning green eyes, and a sailor's mouth. She was, in a word, irrepressible, and Chuck enjoyed her company *very* much. Her brother, Stirling, who sat near the head of the table by Danny,

was a little harder to know. The two had been adopted
when they'd been middle-school age by a couple who
sounded pretty damned amazing. Molly and Stirling
hadn't been related by blood, but they'd gone through
the system together for so long that Molly had clung
to Stirling's hand and insisted he come with her. Although their adopted parents had been killed in a boat-
ing accident a couple of years before, they had stayed
tight even after they'd received money from a trust, and
they'd been Josh's friends since middle school. Both of
them were in theater, but while Molly did costuming
when she wasn't onstage, Stirling—who was a computer genius and the crew's resident hacker—made a
living by setting up lighting and sound plans for half
the productions in Chicago.

Stirling was quiet where Molly was loud, and his
skin was a pale earth color where hers was merely
pale. His dark, thickly-lashed eyes didn't miss much,
though, and although he didn't meet other people's
gazes often, he would live or die for Molly, Josh, or
more recently, Danny. Chuck had learned to be quiet
and kind to Stirling and to accept that, like Hunter, he
wasn't particularly fond of words in sentence or para-
graph formations.

"Well, your boobs are amazing," Lucius said,
laughing kindly. "And the kind of food you should eat
during whatever season is really kind of a silly rule."

"Right?" she replied. "Although I must say I do see
soup in the winter and salad in the summer, but that's
only because summer around here is like a big soggy
wool carpet dropped on you." She shuddered but took
a bite of casserole anyway. "Somehow I can overlook
that for pasta and fat."

"Well, now I really must have a bite," Lucius said, and someone passed him a small plate that he used to serve himself.

After he'd had a bite and generally approved, Chuck said, "So you know Hunter. Um, Hunter, did I tell you we get to fly?"

Hunter perked up. "Like, pilot? A plane? Because I miss that!"

"Right? And we're going to be commuting. I figure there's hours in there for both of us, right?"

Hunter's face—which was square-jawed, narrow-eyed, bold-nosed, and sort of secretive and sly, with lean lips and an almost permanently neutral expression when he wasn't talking about someone he cared about—actually lit up. It was practically boyish.

"That's fantastic. Maybe Grace will come with us once."

Chuck nodded. "Well, I know Felix and Julia have one too. Maybe when Josh is better, we can do a bit of piloting on our own."

And now Hunter was almost luminous. It was creepy.

"I would love that," he said, and Lucius looked at both of them with a gratifying bit of awe.

"You're both braver than I am," he said. "The idea of being responsible for my own fate is one I'm quite comfortable with—as long as both my feet are on the ground."

"Whatsamatter, Scotty Bryce," Chuck ribbed, using his teasing from the cafeteria that day, "afraid to let go and fly free?"

"Yes," Lucius said without hesitation. "I have responsibilities. If I let go, things don't get done."

Chuck cackled, lifting his eyes to Hunter and inviting him to join the fun. "I think that's a challenge, don't you?"

Hunter let a corner of his mouth lift but otherwise concentrated on his food. "Sure. Your challenge. I got my own."

Which left Chuck square in Lucius's scope. "How am I supposed to let my hair down when my company, my people, are in danger?"

Chuck rolled his eyes. "I'm not saying let the whole thing rot, Scotty—I'm just saying that while you're here, enjoy your meal. When we're downstairs eating cookies, get the good ones with the cream filling—"

"The raisins," Hunter said, still concentrating on his meal.

"Or the chocolate!" Chuck added. "But take the richest, most decadent cookie and put your feelings into eating it. When you're in the plane, ask the pilot to take you low enough to see something fantastic, just for shits and giggles. There are lots of ways to let your hair down without getting it chopped off, Mr. Businessman. Don't you agree, Hunter?"

Hunter gave him a beleaguered look. "I miss Grace," he muttered. "Let me talk to Danny." Then he stood up and strode to the end of the table.

"What do you suppose he's doing?"

"Probably trying to see if he can get out of tonight's briefing," Chuck answered with a sigh. "I think he wants to go see Grace and get some stuff from his apartment tonight and then meet us at the airstrip tomorrow."

Lucius tilted his head to see Hunter engaged in earnest conversation with Danny that Chuck wasn't sure was going to go Hunter's way.

"They seem an unlikely pair," Lucius said ruminatively, taking a bite of the casserole.

"Well, you have to know 'em," Chuck said. "Hunter doesn't talk much, but he needs to take care of people. Grace talks *too* much, but he's never been taken care of before. Works great, right?"

Lucius frowned, his smooth forehead developing truly interesting character lines. "Isn't Dylan Li the son of two of the city's richest businesspeople?"

"Grace?" Chuck asked in surprise. "Well, I know he has his own money. But there's a difference between being given a bottle and being sung to sleep and placed gently in your crib, if you know what I mean."

Lucius regarded him curiously and took another measured bite. "No," he said after a moment. "I don't understand."

Chuck blew out a breath. "Well, sir, why do babies cry?"

"Because they're hungry? Or they've soiled themselves?" Lucius hazarded.

"Or they've got air in their bellies," Chuck agreed. "But all of that really boils down to needing care. You can have a robot feed, clean, and burp the baby, but the baby will still cry."

"Because they need to be held," Lucius said in surprise, as though he'd never thought of this.

"Well yeah!" Chuck laughed. "Because babies ain't stupid, son. I remember my sister, Daphne, with her boy, Dougie, calling me up when I was deployed. She was in absolute tears. She'd left her sonovabitch husband, and she was staying with our parents, you know, and she was like, 'He's crying all the time, and Dad tells me it's because I coddle him, and Mom says

I should just put whiskey in his milk, and I don't know what to do!'"

Lucius stared at him. "Whiskey in his mil—"

"Don't act like that's the worst part of that sentence," Chuck said impatiently. "I told her to take the baby to bed with her and feed him when he needed it and hold him until he quieted. And you know what? Dad stopped yelling, Mom stopped trying to poison the kid, and my sister actually got four hours of sleep in a row. Next time she called me up, she said she'd learned her lesson and the folks could fuck off. She was gonna hold that baby as much as he'd let her." Chuck smiled wistfully. He'd missed a lot of Dougie's growing up, but he'd set up a trust for Daphne to have the house free and clear, as well as living expenses, including day care. Daphne was smart as a whip; she'd gone and gotten her AA degree in art, then got a part-time job she really loved as a children's docent in the local museum. She worked enough to not be bored, was off enough to thoroughly participate in her son's life, and was financially sound enough to tell their brother Kevin to fuck right off. Chuck wasn't proud of much, but he was, by God, proud he'd provided for his sister.

"Does she still live at home?" Lucius asked, finishing off his small portion and regretfully pushing the plate away.

"Mm?" Chuck pulled his mind away from Daphne, who was due a letter soon, actually. "Yes and no. She still lives in the same house, but Mom and Dad passed about eight years ago. We write, exchange cards, that sort of thing. Her kid's a riot. Only thing I miss about Cleveland."

Lucius frowned. "Is it so wise to be giving away your... I don't know. Secret identity or whatever?"

Chuck threw his head back and laughed. "Oh my God, no! My real name is Chuck Calder, Scotty. And I've never been implicated in any crime." He winked. "That they could prove."

Lucius shook his head. "Don't you worry about… what you do? Getting back to the people in your life?"

Chuck regarded him seriously. "Two things," he said. "The first is that this crew is mostly too good to get caught. Only one of us has been in prison, and he was there to help Interpol. Julia Dormer-Salinger has no scandal attached to her name, and none of the people at this table would change that." He didn't mention that Benjamin Morgan wasn't Danny's real name, but Danny had been too good to be caught for twenty years. Now that he'd gone (mostly) straight, that wasn't going to change. "The second is that, remember, you need us because *you* aren't too good to be caught. We *caught you*, and your guy not only shot at our unarmed guy, he also ended up part of your security problem, and he ended up dead. So while you might be looking at us like rare and exotic animals, we are, in fact, highly trained racehorses, my friend, and right now, you're trying to take the cup."

Chuck didn't think his tone was too sharp—after all, he was everyone's good ole boy, right? So he was surprised as he watched Lucius's fair skin grow deeper and deeper raspberry-tinted.

"You okay, Scotty?" he asked kindly.

Lucius shook his head and gave him a truly awkward smile. "I… I didn't realize I was looking at you all like zoo animals," he mumbled. "My apologies."

Aw hell, Chuck had wounded the guy's feelings. "No worries," he said, keeping his smile easy. "Just won't do to let you think you're in the hands of amateurs, right?"

Lucius nodded, avoiding his eyes, and Chuck's stomach knotted. Impulsively, he put his hand on the back of Lucius's, mostly trying to gentle him like a wayward colt. Lucius's eyes flew to his, and Chuck's own face suddenly heated.

"It's all good," he said, crinkling his eyes but not smiling too wide. "Look, Scotty—I've been with the bad guys, okay? I've been with the crew who all wore balaclavas and didn't tell people their names. I don't like those guys. Most of 'em are only out for themselves, and they'd sooner shoot ya than ask ya for directions to the john. I'm not with guys like that anymore. Life's too short to be regretting your choices, okay? Trust Felix, Danny, and Julia—they won't steer you wrong."

Lucius nodded, biting his lower lip in what looked like shyness, and gently tugged on his hand.

Chuck didn't let it go.

"We good?" he asked, waiting until Lucius stopped pulling away.

"We're good," Lucius said, capitulating. "I'll, uhm, take my hand back now."

Chuck let his customary grin out and winked. "You sure you don't want me to take it for a spin?" he asked playfully. Then, while Lucius gaped, he pulled Lucius's knuckles up to his lips for a smacking kiss before letting him go.

Lucius's face went beyond raspberry and right into plum, and Chuck let out a sigh of relief. Teasing this man with some flirting was a much better choice than getting awkward because he was telling the truth.

That moment there, when Lucius had blushed and felt bad, that had been way too close to real for Chuck's comfort.

THE REST of dinner was pleasant. Chuck started talking about zoos and taking his nephew to one once when he was four, and Lucius laughed appreciatively. In less than half an hour they were downstairs in the basement den, which looked like the mancave of pretty much any well-off Chicago-based male in the area. The walls were painted red and blue in honor of the Cubs and the Bulls, with an orange-and-black stripe in the corner of one wall for the Bears—or, arguably, the Blackhawks—and another corner done in black and silver for the White Sox.

There was an enormous big-screen television, a wet bar—which Chuck knew held no alcohol but had *all* the sodas, juices, and sweets—and several couches, overstuffed chairs, and beanbags scattered around the plush cream-colored shag carpet.

This was a *den*, comfortable and welcoming, with a stack of pillows and blankets for movie nights in the corner.

And a state-of-the-art media center built into the coffee table for presentations. Add a laptop, the appropriate wires, and voila.

Everybody could be up to date on the game.

The fact that the TV was on (with a screenshot of the Cubs, winning) and the laptop was plugged in told Chuck that Danny had used *his* hour before dinner to check any email from Lucius and prepare.

Hunter had agreed to stay for the first part of the presentation and then to leave as discussion started.

Before he took his usual coiled position in the corner of the room, where he could see the stairs coming down as well as everybody else's faces, Chuck moved over to him before he assumed his own position leaning against the wet bar. Chuck wasn't as deadly as Hunter, but he knew how to handle himself and how to protect other people. He was backup, and he knew it.

As he approached, he pulled out his key and watched Hunter grimace.

"I knew it," he muttered. "What do you need?"

"A sports coat and a nice suit," Chuck said. "My good stuff is at the apartment. You don't gotta touch my crusty undies or socks or anything, but a good suit and the leather oxford shoes would be great."

Hunter rolled his eyes. "You couldn't just have a cheap tux to cater, could you?"

Chuck gave him a wide, toothy smile. "Not my fault the boss lady keeps buying me Brooks Brothers."

"You suck."

"Yes, but you'll never know."

They could have gone on like that for a good hour out of sheer brotherhood, but they heard someone else on the stairs. Both of them turned, keeping their shoulders relaxed, until the man attached to the polished loafers came into view.

"Soderburgh," Hunter muttered.

"Oh yeah!" Chuck grinned. "Carl!" He stuck out his hand. "Good to see you! I wasn't sure if Danny contacted you yet."

Carl "Soderburgh" Cox was a good-looking guy. A little taller than Chuck, he had wide shoulders and a lantern jaw, as well as short-cropped hair that was more blond than brown and wide light brown eyes. While Carl was an insurance investigator most of the time, he'd worked a job with Chuck once, trying to get to the bottom of a ring of car thieves who specialized in exotic cars. Chuck had spotted the po-po right off, but Carl had been cool, keeping Chuck out of his report as long as Chuck gave him some driving pointers and helped him catch the thieves.

The thieves themselves had been dangerous—they'd left some bodies in their rearview—and Chuck wasn't a fan of that. Things had gotten a wee bit hot for the two of them, so they'd fled—and spent a week in bed, waiting for Carl's orders from his company and Chuck's lead on what job he was going to pull next. Carl was a good guy—and a good fuck—but he was also a bit serious for Chuck's taste. Getting the guy to do more than crack a smile was hard work. Chuck liked his lovers to be easily entertained. Lucius, for instance, tended to give him at least a shy smile when Chuck was cracking a joke.

In fact, Lucius's shy smiles always made him feel like he'd won something. Chuck would rather have one of those surprised, bemused smiles—as opposed to the practiced laugh he'd heard Lucius make socially—any day.

Carl smiled at him and took his hand, but left the pleasantries to Chuck.

"Good to see you. I was happy to hear you'd been tapped for this."

Carl gave a direct nod. "Well, you know I'm always happy to help." The corners of his lips pushed up and then fell back down again. "You people are always up to the most interesting games."

Hunter grunted, a pointed reminder that when they'd met, their "interesting game" had resulted in

Carl needing ice and some Band-Aids, and then stuck out his hand to shake too.

Carl shook with him, and his eyes roamed the den. "Oh," he said softly. "No Josh tonight. I'd wondered." His eyes slipped to Hunter. "Grace staying with him?"

Hunter nodded, but to his credit said, "Josh couldn't do what we need you for anyway. We need a security expert—a suit."

"Understood," Carl said, and if he was hurt or put out at all, he didn't show it. "Is there a role for Torrance?" he asked. "He's getting bored again."

Chuck and Hunter met eyes and shook their heads—but not negatively. "You'd have to ask Danny," Chuck said. "We're foot soldiers, he's the general."

Torrance Grayson was like Carl in a way. A successful rogue journalist who had quit cable news to do deep-dive educational pieces on YouTube, he had his uses with the crew, but he had his own apartment in the city. His day job was both absorbing and important, but he did love the little plays of the game that Felix and Danny threw his way. He and Chuck texted at least once a week, because Chuck liked being social, and Torrance wanted an in.

Torrance also had a painful unrequited crush on Josh that he kept hoping would fade so he could throw himself into the crew's adventures with all his concentration. But only Chuck knew that, because people tended to tell him things after a few drinks.

Carl nodded and gave Danny a wistful glance before blinking to clear the softness in his eyes. Poor Carl; he and Danny had hooked up during the ten years Danny and Felix had been on the outs, but nobody could have replaced Felix. It felt as though Carl was destined to be "that guy"—the guy you hooked up with but didn't *love*. Chuck wished him luck with that. He was apparently "that guy" too.

"Hello, are we all here?" Danny asked, glancing around the den. "Has everybody grabbed some cookies?" He motioned to the spread on the coffee table—Phyllis, who usually would rather hire people to cook for her, had been baking up a storm since Josh had gotten ill. There were probably eight different kinds of cookies on the table, and as Lucius sat primly in one of the overstuffed chairs, Chuck noted that he hadn't grabbed a napkin and loaded up.

"Back in a sec," he murmured to Hunter and Carl. As Danny continued to speak, he moved to the coffee table to scoop up some dessert, putting a napkin holding a couple of the shortbreads in Lucius's hand before taking a full plate back to Carl and Hunter. Lucius looked up at him, that sort of pleased bemusement written on his face, and smiled as though Chuck had done this for him and only for him and just for him.

And suddenly, Chuck wished he had.

He almost stumbled going back to the "mercenary's corner," as he thought of it, where the people who thought about security could protect those who knew strategy and tech.

Where had that thought come from? With an internal shake to clear his head, he focused on what Danny was saying.

"So, children," he said, smiling tiredly at them, "this is our puzzle for today. See this?"

An image of an impressive technology business campus came into view, with lots of beech and oak trees grown big enough to provide shade for the three wedge-shaped concrete, stucco, and mirror-glass buildings in graduated sizes. The smallest appeared to be four stories high, the middle one was five, and the tallest was six.

"This is Broadstone Industries," Danny said. "Established forty years ago, right before the tech boom. It was originally a place that manufactured electronic timeclocks and payroll programs. In the eighties, there was a big switch from hand-cut checks, believe it or not, and Broadstone was the death knell of the impromptu break for fast-food workers everywhere." He was probably referring to the fact that while workers used to be able to dodge away for a break, once the electronic time cards came into use, breaks became tightly controlled, if given at all.

"I did not know that," Lucius said, sounding stunned.

"I was reading between the lines," Danny said blandly, and then a voice amplified by an iPad speaker echoed through the room.

"Did you read between the buildings?" Grace said acerbically. "Someone tell Broadstone that his business looks like one of those graduated butt-plug sets. Something expensive and kinky and a little painful, if I know my porn."

There was a horrified silence, and then a rusty amplified giggle. "Ignore him," Josh said. Looking at Hunter, Chuck could see he was holding a tablet face out so Josh and Grace could be at the briefing too.

"I don't know how," Chuck drawled. "If he hadn't said it, we all would have been thinking it, and then when we were undercover on-site, one of us would have just blurted out 'Butt plug!' Thanks, Grace. You saved us from that."

"You're a good egg, Chuck. Keep going, Uncle Danny. I have popcorn. It's getting good."

Danny's smile lightened up a little, and he inclined his head in the direction of the tablet. Chuck looked up to where Hunter was gazing fondly at the electronic object in his hands and winked.

"Good thinking," he mouthed.

Hunter shrugged, face still soft. Well, everybody should have somebody who made them a little soft... and hard at the same time. Chuck tried not to groan. God, it had been a long time since he'd had someone like that.

"So," Danny was saying, bringing Chuck's attention back to the presentation, "Welcome to Butt Plug City. What was once the modest manufacturer of electronic time clocks became one of the country's most promising industries in the field of medical and business technology. Unfortunately, the former captain of this ship was a real bastard, and when he handed the wheel over to his son, our very own 'Luscious' Broadstone, the ship had enough holes to carry it to the bottom of Lake Superior."

Without warning, all of the college students in the room erupted into the first bars of "The Wreck of the Edmund Fitzgerald," including the ones on the tablet.

Danny waited until Molly and Stirling high-fived each other and Josh and Grace whooped over the iPad speaker, before raising an eyebrow. "Was the key word 'Lake Superior'?" he asked.

Molly nodded. "Josh's idea. You should take away his phone."

"I'll do no such thing," Danny retorted, and it wasn't Chuck's imagination: the tiredness had mostly disappeared, and Danny had the bright eyes of someone who really enjoyed his work. "I will instead ask Josh to stay awake long enough to tell me if he's caught anything to help us when I'm done with my spiel."

"Can do, Uncle Danny," Josh said. "I took a nice long nap this afternoon. I'm up for a meeting, I swear."

"Good, because we're going to need your help," Danny said tartly and then returned to the rest of the group. "The thing is, Butt Plug City is under siege. You all know that a side benny of the job we finished a month and a half ago was hopefully to keep Lucius's company from bleeding tech out its asshole until it keeled over and died. Well, we did that. We sealed up one big fissure, but a couple of other wounds are still sucking the life from it. The problem is—as Lucius pointed out—the information leaks aren't coming from one concentrated space. Payroll will lose enough info for a batch of paychecks to not get printed out, and the money will disappear. They'll fix that glitch, and the department that's developing smaller, more portable C-Pap machines will inexplicably get shorted truckloads of parts needed to put together prototypes, and this too can be traced to a computer glitch. It's one irritating act of sabotage at a time, and make no mistake, getting pecked to death by ducks will make you just as dead as getting reamed up the ass with a scimitar."

He gave a look of satisfaction when the entire room grimaced at the awfulness of the metaphor, and then carried on, having obviously paid them all back for the Edmund Fitzgerald thing.

"That actually sounds like some sort of program," Josh croaked over the tablet. "Something that detects vulnerable points in the electronics under a certain magnitude of damage. Stirling, could you develop something like that?"

"Mm...." Stirling's fingers were already twitching, although his laptop sat closed next to him on the couch. Stirling himself was on the floor, knees drawn up to his chin, near where Molly stretched out so they could occasionally touch fingers to shoulders or hair. It was something Chuck hadn't noticed them doing much when he'd met them that winter, but he'd seen them do a lot more after Josh had gotten sick. It occurred to him that the two former foster siblings only needed a little push before they were both once again frightened children instead of the brilliant young people he'd been introduced to. The thought made him sad.

"Any ideas?" Danny prompted kindly, and Stirling jerked.

"It sounds like a geological survey," Stirling said abruptly. "Like something you'd rig to look at fault lines to see which ones were giving miniquakes. In fact, I bet most fracking companies have something like that to know where they can safely drill. This has taken the same principle and adapted it, so instead of tectonic weakness, it's probing for firewall weaknesses. Same concept, different materials, different results."

Stirling stopped talking, his eyes huge, and stared at Uncle Danny as though *he* could explain that strange thing that had just happened when he spoke out loud in public without Josh in the same room.

"Good job," Josh rasped over the tablet. "Stirling, that's brilliant. You and me will have to text. I bet you could rig something up easy to figure out where that program is running and how to stop it."

"Need to set bait," Stirling said, relaxing a smidge. "Give it something to sink its teeth into. Trace it back. I'd need to be there."

"Funny you should say that," Danny asserted, stopping the moment from devolving into a tech conference when that was something they could do far more effectively on their own. "Because a number of us are going to be making a field trip."

Everybody stopped and stared at him as though he'd said something obscene.

"But...." Molly swallowed and her eyes darted toward where Hunter held the tablet. "But, are we leaving now?"

"I'm not dead!" Josh barked through the speaker, but he finished it up with a cough, probably caused by terminal dry mouth from the treatment. They all waited for the cough to stop, and when he spoke next, he'd curbed his irritation. "I'm not dead, guys—I'm *bored*. And while I can't come with you, I'd love to have a puzzle to think over. That's why I told the 'rents to do this one." He paused. "Besides, there's more, and it's important. Tell 'em, Uncle Danny."

Danny nodded, took a breath, and explained what Caraway House was and why the security breaches were so worrisome.

"These women come from prominent families," Danny finished up. "We all know that stalking laws are inadequate in this country, and their husbands are all well-to-do, powerful men. They literally fear for their lives."

"It's not just women," Lucius added. "There are some young men there too, some whose boyfriends proved to be less than ideal, and one young man fleeing from a female MMA fighter who took her disqualification on the basis of steroids out on him. Many of the women are married to police officers. In that case, the money isn't an object, and the scope of the resources devoted to finding them is staggering. The threat of physical violence is real, and the people being cared for on the Caraway House campus are vulnerable in the extreme." He grimaced. "That's why we don't have a picture," he explained apologetically. "The residents are allowed to take pictures from inside, but we've taken every measure to hide the dorms from the road. We want the place to be a hole in the world."

"That's very security conscious," Julia said thoughtfully. She had her legs crossed, and her floral summer-weight dress was creeping up a shapely thigh. She leaned forward, tapping on her lower lip with her forefinger. "How do the residents move on from there, may I ask?"

Chuck watched curiously as Lucius's face became a mask of neutrality, with a twin flag of color in each cheek.

"You forge identities for them and move them to new cities," Chuck deduced, and while the mask remained, Lucius's color swept up and down his pale, patrician features.

"Their escape routes are confidential," he said primly, and the whole room turned to regard him with a little bit of amusement.

"You do know we're criminals, right, Mr. Broadstone?" Molly asked after a weighted minute. "We're not going to turn you in for hiding victims of domestic violence."

Some of Lucius's steely demeanor relaxed. "I know," he said with a brief inclination of his head. "Honestly, I've been practicing my response for when somebody in government asks me that question. We get a lot of donations from anonymous sources that I am pretty sure can be traced back to former residents, but I'm not going to be the one to do the tracking."

"Wise," Felix said, hands in his pockets as he leaned against the wet bar. "You could lead the stalkers right to the victims."

"Yes," Lucius agreed, nodding. "But that means I'm not equipped for the cyberattacks on our books. We have security, although I have the feeling it needs to be updated. I started this endeavor before my father died, and I kept it secret, so I was working with less than full funding. And *I* can't track down our most likely perpetrators because I'd be letting them know that their hacks almost got them what they wanted."

"Is it only hacking?" Danny asked.

To Chuck's dismay, Lucius shook his head.

"I thought you said your security was breached," Chuck said in concern.

Lucius turned worried eyes to him, as though he was the only person in the room. "It was," he replied. "And some of it *was* hacking—a couple of serious attempts to get into the server where we keep things like medical and educational records."

"When did these attacks happen?" Danny said. "Not exact dates. We'll look at that later. But were they close to the other electronic security breaches?"

Lucius nodded, his expression telling Chuck that he'd already thought of this. "About two hours afterwards, as though testing to see if we'd be so preoccupied with one issue that we wouldn't notice the other."

"Why weren't you?" Felix asked curiously. "It seems to me as though the attacks to a business dealing with proprietary information would take all of your security's attention."

"The company and the charity are two different entities," Lucius said. "They're run by different people, they're on different servers. The only thing they have in common—the *only* thing—is that they're on that same ten-thousand-acre packet of land."

"Wait," Hunter rasped, and they all turned toward him.

Grace's voice came from the iPad. "You're not telling them what else is on that land, Rich Man," he said. "It could be important!"

"Well," Lucius said, giving the iPad a beleaguered look, "I was getting there."

"So?" Danny prompted, raising his eyebrows.

"Well, we needed to hide Caraway House in plain sight, and it seemed the most convenient way to do that was to repurpose an already existing building and grounds. My grandfather bought the property from a retiring cattle baron back in the fifties and built his factory and his mansion on opposite ends of it. My father made a fat bundle by capitalizing on the computer age, and *he* built *another* mansion, this one bigger, gaudier, and more ostentatious, between the original mansion and the road."

"So which one do you live in?" Chuck asked, curious.

"My grandfather's has marble tiles and beveled moldings," Lucius said simply. "And only six bedrooms. The bigger one was easily divided into fifteen dormitories with five bathrooms between them and a giant common area for the children. The grounds have been converted. The interior part is parkland, trees and grass and a playground. But my grandfather planted—and maintained—a veritable forest, and we kept that surrounding the house and interior grounds.

There are security monitors, fencing, and motion detectors around the perimeter and periodically through the wooded areas. We want people to feel hidden and secure, but we also want to be able to spot anybody who doesn't belong."

"Who mans the cameras?" Julia asked. "Regular security guards or—"

Lucius gave a veiled glance toward Hunter. "Retired military. Mostly women. We take word of mouth referrals only and run thorough background checks." Lucius shrugged. "I try to be as paranoid as possible," he said. "One of the benefits of running the place on what is supposedly my property is that from satellite photos, it should look kosher. There are enough trees and awnings to shade the number of people who live there. And since I have to pass the place every day to get to my house, which is about a half mile past down the drive, my daily check-ins don't seem strange. For all people know, I've got houseguests. I mean, I can't make it invisible, and I need to keep medical records for possible prosecutions, if nothing else...." He paused to shudder and swallow convulsively, and Chuck suddenly understood what this project cost him. He was *dedicated* to keeping these women and children safe. This was *personal*.

"You've done very well," Danny soothed, that sweet avuncular air that seemed to be second nature to him coming into play. "We're just asking questions so we have a better idea of what we're up against. Because as you rightly assumed, this is complicated. We've got a complex method of corporate sabotage going on, and it seems to mask an equally complex method of breaching the security of people for whom security means everything. But you said the attacks on Caraway's security were more than just virtual. What happened?"

"Chaos," Lucius said grimly. "All three times, there was a dual attack. First the security at the factory started going nuts. Every coder in the building started raising firewalls, and whatever concrete disruption happened—for instance, the hack that turned off all our refrigerators in the wing that tests experimental vaccines—needed to be addressed. While that was still happening, the people who monitored the computer systems and security cameras and alarms started reporting hacks in the servers. Now with Caraway House, the staff's military background stands us in good stead. The first time it happened, when they realized that their cameras were fuzzing in and out, they called the security guards—there are always three on with every shift—to gather the residents together and keep them safe in the house. The electronics expert who was on duty that day had the alarms up and running within a minute, because Lisa is that damned good, and as soon as they went up, the alarms started going off. The cameras caught a glimpse of two different intruders, both dressed in black with facemasks, coming in from two different areas. They vaulted back up the fences as soon as the alarms came back on, and they must have been prepared in the extreme because when the alarms came back up, the fences became electrified. I'm thinking silicon gloves, kneepads, and booties were the only things between these two gentlemen and a very crispy morning. That was the worst one, because we have been doubling and tripling security at every juncture." He let out a sigh.

"But you can't do that forever," Julia said softly. "Hypervigilance only lasts so long."

"It's not fair," Lucius said. "Either to my staff or to the people who only came to Caraway House to find peace."

"Were intruders spotted at any of the other times?" Chuck asked, alarm roiling in his belly.

"Twice," Lucius confirmed. "But both times, they came from different parts of the campus. There have also been other attempted break-ins, each time in places that looked vulnerable."

"But weren't?" Felix asked, sounding impressed.

Lucius compressed his lips into an angry line. "I try very hard not to hire stupid," he said. "Every member of my staff is as dedicated to keeping these people safe as I am." He let out a breath. "But we're exhausted. I thought leaking information would be solved when we took care of the sabotage problem two months ago, but this issue had apparently been hiding underneath it."

"When did the incursions into Caraway House start?" Hunter asked.

"The first information leak was a couple of months ago—but the first Caraway House breach was two weeks ago." He made an unhappy sound in his throat. "We were prepared to deal with the corporate sabotage on our own, but this?" He shook his head and sent Danny and Felix a pleading look. "I promised them they'd be safe," he said, his voice almost a whisper. "Please help me keep that promise."

"Well," Danny replied, "as we discussed this afternoon, I have a plan."

He quickly outlined the idea of Stirling going in undercover as an employee and Carl going in as what he was in real life—an insurance investigator.

"I got called out of my day job for this?" he asked plaintively.

"Well, you'll be working with all of us," Danny said. "And you'll be using your contacts to find out if there have been other jobs like this one. I doubt it. This situation feels very personal. Not just the threat to the shelter, but the technology drain. I can't imagine Lucius is a random victim of this sort of thing—but still, it's possible it happened before, or somebody made a practice run somewhere else. So, Carl, you'll be working with Stirling, and Stirling...." Danny bit his lip, because he obviously knew it was a big ask. "You're going to work for a living. That means you'll need to get trained, hack from the inside, talk to people, and do the job you were hired for at the same time. If you find inconsistencies, point them out to your supervisor, and we'll follow that chain of information to make sure it gets to where it's supposed to be going. If you do a deep dive and find something, turn it over to Carl, Lucius, Chuck, or myself. I'll be working from here, but you can tag me for a face-to-face at any time, understood?"

Chuck had been afraid Stirling would be nervous, or even a little freaked out. To his—and everybody else's—surprise, the kid's face lit up.

"Me? I get to go undercover?"

"Absolutely," Danny said, turning his smile back to him with a 1000-watt upgrade. "We really need you on this."

"Excellent!" Stirling pumped his fist and then shrank back in on himself. "It's just... you know. Everybody else usually goes undercover. Not me." He gave his sister a wistful look, and she turned a gaze of pure adoration back on him.

"You'll be fantastic," Molly said throatily. "Welcome to the front of the house, little brother!" She sobered then and turned back to Danny. "I take it I'll be going undercover at the shelter, right?"

Danny nodded. "We were going to have you go in like Chuck—as a fitness trainer or life coach—"

She shook her head. "Victim," she said simply.

"Feel free to ask for pointers," Julia told her, and while the directive sounded all business, she made eye contact with the younger woman to show Molly that Julia understood what a difficult role this would be.

"From me too," Danny said, and while Molly's eyebrows ratcheted up a notch, she didn't look shocked.

"Stirling and I were in foster care for a while," she said. "But I was in it about two years before Stirling. Don't worry, I've got my own experience to draw from."

There were looks of sympathy, but nobody said anything. Chuck got it, though. They all had marketable skills—the kind that could easily get them a nine-to-five somewhere cushy. They weren't thieves to make money; they were thieves and con men because there was something inside them, some fundamental damage, that made it easier to contribute to the world through breaking the law than upholding it.

Laws were there for a reason. Poor Carmichael. His life would have been so much better if he'd never followed his brothers into crime.

But Lucius couldn't ask the authorities to help him with his problem. Given the statistics for spousal abuse among law enforcement, some of the people in his care feared for their lives from that very quarter.

And that was where thieves who didn't steal for money came in.

Because working under the radar wasn't only for unscrupulous hackers and ninja guys in masks. Sometimes it was for really talented people who took their therapy out in unexpected ways.

"So, good," Danny said, pulling the attention away from the unwelcome revelation that Molly had been abused—much to her relief, judging by her posture. "Molly's going to be staying in the dorms, and Hunter is going to beef up your security. Chuck is going to be a fitness instructor by day and a security monitor by night. Lucius, when were those attacks again?"

"Night, all three times," Lucius said, nodding in understanding.

"So Chuck and Hunter will be there to assist your security team as well. You may need to brief some of them, but I am going to leave that up to you."

"Yes, sir." Lucius nodded respectfully, and Chuck tried not to let that make him any softer than he already was on the guy, dammit. "I trust my security chief, Lisa Sampson, without reservation. But she's been doing deep dives on some of her people to make sure they're not responsible or in any way compromised regarding these incursions. If you and Stirling have any time, she might appreciate the help."

"I can do that if you send me the info," Josh said, his voice sleepy even over the iPad. "Danny and Felix may be running the op, but deep dives on the computer sound like spring break right now."

"I'll send you what Lucius sends me," Danny said. "And that goes for all of you. Right now, that's our plan. Stirling and Carl go in the business side of things as employees, Chuck goes in the shelter, taking on two roles, and Molly, love, I'm afraid you've got the hardest role of all." He paused. "Lucius, about that. I know you are trying to keep secrets here, but the odds rest heavily on somebody's ex-spouse being rich or connected enough to pull this off. Without compromising too many identities here, do you have any ideas—?"

Lucius held up his hand and shook his head, but what he said wasn't the pompous defense of privacy that Chuck expected.

"All of them," he said, his voice burning with fury. "We have a state senator who was abusing his wife and their five-year-old child, as well as his side piece, who is also in our care. We have the wife of Springfield's chief of police, three policemen's wives—they have their own support group—two wives of prominent businessmen, one boyfriend of a stockbroker, and three students from Ohio State, who thought they were dating sweet little frat boys only to get the crap beaten out of them on a bet. One woman's ex-husband runs a drug cartel. He might have been the first person on my list, honestly, but he got blown up about a month ago. We used the opportunity to fake her death, and we're just waiting for an alternative identity to pop up that will suit her and her daughter. It may still be his family, but—"

"It may also be anybody else on that list," Danny muttered, cupping an elbow and gnawing on his thumbnail. "Fucking aces. Why are humans anyway?"

Felix moved fluidly to his side, two cookies in a napkin in his hands. "Here you go. Misanthropy's magic cure-all in a paper napkin."

Danny made a growling sound in his throat and then accepted the napkin. "More like *Danny's* cure-all in a pair of overpriced loafers," he grumbled, "but point taken. Okay, so Lucius has many, *many* scumbags that might be responsible for this. We need somebody that has A) an interest, motive, or familiarity with the *business* side of things, as well as B) a pressing desire to threaten somebody living in the shelter. It's going to take the lot of us to figure this out, including Felix, I think, taking a look at the list Lucius is about to give us and schmoozing his poor face off with some of these villains. Hunter will be here in the morning to drive everybody to the airport, and you all will meet Lucius when you land in Peoria. Lucius, if you could brief everybody on costumes and makeup, they can provide a list to Julia and myself for anything they don't have."

He paused for breath. "Josh, Grace, did you get all of that?"

"He's asleep, Danny," Grace said, his usually quirky, abrupt tones soft and worried. "I'll tell him in the morning."

"Good." Danny's eyes flickered up. "Hunter's on his way to say hi. Be kind to him. He has to drive back at fuck-you in the morning."

Grace's tired chuckle hurt Chuck's heart. "He may be able to walk by then," he announced, and Hunter grimaced and turned the iPod off.

"I top," he muttered.

"We know," Chuck said, his voice dripping with sincerity.

"Grace meant in case I strain something."

"Yes, precious," Chuck told him, nodding. "We understand. Go strain something for the team."

"Fuck off," Hunter muttered before handing Chuck the tablet and stomping off. He was being a tad dramatic, which told Chuck that he was playing it for laughs, which was good.

This case was going to touch everybody a little raw, and they were going to be doing it without some of their brightest and best. They needed as much laughter as they could get.

Stirling and Molly descended on Lucius first, asking about costuming, and Carl caught his eye.

"Do we know where we're staying?" he asked.

"You and Stirling will probably get Lucius's place," Chuck said. "I'm pretty sure Hunter and I get some back room in a security booth. Why?"

Carl shrugged, looking irritated. "I have busted three guys for stealing their own artwork for insurance claims in the last *month*," he said. "This is seriously the most fun I've had since Danny was on the game in Europe."

Chuck laughed. "Well, let's hope it stays fun and doesn't get dangerous. It sure got that way last time." He shuddered. Yeah, he'd kept a good face on it, but defusing that bomb while Stirling and Josh had been in the van had been playing a recurring role in his nightmares during the past couple of months. That was a lot of pressure for a foot soldier who didn't like strings.

"Don't lie to yourself, Chucky," Carl said, looking at him knowingly. "The risk is part of why you like it."

Chuck thought about who he'd been before he'd had to leave Car-Car in his rearview, knowing the guy was going to prison, and knowing he'd set up Wilber and Klamath to be killed by the police.

"Acceptable risk," he said, nodding thoughtfully. "Acceptable risk."

Carl, who probably studied actuarial tables before he went to sleep so he could be top-notch at his job, nodded in agreement. "Concur," he said, which was like him. Carl was all about the action and very little about who was perpetrating the action. It was why he was such an outstanding bedmate—and so very easy to walk away from back in Europe. A cock was a cock after all.

Or it had been, before Car-Car.

At that moment, Lucius broke away from Stirling and Molly, holding out his hands to indicate he would be back to talk to them in a moment.

"Charles," he said, his voice pitching so oddly that the entire room quieted down. "Before you leave—"

"I can wait until you're done with your other conversation," Chuck said, giving a bland smile. He was trying to remind himself that he was nothing special to this man. Yes, they'd some flirting and one hell of a kiss—but this guy had more important things to do than Chuck Calder.

"We're almost done," Lucius said, casting an almost desperate look over his shoulder. Stirling nodded soberly, but Molly, who was better at picking up on unspoken cues, hid her laugh with her fingers.

"Go ahead, Chuck," she said when she'd recovered. "We can wait."

Chuck eyed her blandly. He loved Molly Christopher, oh yes he did, but she had a sense of humor like a rabid pixie.

"What is it you needed?" Chuck asked, and for a moment, Lucius floundered. The room—still silent—grew uncomfortable, so Chuck tried to fill in. "I've got leggings and polos for when I'm a fitness instructor, and a sports jacket and jeans for when I do security—"

"Jeans!" Carl complained, but then Carl always had a thing for tailored suits and shiny shoes.

"Jeans, Carl. Nobody would believe I could lead a unit. Transpo and munitions is the guy in a sports coat—not a suit. All I'll need is electronic key cards and a fake name and I'm good to go."

"Fake name…." Lucius said, his brain obviously shorting out. "Oh. Yes. Charlie Summers. I've got aliases ready for Molly, Stirling, Hunter, and Carl as well. But that's not what I was going to ask."

Oh. "Well, then, uh, what?"

Chuck smiled helpfully, thinking maybe the whole "covert op" part of this had put Lucius a little off his game.

Then Lucius spoke and put Chuck off *his* game.

"A tux, like the one you were wearing at the gala," Lucius said, smiling prettily. "Do you have one of those not covered in grease stains?"

Chuck gaped for a moment and tried to recover. "Uhm, three: basic black, white with silver, and black with a red velveteen jacket. Why?" Julia had been so grateful to him for disarming the explosive device attached to the van that Josh and Stirling had been in, she'd promised him a room full of fitted suits. So far, she'd sent him three—her choice—and he'd loved every one of them.

"Well, probably the basic black, but, uh, the red velveteen jacket would be nice." Lucius's smile grew a little brighter and a little more anticipatory.

"I can have Hunter get it when he grabs my sports jacket," Chuck said doubtfully. "But, uhm, why?"

Lucius's pretty smile came, the one that made his not-quite-crossed arctic-hazel eyes light up and his patrician features look young and sweet instead of adult and powerful.

"There's a function in Springfield in the next week. I, uhm, need a plus-one. I was hoping you could—"

Chuck was still confused. "Is this part of security?" he asked.

"I need a date!" Lucius blurted. "I'm asking you out on a date!"

Chuck gaped, and the rest of the room faded into a Chicago-red-tinted blur. "A… a date?"

"Yes, Chuck—you *have* been on a date before, haven't you?"

"Uhm…." He tried to think. He'd gotten *laid* plenty, but had he ever gotten dressed up and gone out someplace nice and had dinner and conversation beforehand? "No," he said, a little bit of panic creeping into his voice. "No, I don't go on dates. I—"

Carl helped him out by putting a hand on his shoulder. "Don't worry, Mr. Broadstone," he said smoothly. "He'll be all civilized and able to speak like a human and everything by the time we get there tomorrow. You can tell him about the date then."

Lucius's smile grew in wattage, amperage, and general sunshine. "Really? He'll come?" He focused on Chuck, who was staring at Carl like he'd grown another head. "You'll come to the dinner, uhm, Charles? Chuck? You'll come?"

"Sure he will," Carl said, nodding so frantically that Chuck found himself nodding back.

"Sure I will," Chuck said, trying to pull his equilibrium from his ass, his ear, or any other place that would set him back on his feet again. "Are you sure you want me? Carl's bi. He'll go. Stirling's single—"

"Ew!" Stirling said. "He's *hella old*!"

"It's the same age difference as Hunter and Grace," his sister told him, and Stirling's horrified stare at her told Chuck all he wanted to know about how real most other people were to Stirling.

"I'm thirty-two," Lucius said, obviously stung.

"I'm thirty," Chuck said, not quite sure how this entire conversation had veered so far south. "And if you want me to wear a tux and go to a dinner, uhm, sure. I'd, uh, love to." He honestly couldn't remember ever being asked before. Who asked out a good-time Charlie—or a Good Luck Chuck?

"Good!" Lucius said. "Good! I'll, uh, after you get all settled in tomorrow, I'll give you details. The, uh, shindig is, uhm, is in four days. So, if, uhm, Hunter could cover or whatever—"

"We'll make sure he's ready," Carl said and then elbowed Chuck unceremoniously in the side.

"Thank you for asking," Chuck said mechanically, and then Soderburgh, because he was apparently a better friend than Chuck deserved, grabbed him by the elbow and started for the stairs.

"If you don't mind, Mr. Broadstone, Chuck and I have some, uhm, strategizing to do. We'll be in the living room if you need us, yes?"

Lucius smiled that blinding smile again. "Yes, excellent! I'll see you both on the tarmac tomorrow after we land, if not before, okay?"

"Okay," Chuck said. "See you then."

And then Soderburgh hauled him out of the den and out of his misery so he could find his shit with both hands and figure where to put it.

"Oh my God," he said as Carl hauled him to the Italian leather couch in the front room, where he could sit and scrub at his face with his palms.

"What in the hell was that?" Soderburgh asked, genuinely horrified as he sank down in the club chair kitty-corner.

"I don't know," Chuck said, completely off his balance.

"I thought you were a con man! I thought you were supposed to be smooth!"

"I'm a getaway driver," Chuck said sharply. "That's got all the sex appeal I need!"

That rocked Soderburgh back for a moment. "Well," he said, "you're not wrong. But don't you have any moves? Jesus, Chuck, all you needed back there was a 'Yeah, sure, I'd be happy to put on a suit and paint the town with you,' and what you had was—"

"Oh God," Chuck mumbled, burying his face deeper. "But seriously. Who asks the getaway driver on a date? You *fuck* the getaway driver—"

"I recall," Soderburgh said dryly.

"But see? You wanted to *nail* me. Nobody wants to *date* me!"

"Well, apparently that very handsome bazillionaire with the pretty awesome charity wants to date you," Soderburgh told him, and his voice gentled. "So, what are you going to do about that?"

Chuck groaned and fell back against the couch. "Well, I guess I'm going to go. But why hasn't anybody *warned* him about me? Told him I was easy and to take me back in the garage and go for it? I mean… the suit… it's… it's a lot of trouble."

"I don't know, Chuck." Soderburgh patted his knee. "Sometimes the trouble is the point. The getting dressed, the excitement. It means you care enough to worry if you're getting it right. Don't you want that?"

Chuck actually thought about it. "I'm... I don't know. Maybe it comes with the name. I was always in it for a good time." And before Soderburgh could answer, he blew out a breath. "But... you know. Guys like us didn't take other guys to the prom, did we?"

"No," Carl said, his voice quiet. "We didn't. I suck at hearts and flowers myself, which is why my marriage didn't work out. But that doesn't mean I wouldn't want to try some hearts and flowers if it would get me someone I really cared about."

Chuck cocked his head, not wanting to say the name but unable to stop thinking it. Everybody knew everybody's business in this crew. They all knew Chuck and Carl had been a good time to each other, much like they knew Hunter and Grace were "till death do us part." And everybody knew that when Danny and Felix had been broken up, Danny had slept with the wrong gangster and the right insurance investigator, but that even the right insurance investigator paled in comparison to the love he had for Felix Salinger.

"And to answer your question," Soderburgh sighed, "yes. I tried hearts and flowers with Danny, but... I think unless it was Felix, he could never take it seriously. And here you are, faced with a guy who wants to take *you* seriously, and the question is, can you sit still and stop flirting long enough to take him seriously back?"

Chuck thought about it. Thought about Lucius's shy smile and his damned tight security. And the way he'd given his father's monstrosity of a mansion to charity but kept his grandfather's ranch house because it meant something to him.

By all indicators, Lucius Broadstone was a good man. A good businessman and a good person. The fact that he wanted to take Chuck on a date—a real date with nice clothes and aftershave and everything—should not be counted against him.

"It was just so unexpected," he said plaintive-ly, and was *not* reassured when Carl burst into hearty barks of laughter.

Bumpy Landings

LUCIUS ONLY had to wait in the terminal of the small private airport twenty minutes or so before the Salinger plane landed. He and his pilot and mechanic, Saoirse Corcoran, went to meet them after Chuck had taxied to Lucius's hangar, close enough to the fuel pumps for Saoirse to refill.

As he approached, he noted that Hunter exited first, yawning, which probably meant he'd slept for the journey, and Chuck followed Molly, Stirling, and Carl, looking bright-eyed, his swagger possibly intensified by the chance to fly the plane.

Sure enough, although he had a garment bag over his shoulder and was hauling a rollerboard behind him, he paused long enough at the bottom of the ramp to push a pair of aviator sunglasses up his nose with a grin straight out of *Top Gun.* God, he was irrepressible.

Maybe that's why Lucius had asked him out.

Lord knew that wasn't what he'd been planning as they'd hashed out the details and explained the situation in the Salingers' den. No, Lucius had been all business, and more than a little bit of panic. As far as he knew, the women in the two shelters in the heart of Springfield and Chicago had been safe as bunnies in the four years since he'd established Caraway House as a place—or places—that would shelter battered spouses from their violent counterparts. Part of that was that he took security seriously, and part of *that* was that he was pretty slick with hiding the victims in other cities, under assumed identities, while he employed a cadre of idealistic junior lawyers who worked hard to get them disentangled from their spouses legally.

It was hard work and less than ideal. And he was well aware that the company his father left him—the company he loathed—was the cash cow that fed the entire enterprise with its money-milk. If he fucked up Broadstone Industries, all of the equity he'd put into Caraway House would disappear, and the people he was trying so desperately to help would be left without recourse.

He'd been desperate enough to break the law when he realized somebody was stealing technology from the company and selling it to his competitors. And that, of course, was when he'd met the Salinger crew.

Now he was desperate enough to seek out their help when he realized that both branches of his enterprise were in danger.

That was a lot of desperation, but seeing Charles—Chuck—Calder again, getting pulled into the general sense of play and excitement at the dinner table, that had worked like a balm to his soul.

Chuck Calder had been happy to see him. Not the captain of Broadstone Industries. Not the benefactor of Caraway House. *Him.* Lucius Broadstone.

Although Lucius had been so charmed by both his smile and his offer of cookies that he really was thinking about being called Scotty.

Get a grip. Vulnerable people are counting on you!

Nothing had ever been enough for Lucius's father—never enough money, never enough recognition, never enough respect. He'd taken that… that merciless *need* out on those around him—his wife and two sons. Then his one son. And Lucius, desperate to protect his mother, his baby brother, from his father's cruel words and heavy hand, had been… not enough. Not ever enough. By the time he'd grown and gotten his degree, it had been too late to save his brother, to protect his mother, but God, he had enjoyed taking the trust his grandfather had left him and setting up charities his father had deplored.

When the old man had been on his death bed, attached to tubes, unable to speak to call his lawyer, Lucius had shown his father the plans for making his grotesque mansion into a shelter for women very much like the one he'd physically and psychologically abused into an early grave.

His father had died the next day, and when Lucius thought back to that moment, to his father's impotent rage, to the way his heartbeat had labored as he'd fought for breath to scream "Over my dead body!" he wondered sometimes if there was something wrong with him.

Because he didn't feel any guilt at all.

But if these people he'd promised shelter were harmed? That was another story. He'd never be able to forgive himself if he couldn't keep them safe.

The mental shakedown was very needed. He'd sought out the Salinger crew because he'd required help, not because he needed to get laid.

Still… it would almost be criminal to let that tall, long-legged figure swaggering across the tarmac go unremarked.

It wasn't only the muscles—and privately Lucius was forced to acknowledge that they were awfully... muscley. It was the drawled humor, the way Chuck's lean lips were almost always upturned in a smile, and the way he seemed to diffuse any unpleasantness with genuine care for how people felt.

Lucius hadn't grown up with that easiness. He had no idea how to create that for himself. But he sure did appreciate it in others, and to find it packaged in a man who could fly a plane, fight off criminals, and disarm a car bomb?

Well, Charles Calder really was sex on the hoof, wasn't he?

And it had been a while since Lucius had been ridden.

Lucius had to shove that thought solidly to the back of his mind as he crossed the tarmac to greet his new friends.

"A good flight, I trust?" he asked, noting that the two young people in the crew looked relatively happy.

"Smooth as silk," Molly said perkily. "Our father used to fly small aircraft, and shit could get really hairy when he was behind the stick. Chuck, it was like you lifted us into the clouds on the wings of angels."

Chuck let out a hearty laugh. "Oh, sweetheart, you do my ego good." He extended his hand to Lucius. "Good to see you, Scotty my man. You said you'd have us set up with some vehicles?"

Lucius nodded. "Yes. I thought we could carpool to my house. Molly is staying in the shelter, of course, and you and Hunter have a room there to sleep when you need it, and I hope Carl and Stirling won't mind sleeping in my guest rooms."

"Yes!" Carl said, pumping his fist, and Chuck shrugged as though they'd discussed this.

Lucius went on. "Anyway, I'll need to orient everybody, and I thought we could, uhm—" Oh, how embarrassing. This was a job, and he was treating it like a social occasion, but dammit, he *liked* these people! "—have lunch at my place before everybody goes off to their corners."

Chuck and Hunter nodded.

"Excellent. We can use your house as command central if we need to. Meet for breakfast and dinner when we can, trade notes. Good thinking, Scotty boy." Chuck looked up at the two Bentley Bentaygas—one bronze, one green—that Saoirse had brought out to the field. "So, which one of us gets to drive one of those?"

"I do," Carl said happily. "Hunter's still tired, and you got to fly the plane!"

"Yours," Saoirse said. "You take the dark green one. Don't fuck up my vehicles." And with that, she tossed the keys neatly to Carl, who gave a sheepish smile.

"Better me than Chuck," Carl said. "He drives like he's running from the law, even when he's not!"

Chuck's throaty laughter told Lucius that he was not at all offended. "Well then, let's load up. Stirling, Molly, if you two ride with Soderburgh there, Hunter can sack out in the back of the SUV and catch an extra forty-five minutes while we drive to the middle of nowhere, okay?"

"Yes!" Stirling muttered. "That means I get the back to *my*self."

"And I get to look around," Molly agreed. Together they grabbed their roller bags and headed for the dark green vehicle. Lucius held Chuck back.

"This is Saoirse Corcoran," he said. "I'll give you all contact information. She's going to be in charge of keeping your plane housed and fueled and ready to go and keeping your vehicles shipshape. I want you all to be able to come and go freely, and Saoirse is your ticket out of the Peoria/Springfield milieu."

Chuck laughed and extended his hand. "Pleased ta meetya, Saoirse." He paused for a moment and *hmm*d. "Love that name, by the way. You're not a selkie, perchance, are you? From one of my favorite legends?"

Saoirse—who tended toward being taciturn and unapproachable—gave Chuck a flicker of a smile. "Sadly no," she said, her voice betraying just a trace of Ireland. "But I love the old stories too."

Chuck grinned. "Have you seen the Thomas Moore animated feature? Oh, darlin', it's a thing of beauty!"

And Saoirse, for the first time in Lucius's knowledge, lit up like a sunrise. "There's a movie? Animated? I had no idea! It's about the selkie legend?"

"Sweetheart, it will make your Irish heart sing. I promise you that." Chuck pulled out his phone and set it up to enter information. "Now type your digits in there, and I'll text you links about the movie and questions about the cars. That way, you don't have to go, 'Oh shit, that asshole Lucius assigned to me is texting me again.' How's that?"

"That's a plan," she said, her broad-cheekboned face going pink. "Wait until I tell my wife there's a movie—she'll be thrilled!"

Chuck chatted for another moment about animation and selkies, until Hunter barely suppressed a yawn.

"Now I got to go, darlin', cause my friend here is dead on his feet—had to visit his boyfriend last night and got caught in traffic this morning, you know. Anyway, I'll chat with you later and you can let me know how you and your girl liked the movie."

And Saoirse damned near gushed. "Absolutely, Mr. Calder—"

"Sweetheart, everybody who's anybody calls me Chuck. Now I'll see you later, hear?"

And with that, Chuck led the way to the remaining vehicle and held his hand out politely for the keys.

And Lucius, who *owned the damned Bentley*, handed the keys over in a daze.

He'd hired Saoirse five years ago, given her benefits, sent her Christmas cards and fruit baskets—he'd attended her wedding, for Christ's sake—and not once in all that time had that woman so much as cracked a smile at him.

But she'd grinned at Chuck.

He did that with *everybody*, didn't he? No wonder he'd been so surprised Lucius had asked him out. Great. That was just great. This apparently nice, easygoing man dropped a little charm Lucius's way and Lucius latched on like a nursing puppy. Excellent. Lucius got into the passenger seat of his own vehicle and tried not to sulk.

Behind them, Hunter threw his knapsack in one corner of the back and curled up on the seat, using the knapsack as a pillow. He'd brought a rollerboard and a garment bag too, but since Lucius assumed some of that was tools of the trade, he was pretty impressed by these people's minimalism. He would have needed *at least* two more bags if he was going to make it anywhere for longer than a week.

"Out to the main road and turn...?" Chuck asked him as he started the vehicle.

"Left," Lucius told him. "Toward Peoria. Broadstone Industries is sort of smack dab between the two cities."

"Nice," Chuck said. "Bigger recruitment pool."

"Yes, it works out that way," Lucius agreed. "I'm pretty sure my grandfather was just excited about being able to use his cattle land for something else."

Chuck's low laughter still generated warmth in Lucius's belly, but his next question set Lucius off balance.

"Why'd you look like you were sucking lemons there when I was talking to Saoirse?"

Lucius wondered if it was because this man was so much larger than life that he made Lucius feel so small.

"You have a way of making people feel special," Lucius said uncomfortably. "I simply realized that when I asked you out, I had, perhaps, misinterpreted your signals. I thought you were interested, when you were, in fact, simply being nice to me." He let out a sigh. "Disappointment and hurt pride. It won't happen again."

Chuck snorted. "Well, it shouldn't have happened the first time. You were fine. I was surprised, that was all."

Lucius gave him a disgruntled look. "Why would you be so shocked? It surely must have crossed your mind that—" He floundered, and his voice dropped. "—that I enjoyed kissing you."

"Kissing, yes," Chuck said frankly. "I'm a professional criminal, Lucius. Plenty of guys like to get in my pants. I'm the fuckboi in Fuck/Marry/Kill. A date is something else. Especially with a suit. It's special. I was surprised, is all, that a guy like you would want to go to the trouble of wining and dining me. It was...." Lucius turned to study his face while he kept his eyes on the road, seeming to search for words.

There were pink flags of color in his cheeks.

"Was what?" he asked, fascinated.

"Flattering," Chuck said with dignity. "And unexpected. Took me a minute to absorb the significance is all. I'm sorry if you took that to mean I didn't think you were... attractive. Or interesting. Or special."

He swallowed hard with that last word, and Lucius's face was warm as well.

"Special is... premature," he said. "For all you know, I'm excruciatingly boring on a date."

Chuck gave a huff of laughter. "I don't see how, businessman. You are extremely interesting when you're not on one!"

"Not recently," Lucius admitted. "In college, yes. There were expensive and dangerous hobbies—"

"Do tell!" And his enthusiasm seemed real. Lucius wasn't sure how he did that, showed enthusiasm and interest when he was talking to people. Lucius was so grateful for Saoirse's steady, ultracompetent presence. He'd always felt they were a good team. Watching her thaw and bloom under Chuck's sincere kindness had been lovely, but still, it had felt like a personal affront to all of Lucius's natural reserve.

"Cliff diving," Lucius confessed. "I was on the dive team anyway, so that was a natural extension. Bungee jumping—"

"Base jumping?" Chuck asked curiously.

"God no. That's so dangerous. Do you know any-body stupid enough to do that?"

"Not. A. Word." Hunter's grumpy voice from the back of the SUV made Chuck laugh uproariously for some reason.

Lucius tried not to sigh. "Do I want to know?" he asked.

"Well, it's one of the things Grace and Josh did that we're not supposed to know about or tell Josh's parents. But we all saw them on the news. And just because they were wearing specially made microfiber masks and those *Mission Impossible* flying-squirrel outfits so they could slow themselves before they pulled their chutes doesn't mean anything."

Hunter gave a surprisingly satisfied-sounding snort from behind them that lapsed into snores almost immediately.

"Why'd they do it?" Lucius asked.

Chuck checked his rearview, almost like he was checking on Hunter. "Do you remember that day you first saw them on *Good Morning Chicago*? The day Marnie Courtland was arrested?"

"Yes," Lucius said. "How could I not?"

"Well, pretty much everything Danny and Felix said on camera that morning was true, one hundred percent. But there were a few things—"

"The fact that Danny's real name isn't Benjamin Morgan, for instance?" Lucius hazarded.

"A few things," Chuck maintained, his voice neu-tral, "that could have hurt Felix's chances to get control of his company back. And we didn't know about them. But Josh found out because he was working in the back of the house that day. He figured he and Grace could take care of it, and they did." Chuck shrugged. "We, erm—well, I—gave Josh a rather stern talking-to about going out on his own like that."

"Did it stick?" Lucius asked, concerned for the magnetic young man in spite of himself.

"Well, he got sick about a month after that. We'll have to see what happens when he gets better."

Lucius thought about Josh, begging to be part of the op from a distance, or lying in the hospital bed, trying to stay alert and a part of the conversation.

"He seems very driven," Lucius said, recognizing the same thing in himself. "I wonder what drives him."

"I'm afraid that's his story," Chuck said firmly. "But he was raised by Danny, Felix, and Julia, and they made him the center of their world. I think… I think some kids recognize how lucky they are. I know his friend Grace didn't have the same sort of parental devotion. So maybe part of his drive is wanting to give back to a world that was more than generous to him."

"In a most unusual way," Lucius said on a laugh.

"In the only way he knows," Chuck said.

Lucius wanted to ask more questions, but he could hear the finality in Chuck's tone and knew he'd trespassed enough.

"What about your story?" he asked, dying to hear it.

"Well, sir," Chuck drawled, "I'm lazy. Didn't want to finish college, so I joined the army instead. Army was too much work for me, so I quit and began a life of crime. Crime paid, as it turned out, so I retired and became part of a Chicago-based think tank that likes to solve people's problems for them, and that's what I'm doing now."

Lucius felt a stab of disappointment. "That's… that's very attractive-sounding bullshit," he said.

"Well, what did you want from a criminal?" Chuck asked, and he may have been trying to keep his voice light, but it was obvious he was hurt now, too.

"I was hoping for the truth," Lucius said.

"Oh, like you told *us* everything, when you sat in the Salinger's basement and gave us your story," Chuck scoffed, and Lucius was wounded to the quick.

"I told you *everything*—"

"Why is this so important to you?" Chuck demanded, his voice implacable. "You didn't tell us that. I mean, we all know why superheroes have alter-egos, but we sure don't know why Lucius Broadstone wants to keep women and children safe from their stalkers. You could have it easy, guy-in-a-suit. You could be spending Daddy's money and driving his company into the ground. But instead you're fighting to keep Daddy's company afloat for—and I have to say this is what it looks like—the sole purpose of keeping these charities going."

"So?" Lucius asked, feeling defensive.

"So?" Chuck mocked. "I find that really interesting, that's all."

Lucius took a deep breath and tried to get his emotions under control, because right now, he was one deep breath away from forcing Chuck to turn the SUV around and calling the whole thing off.

"It's… personal," he said, his voice stripped bare. "I'm… I'm sorry. It's personal why this means so much to me. You're right. I shouldn't have demanded full disclosure from you when I was not willing to give it myse—"

"My father didn't beat my mother," Chuck said, shocking him badly. "But he may as well have. He cheated on her. He lied to her. And when she confronted him with what she knew to be true, he tried to convince her she was crazy and overwrought. And then he threatened to take our college money away, to move out and leave her and their children penniless. It was abusive and painful. And three and a half years into college, I got myself into just enough trouble to realize I didn't want the education he'd used to blackmail my mother into staying, so I joined the military to get out of trouble." Chuck let out a breath. "And I'll stop there. But *you're* right. You got me where I hurt, so I struck back. I shouldn't have. Forgive me."

Lucius swallowed that for a moment and allowed it to digest. It was… an offering of sorts. A peaceful gift of information. Something real. There was plenty of bullshit left to sort through, but what Chuck had given him—the diamond in the pig wallow, as it were—was that Chuck knew his pain.

He took another deep breath and opened his mouth to say as much when Chuck spoke again.

"I know why this is important to you," he said softly. "Everybody in the basement knew. I get that this is personal to you, but think about it. We're sending a twenty-year-old girl into a dangerous situation to play an abused girlfriend, and when she volunteered to do that, Julia and Danny both told her they could give her pointers on the part. And it turned out, she had her own life experience to draw from. We know why you're doing it. Just remember. It's why we're doing it too."

Lucius's breath caught, and his eyes burned. Unconsciously he wiped underneath them with his palms.

"I'm sorry," Chuck sighed. "I… I bungled this. From the very start. I should have told you—"

"Just let me talk," Lucius said thickly. "Thank you. I… when you grow up rich and privileged, and your life is a nightmare, you… you think you are all alone. You think the things that drive you are yours alone and you have to deal with them yourself. I had not realized, until just now, that… that you and your friend in the back and those people in the car following us—you make me not alone. It's… it's humbling. It's a gift. It's enough."

Chuck let out another breath. "It's not," he said. "I was rude and an ass. I was trying to get out of being honest. You may be used to playing the boss man in a business suit, but I'm used to bullshitting a big enough hill to coast down. Let's take a breather from honesty for a bit, and I'll tell you the story of how I ended up in the military. Then you can laugh at my expense and start again."

Lucius took a moment to watch him, his eyes resolutely on the road, his big hands capable on the wheel, and while part of him was disappointed, another part of him was relieved.

This was, after all, Chuck's gift: putting people at ease. Lucius should allow him to use it and see what happened from there.

"That sounds good," Lucius said. "But I reserve the right to ask questions."

"Fine, fine, but when I'm done." Chuck nodded and Lucius did too, although Lucius was pretty sure Chuck wouldn't let anything derail him from the whopper heading down the pike. "Now, Mr. Broadstone, let me tell you about a college senior in chemical engineering who enjoyed his classwork but who did not enjoy some of his fellow students."

Chuck went on to tell him a story about an exploding frat-house toilet—and an exploding frat house—that left Lucius by turns in stitches and in shock.

When Chuck was finished and Lucius had stopped laughing, he managed to pull a coherent thought out of his head.

"Wait a minute," he said, trying hard to take a good breath. "I've heard about that. Didn't it happen in… wait a minute. Ohio? This really happened!"

Chuck made a noise of complete noncommitment. "Mm, I said."

"But… wait." Lucius's breath caught. "Kyle Miller. Was the guy you were trying to get back at named Kyle Miller?"

Chuck's neutral expression grew more guarded. "And if it was?"

"What did Mr. Miller do to piss you off, Chuck? This is important."

"Beat the shit out of a friend of mine because she wouldn't put out for him. Why?"

Lucius's laugh had more than a little bitterness in it. "Because remember how I said one of the women was a senator's wife?"

"Yeah. You didn't say if it was state or federal, but—"

"State. And her name is Heather Miller. When we sat down for the briefing, I was going to make him our first suspect for trying to break in."

Chuck grunted, and a sly, evil, *real* smile twisted his lips. "Why, Mr. Broadstone, I do believe we have something in common."

Well, having a common enemy wasn't what Lucius had in mind for romance, but it was definitely a start.

Places I Remember

SURE ENOUGH, about midway between Peoria and Springfield, Lucius had Chuck take a left into what appeared to be a giant stretch of nothing but cattle country. The impression faded about ten miles in, as a small suburb formed, one with outlet stores and grocers and gas stations, with a healthy dollop of homes nearby. Chuck studied the area with a little bit of awe.

"You're… you're like the king here, aren't you? They built this little town of…." He paused and looked at the signs on some of the stores and the gas station.

"Fuck," he said.

"I'm not the king," Lucius told him, obviously squirming uncomfortably.

"This town is called Broadstone."

"It only has about 10,000 people in it," Lucius said. "You know, three thousand employees, support industries, families—"

"Look!" Chuck said, appalled, seeing the big white board announcing classes starting in a couple of weeks. "There is a *high school* named after you!"

"Technically, it's named after my grandfather," Lucius muttered. And then, his voice dropping, he added, "Kenneth Broadstone Middle School is named after my brother."

That stopped Chuck. "You have a brother?" he asked. "Older or younger?"

"Younger. He, uhm, passed away when we were both young."

Gah! Would this man for fuck's sake stop tying his heart into knots? It was bad enough when Chuck made him confess his most painful secret because Chuck didn't want to talk about himself, but augh! "I'm so sorry," he said inadequately.

"Yes, well, it was a long time ago. It's not like you could have known."

The way he said it—so practiced—told Chuck that was not all there was to it. But he was done with ripping Lucius Broadstone's guts out for the day.

"Still," he said instead, "you really *are* rich, aren't you?"

"Mm… more established than really rich. Like I said, my grandfather owned a huge whack of cattle land. Some of it went into the factory campus and the mansion grounds, and, well, the rest of it went here."

"That's impressive," Chuck told him.

"Not really." Lucius blew out a sigh. "When you trace old money back to its roots, it inevitably has blood on it. I'm proud that I've been able to do something constructive with it—keeping the company afloat in tough financial weather, putting the proceeds into a cause I believe in. Getting praised for being born rich is like getting praise for having blue eyes. It's nice that people want to say something nice about you, but I would rather get praised for something good I *did*."

"Mm," Chuck nodded, getting it. Then he gave a quick smile, hoping to let Lucius off the hook a little.

"I haven't done much good in my life, Scotty, so I'd be happy to spend all the time praising you."

Lucius snorted, and Chuck, remembering the tenseness—the defensiveness—of the first few minutes of conversation, wouldn't let it go.

"It's true, Lucius," he said softly. "You do deserve praise. I'm an asshole. Don't let the shit I say get you down."

"You're not an asshole," Lucius snapped. "You just… just don't want me to know you."

"Well yeah! My good deed in college was blowing up a frat house! I mean, besides giving Miller second-degree burns on his ass, that's not much to brag about."

"Give it up, Chuck" came Hunter's voice from the back seat. "Even I know you were protecting your friend."

Chuck's cheeks heated. "Are you or are you not supposed to be asleep?" he asked irritably.

"Well, if either one of you was any good at small talk, I could have caught a nap," Hunter groused, sitting up. "But even *I* know that courtship talk needs to go a whole other way."

Great. The world's most taciturn man was giving Chuck lessons on how to bullshit. Wonderful.

"Well, since you're up," Chuck muttered, "did you happen to hear what we were saying about Kyle Miller?"

"That he's running for state office in Ohio and his wife is at the shelter? Yeah."

"He didn't say Ohio!" Chuck said, baffled.

"Well, I looked it up on my phone. It's handy. It's got a little computer on it now. Even muscle can use it.

It might even have a map thing you can use in your line of work, Chuck. You should try it."

"Remember before you and Grace hooked up and you never talked? I miss those days."

"Josh doesn't. Now Grace shuts up occasionally. Everything's a trade-off."

"You wanna know what I'd trade to—"

"Boys, boys," Lucius intervened, unsuccessfully hiding his laughter. "As much fun as this is for all of us, we need to decide. What should we do about Chuck and Kyle Miller? Also, Chuck, turn right at the light. You'll be going for a good twenty minutes. We'll see the company first. Pass it, go down to the next big road, and turn left."

"Gotcha, big man," Chuck said mildly. He needed to think of something good he could give Hunter for rescuing him from the awkward sinkhole that his conversation with Lucius kept descending into. It was like they couldn't avoid a serious subject if they tried! What in the hell was *wrong* with him?

"But about Kyle Miller—"

"Well, if we do our job," Chuck said, "he'll never know I'm there. But he's very capable of hiring people and doing shit like trying to sabotage your company. We should have Stirling or Danny do a rundown on who his friends are and if any of them stand to benefit from you going under. But the fact is, I'm there to protect the residents from hired muscle. Kyle Miller isn't going to get his hands dirty with the physical break-in, and I'm not the computer genius who's trying to defeat him with the other stuff."

"If it is him," Hunter reminded them both.

"Exactly!" Chuck nodded. "So don't worry about me. And even if he *does* find out I'm there, it'll be to our benefit. He'll likely split his focus, making him easier to take down."

"But aren't you afraid he'll try to get... I don't know. Revenge or something?"

Chuck snorted. "We are making an awfully big assumption here that he actually found out it was me in the first place. Nobody came after me after I enlisted, and his father was a big enough deal to do it. So no. No borrowing trouble. We look into Miller as a possible suspect, but we don't worry about the two of us tangling. The odds of me and Miller coming face-to-face are impossible to three."

Hunter snorted. "I'll take odds on that. I'll let you know how the house runs."

"Put me down for fifty," Chuck said confidently. "I'm good for it."

"Put *me* down for fifty," Lucius said, sounding decidedly dour. "I think if there's a chance for Charles here to get into trouble, it will show up on the porch with bells on."

"Why don't you call me Chuck?" Chuck asked.

"Because Chuck is a guy who blows up a toilet in college," Lucius retorted. And then his voice grew soft. "Charles is the guy who would crack jokes so his friends don't worry too much about their young friend who's ill."

"Left here?" Chuck said desperately.

"Yeah, Chuck," Hunter said, his voice gentle. "Left here."

"Does anybody want to listen to music?"

"Yes, absolutely," Lucius said. "I've got Mahler on Spotify."

"No!" Chuck and Hunter burst out in tandem. "C'mon, Hunter," Chuck added. "Save us."

Hunter handed Lucius his phone over the seat. "It's all cued up. Led Zeppelin, Pink Floyd, Greenday, the Killers, Imagine Dragon, and The Who. Everything Chuck needs to drown out conversation."

Oh, bless him. Chuck was going to have to get this boy an area rug for his kitchen or something. It was the only thing he could think of that Hunter might need that Chuck could give him in bald gratitude for saving his dignity.

EVENTUALLY LUCIUS directed them past the company campus. The campus itself could be seen from the road, and aside from the "butt-plug" configuration, it looked lovely—lots of old-growth beech trees with shady canopies and open picnic spots near the buildings. The parking lots had solar-powered overhangs and charging ports for electric cars. Chuck said something about how forward-thinking that was, and Lucius said he'd made an arrangement with the local car dealerships to offer a discount on their electric vehicles to employees of Broadstone Industries.

Nice.

Chuck also spotted basketball courts, a running track, soccer fields, and a gym that looked big enough to house an indoor pool plus weights. When he asked Lucius about it, Lucius told him that he hired health workers to help his employees keep fit, and Chuck was impressed yet again.

"If all the bosses I'd been exposed to coming up through college had been as cool as you, I might have been a little more careful not to blow up that toilet," Chuck told him.

Lucius had snorted softly, but he'd looked pleased. After they turned left onto another straight country highway, the trees and manicured lawns of the campus morphed into a slightly wilder topography.

It was funny, Chuck noted. On the inside of the roads bordering Broadstone land, there were green trees, green grass, and wildflowers.

Go outside that perimeter and there was the scorched grass of cattle country.

A good bit past the turn, Chuck spotted the long driveway that led to the mansion. The mansion itself stretched over the treetops, almost too big to be a residence. Damned near a hotel.

It was surrounded by trees deep into the acreage, and Chuck knew he should be outraged by the expense of watering all that green, but instead he was enchanted.

"That's amazing," he said, a little bit awestruck. "That's—did you ever go out in there and get lost?"

"Well, yes," Lucius admitted. "On purpose. There's a stream there. It runs up from an underground spring. I know the dividing lines are a bit harsh, but the oasis in the middle of the flat lands was actually a natural feature. Grandfather just developed around it, that's all."

"How deep does it go?"

"The business campus is a little more than half of the parcel—and the parcel is 10,000 acres. So about 10,000 acres, give or take."

Chuck let out a low whistle. "Wow. That's a lot of fuckin' land."

"There was a lot more." Lucius shrugged. "The town, the surrounding cattle lands—all of it Broadstone. My father sold most of it as the factory made good, and the cows that went with it. But this—this he kept."

"Well, he did keep the good stuff," Chuck said. "Now tell me how to get to your part of it."

"Keep going down this drive," Lucius said, "and ignore the right turn. That will take you to the shelter. Like I said, there's a great deal of tree cover and a lot of fences. When I bring you back later, there will be layers of security, key cards, the works."

"You said you passed this off as a place to entertain guests?" Hunter said doubtfully from the back, and Lucius gave a sheepish shrug.

"I… bribed somebody who works for Google Maps," he muttered. "An old… friend."

"An old flame," Chuck said, enjoying this game.

"Yes, well, on Google Maps it says it's a hotel. The rumor in my circles is that staying over is exclusive and hush-hush. You would not believe the people I've supposedly had in my father's mansion."

"Royalty?" Chuck asked, chuckling as they passed the promised right turn. Both sides of the driveway were lined with a twelve-foot wrought iron fence for a good quarter mile, all of it overridden by foliage. It changed to chain link fencing after the need for decoration had passed. Chuck's practiced eye—and probably Hunter's as well—picked out remote camera stations, small antennae filaments, heat sensors, motion sensors. The gamut of security measures available to man were in place along that fence line—but Chuck could already spot some holes. The gap between the wrought iron fence and the gate, for instance, was nearly a car's width. Sure, a driver would have to go through some pretty rough terrain as they were squeezing a two-ton vehicle through the eye of a needle, but Chuck could do it easy, and the security kiosk on the other side of the gate wouldn't stop him either.

Behind him, he heard Hunter grunt unhappily.

"What?"

"Coms just went out. I was texting Stirling, and his phone went dark. That intentional?" he asked Lucius.

"I'm afraid so," Lucius said. "We actually have the residents ditch their phones before we bring them here. If they need to contact family, they do it from a landline that shows up as someplace in upstate New York—or, alternately, Arizona—when it hits someone's phone."

"Handy," Hunter muttered. "But it's going to make our jobs really fuckin' hard."

"You and Chuck will have radios," Lucius said. "All of the staff do."

"But Molly won't even have an earbud or a phone!" Chuck muttered, about ready to pull the plug on the whole thing.

"I know," Lucius said simply. "However, the women do have access to computers—the IP addresses are rerouted several times, of course. And there is always pen and paper. They do journal extensively."

"Well, that's going to be great if someone breaks in," Chuck retorted. "Dear Chuck, he's got a gun. Please kill him now."

"That one would be addressed to me," Hunter told him mildly. "You'd get the one that said 'Pull the car around, hurry!'"

But Chuck couldn't laugh—not about this. "She'll be trapped!" he argued. "In a 10,000-acre prison!"

"Molly can run ten miles like a fucking deer," Hunter said, his implacability actually a comfort. "And she won't even need that to get to us. Remember that. It's fifteen miles squared, and she's not even dead in the middle. She can get out of there. And she won't have to, because we'll be there. Now Molly's got a reason to want to do this, and Julia and Danny do as well. We need to leave it up to her."

Chuck nodded, but all he could think of was the look on Carmichael Carmody's face as he put on his mask and slid out of the car on the way to the bank. He'd given Chuck one last glance before nodding hard, giving Chuck permission to call the cops and tell them to use snipers after giving the signal. The plan had worked, but in pulling it off, Chuck had sentenced his friend to prison, and he'd wanted to die.

This felt the same.

"Fine," he said as he piloted the SUV toward the smaller, more "modest" mansion behind what was now a shelter for abused spouses. "We'll let Molly decide."

"YEAH, SURE," Molly said, sitting in Lucius's *informal* dining room, which still boasted marble tiles, a marble kitchen table, and light fixtures that were bordering on being chandeliers. The wallpaper was a dusty rose color that Chuck had to admit always made him think of money and grandmothers for some reason, and the food—grilled salmon, rice pilaf, and a vegetable dish that might even make *Hunter* like vegetables— was damned good.

But Chuck's stomach was roiling almost too much to enjoy it.

"Molly girl, do you know what you're risking?" Chuck asked, looking around the table. "Stirling won't be able to monitor our coms."

"I'll know where you and Hunter are," she said. "You'll both be there, full-time. Except when you and Lucius are on your date, of course."

Chuck almost spit up his salmon. "You know about the date?"

"I was there, Chuck. I've never seen anybody choke so badly. It was epic. You have to redeem yourself. I almost apologized to Lucius *for* you. I wanted him to know that you were a real boy and you *could* form a complete sentence."

"Charming," Chuck muttered. "But are you—"

Molly set down her fork. "Look, Good Luck Chuck, you're being a good guy, and I appreciate that. But remember, I only look like a mild-mannered college student. In reality, I've taken just as many dance and martial arts classes as Josh and Grace, and so has Stirling. And I have the one thing someone needs when practicing self-defense."

"What's that?" Stirling asked, eyes wide. Chuck had a sense of the kind of responsibility the girl had faced simply being his older sibling. She would *not* have wanted to let that sort of trust down.

"Commitment," she said, picking her fork up again. "Don't worry, Chuck. Nothing's gonna hurt me that I don't take out with a solid right hook and a kick to the jaw."

Chuck nodded and exchanged looks with Hunter and Carl.

"Men, stop," she said firmly. "Stop trying to make this decision for me. It's mine. Conversation over. Lucius, tell us more about the job."

And that, Chuck had to concede, was that.

"Well, I've got a couple of electric vehicles in the garage. Carl and Stirling can take one of those down the back road that leads straight from our driveway to the campus. I'll take them after they settle down in their rooms after lunch. I'm introducing you both to Linus Catton, my head of personnel. Linus—unlike my head of security, whom you may remember—"

"The murderous scumbag," Hunter filled in darkly, because the guy had taken a shot at Grace.

"The now-dead murderous scumbag," Molly amended, because that story hadn't ended well for Mikey Jenkins.

"Yes," Lucius confirmed. "The deceased murderous scumbag. He was picked by my father. Linus is somebody I knew in school, and frankly, although he's a wonderful head of personnel, I almost didn't promote him because he was much happier as an engineer."

"Why'd you do it, then?" Chuck asked.

Lucius grimaced. "Because he was a friend, and I trusted him, and I didn't trust any of the people my father had hired. And for good reason. Morale was hideous two years ago when I took over—backbiting, undercutting, bullying. Linus is so good with people, so good at using teamwork and choosing the right personalities to mesh. He was taking a single management class as I was getting my MBA, and I could tell then that he was going to be very necessary to somebody, and I decided it should be me. Anyway, he's got a nice house in that suburb we just passed, and he likes it there. When we realized that we were in danger of losing the company—and the safety of Caraway House— well, he's the one person I've confided in at the company. He's going to put Stirling somewhere he can spend most of his time checking for weaknesses and combating hacks, and he's going to take Carl on a tour of the plant and give him access to our personnel files."

"I'll be looking for red flags," Carl told them. "Anybody who has a wife or a sister or a brother who might be in Caraway House, anybody with outstanding debts they might be trying to pay off by conducting a little espionage, anybody with any contacts to Lucius's competitors," Soderburgh was all business. "Am I allowed to use outside sources to do this?"

Lucius sucked air through his teeth. "Can we be sure they don't abuse their spouses or know somebody rich who does?" he asked.

Carl's countenance, smooth, Germanic, with cheekbones that could cut steak, went blank. When his mouth started moving again, it was clear he hadn't thought about that.

"I, uh... well, I don't think I can. I mean, most of my connections through the insurance company *seem* like good people...." His voice trailed off, and he looked unhappily around the table. "Well, that's disheartening."

"What is?" Chuck asked.

"Turns out the only people in my life I can trust not to be scumbags are in the crew of a mostly reformed jewel thief. How wrong is *that*?"

Chuck and Hunter exchanged shrugs. "Works for us," Chuck said. "Stirling, Molly, how about you?"

"We'd pretty much die for Josh Salinger," Molly said, like she might have said "We pretty much love salmon." "Doesn't seem odd to us."

Carl gave a beleaguered shake of his head. "Well, lucky you," he muttered. "I'll just have my little life epiphany all by myself."

"You do that," Chuck said frankly. "So I know Hunter and I are sleeping in the shelter like most of the staff."

"There's a room. You'll have to share," Lucius said. "But you won't be in it much, I assume. Molly, you'll be in a dorm-style room. I'm going to introduce you all three to Lisa Sampson. She should be at the shelter by the time I get back from dropping Carl and Stirling off."

"Good," Hunter said. "Either me or Chuck will be in the shelter with Molly at all times. I know one of us needs to come up to the house for the briefing, but the other guy will stay there."

Chuck nodded in agreement, relieved, and Molly did too, which was *also* a relief because it meant she was taking this seriously.

"Hunter and I will be looking for weaknesses in the security," Chuck said, "and all of us will be keeping an eye out for residents who may have more to fear than some of the others—anybody who is super paranoid or who had a link to a super-resourceful, epic bad guy. Once we get the names to Josh and Danny to have their financials and activity run, we can see which asshole is doing what, and who's trying to put you out of business and hurt your people."

Lucius nodded. "Thank you," he said. And like it had the night before, some of his world-weariness and exhaustion eased off his shoulders. "I spend my days at both sites, so I will have a chance to pass messages between you before dinner and the nightly briefing. Carl and Stirling will be able to contact Josh and Danny, so let me know if you need them to run down any information for you. And also, tell me if you need anything *I* can provide." He smiled briefly. "And, uhm, let me know if there's anything you want for dinner. I can have Cheri—that's my cook—put together care packages for whoever can't attend, but the food at the shelter isn't bad."

"Are there cookies?" Molly and Chuck asked in tandem.

"Always," Lucius said, laughing a little.

Chuck high-fived his girl across the table and tried to put his misgivings aside. "Have you given any thought to your cover?" he asked.

Molly nodded. "Maisy Blanchett," she said. "Well-off girl from the suburbs, snagged herself a sugar daddy, dropped out of college, didn't reckon on getting pushed around. Sugar daddy has deep pockets—and a wife—and I ended up here." She frowned. "How did I end up here? Who would have recced me?"

"Someone who's been here before," Lucius said. "Which is convenient for you, because that means nobody wants you to give them any names."

She grinned. "Gosh, you're nice to us con men. Well done!"

Lucius inclined his head modestly. "I try."

"That means nobody's gonna want the name of my sugar daddy, right?" Her eyes widened happily. "Because that's great. I have to use one of those computer-generated name things to think of something good anyway. I mean, I already know Lucius Broadstone and Felix Salinger. I'd have to start looking off a political roll call to get something that sounds remotely legit."

"Say he's a stockbroker," Hunter told her. "I've guarded a lot of those guys, and they're pretty tightly wound. If there's good ones, they're not the people who call private security."

Chuck snorted. "Naw, man—finance. The muckety-mucks in banks are some cold-ass motherfuckers. I was on a job once where we practically danced out of there because the bank CEO told the police that he didn't care about the human cost, he needed to protect the investors. Cops lowered their weapons and turned their backs, and not one of them so much as looked at the license plate as I drove away."

Lucius choked on a sip of coffee. "That's...."

"Unbelievable?" Chuck asked, nodding, because even though it had been years ago, it still stuck in his craw.

"Sadly not," Lucius said. "I was going to say reprehensible. But I believe it happened, most definitely."

"A banker," Molly said, looking at her brother. "Definitely a banker."

Stirling's expression, which was usually closed and observant, suddenly grew narrow and sly—almost evil. Chuck wondered who in their past had done them wrong, but he refused to feel sorry for whoever it was. He was firmly in Molly and Stirling's corner.

"A banker it shall be," Lucius said, a quirking in his eyebrow letting Chuck know that their byplay wasn't lost on him.

But he also didn't seem to disapprove.

"And on that note," Lucius said, finishing off his coffee, "I think we need to get a move on. If we leave now, we can get to Linus's office right when he returns from lunch, and he can get you two situated." He smiled at Carl and Stirling, who both followed his lead and stood.

Stirling surprised them all, though, by circling around to where Molly sat and wrapping his arms around her shoulders tightly. Molly stood and returned his embrace.

"I'll be okay, little brother," Chuck heard her whisper. "Go have fun being an ubergeek, 'kay?"

Stirling pulled back and gave her a watery smile. "I never get to be front of the house," he said.

"You're going to be fantastic." She leaned her forehead against his briefly and then pulled back. He turned toward Lucius then and nodded briefly, and Lucius headed for the front door and the SUV parked outside.

Hunter, Chuck, and Molly were left behind as a nice young woman wearing shorts and a polo shirt came in to clear the table. She introduced herself as Cheri, told them she was earning money for school and that Lucius had agreed to match whatever she made as his domestic worker with a scholarship donation as well. As chirpy and blond as anybody could wish for, she brought out a plate of cookies and then disappeared into the kitchen to do the dishes.

Silence descended, and for a moment Chuck felt relief. Then Hunter spoke up and jumped right into his damned business.

"What in the fuck was that bullshit on the drive over?"

Chuck and Molly stared at him.

"What?"

"There you guys were, having perfectly normal courting conversation, and suddenly you get in the guy's face over not being honest?"

"I thought you were asleep!"

"I was *trying* to help a brother out, but he had to pick a fight with one of the best catches I've ever met!"

"He was trying to get to know me!" Chuck argued back, like that was a reason for his defensiveness. Hunter stared at him. "There's not that much to know," he muttered.

Molly snorted. "Oh, I doubt that very much. Chuck, if Hunter said something about it, it's got to be bad."

"He just… you know. Asked about my past. I know you're young and fresh, darlin', but some of us have done some… some not-so-great shit."

Hunter let out a sigh, tilted his head forward, and rubbed his neck. "Look, man, whatever it is you think you've done in the past, it cannot possibly be bad enough to fuck this guy up in the present. Do you understand me?"

"I bit my foster father's penis," Molly said. "And he broke my jaw. That's how I ended up with Stirling's foster family. I don't need a fainting couch, Chuck."

Chuck stared at her. "But now I need a hug!" he said wretchedly, and she stepped into his arms with no hesitation whatsoever.

"Better?" she asked.

"No. Darlin', I'm so sorry."

"C'mon, tell us. When we tell you it's okay, it'll be easier to tell Lucius."

What if Lucius doesn't want to hear it?

"I—"

And at that moment the front door opened and closed. Molly stepped out of Chuck's hug, and they all had their game faces on when Lucius stepped through the door.

"Oh, you're all ready, then?" His face fell. "I… uhm, was sort of hoping to have time for a cookie."

It was the dumbest thing. Lucius Broadstone— CEO of Broadstone Industries, philanthropist, captain of this magnificent house that must have been half of a sustainable forest in paneling alone—looked disappointed.

And Chuck's heart twisted, because apparently, he was also the world's dumbest thing.

"We can certainly stay for cookies," he said, going back to his seat with a sigh.

He looked expectantly up at Hunter and Molly, but they both shook their heads.

"Grab me one," she told Chuck. "I'm going to go update Danny and Julia on the sitch."

"I'm going to go tell Grace," Hunter said. "They need to know we'll only be in contact once a day."

"Good thinking," Chuck said, and he tried to ignore Hunter as he made little shooing motions with his hand.

"Ooh, almond cookies," Lucius said happily. "Did you have one? Cheri's really amazing. Did she tell you she's going to bakery school next year?"

"She told me you're paying half her way," Chuck said. He took a cookie, which melted in his mouth with the aftertaste of almonds and honey, and he gave a little smile. "They're really good."

Lucius eyed him quizzically through those hazel eyes Chuck had thought of as cold once.

Not anymore.

"What's…? You seem to have something on your mind."

"Hunter and Molly want me to tell you my big bad. You know, everybody's got one."

Those hazel eyes widened. "Yes," he said softly, pausing in the act of taking another cookie. "I do."

"I… I don't want to," Chuck confessed baldly. "Not yet. Eat the cookie, Scotty. It's not a bad thing."

Lucius lifted the cookie up and took another bite. He'd stripped off the business coat he'd worn that morning and had rolled up his shirtsleeves to drive Stirling and Carl. He still looked like a powerful businessman, but he also looked relaxed and a little vulnerable, and Chuck was still raw from Molly's confession and hug.

He wasn't sure he was feeling large enough to protect Lucius Broadstone and still protect his own heart.

"It's not a bad thing?" Lucius asked, pouring milk from a pitcher that Cheri had brought out. Chuck thought about how having a little bit of sweet with his meal must have been one of the things Lucius looked forward to every day, and he wanted to bang his head against the giant hand-carved table.

Why this man? Why did Lucius have to take a fancy to Chuck? And why did it have to be the kind that Chuck couldn't blow off with a quickie in a supply closet or something?

"I liked the idea of a date," Chuck said, feeling forlorn. "Can't we just… you know. Dress up. Look good. Go eat some fancy canapes or something?"

Lucius gave him a winsome smile. "Sure. We don't have to go any deeper than you want, Chuck. I wasn't trying to pressure you."

"You discombobulate me," Chuck told him, feeling wretched. "I like you. I like you fine. You're easy on the eyes, fun to talk to when I'm not being in meltdown, and you're a genuinely good guy. I just… you look at me and smile at me and I can barely remember my own damned name."

Lucius gave him the most amazing look, sliding his eyes sideways as he bit into his cookie. After chewing and swallowing and then taking another swig of milk, he said, "Charles. Your name is Charles."

Charles groaned and buried his face in his folded arms as they rested on the table. "You're a terrible, terrible person, Lucius Broadstone."

Lucius's hand in his hair was odd… and soothing. "But I understand your friends call you Chuck," he said softly. "I would very much like to be your friend."

"We have to catch a bad guy first," Chuck said into his folded arms. He sat up a little and finished, "I'm just saying. I'll get to the big bad eventually, okay?"

"I look forward to it."

Chuck turned his head quickly, realizing Lucius had scooted his chair and was suddenly very, very close. Chuck reached up and rubbed his finger on a bit of cookie crumb that lingered on a lean lip, and Lucius smiled.

The awkward moment—the accretion of them, actually—turned tender. Chuck dropped his hand and captured Lucius's chin, holding him still so he could place a kiss on his lips just… there.…

Much like it had that night at the gala, Lucius's mouth opened for him, and he became lost. The job faded into the background and it was only him and the male heat and the charm of the man he was kissing.

The charm beckoned, and when Chuck had planned to pull back, he found himself plundering forward, Lucius's hearty groan echoing up from his stomach as he leaned forward in his chair, his hands splaying against Chuck's chest and kneading happily.

Chuck sighed happily in return, and behind him his chair tilted dangerously. He jerked back to keep it from spilling him forward, and Lucius tumbled out of his chair and came to a rest on his knees, his head practically in Chuck's lap.

"Ouch," he mumbled, his words muffled by Chuck's knee.

"Wow." Chuck stood, careful not to knock his teeth or anything, and helped him to his feet. "I swear to God, I am usually smoother than that."

Lucius gave a choked laugh. "You know, me too! I am not an ingenue. I… I've had dates. Lots of dates. Sex even. Lots and lots of sex! I just… every time you and I are together…." He bit his lip.

"Things get serious for no reason," Chuck said gruffly, wanting to lick the abused lower lip at the same time he wanted to run the hell out of there. "I have never known anything like it."

Lucius gave him a level look, as well he might as he was only one or two inches shorter. "I think it means that yes, we can go on a date and pretend there's nothing to see here, folks, but something in the two of us wants very much to be seen."

Chuck shook his head. "Molly and Hunter depend on me right now. That part of me, the part you want to see so badly? He needs to stay hidden for a little while yet. You understand?"

Lucius nodded and cupped Chuck's cheek, rubbing his lower lip with a thumb. "I do, but I think you need to understand that the big bad that you keep putting off, like doing your taxes or filling out paperwork, is a thing you're going to have to face. I've faced my big bad. Have you faced yours?"

Chuck grimaced and stepped back. "We need to get situated at the shelter," he said, in the world's shittiest evasion.

"Of course you haven't," Lucius murmured. "Because that would be too easy."

Chuck pretty much fled the room.

Outside Forces

LISA SAMPSON was a trim, fit woman in her early fifties with close-cropped curls, sharp brown eyes, and skin the color of teakwood—midnight with hints of earthy brown.

Even without the uniform of khaki pants and a crisp white shirt, complete with a badge that read Security, Chuck recognized her military shoulders and no-bullshit chin and told his inner authority rebel to stand down. This woman was a badass for the forces of good.

She was waiting in front of the mansion, and the building that housed the shelter really was a mansion in the biggest, most antebellum sense of the word, with giant Grecian columns and aspirations to Tara, Monticello, and Mount Vernon in the front and an ivy-covered English boarding school in the back. Chuck was going to have to ask Lucius about the dual personality of the architecture, but first, he had to get the lay of the land.

Lisa greeted Lucius with a handshake and a warm smile, which helped Chuck overcome that authority thing almost immediately. Anyone who liked Lucius was okay in his book. Then she turned gravely to

Hunter, Molly, and Chuck himself and extended a cautious hand.

"Hi," she said. "I have to tell you, I am not excited about having strangers here."

"We promise to be respectful, ma'am," Hunter said.

Molly added, "I promise you we want your residents to be safe and not feel violated in any way."

"Our entire concern here is their safety," Chuck added, and Lisa took a step back and eyed them all suspiciously.

"Did you *practice* that?"

Chuck laughed. "No, Ms. Sampson, but two of us are former military and one of us is barely old enough to drink. You do bring the 'yes, ma'am' out of us. You get that, right?"

And that brought out the faintest smile.

"Understood," she said with a more relaxed nod of her head. She sobered. "Those security breaks have us all upset here," she said. "I understand why Lucius didn't want to contact the police, but I have to admit, I don't know who that leaves."

"We're the people you don't hear about," Molly said cheerfully. "Which is fine with us. Now, my real name is Molly, but you're going to have to call me Maisy Blanchett. I'm on the run from an abusive sugar daddy who wants to control my life." She fluttered her lashes. "Get me in orientation like any other newcomer, and I'll be fine."

Hunter introduced himself. "I'll need a uniform like yours," he said, indicating her khakis, pressed shirt, and security badge. "And I'll work in the booth like you. Chuck and I are sharing quarters, I guess, so tell us where we can stow our shit—erm, stuff."

"And I'm Chuck." Chuck winked. "I'm your new self-defense and fitness instructor. I'll teach three classes a day to whoever wants to learn." And he sobered. "And I need the same orientation Hunter gets. We need to know where the motion detectors and relay stations and heat sensors are so we know where the weaknesses are. Next time you have one of those little electronics breaks, Hunter and I need to be able to try to get the guys who are coming in the fences."

"And what are you going to do with them?" Lisa asked, still suspicious.

"Bind them and blindfold them and take them to the authorities," Chuck told her with a bland smile.

Hunter held up his hands. "I swear, ma'am, we won't do anything that will bring attention to Caraway House. We want these women safe, just like you do."

Lisa's mouth relaxed again. "Okay," she said finally, looking at Lucius and nodding. "I still have some doubts, but they've managed to convince me they can't make anything worse. Mr. Broadstone, you can go. Tara-Lynn and I have this covered."

Lucius nodded, but before he could leave, a gently rounded, fiftyish woman with pink cheeks and gray-threaded blond hair came out of the house, wiping her hands on an apron tied around her waist. In deference to the thick summer heat, she was wearing walking shorts and a flowered sleeveless blouse, as well as orthopedic sandals and a badge clipped to the V-neck of the blouse.

Everything about her seemed maternal and sweet, except the places where her nose had been broken and the way she limped as though she'd recovered from an untreated hip fracture at one point in time.

"Lisa, are you going to introduce me to the newcomers?"

Lisa smiled at her warmly. "Tara honey, come meet the people Lucius brought to try to get to the bottom of the break-ins. Everybody, meet Tara-Lynn Watkins, our director."

"Director of what?" Molly asked, eyes bright and interested.

"Well, everything," Lisa said, frowning slightly. "I don't know, Tara-Lynn. What *is* your official title?"

"Residential Director," Tara-Lynn told them. "Think of me like a headmistress in a boarding academy, but I give out cookies, hug a lot, and will share a smoke with you after curfew, even though I quit twenty years ago."

Lisa took them all through a round of introductions, pausing when she got to Molly. Chuck and Hunter broke the con man's code by exchanging nervous glances, but Molly took the decision out of her hands.

"You can call me Maisy," she said, giving Tara-Lynn a direct look.

Tara-Lynn nodded. "Then that's what I'll call you. We don't do last names here. Maisy will do just fine."

Chuck caught the slight wrinkling of the nose that indicated Molly was disappointed her entire role wasn't going to be used, but he figured she'd get over it.

"So," she said, taking them all in. "A new security officer, new fitness instructor, new resident. Since I know you're all doing extra jobs, I'll try to keep people off your backs, but there's only so many 'errands,'"—she emphasized the words with air quotes—"I can send you on. I do hope you know how to do those jobs."

Chuck grinned. "Army, ma'am. I can most assuredly lead a PT and physical self-defense session. I'm good for it."

Tara-Lynn burst into a delighted cackle, and Lisa Sampson did too, and Chuck felt a sense of release. He'd gotten these women—who looked scary competent—to trust him and Hunter. It was like getting your crew to trust you to be outside the bank when the job was done. Having that backup, having that synchrony going for you, that could be the difference between a clean getaway and a botched job.

"Well, sweetheart, let me get you settled," Tara-Lynn said, and Molly grabbed her rollerboard and her giant purse and followed the woman in.

"And if you follow me, you can stash your gear and get the lay of the land," Sampson told them. Chuck grabbed his own duffel, only to be paused by Lucius's hand on his elbow.

"You'll be okay?" he asked, biting his lip.

"I'm always okay," Chuck told him, because he did have an uncanny knack of landing on his feet. "But I'll have Hunter and Maisy's back, I promise." Because that was the thing he worried about most. He didn't want another Car-Car on his conscience, and this would be even worse. Carmichael Carmody had been a thief because he couldn't stand up to his brothers, because he'd lacked the backbone to stand up to anybody, really. Molly and Hunter were competent, and they were running this mission to help the helpless, the bullied—people like Car-Car in a way, but who had not yet picked up a gun and done something desperate.

They needed Chuck at his best, not his panicked, half-assed worst, to keep them all in one piece.

"I know you will," Lucius said, but Chuck couldn't explain to him why he was wrong. With a little tug, he pulled away and winked and then followed Sampson into the house.

HE HAD to admit the house looked much more human inside than it did outside, and he figured they had Lucius to thank for that.

The outside lent itself to heavy antique furniture with an excess of curlicues and dark wood, but nothing could be further from the truth. The floors had been repaneled in a sturdy amalgamate that looked like wood but would withstand the patter of little feet.

There were plenty of those.

A pegboard lined the front hallway, as well as a shoe rack and a couple of benches to facilitate with the putting on of the shoes. The hallway was white, battered but clean, and the hall almost immediately opened up into what Chuck thought must have been a sitting room and a grand dining room combined. Instead of an enormous, awkward table, the dining room consisted of several standard-sized kitchen tables with a couple of plastic kids' tables scattered about. The tile—more sturdy decorating here—was white and nonslip and easily washed. The kitchen was separated by a partial wall with a counter, probably because the support posts were load-bearing and it couldn't be completely eliminated, and the whole works opened up into a living room, complete with a big-screen television, several couches, beanbag chairs, and a corner dedicated to colorful toys.

The entire area must have taken up a quarter of the first floor, and Chuck was impressed.

"We have a couple of other areas on the first floor," Lisa said. "A room for grownups who want to watch grown-up damned movies or series, and a game room for teenagers' after-school hours."

"You have classes?" Chuck asked, impressed. Molly had disappeared as they'd walked in the front door—he assumed to be taken to her room and get the residential tour, and he missed her. She could have made that question sound adorable instead of dumb.

"We have an agreement," Sampson temporized. "Essentially, we have a contact in the local school system who gets us home-study packets for the grades we need, and keeps records for us. When a family is ready to move on, there's a record ready to go with...." She gave them both a look.

"Whatever ID is necessary," Chuck murmured, getting it.

"It helps the kids," Sampson said, nodding, "to have school, to know that the world isn't all chaos and fear. We've got two teachers who were former residents to make the classes formal, and one art therapist who comes by twice a week to help the kids deal with what they've been through." She shook her head. "People who work with children do not get paid enough, I don't care *who* they're working for!"

Chuck unsuccessfully hid a smile. "If those kids are anything like me, roger that."

She pulled them through the front room, introducing them to residents by their first names, telling them that Chuck was doing self-defense and fitness training and Hunter was their new security guy.

"Will you have yoga classes?" said a slender, wispy woman, looking at him with hopeful eyes.

"Absolutely," Chuck said. "Give me two days to work one into the rotation."

"Do you even know yoga?" Hunter asked as they moved through the well-stocked, child-proofed kitchen.

"I've taken classes," Chuck murmured back. "Give me time to work up a routine and I can give a basic hour."

Hunter rolled his eyes. "Forget 'Chuck.' We should have called you 'Jack.'"

Chuck grinned. "Except I've mastered more than a few," he said suggestively, and Hunter elbowed him in the ribs.

Chuck grunted when he wanted to yelp and then paused.

One entire wall of the kitchen was devoted to student art, probably because a refrigerator wasn't big enough, and Chuck was pulled to it by a brightly crayoned string.

"Art therapy," he said softly, looking at the pictures. Most of them broke his heart. Happy families… scribbled over in red. Misshapen stick figures… with casts on their arms or big blue marks on their faces.

Mommies lying on the ground, crying.

He swallowed, understanding the enormity of Lucius's panic. These women, these children, they had safety here. They had order and gentleness and security. Chuck hadn't been abused, but he knew what it was like to walk into the house and feel like you were tip-toeing on quicksand. His mother had been made tired, exhausted by her husband's constant straying, constant lies, constant mockery of the home she'd been trying to build.

These children who lived here, they'd had their entire lives upended, possibly had never known peace or security. This place was a way for their mothers to give them a home, a sense of safety that they'd been robbed of, maybe even since birth.

No wonder Lucius was so upset. He'd created this safe space—this healing space—and it was being attacked by both brute force and cunning, and he was *scared.* He didn't want these people to be hurt any more than they already had been.

"Do you like my picture?" Chuck looked down in surprise at the little boy at his knee. He couldn't have been more than seven.

"I don't know," Chuck said. "Which one's yours?"

The boy's face—round, apple-cheeked, freckled, and mildly sunburned on the tip of his nose—lit up. "This one!" he said, pointing to one to the left. Stick figures again, this one a small figure that was obviously the boy and a larger one with long yellow hair, sitting on a blanket outside with scattered colored squares on the blanket.

"Those are my Legos!" the little boy said excitedly. "I can have them here." His voice dropped. "Daddy didn't like them at home. Said they were useless. Me too." He brightened. "But here I can have Legos. Mommy says I can have Legos wherever we go after here too."

Chuck grinned, but inside he remembered his own father, in a rage, throwing away all of Chuck's model cars when he hit twelve because he was "too old for that bullshit."

"Every boy should have Legos," he said soberly. "For as long as they want. I think grownups should have Legos too. They're good toys."

The boy's wide smile revealed missing teeth. Seven. He was definitely seven. "Tha's what I think too!"

"Matty, c'mon, sweetie. It's quiet time."

Chuck looked up to see a pretty woman with blond hair in a ponytail and a sweet elfin face, holding her hand out to her son. He could still see the lump on her arm from a healing bone.

"Can I play with my Legos?" Matty asked, lisping a little from all those missing teeth.

"'Course, baby," she said softly. She gave Chuck and Hunter a worried little glance and slipped away with the other mothers and children, and Chuck's heart twisted.

Quiet time after lunch. Kindergartners might take naps. Teenagers might read a book. Peace. This place was all about peace.

"This is why we're here," Hunter said softly.

"Yeah."

Lisa Sampson paused at the doorway she'd been trying to lead them through and cleared her throat. "This way, gentlemen."

As a unit, Chuck and Hunter turned to follow her.

Behind the kitchen, in what had probably been a study before renovations, was what should have been a state-of-the-art security room.

Every window and hallway was monitored, as well as the bedrooms themselves.

"Do the women know they're on camera?" Hunter asked.

"There's a button in the room," Lisa said. "See there?"

Chuck looked at the camera indicated and saw that only the window was visible. "They can mute the camera?"

"We need to see the windows," Lisa said, nodding, "because that's security. But no-damned-body wants the world to see them after bra o'clock. The women have the power to turn the cameras off. It's almost...." She frowned. "Almost like a security blanket for some of them. They get here, and they're so scared, all the time. They use the bathroom to change and keep the camera on twenty-four seven. It makes them feel better to know we're here. After a couple of months, when they get their feet under them, they start to want their lives to be their own. They mute the camera more and more, until they move out."

There were twenty monitors, many of them with revolving views, but Chuck couldn't seem to follow a pattern. The little labels under each screen said which room the view covered, but the labels were a mess: "Blue room and hallway by the big oak" or "Hallway by the leaky toilet" or "Schoolroom—maybe little kids." Hunter snorted. "This is a disaster. Who did this?" he asked, and it was a fair question. Every camera showed activity, and even a trained eye could get confused.

"This was free labor," Lisa said, acknowledging the problem. "Somebody's nephew had an internship with a media company, and when Mr. Broadstone was setting things up—about four years ago, before he had the reins of the company—this here was a shoestring operation. He was using his trust fund money, and he'd put everything he had into just making the house livable. It used to be a death trap. I swear, our first month here, I fell through one of the bathroom floors. Once he had the company and all the tax breaks he got for giving to an already established charity, the money came pouring in, but...." She shrugged.

"Once it's in place, it's not something you think to fix," Chuck said. "We get it." He sighed and met Hunter's eyes. "This is where we need Josh."

"Right?" Hunter replied. "Or Danny or Stirling."

"You're bringing *more* people?" Sampson asked, sounding alarmed.

"We all have our specialties," Chuck said with a nod. "Turns out that the folks who couldn't make it are damned good with things like this." He looked at Hunter, who nodded. "If we get Lucius's permission, maybe we could give Josh access to this setup? If nothing else, he or Danny could be another set of eyes if there's another attack."

"Why can't this 'Josh' get his ass down here to help you?" Lisa Sampson was obviously not impressed.

"He's in chemo, ma'am," Chuck said, the words taking a gouge out of his heart like they always did. "Some of us are working in the main company, but about half our crew stayed in Chicago to take care of him."

"Oh," she said softly. "Oh. I'll ask Mr. Broadstone. And Bianca Grimes, our on-site techie. If you think your folks in Chicago can help, and Mr. Broadstone trusts them, I think we can do that."

"He's damned good with media and multiple viewpoints," Chuck told her. "And his Uncle Danny isn't far behind."

"Josh had the formal training, Danny has the instincts," Hunter voiced, and Chuck couldn't have put it better himself.

"Okay then." Lisa nodded. "But in the meantime, this is what we have. You may notice the outer perimeter cameras leave some gaps. If you can figure out how to cover those gaps without giving away that there are cameras up the yang, I will be very grateful."

"If there's a hole in your setup, we'll catch it," Chuck said. "And if nothing else, Josh could probably talk your techie through reorganizing the screens to make them easier to follow. See Molly?" Lisa and Hunter scoured the screens and found her at the screen on the far-right corner where Molly was setting her luggage in a pin-neat room with a cotton quilt on a double bed, a dresser, a small desk, and a TV on the wall. There was a sign that listed the streaming services for the television but told residents they needed to go to the computer room during certain hours to get internet.

Fascinated, Chuck and the others watched as Molly exited the room and appeared....

On a screen two rows down and three monitors to the left as she followed Tara-Lynn down a hallway to a set of stairs.

Tara's hand appeared in another monitor, two screens up and to the left again, as she gestured to what looked to be a recently installed lift to guarantee access for all the residents.

And then it disappeared, as did Molly and Tara-Lynn as they appeared one monitor up and four to the right while walking down the stairs.

Chuck and Hunter both made grunting sounds and stared at Lisa, who appeared to be shifting from foot to foot.

"Right," she said. "We, uhm, got used to it, I guess. I'll talk to Mr. Broadstone—"

They both stared at her with hard eyes.

"—tonight, when he comes to pick one of you up."

"He thought this was taken care of," Chuck said, feeling injured for Lucius.

"Well, when you see it through someone else's eyes, it looks a lot worse."

At that moment, two other women walked in, both of them dressed like Lisa, but their khaki pants were shorts in deference to the thick August weather. Both in their midthirties, the women, like Lisa, were fit and muscular and moved like they could handle themselves. They were introduced as Kenzy and Jamie, and while Kenzy was petite, pale, blue-eyed and blond, Jamie was a little taller, with dark hair she'd tamed straight, dusky skin, and round brown eyes.

They had strong, no-bullshit handshakes, and when they saw Hunter and Chuck checking out the monitors, they both gave a little whimper of mortification.

"It's terrible, isn't it?" Kenzy said. "But Lucius is so good, and it was a choice between updating the monitors or having an art therapy teacher on staff. Guess which one we voted for?"

"That's a rough choice," Chuck agreed. "Don't worry about it. Hunter can talk about it when he goes back to the house tonight."

"I'm not going back," Hunter said.

"Yes, you are. It's your only chance to talk to Grace."

Hunter narrowed his eyes. "You're going back. Don't argue." Then he turned back to the women. "Okay, people. Chuck and I need to be updated on everything. Even though he's going to be teaching fitness and self-defense, you need to keep him alerted, as if he's wearing the uniform too. He *will* be carrying a radio, won't he?"

"Yessir," Lisa said, and just like that, Chuck sensed the transfer of power from Lisa's shoulders to theirs. On the one hand, it was good because they *could* fix the problems that had apparently built up over time. On the other?

They had better not fuck this up.

LUCIUS WAS pulling the SUV around the driveway to pick up one of the men for dinner while Chuck and Hunter were still arguing sotto voce over which one of them it was going to be.

Chuck was insisting that Hunter deserved to talk to his boyfriend, and Hunter was calling him a whiny little bitch for not wanting to own up to a thing going on with Lucius, and in general, their inner fifth-graders were coming out to play.

The fight ended with Hunter putting his hands on Chuck's shoulders and shoving him forward a little, so Chuck was forced to look at Lucius through the open window and smile greenly.

"Hey, Lucius. Good to see you."

He looked good but tired. His suit coat had never come back on, apparently, and his short hair was rumpled. His five-o'clock shadow was sexy, but it also added to the weariness, and the circles under his hazel eyes didn't help.

Carl and Stirling's news must not have been good.

"Go ahead," he said to Chuck, and then to prove Chuck right, he added, "Get in. It can't be nearly as bad as the news from the business side of things."

Chuck rolled his eyes, because he doubted Carl and Stirling could have found anything worse than the security clusterfuck that was the camera system at the shelter.

He slid in, though, and said, "Do me a favor, will you? Roll up the windows and crank the AC. We've been tramping through the brush, and I feel like I'm sweating all over your nice leather seats."

Lucius laughed a little and did as he asked. "Chicago has the lake to cool you off most nights."

Chuck gave a grunt of agreement, happy to let the weather be a distraction. "Yeah, but this is embarrassing. I grew up in Cleveland. They've had summers that have melted the light fixtures. And Texas, where I was born? Forget about it. I got spoiled the last couple years."

"You have all that Texas accent from just being born in Texas?" Lucius asked, laughing.

"Well, we moved to Cleveland when I was ten or so, and I spent about two years in Texas before moving out to Chicago." He would have considered staying there if Car-Car had been able to leave his wife—and stay out of jail, without getting beaten to death and left to bleed in an empty field, which Chuck had no doubt his brothers would have done.

"Why not San Francisco or Portland?" Lucius asked, pulling him out of Texas. "I mean, if you're not a fan of the heat, there are other places to live."

"Yeah, but Chicago is Chicago," Chuck said, nodding in satisfaction. "You can hit the natural science museum, the aquarium, and the Art Institute in one day!"

"Well, it would be a big day," Lucius laughed.

"Haven't you ever seen *Ferris Bueller's Day Off*?" Chuck demanded. "Where else could that movie have happened? I mean, I've been to New York, but the streets and sidewalks are too narrow. Nope. Chicago. Plenty of breeze coming off the lake—"

"It will push you uphill in the winter on the ice," Lucius warned.

"Lots of history," Chuck countered.

"Lots of it illegal."

"Lots of culture."

Lucius snorted. "Lots of violence."

"Well, yes, and a pretty brutal police force too. But that's what we're here for, right? To right the wrongs? To give the underdog a chance? I mean, we're not in a position to broker peace at the moment, but give us some time. We might be."

Lucius sighed. "You're probably correct. And I love the city too. It's just…well, Stirling and Carl have a to-do list a mile long, and given the way you and Hunter were arguing, I could tell that neither one of you wanted to tell me what you'd unearthed."

Chuck sighed. "Over pie," he said. "Hunter and I spent all hot, sweaty, mosquito-y afternoon tramping around the fence perimeter, and I have worked up an appetite. We're literally in the dead center of corn-fed beef on the hoof. I'm begging you—"

"New York strip," Lucius said, and Chuck whooped.

"There is a God after all," he proclaimed, and given the carefree way Lucius laughed and the easing of stress lines on his forehead, it had been the right approach.

It would be a shame to break him completely before they protected the business he loved most, which had nothing to do with computers and everything to do with the women and children in the giant converted mansion with the shitty security.

Dinner was great. Cheri did an amazing job with the steaks, which Chuck understood to be grilled outside near the kitchen. He hadn't been lying about being grateful for the air conditioner, and sitting under the comfortable whir of the high ceiling fans in the AC took some of the discomfort out of the coming conversation.

When pie arrived, Stirling set up a tablet at the end of the table with a screen broken up into five faces: Danny, Julia, Felix, Josh, and Grace. Josh was home again; he and Grace were sitting next to each other on the couch in the den. Julia and Felix were sharing a screen by the wet bar, and Danny was seated at the coffee table in another chair and obviously had his laptop open so he could look things up while they were speaking.

Once their window to the rest of the crew was established, Chuck let Stirling and Carl go first.

"Someone has simulated the key cards," Carl said. "Those small moments of espionage were just the tip of the triangle—"

"Isn't that iceberg?" Chuck asked, and Carl rolled his eyes.

"Sure, if that's your idiom. I'm saying I found three different places where the simulated key cards had been used, and there was everything from a petri dish left outside to spread mold to a clean room, to the fuse removed on an ionizer that would have eventually led to humidity destroying a new microchip. The sabotage is small. It's irritating. And if it wasn't so deliberate, it might have been dismissed as incompetence or bad luck. But it's not. It's insidious, and I'm going to get the fucker who's doing it because it's an affront to everything I stand for."

Chuck grinned at him. "It's like you're a superhero."

Carl preened, and Grace's voice echoed from the speaker. "It's almost like the guy he's after is me. I'd totally do that shit." He paused. "If I wasn't reformed—reformed, I tell you—and now working for the good guys."

"You'd totally still do that shit now," Josh said, "but only to douchebags."

"Lucky me, I'm not a douchebag," Lucius said mildly, and Chuck had to give him points. He was still smiling. Grimly, but smiling.

"Good to know." Grace sounded bored now, but Chuck realized he had a question.

"Grace, how would you stop this guy?"

Grace looked up from a tablet he was playing with and blinked, his uptilted eyes almost alien in the small confines of the meeting window.

"I wouldn't," he said after a moment. "I'd leave the hole open for the key card to get in, but I'd put an alarm on it so you'd know when he entered. Then I'd track him down and beat the shit out of him."

"You lie," Josh said. "You'd have Hunter beat the shit out of him."

Grace gave a truly feline smile. "I'd enjoy watching."

Chuck arched an eyebrow at Carl and Lucius. "Do you like this plan?"

"I do," Lucius said thoughtfully, and Carl nodded with great enthusiasm.

"Can you set that up, Stirling?" Danny asked, and the young man practically sparkled.

"Absolutely, Uncle Danny. Carl is going to have to give me the specs on the key code, but I can do that tonight after dinner."

"Most excellent," Felix said. "Next item on the list?"

Stirling spoke up. "Your business culture sucks," he told Lucius. "But it's not your fault. You and Linus have done all the good things in hiring—solid recruiting, a diverse population, good benefits. But the holdovers from your father's era are shitting on all of that. You need to have Linus fire half of them."

"Only half?" Lucius asked curiously, although Chuck noted that his tan had dropped a few degrees in intensity and warmth. This bothered Lucius. The fine white lines at the corners of his eyes confirmed it.

"Like with any clique system, there's the leaders and followers," Stirling said, his voice clinical, although Chuck imagined that, like his sister, Stirling had some experience with bullying and the culture that allowed it. "Get rid of the key players and the people left are usually happy to have a new start. Get rid of the followers and the leaders just pull the new people into their vortex and suck everybody back down again."

"Are they a danger?" Felix asked. "When I came back to the network, I had to fire two station managers who had revealed their inner prejudices while I was gone and they thought they had free rein. Then I had to hire back the dozen people who had quit and were threatening to sue the station. Stirling, if you could round up a list of potential victims and sound them out, that might be a good thing too."

Stirling nodded soberly. "I can do that." His eyes flitted to Lucius's. "Would you like me to have that tomorrow night, Mr. Broadstone?"

And Lucius's jaw unclenched long enough for him to show kindness. "Yes, Stirling. I would be very grateful."

"Was there anything else?" Danny asked. "Any more hacks?"

Stirling's expression grew sly. "Not anymore," he said, sounding smug.

"I take it you found a hole?" For the first time, Lucius sounded like he was shedding some of the weight of the world.

Stirling nodded. "It was a backdoor, an old password from an employee who no longer works there. I didn't plug it, exactly. More I sort of put in a… a receptacle, I guess you'd say. Whatever code they try to insert via that password will get a dummy landing page saying the code is activated. But it's not. It's just recorded, and we can see what it was going to try to do."

Chuck knew he wasn't the only one at the table with his mouth open.

"My God, you're brilliant," Lucius whispered. "Are you sure you don't want to come work for me?"

Stirling wrinkled his nose and shook his head. "Maybe once a month for kicks," he said. "It's really boring. And no offense, but you're out in the middle of nowhere. I'd miss Chicago."

Lucius let out a laugh. "Understood. You are welcome to come fiddle with our code anytime." He sobered. "Can you figure out who it is?"

Stirling and Carl exchanged a look, but Carl was the one who spoke.

"Stirling and I talked about that. He's going to spend tomorrow trying to trace the signal and find the IP address of the computer that initiated the hack, but it's being bounced off of a million places, and he's limited by what his station here can do. Your campus is set up so we can't do anything illegal. It would set off alarm bells everywhere. But even if we could, we're not sure it would net us who and where this is. The IP address, that we can do."

"You have another plan?" Danny asked.

"Well," Carl said, with another nod from Stirling, "while he's getting the IP address, I'll be looking up the old password—who used it, who their friends are—and then cross-referencing it with the names of the people Lucius provides me with tonight. Our most likely suspect list. Hopefully using Stirling's IP address, the source of the password, and our most likely suspects…."

"Good angle," Felix said, surprising everybody. "Thank you, Carl. That's good thinking."

Carl smiled a little. "Thanks for letting me come play, sir," he said respectfully, and Chuck wanted to do a happy dance. He *liked* Carl; the guy had potential to be a good friend, and Chuck had never been so deep in friends that he could overlook that.

"Oh my, Lucius," Julia said before the silence could become awkward. "You are having a rather trying day. Chuck, I hope you have better news."

Chuck grimaced in apology. "Sorry, Julia. The thing is, Lucius hired good people—he really did. But in an effort to protect him, they've done some shit half-assed, and it's going to get in our way."

Lucius gaped at him. "But…."

"Your cameras are a mess, Lucius." Chuck looked at the computer. "Josh, if you're up to it tomorrow, we can send you a schematic of which camera goes where, and you can tell us how to—"

"I'll fly down tomorrow," Josh said. "Grace'll come with me—"

"Josh!" That was Felix, Danny, and Julia, pretty much in tandem.

"I have a week break between rounds," Josh said. "And no, I don't expect to feel fantastic. In fact, Mr. Broadstone, if you've got barf bags handy, I will probably use them. But Grace misses Hunter, and I'm tired of being treated like I'm dead already."

"One of us is going with you," Julia said, her tone brooking no argument.

"You, darling," Felix murmured. "You go. I can front for you at the network, and Danny can do lots of digging from here." And everyone knew she wanted to be with him, more than anything in the world. It was unspoken—and probably true for all three of them— but while Danny and Felix had each other to cry on in the darkest parts of the night, Julia was alone.

"Okay," she said, without arguing. "Josh, any protests I need to mow over?"

"No, Mom," he said reluctantly. "You'll do the thing you do."

"Glad you understand," she said. "Okay then, anything else we may need to know about?"

Chuck and Lucius met gazes, and Chuck told them about Kyle Miller.

Game Plans

IT WAS only two miles from Lucius's front door to the shelter. He knew, he'd clocked it. In fact, he could probably drive the stretch of property drunk *and* asleep, not that he'd tried it in either condition. But by the time he pulled up to drop Chuck off at the grand entrance to the ungodly ugly Georgian building, he felt like he'd run the distance four or five times over.

"That was…."

"Painful?" Chuck filled in, but his voice was kind, and Lucius blessed him for it.

"Embarrassing," Lucius replied honestly. "My God. I thought I had my shit together—I really did. I thought I could run the company and run the charities and not make a hash out of both of them, but…." He groaned, tilting his head back as the engine idled. "God, was I wrong."

"Good Lord, boy, cut yourself some slack," Chuck told him, and Lucius could barely manage to tilt his head and look Chuck in the eye.

"For what? The shitty camera system or the shitty corporate climate?"

"The corporate climate you inherited," Chuck said frankly. "And you've been doing your best, but frankly, you would have needed an inside guy to fix it. And how would you know who to trust?"

Lucius grunted because that was true. "Linus has been doing his best," he muttered, "but apparently the job is bigger than one man."

"And Stirling and Carl both told you that he's working his ass off, and effectively too. The two of you could probably fix this if you had another two years, but you're hemorrhaging money, and you don't, so that's why you needed us. Don't sweat it. That's what we're here for."

"And the fucking cameras—"

"I've seen that sort of thing happen," Chuck said frankly, "when a company or a group has to fight for money or resources. Some people will come in every day and be the squeaky wheel. And some people will figure out how to run without grease. Your people chose option B because they believed in what you were doing, and I gather you were doing a lot of it on your trust fund, which while sizable is not the same as having the entire company to back you."

Lucius nodded. "I'll be honest. I found my father undercutting my bids for work done on purpose, just to be a bastard. He didn't even know what the work was *for*."

Chuck sucked air in through his teeth. "My God, Lucius. I mean, my old man wasn't a picnic. Lots of yelling, lots of hearing how we—my mother especially—were all worthless pieces of shit. But *your* old man? Well, he was a special shape of bastard, wasn't he?"

Lucius heard that, *felt* it keenly, in his chest. "He never hit my mother in the face," he said after a moment. "Nor me, nor Kenny. Broken wrists, yes. Broken noses, no."

"Your poor mother," Chuck murmured. "That big old house out in the middle of nowhere. Nobody she could tell. She must have felt so alone."

"Cheri's mother was her personal maid," Lucius said softly. "My mother's only friend. She helped Mom wrap broken ribs, set shoulders. Learned how to make excuses like a pro." To his horror, Lucius heard the wobble in his voice. He was over this. Years with a shrink, cursing the old man's name, planning his revenge by helping the very people his father despised. He'd cried. He and Kenny and his mother had all cried. Until finally Kenny had had enough crying and leukemia had given him an out in the seventh grade.

Lucius and his mother had been alone then, until the year Lucius went off to college and she'd died of a heart attack.

Or a broken heart. Lucius was never sure which.

"Nobody you can go to," Chuck said, sighing. "Everybody you'd talk to was a friend of your father's. 'Oh, that guy? He's great! We go to the same club—always good for a laugh.'"

Lucius let out a harsh breath. "It's like you were here," he said, the acid in his voice threatening to unmake him at the seams.

To his surprise, he felt Chuck's warm hand on his as it rested on the center console. Uncomfortably, he realized his own hand was sweaty—and shaking—but Chuck didn't seem to notice. He threaded their fingers together and softly began to stroke the back of Lucius's knuckles with his thumb.

"You are doing a good job," Chuck said kindly. "And I get the feeling you have been all alone without help for too long. You've got help now. You've got a squadron of help. Your pilot is flying to Chicago tomorrow to get more help, help that has all but promised to throw up on your nice upholstery. But it's help just the same."

"I can't believe they're coming down," Lucius said wretchedly. Of all things, that brought tears to his eyes. "My brother, he died of leukemia. A more insidious form than the one Josh has, I suspect, but… but it was so hard, watching him just waste away. I have no words of gratitude or respect or—"

"Hey, hey, hey…." Chuck released Lucius's hand long enough to kill the engine, before leaning over the console and wrapping Lucius in his arms.

For a moment, Lucius was stunned. What was he supposed to do here, pulled against the broad chest while this nice, easygoing, mysterious man took him into an embrace?

But after a moment of holding himself stiff, of trying to master everything—the fear, the disappointment, the bitterness, the anger—Lucius's body gave a hard shudder, and he let himself relax.

Ah God. That chest. The soft words. The kisses in his hair. His whole life he'd been waiting for somebody to hold him and tell him it was going to be okay. He, his brother, his mother—they'd clung together in fear and pain. But his mother had never lied to him, and all she'd ever told him was that she'd do what she could to protect them all.

She had. She'd taken blows that had been meant for Lucius and Kenny both, but that wasn't the same as promising safety, promising help.

Lucius shook in his arms, letting Charles Calder's kindness, his strength, wash over him, letting it seep into his body and replenish his bones. God, he was fascinated with this man. Every moment in his company, no matter how awkward, only filled him with a bigger hunger to know more, to grow closer.

He spoke rustily, both mortified and embarrassed by what came out. "Dammit! I was looking forward to our date."

Chuck's chest rumbled with his laugh. "Well, we're still going," he said. "But, you know, we'll be working too."

Kyle Miller had moved up on their suspect list, and as it turned out, he was going to be a guest at the same chamber of commerce fundraiser that Lucius had been going to drag Chuck to. Boom! They already had invitations, and suddenly Chuck was going to be miked up and on the job.

"I wanted it to be personal," Lucius grumbled.

"Mm…." Chuck nuzzled his temple. "Don't fool yourself, Mr. Broadstone. Everything between you and me right now is personal. And don't worry about the soiree. I wouldn't stick with a crew unless they were having fun together. Believe you me, when we get prettied up and put our dancing shoes on, we're going to have some fun."

Lucius pulled back enough to search his face. "I have never met anybody like you," he said after a moment. "You seem to make the best out of everything. To forgive people for their flaws. You have all these opportunities to be larger than life, but you play off the aw-shucks thing until I could almost believe you're no one of consequence."

"I'm not," Chuck said soberly. "If we're going to go any further here, Scotty, you've got to believe that I'm exactly who I say I am. I'm a low-level criminal who squandered all his chances at anything better. That I get to hang with a crew as classy as the Salingers? That is purely coincidental."

Lucius smiled slightly. "I don't believe you," he whispered, and then he raised his head and kissed Chuck, hard and no bullshit, and he sensed Chuck's moment of surprise.

Lucius meant this to be a *real* kiss. It wasn't playing, and it wasn't fucking around. This was the kiss of somebody who meant to take Chuck somewhere private, get naked with him, and do hard, muscular, pleasurable things.

Which was why it surprised Lucius that there was something teasing in Chuck's response. Something tender. Lucius took Chuck's lower lip between his teeth and nibbled instead of nipped, and Chuck gasped, almost shocked. Lucius was not surprised at the sudden unfurling of a very ripe, very adult hunger in his belly. Chuck allowed Lucius inside for a moment, his barriers dropped, his aw-shucks nowhere in sight.

Lucius was hungry for this, for the honesty, for the diffidence and even the teasing. He wanted to know Chuck's secrets, the things he'd held back, the real person. But he had no tools with which to power that honesty out of Charles Calder. Chuck framed Lucius's throat in the vee of his thumb and forefinger, and every inhibition, every thought of propriety Lucius had, went flying out of his head and into the vast and starry night.

Chuck started to ruck the front of Lucius's dress shirt out of his pants, his fingers rough on the tender skin of Lucius's abdomen, and Lucius gave a faint moan and gathered Chuck's shirt in his hand. He had a wild thought of pushing Chuck back in his seat, shoving his pants down, and straddling him like a horny teenager, but no sooner had the thought crossed his mind than he remembered where they were.

Chuck apparently did too. He pulled back a moment and tried a smile. "Lucius, my man, you *do* remember that we're parked in front of a place where kids might see us, right?"

That quickly, Lucius threw himself back into his seat and covered his face with his hands.

"Augh! My God, Charles, you really do destroy my equilibrium." He glared at the man while tugging his shirt back into place, at least over the bursting fly of his slacks.

Chuck grimly adjusted himself in his khaki shorts. "Sure. That's where I'm having trouble. My equilibrium."

Lucius cast him a sideways glance, a tight smile pulling at his lips.

"I have the feeling nothing bothers *your* 'equilibrium,'" he said dryly.

Chuck's reply surprised him. "You do," he said seriously. "You… you have the potential to wreck me and wreck me hard, Lucius Broadstone. If I seem a mite skittish, it's because I have let people down before. And I do not want to let you down, not as your employee and not as your lover. So I'm going slow so I make sure I can do what's right by you. I know you wanted me to open up this afternoon, but believe me, there are some things you do not want to know."

Lucius gnawed on his lower lip for a moment before making himself stop. It was one of his tells, a throwback to a childhood spent in fear.

"You know, sometimes, you simply have to close your eyes and jump." Brave words, he thought ruefully, but then, they'd been his touchstone when he'd taken

162 **Amy Lane**

the reins of his father's company, and they'd gotten him this far with Caraway House.

Chuck gave a humorless laugh. "That's the philosophy that has gotten me where I am today. I've been trying really hard to think a little first and see if I can save you a world of hurt."

Oh. Well. That was a hard thing to argue with. But God! Look at him. Broad shoulders rippling, auburn hair mussed. Lucius just… just *wanted* him. His entire life, his wealth and his privilege had given him nothing but a burden of secrets and pain and more responsibility. This once, he wanted to *have* something, have *someone*, who would hold him through the pain and help him shoulder the responsibility and maybe—just maybe—share his secrets.

"I've lived through a world of pain, Charles. I've helped these women in the shelter escape their own world of pain. Sometimes you don't need a hero. You need a decent man who refuses to hurt you to make himself feel bigger. I know you're capable of that. I have no doubts."

Chuck sighed and reached across the console to cup Lucius's cheek and rub it with his thumb. Lucius leaned into the touch, covering his hand and trapping it. God, there was nothing wrong with this man's heart. How could he not see that?

"Just because you're strong enough to survive all the bad doesn't mean you don't deserve a world of good," Chuck said softly. "I'll try to be good enough." He dropped his hand. "But not tonight. Tonight, I've got to go brief Hunter and help keep Molly safe. You and me have got to wait."

Lucius nodded, understanding in his head, if not his heart. On autopilot, he started the car, which was nice because the night hadn't cooled down much and he could feel sweat staining his underarms.

"Hunter's probably going to the house for dinner tomorrow," Chuck warned. "So I'll see you the day after."

"Well, I'll think of you tomorrow," Lucius told him, mouth pursed. He sent Chuck a dirty look, but Chuck winked and some of his irritation faded.

"I'll think of you tonight," Chuck said, his gaze sultry, and Lucius found the tension in his shoulders, back, and forehead relaxing.

"You do that," he said, breathing out. "And I'll think of you."

Chuck's smile was damned sinful. "Think of me hard and hot, all right? I'm good for it."

Lucius groaned. "Augh! Go. You are *killing* me!"

Chuck's laughter chased him down the driveway. Damn the man.

LUCIUS DROVE to the airport the next morning to pick up Josh Salinger, his mother, Julia, and Josh's friend Grace. Josh slept most of the car trip and then went upstairs to rest some more the moment they hit the front door. Julia went with him, leaving Grace standing in Lucius's sitting room, which was, Lucius gathered, a bad thing.

Lucius made sure Julia and Josh were settled and that Josh had water and juice before practically running down the stairs.

Grace was looking at the tchotchkes Lucius kept on the fireplace mantelpiece, his hand out as he touched each one, lifted it, tested its weight, and then returned it exactly where he got it.

Lucius knew that Grace—a slender, graceful young man whose real name was Dylan—was their "grease man," their thief, the member of their crew who could get into tight places and get out with anything that was needed, and he'd also gathered that the young man, Josh's dearest friend, was unpredictable at best.

Lucius girded his loins to have half his inventory of small valuables raided.

As though to confirm his deepest suspicions, as Lucius came down the stairs, Grace asked, "I don't want to piss you off, because Josh's family likes you and you're not a douchebag. Is there anything here in the mansion that I absolutely can't steal? I mean, if you ask, I'll give it back, but is there anything that's sacred or something?"

Lucius thought about it. "My mother's locket," he said, surprising himself. "I keep it in the safe behind my computer. It's got a picture of me on one side and my brother on the other. My, uhm, brother passed away when we were young. It's one of the few pictures my father let her keep."

And to his dismay, the expression Grace turned to him was stricken.

"You should have all the pictures," he said, his voice thick. "Josh and I have hard drives full of photos. You should be able to swim in them when you need to."

Lucius swallowed. "I would rather have my brother."

Grace gave him a sad smile, something at odds with his pixyish features. "So would I."

"Your friend should recover," Lucius told him, feeling a strange tenderness for this almost ethereal young thief. "I… my brother's illness was much more malignant. Josh should be okay."

"He needs a bone marrow transplant," Grace said. "If we were really brothers, I could do that for him, but we're not, so I can only be his good-luck animal and hope."

Lucius wanted to rub his chest. Of all the things he'd expected when asking the Salingers for their help, ripping this wound open had not been on the list.

"I'll hope with you," he said softly. "Dylan, erm, Grace, is there anything I can get you? I was going to go back to work and see where Stirling and Carl are today, and then hopefully after lunch Josh would be good to go to the shelter and see how to fix the cameras. I know usually you hang by his side, but I think he's going to be asleep for a couple of hours. What can I do to make your stay here—"

"Not suck?" Grace asked.

Lucius shrugged. "If I can."

Grace nodded. "Can I try to break into the shelter?" he asked. "I mean, Hunter's manning the cameras, and Chuck's there too. If I can break in, I can tell them where to shore up the sensors and things. Trust me, I can find the hole in a steel door."

Lucius hesitated, and Grace hastened to reassure him.

"I promise, no scaring the residents. They won't even know I'm there."

"There are other young men in the shelter," Lucius said after a moment. "Women aren't the only ones who get trapped in abusive relationships."

Grace nodded. "Yes, I understand. I'll be good. I promise." He gave an almost sweet smile. "I'll be back in time for lunch, probably before Josh wakes up."

Lucius nodded. "I'll tell the people at the security booth that you're—"

But Grace had already turned and slipped out the door, running lithely in what looked like dance shoes. As the heavy front door closed behind him, trapping the cool air in the house, Lucius wondered exactly what he'd done.

At that moment, Carl texted. He and Stirling asked not to be pulled in for lunch; they were getting their meal at the cafeteria and working through until a late dinner. Lucius didn't want to bother them. He'd hired Linus to free him up to work on Caraway House, but he couldn't do that either.

Restlessly Lucius wandered up the stairs toward his home office, only to bump into Julia Dormer-Salinger as she emerged from her son's room.

"Oh!" he said, surprised. "I thought you'd be resting with him."

Julia wrinkled her nose with an expression very much like the young people she surrounded herself with. "Are you insane? It's only ten in the morning! I have at least two phone meetings to attend before lunch. Do you, uhm—?"

"I have an upstairs den with outstanding phone reception and a downstairs den with perfect internet. I do not know why both things are not perfect in both rooms, but I take what I can get."

She gave a delicate snort. "Do tell Stirling and Josh about it while they're here. That sounds almost intentionally inconvenient. I'll take the upstairs den if that's okay with you."

"That's fine. Follow me!"

Truth was, he liked his upstairs study best. The paneling was maple, so not too dark, and his grandfather had known and been known by the craftsmen in the area. It was hand cut and placed in geometrically shaped precision over the walls and floor, leaving the ceiling open, with raw beams and pale cream-colored plaster. The couch was a gentle blue color, which didn't exactly match the paneling, but it was comfortable as hell, and his roll-top desk had been restored and customized so it could fit modern desk equipment, including a charging station and a router that *did* match the paneling. Two fully ergonomic desk chairs and a smaller secretary-sized desk, tucked in the far corner, completed the setup.

"Oh, this is perfect," Julia exclaimed, drawing her laptop from a bag at her hip and setting it up on the secretary.

"Can I get you anything?" he asked. "Water, coffee, some fruit perhaps?"

She winked at him and pulled a bottle of seltzer water from her bag, setting it up on the desk before slipping off her modest heels and settling down into the chair with a hedonistic sigh.

"Oh, this is wonderful. Felix keeps trying to make me get one of these, and I keep putting him off. The one in my office at home is horribly uncomfortable, but...." She shrugged. "It matches the furniture in the rest of the room."

"Well, I'm on Felix's side," Lucius told her, charmed. He remembered his and Julia's first meeting and how Julia, with her winsome smile and kindness, had pretty much pulled him into the crew when he could have been very much their opposition. His impression of her—and his desire to be near her, to soak up the sunshine of her smile—wasn't a mystery. He missed his mother so very much, and it didn't matter that Julia was not even ten years his senior; she was a mother to her core. The way she'd opened her home to her son's friends and appeared to fret over and embrace each one in their very individuality was as motherly a trait as he'd ever seen.

And her strength was undeniable.

Unhurriedly she plugged her computer into the charger. He realized he was staring and moved to grab his own laptop when her voice stopped him.

"What are you thinking, Mr. Broadstone?" she asked.

He eyed her again, her hair pulled up into a smooth knot at her nape, her sleeveless coral-colored summer dress both practical in the heat and demure. She'd put on makeup—understated—and wore a locket at her throat much like his own mother had, and he was tempted to sink to his knees and confess everything to her, including his confusion over Charles Calder.

"I was thinking that you're a born mother," he said baldly, and to his horror, her eyes grew bright and shiny.

"What a lovely compliment." And then to prove to him that everything he believed was true, she said, "My son is sick, and I'm worried as hell. It would please me to do something useful, Lucius. What kind of mothering do *you* need?"

Lucius's own eyes burned, and he was suddenly the bashful schoolboy who had grown so awkward during the car trip the day before. "You're busy," he said, looking away, and she shook her head.

"Sit." With brisk movements, she picked up her phone and texted deftly, smiling when the phone buzzed in reply. "There we go. My ten fifteen is now my three fifteen, and you have an hour at the very least to pour your troubles into my lap."

He smiled and sank onto the comfortable blue couch. "Well, since you insist...."

She chuckled and opened her fizzy water, taking a dainty sip before wiping the lip of the bottle and offering it to him.

"That's kind," he said, "but no. I need to go down and have an online meeting in twenty. I was going to get a snack then." It was a lie. He wanted the excuse to flee if things got too emotionally difficult. But God, did he want some advice.

"Sure you do," she said gently. "So use your time wisely."

He smiled at her a little, appreciating her, appreciating her entire family. "Chuck," he said softly. "I... I can't get a handle on him. I think he wants me, you know?"

Julia nodded. "That's very much *my* impression."

"Was it?" he asked, heartened. "Because now I get the feeling he's a...." How did Chuck phrase it?

"A mite skittish?" she asked, her full lips twisting.

"Well, yes."

She looked away for a moment and then faced him, her dark blue eyes taking in every nuance of his expression. "Do you know why Danny and Felix split up for ten years?" she asked, and he widened his eyes in surprise.

"I thought it was twenty. Because you and Felix got married?"

She pursed those full lips and shook her head. "Oh no. It was ten, because Felix and I *were* married, and Danny was honing the craft of being a thief and a con man by stealing into our home under my father's nose so he and Felix could be together."

"For ten years?" Lucius squeaked.

She nodded. "Yes. For me, you see. Because if Felix and I hadn't married, the odds were very good my father would have beaten me to death when he found out I was pregnant with Josh. Felix and Danny were on the grift then, you understand? They were going to steal from my father because Hiram Dormer was a fucker in every sense of the word. Instead, they saved my life, and Josh's too—and came into part of a fortune that Felix turned into a *real* fortune, and a legacy for that matter, because the network empire he's built out of my father's two crappy cable stations is truly a thing of beauty."

"I believe he's had some help there," Lucius said, and Julia inclined her head gratefully. It was well known that Dormer-Salinger Network was run with two geniuses behind the helm, but Julia stayed away from the pushing and shoving and catfighting that often came with corporate culture. And now, hearing her talk so matter-of-factly about a father who, by all accounts, was monstrous, he understood why.

Julia knew her own strength, but she was not interested in proving to another human being how strong that was.

He respected the hell out of her.

"So Felix wasn't able to leave me yet. We were both still afraid of what my father would do. He might have taken Josh away from me, and he might have taken the company away from Felix—illegally, because Felix is really very canny, but still. All that we'd spent ten years working for, my father might have taken from us. But Danny?"

"Couldn't wait that long?" he hazarded. God, ten years living in the shadows was long enough.

"He was dying by degrees," she said softly. "The situation was killing him, and he was drinking enough to help it along. He picked a fight with Felix, made Felix throw him out. Then he left. And Felix and Josh and I were…." She shook her head, her eyes growing red-rimmed.

"Devastated?" he asked softly.

"Yes." She nodded. "All of us. And not one of us blamed him. Not then, not now. Because he stuck it out for ten years. And I honestly think that if he'd tried to stay for the two more years that the old fucker took to die, Danny would have been dead or worse. He was miserable. The person he loved most in the world couldn't even look at him if they bumped into each other in public. When we were all inside the house and my father was gone, we were so happy," she said, her voice throbbing with it. "When Danny came back, half-feral, wanting to help Felix recover from that setback with that awful woman, wanting to see me again—"

"And Josh!" Lucius said, because he'd seen how much Felix's lover adored Felix and Julia's son.

"Oh, he saw Josh," she said, her voice dry. "He snuck into Chicago four times a year. Do you know that rat bastard came to the grad-night party *Felix and I* threw for Josh, and we were none the wiser? Looking back at it now, I could throttle him." Some of her wry amusement fell away. "But I could also kick myself. Because we put him in that situation, and we were so… so afraid to try to set it right again."

Lucius nodded. "I'm not sure what this has to do with me and—"

"With the billionaire businessman and the getaway driver who has a knack for getting things done?"

she asked, so mildly he almost didn't feel the cut two breaths after it landed.

"But I'm not…," he began, trailing off as it set in. He was taking a *bank robber* to a public function. Had he even thought about how he'd introduce Charles? Had he thought about how Charles might not like being lied about?

"Yes, I know you're 'not like that,' Lucius. Nobody *thinks* they're like that, until they have to come up with a truth that the public can swallow and live with the truth that's real in their own lives. Now, I know Chuck is a good person, and so do you. But I would bet he's got some skeletons in his closet you might not anticipate. Or understand. So of course he's skittish. He's never dated anybody like you."

"Has he told you that?" Lucius asked. It would be *wonderful* if Charles had confided in *somebody.*

"Darling, unlike you, I don't think Chuck has ever seen women as protectors and confidants. Unless I very much miss my mark, it's the other way around for him. He does what he must to protect the people in his life and then escapes before anybody notices he was there or the blow lands to pay him back for standing up for someone. I think getaway driver is possibly his most apt description, don't you?"

Lucius's heart had fallen to his stomach. "Because he's so good at running?" he asked numbly.

"Not because he wants to," she said, reassuring him. "In fact, I think that's why he seemed so happy to simply blend into our household. I think he'd floated around long enough. He was looking for a place to land. Decide now if you want your date—your thing, whatever it is—to be a bit of floating in the breeze, or if you want it to land and grow roots. Once you've decided that, I would imagine Charles will be a little happier about putting his feet down."

Lucius didn't answer her for a moment, thinking about the things Charles had said, his willingness to protect and be kind.

Julia, the true mother that she was, apparently knew all the "children" in her orbit, and she knew this particular wayward son in a way Lucius imagined Charles would not be comfortable with.

"How do you think he got like this?" he asked, feeling hopeful for the first time since she'd told him the ridiculously sad story of Felix and Danny, two of the happiest men he'd ever met.

"You will have to ask him," she said softly. "But I suspect that people get like this because they've hoped for love or security so badly but it has never, ever come to be." She paused. "Good people. Bad people turn this into an entirely different thing, I would imagine. It's not the experience that makes somebody good or bad, I think, but how they react to it. Chuck's reaction is to drive in and save the day and then get the hell out. Make of that what you will, but that's how I see him."

"You're very wise," he said, and she put a gentle hand on his knee.

"You're very kind to ask me," she told him. "I was feeling quite woebegone when I left Josh's room. It's so hard to see him feeling this shitty. But you've reminded me that there are other people who need me, and—" She swallowed hard. "—I think I needed to remember that."

He stood and was surprised when she did too, throwing herself into his arms for a hard sisterly hug. He returned it, a little awed, because it felt like the exact thing he needed at the exact time, and he wondered what magic these people produced that allowed that to happen.

The hug was interrupted when the radio at his belt buzzed harshly, and Julia stepped back, looking at her phone in the charger, which was doing the same.

Eyes wide with alarm when he saw Charles's name, he hit Call and got an earful of irritation.

"Did you actually sic Grace on the shelter's security system?" he asked.

"Why? Is that bad?" Oh dear.

"Only when he slips in completely unnoticed and Hunter almost trips over him as he's coloring with the six-year-olds. Good God, man, could you have *warned* us!"

Lucius put his hand to his chest, feeling the retroactive panic. "Well, I was going to, but I had a conversation with Ms. Dormer-Salinger first, and—"

"Yeah, yeah. Look, you're about to get a *laundry list* of things that you need to fix, and you know what?"

"I have only myself to blame?" Lucius asked, making sure.

"You're damned right you do. Jesus, man. Hunter yelled his name, and all the kids burst into tears, and now he's sitting on the *floor*, apologizing to the children, telling them that his boyfriend worried him and he didn't mean to scare them. He's almost in *tears*, you understand?"

"I'm so sorry," Lucius said, feeling it in his bones.

"Communication, Lucius. I'm saying. It's a big fuckin' help."

Lucius scrubbed at his face with his hand, part of him trying not to smile at the thought of dark, mysterious, *dangerous* Hunter sitting on the floor and trying to make things right with children he'd startled, and part of him genuinely appalled.

"I understand," he said, feeling it in his bones. This was what Julia had been talking about: being upfront with people, telling the best truth you knew.

Not keeping people in the dark about your motives.

"I know you do," Charles said, letting out a breath. "I'm sorry for yelling. I'm just saying, man—"

"You needed warning," Lucius said.

"Next time?"

"I promise, Charles. I swear to God, next time I will keep you apprised of what your team is doing."

"Thanks, Lucius," he said, his voice mellowing now that the initial surge of upset was over. "We'll take care of your people, you understand? We don't want anybody to be afraid."

Especially you, Charles, because I think you're afraid I won't see you for the good that you are.

"I get it completely," Lucius said softly. "Charles?"

"Yes?"

"Thank you for taking care of the people in the shelter. For taking it seriously. It means everything to me."

"Well, you know. It's a thing I'm good at."

"It is. Will I see you tonight?"

"No. Hunter and Grace might need to hold hands and moon a lot. I think Hunter's heart is still pounding. But, uhm…."

"What?"

"I *want* to see you."

Lucius smiled. "I want to see you too."

"Good," Charles said. "Later."

He signed off brusquely, and Lucius put his phone in his pocket with a sigh.

"Grace?" Julia asked, a certain grim humor in her voice.

"Grace," Lucius confirmed.

Julia shook her head. "As much as he's trying not to lose his shit over Josh, we're probably lucky he wasn't robbing a bank."

Lucius slow-blinked. "You know, your family has the most interesting ways of dealing with stress."

"A good robbery can make you feel ten years younger," she declared. And then she winked, as though she were kidding.

Lucius suspected that she was not, but he smiled in return.

He could get used to Charles's family. He could, in fact, very much enjoy having them as his own.

Break-ins and Escapes

CHUCK EYED the group of women—and one man—on the lawn in front of the mansion with what he hoped was a benign and friendly expression.

They did not look happy.

"Heya!" he said, encouraged when Molly trotted up, beach towel under her arm. He understood yoga mats were on their way, but in the meantime, the grass was soft and a beach towel would do.

"Not namaste?" asked one woman. Platinum blond, thin as a steel blade, with an equally sharp expression, this woman had obviously had yoga, Pilates, strength training and cardio, probably religiously, before she'd ended up here. Something about her expression made Chuck want to point out that she wasn't any better than any of the other people in their little group, but he didn't think she'd take too kindly to that.

"Not my thing," Chuck said evenly, "but feel free to namaste all you want. This is a beginner's yoga class—nothing too fancy. This is all about stretching and flexibility and finding ways to release your stress through movement. Now, I want everybody to spread out your mats and towels, and make that little spot on the ground your center for the next hour. Remember, the rule of thumb is 'don't do anything that hurts.' When you have a position right, you will feel the stretch and the tension releasing from your body. If you've got it wrong, adjust until things start to feel good. I want you to walk away from this class refreshed and happy, not hurt and twisted into knots, y'all hear?"

Everyone *except* the namaste woman nodded in something like relief, and Chuck led them all through basic stretches, making them hold the stretch, repeat the stretch, and hold it again. He walked back and forth, asking permission to correct a pose with his hands, accepting no for an answer and offering verbal encouragement when a few of them refused his request to help. Chuck had spent a lot of his life making himself as unobtrusive and laid-back as possible. It had served him well as a kid when nobody knew what would set off his father's temper, in the military when he didn't want anybody to do something stupid like promote him, and as a getaway driver, when he didn't want to get in too deep with a crew because he didn't like the leadership or the direction.

In this case, his ability to make himself small worked well, because he could feel the tension vibrating from his students like a tuning fork. These people had been beaten, and they were not okay.

He kept his voice soothing, his touch light, if needed, and his directions concise but gentle. This was all about feeling good, and he repeated that a thousand times, because he knew from experience, if you were a cat on a hot tin roof, the slightest bit of criticism could make you freak out and fall off.

When he was done, he had everybody salute the sun and shake themselves out before he bowed slightly, hands together, and told everybody to have a good day.

Oh sure, he could have said "namaste" to the woman who apparently lived her life in a gym, but he really wasn't in the mood.

But he did remind folks to come later that afternoon for his self-defense class, and the looks he got were... hopeful.

Molly noticed too as she walked up to him, smiling diffidently.

"Thanks, Mr. Summers," she said breathily. "I really do feel much more relaxed."

He gave her a benevolent smile, like he would any other student. "That's good to hear, Maisy girl." He dropped his voice. "You got any information for me?"

"Yeah," she muttered, folding her towel as a pretext to keep her eyes down. "Don't piss off the namaste woman. She's the trophy wife of a prominent doctor who's on a thousand committees in the Chicago city council. He could make Felix and Danny's life really difficult if we slip up."

"Well, fuckin' na-ma-ste," Chuck muttered, and her smirk made him feel better. "Anything else?"

"Well, her husband is out as our guy. He smacked her around once. According to the gossip and a check with the hospital, this is true. So she set up a hue and cry and got placed here. Her maid, apparently, had a friend who was getting relocated. But her husband is already in the Bahamas with his next trophy wife. I think she's hiding out so she can spring the big divorce on him. That's fine, more power to her, a douchebag is a douchebag, but...."

She gave him a look he easily interpreted.

"But he's not hiring hackers to get back what's his," Chuck agreed. "I gotcha. Anyone else?"

Molly grimaced. "The three girls my age, toward the middle?"

Chuck nodded. They'd all had straight brown hair pulled back in a ponytail, oversized T-shirts, and cotton Lycra bicycle shorts that looked like shelter hand-me-downs. Two of them had also been his most skittish, one of them begging him not to touch her to help her form.

"Bad?" he asked quietly.

"So bad," Molly told him, voice soft. "They went to Ohio State, and their college boyfriends, all three of them, just beat the crap out of them one day. It was like some sort of fraternity ritual for the guys. Some sick little pact."

She shuddered, and Chuck's jaw hardened. "Are the guys in custody?" he asked.

Molly's eyes narrowed. "No," she said after a moment. "In fact, they all graduated from State and got jobs this spring."

"Think there's anything wrong with that?" he probed carefully.

"Yes, Charles. Yes, I do."

They both nodded. "I'll see if Stirling can look them up," she said into the grim silence that followed. "You, me, Hunter... we could do some reckoning."

"I agree." He sighed. "But we're getting off track."

"Yeah, speaking of that, you know the woman in her forties, sort of namaste-woman's friend, but that heifer wouldn't give her the time of day?"

"Yeah," Chuck said. "Sweet lady. Curvy. She's got one of the teenagers in the boy's section."

"Exactly." Molly pulled out her water bottle and took a swig. "Well, her husband was the police chief who looked the other way when our college girls got beat up. Joanie had, apparently, been taking the odd hit for years, but, you know…."

"Police chief," Chuck supplied grimly.

"Yeah. Anyway, their son came out three months ago, and Daddy apparently tried to go through her to get to him. Put her in the hospital, so she got the boy to steal her husband's car, left AMA, ditched the car, bought a shitty Toyota, and followed a nurse's directions here. From what I understand, she practically drove through Lucius's hedge, she was in such bad shape before she got here. She and the boy, Troy, are terrified, and I don't blame them."

"Sounds like a *prince*," Chuck muttered. "Do you know if he was the chief of Springfield or Peoria? We're almost dead in the middle of the two of them."

"Springfield," she said. "So you might meet him at Lucius's little shindig tomorrow."

"That's in Springfield?" How had Chuck not known that?

"Yeah, idiot. It's some big society thing. I got invites in Chicago. It's a big deal."

Chuck tilted his head back and groaned. "God, why did I agree to go to this again?"

"Because Lucius is hot, and he's not a bad guy."

Chuck glared at her sourly, not even sure if he could explain the grumbling in his stomach.

"Look," Molly said kindly, "I know you like to play it fast and loose with the guys you date—"

"Bang," he said in the interest of full disclosure. Even Car-Car hadn't been a date.

"That's my point," Molly said, her big green eyes fixed soberly on his face. "I mean, all your stories are about how you did a guy and ran out and robbed a bank. But…." She bit her lip, and to a stranger, it would have looked like she was being diffident and self-conscious, like her cover. But those weren't really Molly's emotions, so Chuck knew she was going to say something serious.

"What?" he asked, knowing they really couldn't afford to linger any longer on the lawn.

"You… you seem to really like it in Chicago. Maybe you could, I don't know, find someone in particular to like while you're here."

"We're in Springfield, darlin'," he said with a wink, although inside, his chest felt all achy, as if maybe, she had a point.

"Don't be an ass," she said pertly, and he knew that if they'd been back in Chicago, she would have smacked his arm or something. As it was, she raised her voice a little higher and said, "Thanks for your advice, Mr. Summers. I'll be back in half an hour for your self-defense class."

He almost expected her to flounce off, but she was a pro, and her walk across the lawn was a little more uncertain, a little subdued. He wondered how much of a relief it had been to talk to him, someone who knew her as the powerhouse of laughter, sensuality, and will that she was, and who thoroughly approved.

Then he got his brain in the teaching place, began to plan for his self-defense class, and tried not to yawn.

Hunter had stayed up at Lucius's house the night before—probably to reassure Grace, after the near-disaster before lunch. Although Chuck hated to admit it, Grace had brought a *shit-ton* of important things to their attention. Hunter had spent the morning working with the fence electronics people, fixing the obvious holes, including an actual *hole* in the chain link fence facing the driveway that had been cut sometime in the past month. Set in a blind spot between motion sensors, the break hadn't been obvious because it had been covered with holly, but Grace had used the space to sneak in without so much as a hiccup.

The spot bothered Chuck, and Hunter too. Lucius hadn't suspected inside help for the intruders because the women had so much to lose, but this definitely made it look like somebody could make things sticky. One of the things Hunter was doing was putting their *own* surveillance cameras in the area—ones that reported directly to Josh's and Stirling's computers—and leaving the gap partially open to see if anybody inside the fence tried to get out.

Or one of the things Hunter *had* been doing. After Chuck taught the self-defense class, he found Hunter in the surveillance room on his hands and knees, unplugging and replugging in monitors while Josh looked at a schematic on his keyboard and said, "Yes. Yes. The one below it. No, not that one. The one to the left."

Suddenly they both paused, and Josh said, "Walk from the back hallway to the elevator. Fine, dance from the back hallway to the elevator." And then, on the thin edge of patience, "Look, asshole, you can grande fucking jeté if you want, as long as it's from the *back hallway to the elevator*!"

The chatter that met that statement was loud enough for Chuck to hear through their earbuds.

"*Grace!*" Hunter barked, and Josh and Hunter both breathed in and out slowly. Chuck looked up at the monitors and was relieved to see the slender thief, dressed in his signature black, dance fluidly from the back hallway to the elevator, his motion displayed from monitor to monitor to monitor across the bank of them in one continuous arc.

"Works for me," Hunter said gruffly.

"Me too. Thank God. How much acid did the unpaid intern drop to do this the first time? That's all I want to know so I can go tell them to stop."

Chuck let out a low rumble of a laugh. "The machine has not yet been invented that can measure the quantities of incompetence here, my friend. Thank God we have you to stop it."

Josh rolled his eyes and then yawned.

And then Chuck yawned. "Dammit," he complained when he was done. "That's catching!"

"You took the night watch for me, didn't you?" Hunter asked. When Chuck yawned again, he said, "Do you have any more classes to teach today?"

"Nope," Chuck said. "And I see where this is going. I just wanted to be here when Lucius came to pick up Josh and Grace."

He really had missed seeing Lucius the day before. Every conversation they'd had felt like a solid stone set in the bridge that spanned the gap between them.

You know that means he's getting close, right?

Chuck ignored that little voice and tried to concentrate on what Hunter and Josh were saying.

"He'll be here in two hours," Josh said, "so I can rest before dinner. Go nap, Chuck. We'll get you for the briefing when he arrives."

Chuck smiled gratefully and headed for the bunk behind the surveillance room, on what he understood had once been a porch. It was a small space, big enough for two twin beds with footlockers underneath to stash their gear, a pathway at the foot of the beds that led to the tiny bathroom, barely big enough for a shower cubicle, a sink, and a john, and a linen closet that stashed spare bedding for much of the house. There was a connecting door to the laundry room, but that was locked while the porch bedroom was occupied, and Chuck and Hunter gave Tara-Lynn permission and a key to use the shortcut, since the woman was chronically overworked as it was.

Chuck walked into the room, gaze scanning restlessly out of general habit, and he noticed a movement from the corner of his eye. As he whirled to pin down where the movement came from, he caught the door to the laundry room clicking closed. He was there in two strides, cranking the door handle, only to find the door locked from the other side. He gave a grunt and pulled out his key, but he knew what he'd find: the laundry room was empty by the time he'd opened the door, and both the back entrance and the entrance into the house were commonly used routes of cross traffic for anybody going anywhere in the mansion.

"Goddammit," Chuck muttered. Then he called, "Hunter! Hunter, get in here."

There was a thump and a "*Fuck!*" and he grimaced at the thought of Hunter bumping his head. Still, the man was in his room in two strides, and Chuck gave him a brief nod.

"Look around and tell me if you see anything out of place," he commanded, and while Hunter conducted a brief search, Chuck told him about the intruder.

Hunter growled. "Oh my God. Tell your boyfriend that the security in this place is for shit."

Chuck gave a weak laugh. "Well, that's our job, right?" he asked, and Hunter just shook his head.

"Get some sleep, Chuck. We'll be right here on the other side of that wall, and the air conditioner is going full blast or we'd already be people stew."

Chuck gave a sleepy grin. "Am I the carrot in the people stew?" he asked, referring to his auburn hair. "You can tell me. Be honest."

Hunter growled. "You know, between you and Grace, I can't believe anybody else I know tries to be a smartass. You two think you've got a corner on the market."

"Well, we're the originals," Chuck said, grateful for his presence. A buddy who had your back, that you could trust—wasn't that the one thing he'd wanted since he'd left for the military nearly ten years before?

But as he kicked off his shoes and settled on the narrow bed, he thought about that luminous, needy look on Lucius's eyes before he'd left two nights before.

He wanted that too. Was it too much to ask of life, to get the good friends and the good lover and a job that gave him the chance to beat up on real bad guys?

Maybe. But as he dozed off, he thought, *Maybe not.*

LUCIUS WAS attentive that night as they met to debrief.

Stirling and Carl were making progress, they said. Stirling had planted the alarm on the forged key card; a lot of their job now was waiting for their perpetrator to mess up. Carl was creating dossiers on some likely employees, doing financial and personal background checks on the ones who pinged his radar.

"We've got a couple of guys in communications who have an undisclosed source of income that we can't trace," Carl said. "Steve Kubler and—"

"Rob Wopat," Stirling filled in for him. "They're selling weed."

"How do you know?" Carl asked, sounding aggrieved.

"They tried to sell to me," Stirling said, unperturbed. "It's because I'm quiet. They think I'm either a stoner or a serial killer."

"Did ya buy weed from 'em, Stirling?" Chuck asked, trying to keep his smile under wraps.

But Stirling made a rare attempt to meet his eyes and grinned. "Nope," he said, and they both burst out laughing.

"Well done," Lucius told him, smiling too. "Keep 'em guessing."

"Why don't people tell *me* this shit?" Carl asked in disgust. "I spent an hour running their financials, dammit!"

"You look too legit," Josh told him, his voice growing rough like it did toward the end of the day now. Chuck thought it was because he got sick so frequently, and it pained him to see the young man eating practically nothing on his plate. "Don't worry, that comes in handy when we have to deal with police or other authority. That's why you and Stirling make a good team."

"Well, I *have* figured out some things in my capacity as a 'legit' investigator," Carl said, looking barely appeased.

"And…?" Julia teased. "Come on, Soderburgh, we're dying to hear from you."

"A couple of high-profile investors—not competitors—have been watching your stock closely," he said, cocking his head at Lucius.

"They have alarms set to buy it up whenever it falls."

"You can track that?" Lucius asked, surprised.

Carl gave him a pretty smile, highlighting his high-cheekboned Nordic features. "No. No, I can't."

Lucius rolled his eyes, and the rest of the table made throat-clearing noises, letting Lucius know that this wasn't exactly on the up-and-up.

"Well, it's a pity you can't," Lucius said blandly. "I wonder who, if anybody, would be tracking my stock like that."

"Fielding Stans of Stanfield Investor Corp," Carl said crisply. "And well as Miller Corp—an investment firm based in Cleveland, and Charleston Subsidiaries, which manages most of the pension funds in the Springfield and Peoria suburbs. Teachers unions, medical—"

"Law enforcement," Chuck said, his conversation with Molly fresh in his mind.

"Yes!" Carl focused on him. "How did you know?"

"Well, Molly picked up some information today," Chuck said, thinking quickly. "I don't know who's at Stanfield Investor Corp, but Miller Corp is managed by Kyle Miller's father. We told you all about Miller the other night, and he's a nasty entitled piece of shit. From what Lucius tells me, his wife is one of the people in the shelter here. And a nice lady Molly and I met today—and her teenaged son—are both running from her husband, who is chief of police nearby."

"Springfield," Lucius said, his eyes a little glassy. "But they live in Collingsworth. It's an incorporated suburb about twenty miles from here."

"So at least two of those three companies are connected to somebody who has an agenda against Caraway House," Julia said thoughtfully. "And they know that attacking Lucius's company has the potential to make the women's shelter more vulnerable."

"At the same time, they want into the women's shelter," Lucius mused. "Are they trying to get somebody there? Is someone trying to kidnap an abused spouse?"

"How did they know?" Chuck asked suddenly. "How would somebody find out who is in the shelter? I mean, if these three companies are trying to buy Lucius's stock and initiate a hostile takeover, using corporate espionage as a means to do it, how do they know to go after *Lucius*? I know *we've* been finding a fuckton of security vulnerabilities, but ninety percent of the crews out there would have given up as soon as they saw the motion detectors. Josh has already checked. You really *can't* get a satellite shot that reveals anything about the people on the grounds. Well done there, Lucius, and—"

"You're all dumb," Grace said, derailing Chuck's train of thought and leaving him to try to set it right.

"Don't be rude," Josh muttered. "Tell them why."

Grace grunted and buttered a piece of fresh-baked wheat bread that had been placed on the table, setting it on Josh's plate as they all looked at him expectantly. "Eat that," he said, his voice assuming a stony obstinance that even Chuck knew nobody tested.

"Is it good?" Josh asked plaintively.

"It's good," Grace said, a sort of tenderness in his eyes that someone who didn't know him well would have assumed he wasn't capable of. "Eat it."

"Okay. Tell them what you're thinking." Josh picked up the bread obediently and took a bite, and Chuck didn't realize how tense the entire table had gotten watching him not eat until his own shoulders relaxed.

"I found a person-sized gap in the fence yesterday," Grace said. "You know that. It's how I snuck inside. Thing is, it was perfectly placed. Between motion sensors, between cameras. I know I give Mr. Business Guy a lot of shit, but there's not a lot of places along the fence this hole could be. It had to be under vegetation, it had to be within walking distance of the road, and it had to be invisible to the tech. Anyone but me trying to get in from the outside wouldn't have seen it."

He took a small bite of whatever was on his plate then and gazed back at all of them, expecting them to make the intuitive leap that Hunter's boyfriend seemed to do effortlessly.

Chuck was the first one who got it.

"It's an inside job," he said, anger starting in his gut. "It's… someone on the inside of the shelter is giving information to someone on the outside, and that person is sharing the info with the investment companies. They've got somebody in the company with the forged key card trying to sabotage the company, the money men swooping in to bankrupt Broadstone Industries, and an inside source telling…."

His heart froze. Stopped beating. Fear sweat sprang out on his brow.

"Telling the abusers where to find the people they're abusing," Lucius muttered. "Oh my God."

For a moment, the entire table was silent. Josh was the one who spoke up, and Chuck blessed the boy a thousand times over.

"It's bad," he said, agreeing with them. "But the plan isn't ripe. Not yet."

"How do you know?" Lucius asked, and Chuck could hear the naked exhaustion in his voice. Oh God. Poor Lucius. He'd obviously been working so hard to make his business profitable, and Caraway House was so dear to his heart. Without thinking, Chuck pressed his knee to Lucius's under the table, but nobody was more surprised than he was when Lucius squeezed his knee in return.

"Because your finances aren't in that bad a shape, for one," Josh said. Very carefully, as though surprised that it tasted so good, he took another bite of the soft honey-flavored bread. "And because your saboteur isn't doing things on a grand enough scale to speed up the timeline. We're going to need *you* to take a look at what and where you're the most vulnerable—even on the inside, Stirling can't get all the good stuff. Things like clean rooms and refrigerated components and controlled environments are completely out of our... what's the word, Mom?" he asked, revealing how very tired he was.

"Purview, sweetheart," Julia said softly.

"Exactly. Whoever's fucking you over, he either doesn't have the brains or doesn't have the balls to do it big-time yet. And the people trying to hack the security systems haven't come close. These things could change, I'm not gonna lie. But the whole reason we're here is to stop this person before they bankrupt you and hurt someone."

"But why pick an incompetent saboteur!" Lucius asked, clearly frustrated.

"Maybe he wasn't picked," Carl said, frowning. "We ran background checks on all the employees, and nobody popped. Maybe he really *is* an employee because he got the job. Whether it was so he could sabotage you or whether that came later, maybe he was just handy."

"But if he's handy, and his financials aren't popping, he'd have to have a vendetta too," Carl argued, and Chuck sucked in a hard breath of air.

"People, we all owe Molly the shopping trip of her dreams. Because she really frickin' came through," he said. He outlined the story of the three girls from Ohio State who'd been beaten up as part of a frat-house pact made by their boyfriends.

"What if one of them graduated in June and got a job here," Chuck said. "And then somebody else found out and…."

"Wait. That other investment company." Carl looked around excitedly. "Don't you see? Fielding Stans doesn't have anything against Lucius, but what if—"

"Someone young, related, and fresh out of school does," Chuck said.

"Yes!" Julia clapped her hands in excitement. "Oh yes. Gentlemen, this is all coming together, and Molly *definitely* gets the shopping trip of her dreams. We have places to look now, leads to follow. Oh, I'm so excited."

She smiled around the table, and all the men smiled besottedly back.

"Great!" Carl said, looking very pleased with himself. "Okay, Julia. Josh, tell us where to start."

Josh made a pained grunt. "I'm afraid you're going to have to call the dads," he said apologetically. "Grace, if you could help me…."

And Grace, for all he had the body build of a reed in the wind, literally picked Josh up and swept him to the downstairs bathroom.

Julia's momentary happiness dimmed, and the table was silent in pained sympathy.

"Here," Stirling said after a moment. "Let me get my laptops. One to talk to Uncle Danny and one to keep a list, how's that?"

"Of course," Julia said, her beautiful eyes infinitely sad at the corners. "That is a good place to start."

This time, it was Lucius's knee pressing against Chuck's in reassurance.

This time, Chuck reached over and squeezed.

THEY WERE so busy making a list of leads to pursue that Chuck didn't think to mention the intruder in his room until well after dessert, and after Danny and Felix had signed off of their computer call.

When he'd reported the break-in, Lucius seemed the most upset.

"You... you can't go back there!" he said unhappily. "You have to stay here for the night."

"And leave Hunter and Molly without backup?" Chuck snorted. "No, Lucius, I don't think so. It'll be fine. In fact...." He glanced at his wristwatch. "I caught a nap, and Hunter didn't. I should get back so he can get some shuteye. We'll keep a lookout. The intruder might be our mole, so that's actually encouraging, right?"

"No," Lucius said. "Not really."

Chuck gave him a grin and a wink. "Now relax, Lucius. Me and Hunter, we can handle bad guys. It'll all be okay."

Lucius shook his head in frustration, and Chuck turned his attention back to Carl, who wanted to hear the story of Kyle Miller and the exploding toilet one more time.

Grace came back to the table then and told them Josh wouldn't be rejoining them, and that seemed to be the signal for everyone to get up. Chuck moved quietly to Julia and accepted her hug and her conveyed good wishes to Molly and Hunter, almost as though they were out of town on business and not undercover not two miles away. Chuck saw the faint absence in her smile, though, and knew where her thoughts really were.

"He's going to be okay," he reassured her, and her mouth twisted.

"We're looking into some things that might help," she replied with dignity. "Right now, he's at the worst of it, and odds are good he'll come through. But it never hurts to stack the odds, does it?"

"Never," he said. He took her hand and kissed the back of it, flirting because he knew she enjoyed it. "You, my lady, deal a mean deck."

She laughed, as he'd meant her too, but he could feel the effort she'd put into it. Hurting inside, he kissed her cheek.

"We'll do anything to help," he told her. "Anything. I mean that."

"Thanks, Charles," she said softly, and then she nodded to where Lucius was talking to Soderburgh. "For starters, you could perhaps give him a break. He's a good guy."

"As I am not," Chuck said, keeping his flirt solidly in place. But Julia was too worried and too sad for that to stand.

"As you are, truly. There are worse things, you know. Worse than flying back and forth between Chicago and Springfield? Imagine the possibilities, Charles, and then make them so."

And with that, she excused herself to go look after her son, and Lucius came to his side to walk him out to the SUV.

As they stepped down off the wide tiled porch, Chuck looked up at the sky. In the distance he could see the light pollution from the suburb, and further than that, he could see Peoria, with Springfield in the opposite direction.

But right here, the sky was a carpet of stars.

He stared for a moment, enjoying the slight breeze, enjoying the scent of greenery nearby, and beyond that, the scorched grass that came with cattle country. He closed his eyes and took a breath and was unsurprised when Lucius's mouth covered his own.

He smiled slightly and responded to the kiss, soft enough to gentle, insistent enough to rouse a fire inside that, with a little encouragement, he wouldn't want to bank.

Lucius slid his hands up Chuck's polo, palming the heated skin in the small of Chuck's back, and Chuck's yearning for the two of them to be alone, skin on skin, hit him like a cannonball.

He slid his fingers into the short hair at Lucius's nape and pulled him closer, and Lucius moaned in his throat in total surrender.

Now Chuck plundered, grinding up against Lucius, his cock aching and needy. Lucius ground back, groaning a little when Chuck undid his belt one handed, thrust his hand down the placket of Lucius's slacks, and found him—squeezing, stroking.

"Ah!" Lucius pulled away, panting. "Anyone can see us!" Of course he meant anyone in the house. The driveway was isolated and private, and the hedges on either side of the porch steps kept that impression of privacy as a person walked up.

Chuck pulled his hand out of Lucius's slacks long enough to tug on Lucius's hand, pulling him into the shadows on the side of those hedges, out of sight of the house. Out of sight of anyone coming up the front drive to visit Lucius.

Once they were there, Chuck resumed kissing him, enjoying how pliant he was, how eager, in spite of the interruption. Once he knew Lucius was under again, lost in passion, gasping helplessly, he undid Lucius's slacks completely and stripped them down, sinking to his haunches on the lawn.

"Charles—augh!"

Oh Lord, Chuck needed this. He loved these things—long, short, fat, slender, mushroom-capped or uncircumcised, Chuck *loved* the feel of a cock in his mouth. He loved to look at them, to lick them, to taste them. He loved the way they twitched, the way they thrust, the way they sought out the cavern of his mouth and the back of his throat like they knew where home was.

Lucius's cock, pale and circumcised in the moon-light, was just as much of a delight as he'd hoped, and he pulled it into his mouth because he was starving for it.

There was no questioning his feelings when a man's cock was in his mouth. There was no doubting his worth or worrying that he couldn't protect his lover from all the dangers in the world. There was just the taste of salt and precome, the feel of hard flesh and soft skin against the palate, and the knowledge that Chuck and only Chuck could bring this man the pleasure he so desperately craved.

He pulled at Lucius's buttcheeks, urging him deeper, knowing he wouldn't gag because he'd practiced this, loved to do it, and Lucius obliged. Chuck sucked him harder, then released. He plied his tongue at the base, pushing hard, licking up the underside, teasing the frenulum until Lucius dug his fingers into Chuck's hair and grunted softly.

"Want it?" Chuck teased, pulling his head back and stroking firmly up, licking madly at the head on the upstroke.

"Yes!" Lucius begged, and there was something so innocent about him, something so unguarded. Lucius may have been a business god and a zillionaire, but he was vulnerable here. He trusted Chuck in a way that Chuck understood—and would never betray.

"Good," Chuck whispered and sucked him in hard again, bottoming him out in a series of short, hard thrusts that left Lucius sobbing for breath.

"Charles," he pleaded. "Yes…. God… now…."

Chuck moistened a finger with a little spit before he groped gently, parting Lucius's cheeks and looking for…. Where was it?

"*There*!" Lucius gasped as Chuck found his entrance and pushed, just a little, enough for friction to do his job for him.

Chuck pulled him even deeper and thrust a bit more, and….

"Oh!" The rest of Lucius's cry was muffled as he bit down on his palm, and Chuck kept sucking, kept pulling, milking that sweet cock for all it was worth.

Finally Lucius gave a little sound of discomfort, and Chuck pulled off, wiping his face deliberately on the underside of Lucius's shirttails while making eye contact with him. Chuck got to go back to the shelter, but Lucius? He had to go back into his living room and be polite to all the guests in his house and not betray, not even a little, that Chuck had wiped Lucius's come off his own lips and it was currently wet against the skin of his stomach.

When that was done, he pulled Lucius's briefs up, placing a little kiss on the end of his new best friend before tucking it in for the night. He stood and solicitously tucked Lucius's shirt into his pants and zipped him up before fastening the stay and doing the belt.

He pulled back and grinned wickedly, thoroughly enjoying the dazed and dreamy look on Lucius's face.

"That was… I mean, wow. I mean…." Suddenly his eyes sharpened. "Why?" he asked, sounding confused but not dazed. "Wasn't that a little fast?"

Chuck swallowed, because he'd hoped that Lucius wouldn't ask this question. "Because life is short," he said, thinking about Josh. "And because I would hate to miss out on that." He smiled a little, enjoying his own version of afterglow, in spite of the fact that his erection still strained against his briefs. "In fact, I'd like to do it a few more times."

Lucius let out a little sound of exasperation before resting his forehead against Chuck's shoulder and putting a hand on each hip. "I'd like to do more than that," he confessed. "I was just…."

"Don't worry, businessman," Chuck said, dropping a kiss on his crown. "We'll get to that date. Tomorrow, actually, but we can get to another one when this is all done. I just…." He sighed and wrapped his arms around Lucius's shoulders, pulling him in for comfort and not for lust this time. "I wanted a moment now. I know you have plans, and you want to put a name on things and a pin in that, but I just wanted a moment now. I hope that's okay."

"Yes," Lucius said, melting against him and turning his face against Chuck's neck. Oh, he felt nice in Chuck's arms. No awkwardness here, no weird position because they were in a car, no scary courting conversation, just a warm, slender man in his arms, one who liked his company and the pleasure Chuck could bring to his body.

"Just yes?" Chuck teased.

"There will be more later?" Lucius all but begged.

This time Chuck kissed his temple. "I promise you."

They stood for a few more minutes before Chuck pulled back, kissing his forehead and stepping away. "Go on inside, Lucius," he said softly. "I'm going to walk back, clear my head."

"But that's over a mile!" Lucius protested.

Chuck shrugged. "Can't let Grace show me up, can I?" He lifted his knee—bare in his uniform khaki shorts—and swung his foot back and forth, showing off his white tennis shoes. "I'm even dressed for it."

"Yes, Chuck," Lucius told him dryly. "You shouldn't let that uniform go to waste."

Chuck grinned and winked, and dove in to kiss those lips—now swollen and puffy—one more time.

"Mm… I could stand to kiss you more, sir," he said, before turning down the driveway and swinging his legs into the night.

Calamity Charles

THE PROPERTY Lucius had demarcated for the larger mansion—for the shelter—started about two hundred yards down the drive from Lucius's own manor.
Once Chuck came to the fence—chain link for security after the show of wrought iron at the beginning of
the property—and moved to the long gravel drive, the
fence stretched to his left, running alongside a drainage ditch that kept it slightly lowered from the paved
roadway. He strode quickly, trying to mark any places other than the one Grace had discovered, but the
foliage behind the fence—and the holly and ivy that
wrapped around it—hid a lot of sins in their shadows,
and Chuck realized how lucky they'd been that Grace
had run this perimeter for them. He wasn't even sure
he could spot the place Grace had found, and he knew
where it was!

About three-quarters of a mile from Lucius's
house, Chuck spied the break in the fence—but only
because there were shadows moving close to it.

Cursing the fact that he was wearing bright white
tennis shoes and khaki shorts, he practically dove into
the drainage ditch, grateful for soft grass and the absence of snakes.

Mindful of the vegetation—and cursing the well-irrigated ground and the moisture seeping in through his clothes—he combat-crawled closer, finding better cover in the leaves of an overgrown jasmine bush that cloaked both sides of the fence. The figures in front of him were about fifteen yards away, bent together and speaking in hushed voices. If he'd kept walking down the road, he could have walked right by them and feigned not seeing, but this was way, way better.

"I'm tired of this stalling bullshit. I need some fucking info!" snarled the larger figure. Chuck could see a tall, well-built man from this distance, someone who spent some time in the gym. If he was talking to the police, he would use the word "menacing," and even if he wasn't, he knew a shakedown when he saw one.

"No," snapped the shorter, slighter figure. Chuck recognized him but didn't know his name. He'd been in the yoga class that morning, and Chuck had seen him hovering on the fringes of the self-defense class that afternoon. A young, skinny white male, with a pretty face, hazel eyes, and brown hair. He had a way of smiling—a jerky, sudden smile that was more of a flinch—that reminded Chuck of a frightened animal.

Chuck recognized fear in someone who'd been beaten, and the harder, deeper fear that standing up for yourself would just result in something worse. But worse for whom was really the question.

This kid—he couldn't have been older than twenty, as young as those poor coeds who huddled together for protection—was walking a tightrope between fear and fury.

"Whaddya mean, no? Larry, you sniveling piece of shit, you don't get to say no. Didn't he explain to you that you don't get to say no?"

"I came here to get away from him!" Larry spat. "Not to turn over mothers with broken bones or kids so scared they freak out when they hear someone stub their toe. One name. I gave him one name, but not any fuckin' more, do you hear me? He doesn't get to send his fucking goon here to terrorize me. I'm sayin' *no.*"

In Chuck's head, he heard the lesson he'd taught that afternoon, clear as day.

The most important thing about self-defense is commitment. You have the right to say no, but nobody's going to hear it unless you back it up. When you say no, when you defend yourself, mean it!

Well, apparently Larry had been listening.

"Nobody says no to your boyfriend, you know that." The threat was implicit and awful, and the larger figure spun Larry around and pinned his shoulders to the fence in a heartbeat. Larry whimpered and cowered, and Chuck sighed. You couldn't turn a bunny into a wolf overnight, particularly over one half-attended self-defense lesson. Chuck pulled his knees up to his chest, ready to spring. Whoever this guy was, Chuck was going to have to take him out.

"I do," Larry said, but whatever fury had possessed him, it seemed to bleed out now. His head drooped, his shoulders fell; he was already curling forward inwardly to protect his soul from whatever was going to come from outside.

"You don't say no to shit," the assailant hissed. "Now give me what I want or I won't even spit on your hole."

Larry whimpered, and his tormenter yanked at his clothes, and Chuck launched himself across the space so quickly he didn't even remember running it.

He shoved the goon off the kid's shoulders and onto the ground, not grunting, not even breathing hard. He fell on the guy's back with one knee, pinning him to the ground while he seized one flailing arm and then another, hauling them behind the attacker until he howled in pain.

Goddammit.

Where was a pair of restraints when you needed them?

"Larry!" Chuck snapped, risking a look over his shoulder to see if the kid was still there.

"Mister… Mister Summers?" Larry squeaked, and Chuck gave him a reassuring smile.

"Good, kid. Great, kid. Look, Larry, you want to reach in my back pocket and grab my radio?" His prisoner—no longer an assailant of any kind—gave a grunt and tried to wrestle his way out of Chuck's grip. Chuck gave his arm another haul, reveling a little in the guy's howl before he went limp.

Dislocated shoulder. Yup. Those hurt like a fucking bear.

Chuck wasn't about to let go of his wrists, though, but before he could ask Larry again, he felt tentative, shaking fingers in his back pocket, and then his radio unit was placed under his nose so he could unlock it.

"Good," Chuck told him. "Now press the voice command button." And after that, it was as simple as, "Hunter, wake the fuck up!"

"What?" Hunter snapped as he picked up. "What in the hell—"

"Get your ass to the gap in the fence, and bring me some fucking handcuffs."

"You can't take him to the cops," Larry begged, his teeth chattering. "You... you can't. He knows where this place is. There's... there's people in there—"

Chuck shook his head. "Larry, I swear to you, we'll find someplace for this scumbag to disappear to."

Said scumbag whimpered under his knee, and Chuck bounced a little. "I didn't say we were gonna kill ya," he taunted. "I just said we were gonna make ya disappear. Now shut up and let the grownups talk."

"Can I kick him?" Larry asked, and Chuck blinked at him in surprise.

"Kick him?"

"He... he was gonna... again. I... I don't know how my ex found out where I was. But he sent his buddy to... to threaten me, and this is his buddy, and he was gonna... and I had to test for HIV last time, and...."

"Kick away," Chuck said, sickened. "Kid, this shoulder over here?" He gave the guy's dislocated arm a jerk. "It's super fuckin' sore."

Larry came over tentatively and pulled back his foot, swinging it like a kid who'd been in soccer all his life.

The scumbag eating crabgrass in the dirt howled so hard, he threw up, and Chuck told Larry to kick him again.

THEIR SCUMBAG was in sorry shape by the time Hunter drove one of the security SUVs around the corner and they shoved him in it. Hunter had zip-tie handcuffs and ankle shackles, which they used in spite of the guy's whimpers for the much-abused shoulder.

"We found his car parked on the side of the road about half a mile from the turnout into the driveway. I'm having you-know-who drive it to fuck-all-wher-ever, and we'll pick him up after we dump this guy. Where are we dumping this guy again?" Hunter asked.

"Hospital," Chuck said. "He can tell them he was attacked all he wants, but if he drags the authorities here, we won't have seen a thing, will we?"

"I've never seen Clive Hudson before in my life," Larry said on a partial sob.

"I'll tell... I'll tell the cops everything," the guy, who was apparently Clive Hudson, sniveled, and Chuck snorted.

"I don't think so. Because then we tell them what you did to Larry here last time you broke in and tres-passed on private property. And we tell them Larry's underage—"

Larry sucked in a breath, and Chuck gave him a bored look.

"How did you know?" Larry asked.

"Because that was a kid's soccer kick if I've ever seen one," Chuck drawled.

"I didn't know!" Clive whined, and Chuck wished he was one of those criminals who got off on casual violence.

"I don't care," Chuck said. "You can go to the hos-pital and find a way to never come back here again, or you can go to your boss and tell him we know who he is and we're coming for him, or you can go to the police and we'll tell them what you did and make sure you get locked up in gen pop."

Clive's gasp of dismay was eloquent. "I didn't know he wasn't full grown!"

Hunter, who had started the car and was driving toward Peoria in the dark labyrinth that was country roads under the moon, pulled off on a cattle road. He undid his seat belt and turned around, then cuffed Clive's ear hard enough to break the ear drum.

Chuck sucked in a breath, because he'd thought he couldn't do something like that, but boy, he was glad it had been done.

"Asshole," Hunter growled. "You are looking at this the wrong way. One way or another, we are going to find your boss and take him down. This, right here, is your chance to find another boss. He won't know where the hell you are. We took your cell phone, your radio, and I've got a friend who is currently dumping your car. You can for now and forever keep your dick to your fuckin' self, and you can get out of this sitch and find a new drug lord or whoever to work for."

"Aw, fuck you!" Clive Hudson snarled. "I work for the goddamned chief of police, and I report to a state senator, so who gives a fuck what you say!"

Hunter and Chuck made eye contact, and Chuck nodded grimly, once.

"I'll do it," Hunter said. "I know the perfect place to drop him. No blood on our hands, but I'm pretty sure they'll get the job done."

"What… what are you going to do to me?" Clive Hudson sounded terrified.

"I know where every chain gang in the state is working," Hunter said, and Chuck knew he had his earbud on. Once they were off the grounds, as long as Stirling was at Lucius's house, it would work. Stirling was probably giving him locations at lightning speed even as he said the words.

"Chain gang?"

"Yup," Hunter said with great satisfaction. "I may not enjoy cold-blooded murder, but believe me, those guys will not hold back."

"Wait!" Clive cried. "Wait! I'll tell you! I'll tell you who I work for!"

"You idiot," Chuck muttered. "You just did."

Clive gaped for a moment. "I never said Miller's or Newman's names," he muttered, and next to him, Larry let out a disbelieving snort.

"Oh my God."

"Right?" Chuck encouraged.

"So dumb."

"Too stupid to breathe," Chuck agreed.

"Are we really going to leave him for a chain gang to find?" And to Larry's credit, he didn't sound happy with that.

"We can't take him to the cops," Chuck said. "If he's one of them, or working for the police chief, he's got a free pass. And he knows where you were, so if we take him somewhere else, we'd have to explain to too many people what he was doing there."

"But…." Larry shuddered. "I don't want him near me. I don't want him touching me. But… but he could get killed. I… I'm better than this asshole, you know? I give a shit that he's going to be killed."

Hunter grunted. "You *are* better than this asshole," he agreed. "Hang on a sec. I got an idea." He tapped his earbud. "Tech kid," he said, obviously still keeping their names from the idiot in the back seat, "do me a favor and ask my boyfriend if he or his buddy can patch me in to the cop they know in Chicago."

Chuck blinked. He remembered that cop. Nick Denning, who worked theft, was a young married father with a rather baffled crush on Josh. Josh's crush was not nearly so baffled, but it was also kept very close to his vest. Chuck understood that. Unlike himself and Car-Car, Josh drew the line at a married man, and while Josh had never, not once, spoken a word of judgment, Chuck had taken his moral code to heart.

Never. Again.

Still, that didn't mean Nick wasn't an ally. He was one of the few people in law enforcement who knew about Josh's crew—and who was willing to overlook small laws being broken in order to protect people that the law didn't really protect.

After a hurried, coded message to Stirling, and then, if Chuck could read voice tones, to Grace, Hunter grunted. "Good. I'll take the plane and bring it back in the morning." He shot a look to Chuck. "You call your boyfriend and have the thing fueled up."

"He's not my boyfriend," Chuck protested.

"Wait!" Clive called desperately from the back seat. "Where am I going *now*?"

"Kid, could you gag him?" Hunter snapped. "You and your damned sensibilities. I could have just kicked this asshole out on the side of the road, but no, I have to fly him to fucking Chicago."

"Not Chigaglllg...." Because Larry, thank God, had apparently gagged him with a dirty sock, from what Chuck could see.

"What's in Chicago?" Larry asked quietly.

"An honest cop," Hunter said. "One who's willing to run this guy's DNA. What about it, idiot henchman? You got any swimmers swimming around an FBI database you don't want anyone knowing about?"

The whimper that came out from behind the dirty sock was pretty encouraging on that front.

"Yeah," Hunter agreed. "Guys like you, they're not smart enough to be discreet. You're probably wanted on multiple counts of something. Your antics get swept under the rug by your cop friend out here, but in Chicago, they don't know you from dick. That answer your thirst for vengeance without bloodshed, Larry?"

"Oh my God, yes," Larry said, and the tenseness, the misery on his face faded a little. "I really didn't want to bring attention to the shelter. God, that was what they had on me in the first place—the women there, the other boys." He shuddered.

"Who were you supposed to give information about?" Chuck asked. "And how did they know you were there?"

"I was stupid," Larry told them bitterly. "He put me in the hospital, you know? His wife disappeared, and he was raging, and I… I was so stupid." He gave half a wormwood laugh. "I thought, with her out of the way, we could be together. And I told him that, and he… he said he wasn't a faggot, I was just… just some strange on the side. And then he hit me and…."

"Lights out?" Chuck asked softly.

"Only merciful thing he ever did," Larry admitted, his voice breaking.

God. Poor kid. Seventeen, and he knew this about the world?

"Did he know how old you were?" Chuck asked. He could see that Larry's face, in the light from the occasional streetlamp, was drawn, his mouth pinched. He looked older than he was. Chuck's only clue had been the way he'd moved during class that day, and the kick he'd aimed at Clive. Something about his shoulder joints and hip joints looked unfinished.

And the resigned way he'd turned to the fence and begged not to be assaulted broke Chuck's heart.

"No," Larry said softly, leaning his head against the window. "Met online. Told him I was twenty."

Chuck blew out a breath. "Seventeen should be more fun than twenty," he said gently.

"Not when you lived at my house," Larry told him. "But I knew that my old man was a bastard. I didn't know this guy would beat me too."

The words fell in the SUV like barbells.

"Who's he?" Chuck asked, knowing it but needing it said. Lucius had said that the state senator had a wife *and* a side piece in the shelter. Clive Hodges squirmed and tried to shout from behind the sweat sock, but Larry gave him a look of contempt.

"Kyle Miller. He's a state senator in Ohio."

"Oh, I know who he is," Chuck said darkly. "And don't worry, we'll keep you safe from him. Garbage humans like this fucker will not know who you are. Not ever again."

Larry was still leaning his head against the window, crying. "It's my fault," he whispered.

"Kid, getting beaten is not your fault—"

"That he found me," Larry insisted bitterly. "I woke up in the hospital, terrified, and a nurse helped me find this place. I was safe, Miller's family was safe— and I was so stupid."

"How did you call him?" Hunter asked, which was a good question, because Lucius had told them that phones were confiscated.

"About a week after I got to the shelter," Larry said, "I found a phone next to my door—there's blind spots in the cameras. I mean, we're not supposed to know, but all the women know where they can sneak a smoke. So there was a phone in the blind spot next to my door, and a Post-it with a map to the hole in the gate." He sighed. "He told me to call back the next day—I thought so he could say he was sorry"

Oh, baby. "And he tracked your phone," Chuck filled in.

"He tracked my phone," Larry repeated, so much anger in his voice. "I came out of the crack in the fence to have a real conversation, to tell him I was okay. That his wife and kid were okay. And he tracked my phone. And *this* asshole showed up, and…." His voice broke, because Chuck had heard this part and he was still wishing he had the stomach to beat that bastard to death. "Anyway," Larry finished, "Miller told me to get more info and call him again and… God, I've made a mess of things."

"Don't worry, kid," Chuck said, voice soft with compassion. "We can help you fix it." Then he remembered that afternoon. "Was that you in my room? Around three?"

"No," Larry said, confused. "No, why would I be in your room? I don't even know where your room *is*!"

Chuck and Hunter met eyes before Hunter turned his attention back to the road.

Welp. Their job was not quite done.

SAOIRSE HAD the plane fueled up and running as they pulled into the airstrip, and she watched without comment as Hunter and Chuck grabbed Clive under the arms and hauled him up the ramp before laying him out in the aisle.

He whined under the gag, but Hunter gave him a good kick in the ribs on his way to the cockpit, and that shut him up.

"You're lucky that kid's a better person than we are," Chuck told him. "I really did like that chain gang idea. But no, you get Federal lockup, and that's a blessing."

Chuck kicked Clive, too, for good measure before turning to Hunter. "Fair skies, brother."

"Tell Grace to pick me up around ten," Hunter replied. Then, after a pause, "Nice job with Larry, by the way. That kid… God. He's gonna need more than a few months in a shelter and a new name."

"Yeah. Hopefully we can get him some skills or something before we let him back in the world." Chuck thought unhappily of Car-Car. It hadn't been an accident that Car-Car had run to his wife immediately after high school. Beaten by his father, bullied by his brothers, Carmichael Carmody had a lot of strikes against him before he'd chased Chuck down behind his garage and given him an awkward blowjob.

And Chuck still couldn't figure out if he'd been the hero Car-Car had made him out to be, or just another user, trying to make everybody happy but never owning up to the truth.

Chuck's brain veered away from that subject and landed on something he and Hunter should have been thinking about. "Hunter, before you go, you got your earbud in?"

"Yeah, why?"

"Because Larry found that hole in the fence, but he doesn't know who made it—or who slipped him the phone. Now you looked at it. Did it look rusted out or recently cut?"

"Recently cut," Hunter mused. "Which means...."

"It means we need to find out when Larry made that first call, because I'm betting it was after the attacks started. So Kyle Miller, while part of our problem, and the chief of police, while also part of the problem...."

Hunter scowled. "Are *not* our original scumbags," he muttered.

"Or if they are, they're not our *entire* problem," Chuck told him.

They both heaved a sigh. Hunter scowled at the baggage on the floor and pulled his foot back as though to kick it in the head again, but then thought better of it.

"What are we going to do with these guys when we pin them down, anyway?" Hunter asked. "It's the same problem we've got with this asshole. Nobody's going to arrest him for what he *should* be arrested for."

"What we need," Chuck mused, "is a fitting revenge. Once we pin them down, we need to take away something important to them. They took away Larry's safety, and the safety of everyone Lucius is trying to protect. We need to take something *that* important away from them."

Hunter gave him a slightly evil look. "That sounds like an excellent idea. Why don't you ask Lucius what that should be when you're on your date tomorrow. What do you say?"

Chuck groaned. "I hate you."

"Sure you do."

"You have no idea how much."

"I have some. Now get off my plane. I have to go deal with the po-po, and even though he's Josh and Grace's friend, that still gives me jock itch."

Chuck blinked. "You're sleeping in the mansion tonight?"

Hunter blinked. "It's closer to the airstrip, so yeah."

"Then ask Danny for some of Julia's loofahs. They'll help you wash your private places so that jock itch'll clear right up."

Hunter's gray eyes got *enormous*. "That conversation took a left I did not expect."

"I know it did. *Now* I'll get off your plane."

Cackling to himself, Chuck sauntered down the ramp and then got out of the way as Hunter hit the button that would help it retract. He and Saoirse stood by the SUV and watched as Hunter took off, practically textbook, and she gave him a grin.

"You fly that pretty, sweet-talking man?"

Chuck shook his head. "I'm a right mess, Miss Saoirse. I'm practically doing barrel rolls before I hit free air."

Saoirse guffawed, obviously happy to think he was *that* guy, and he winked before swinging up into the vehicle. Larry had moved to the front seat while he and Hunter had been taking out the trash, and Chuck got another good look at the kid as they buckled up and he turned on the air-conditioning.

"So," Chuck said as he pulled away from the airfield. "What do you feel like tonight? A hip-hop station? The golden oldies on my cell phone? Or a deep, meaningful talk that will help you feel better about your life?"

Larry laughed weakly. "You got one of those? You jump out of the bushes and save me, and you apparently teach yoga and self-defense, and I don't even want to know what you and that other guy have going to keep us all safe. And you've got a deep, meaningful talk in your back pocket? I'm *impressed*."

Chuck liked this kid, butthurt bitterness and all.

"I've only got the same shit that's got me by," Chuck told him.

"What's that?"

"Have a plan." Chuck cringed as he said it; from him, it sounded like the worst sort of hypocrisy. "Even if it's short-term," he qualified. "I didn't jump out of that bush without knowing Hunter or the other security could see me. We didn't just pull an airplane out of our ear. I'm not saying you can't improvise, and definitely don't expect all your plans to come out right. But have a plan so you know what you want things to look like when you're done."

Larry *hmm*d, like he was thinking about it. "Like what, exactly?"

"Well, you know you don't want to be a big shot's punching bag, and you know you don't want to be a boy toy. So, Larry, what *do* you want to be?"

Chuck could almost hear the boy thinking.

"I want to be someone who can help people like me," he said after a moment. "They were trying to get me to name names, and the last time I just…." His voice cracked, because sexual assault was sexual assault and Chuck was not the person in his life who could make that better. "I wanted to keep them all safe."

"What about keeping yourself safe?" Chuck asked gently.

"Yeah," Larry whispered. "That too."

"So a doctor, a bodyguard, a social worker— what're you thinking?"

Larry sighed. "I'm not sure. I'll have to chew on it a while."

And that was fair enough. "You ready for that music choice yet?"

"Can I play with your Spotify?" the kid asked plaintively.

"Yeah." Chuck unlocked his phone and spent the next thirty minutes screaming "Fuck me with an anchor!" at the top of his lungs. Until Larry pressed Play, he'd had no idea that Gaelic metal even existed.

HE GOT Larry back to the shelter and had Lisa go wake Tara-Lynn.

"Oh God," Larry muttered. "Do I have to tell her?"

"Kid," Chuck said, "that nice woman is dying to mother the everlovin' shit out of you. Let her. Let her help you feel better. This entire facility is here to help you pick yourself up, but you can't do that with the weight of everything that's happened on your back. So yeah. Go talk to the nice lady and get yourself a counselor and all of that. And then start working on a plan."

Larry nodded reluctantly, and Chuck held up a fist to bump. After a few suspicious moments, Larry didn't leave him hanging.

Chuck blew out a breath and moved to his bedroom to change his clothes—and swore.

Whoever had been through his and Hunter's things had been back, and the place was tore up. His suits were thrown across the bed, his shoes, the contents of his and Hunter's duffels. All of it, scattered across the room like somebody had been searching for something.

Goddammit! Did somebody have a thing against Chuck getting any fucking sleep?

Bad Boys

LUCIUS COULDN'T seem to get enough spit in his mouth.

Oh, he'd known things had gone down—Hunter had briefed him after Grace had brought him to the small house, and he was aware that one Clive Hudson, confidential informant of their local police chief and apparent henchman of Kyle Miller, had been arrested in Chicago the night before on suspicion of sexual assault and indicted that morning when his prints and DNA went through.

How they'd gotten their hands on Clive Hudson had been something of a mystery. The fact that two of the people in the shelter had been assaulted by the same high-profile abuser had been something he'd known, but that one of them had been coerced into giving information was an unpleasant surprise.

And the knowledge that someone had ransacked the security room while Chuck and Hunter had been out was, frankly, terrifying.

And Chuck's blasé attitude toward it made him want to hit something, which was a novel experience in itself.

"No, Hunter and I aren't in imminent danger!" Chuck protested as Lucius piloted the Bentley down the main highway to Springfield. "We have each other's backs. Grace is there in our rooms tonight, and Molly has her earbud in."

Lucius took it that the earbud had been something of an argument. Molly had argued that she didn't need it, she could take anybody there except Chuck and Hunter, and Chuck and Hunter had argued that even Chuck had called for backup. That had been the angle that had tipped the argument in their favor. If she kept in contact, either with them or with her brother and Carl, nonstop, they wouldn't pull her cover.

Her argument—that she was the one best placed to figure out who was so interested in Chuck and Hunter—had been the only reason they hadn't.

"So what did they take?" Lucius asked, with what felt to be a 200-pound boa constrictor wrapped around his chest.

"Nothing," Chuck said with some satisfaction. "Because they were *amateurs*."

Lucius let out a laugh at the smugness in his voice. "Tell me some more about how brilliant you are."

Chuck nodded appreciatively. "Well, most of it is the crew I run with. Our phones have a lot of our security tech. Not all of it is bought in the regular app store, if you take my meaning, but it's on us. We have earbuds and backup earbuds and backups to the backups, but they're all hidden in James Bond places: false heels in dress shoes, the hems of suits, special compartments in our shaving kits, that sort of thing. And Hunter's slick leather jackets? Those are tactical wonders right there, and he hates guns. He can do more damage to an assailant with the tactical pen he carries around in plain sight. And since he didn't know how safe the situation was, he didn't bring any guns with him. For the most part, we *are* the weapons, and we don't have anything but our wallets and our phones to ID us. So I picked shit up, inventoried our earbuds, used my phone to scan for monitoring devices—none, by the way—and then I checked the security footage. Nothing was there we could spot, sadly. Hunter, Josh, and Grace spent the day installing a couple of cameras so that can't happen again. And the ransacking of the rooms?"

"Netted whoever it was, nothing," Lucius said, but he was still scowling about it. "I don't like it. We know Larry used the gap in the fence, but we still don't know who put it there! And somebody in the shelter isn't who they're pretending to be."

"Or they are," Chuck said, "but they're not actually an abused spouse, but a complicit one."

Lucius grunted. "Would a woman really do that to another woman?" God, that was a betrayal.

"There's even a term for it," Chuck said. "An Aunt Lydia. It's a woman who enables a system that abuses other women. I mean, it could be one of the men, but that would be a bad move."

"Why?" Lucius asked, interested. "And how do you know all this?"

"Because the men are rare enough and frightening enough to the women who've been injured that they're under a lot of scrutiny. They're also isolated. I noticed it today when I was giving my self-defense class. The guys need the talk-up as much as the women do, but they stand off to the side. All sorts of bad social systems at work there, I suspect. Toxic masculinity makes them afraid to accept help. And the women are justifiably afraid to have a man, even a young man who was abused like themselves, near them. You may want to have a separate place for the men."

"They… well, the three young men here, including Larry, were all recommended by a nurse who knew they had a high-profile abuser. Originally, I wasn't going to accept them, but my source was genuinely afraid for their lives."

Chuck *hmm*d. "Well, maybe find another place for them, like a mother-in-law cottage or a smaller area wholly dedicated to them. I don't know. I just know that right now things are a little weird. Maybe we need to have a big counseling circle to address that. I'm spitballing here."

Lucius had to smile. He would have turned to look at Chuck if he hadn't been dealing with some traffic on the way to the party. Chuck had been waiting for him as he'd pulled up, wearing a truly spectacular red-brown velveteen suit with a crisp white shirt and a tie that looked like cinnamon candy. With Chuck's auburn hair and tanned skin, he looked altogether delicious.

"They're good ideas," he said mildly. "But that brings me back to how do you know all these things?"

"I've been taking pretty much all the humanities that U of C has to offer," Chuck said proudly. "Women's studies, ethnic studies, history of oppression, and pretty much all the literature and psychology you can think of."

"Good Lord!" Lucius exclaimed. "Whatever for?"

Chuck scratched the back of his neck. "I don't know. I'm not planning to get a degree. Just, you know, I got out of the Army and, uhm, came into a little bit of money. So I decided to learn more about the world, that's all."

"Came into a little bit of money," Lucius repeated.

"Yessir, that's what I said."

But Lucius heard the caginess in his voice and sighed. "I'm not going to haul you to the nearest policeman and tell him what you did to get the money, Chuck. I do wish you'd trust me."

"You can't haul me off the nearest policeman," Chuck pointed out, "because he's probably being paid off by the police chief, who's an abusive bastard and all-around corrupt piece of shit. And on top of that, he sort of wants your head on a platter."

It sounded so reasonable, and Lucius knew without asking that Chuck would have that good-ole-boy smirk on his face that said he'd thought of everything.

"I'm just saying that you can trust me with the real story, Charles," he said softly, and some of Chuck's bravado seeped out.

"The real story is long and sad," he said after a moment. "It's the same story you asked for a couple of days ago. We just... you know... had such a nice time the other night, I didn't want my story to leave a bad taste in your mouth."

For a moment Lucius wanted to bristle; he was a big boy, and dammit, he didn't need shielding from this part of Chuck's life! But then he recalled Julia's conversation about why people kept secrets, and what someone without power might know that the person with the fancy car and a lot of money might not.

And in that moment, he heard the vulnerability in Chuck's voice that he'd been trying so very hard to keep hidden all this time.

"Later," Lucius murmured, taking Chuck's hand from his lap and bringing warm, battered knuckles to his lips to kiss.

"Later what?" Chuck asked warily.

"Later, when you're comfortable, you can tell me that story. Then you'll see that I don't hold it against you."

Chuck pulled his hand away and briefly cupped Lucius's face. "That's fair," he said. "Now ask me something else, something I can answer."

"Fine," Lucius said brightly. "Where did you get that *stunning* suit?"

Chuck's low rumbling laugh was both charmed and charming. "Believe it or not, Julia bought this for me."

"Just bought you a suit?" Lucius wasn't jealous. Not after spending the past three days with Julia Dormer-Salinger, watching her work from a distance and care for her ill son at the same time. There was nothing salacious or inappropriate about that woman. She was a class act to her toes.

"She bought me a shit-ton of them," Chuck said, the affection in his voice evident. "I dismantled a bomb underneath the van in which her baby boy was trapped, you remember?"

"I do indeed," Lucius murmured.

"Well, she'd bought me a tux for another adventure, and I sort of ruined it in the parking lot that night because I'd set the jacket in a grease spot to hold bomb parts. Julia told me she'd buy me a thousand suits, and it's become a thing with us. She'll see something pretty and order it for me, made special. I have tailor fittings and everything. And it's a little rich for my blood, on the one hand, but…."

"You like spending time with her," Lucius said, getting it.

"She really is a delight," Chuck admitted. "The big sister I never had. The entire family, in fact. I've always been a big fan of spending time with people whose company I enjoy. It's not a big deal, but until now, I haven't found so many of them in the same place."

"Sounds like a family," Lucius said wistfully. He and his mother and brother had never really felt like that. They'd been close, yes, but in the end, particularly after his brother died, they had felt more like survivors of the same trauma than family. There hadn't been the back-and-forth at the dinner table like he'd seen the Salinger crew participate in, and he couldn't remember the last time he and his brother had laughed. Kenneth had been sick, yes, but so was Josh Salinger. And while the family was subdued and a little sad, they still tried hard—damned hard—to play together as they worked.

"It is," Chuck said, sounding surprised. "But not like my family." He shuddered. "God, the tension at the dinner table. You could cut it with a knife."

"One false move," Lucius murmured. "Most of the time, it was just yelling or some nasty remark. But not always."

"But even if it wasn't a whoopin'," Chuck said, some of his Texas emerging, "it made you more excited about getting the hell out of there than hanging with your family."

"Yeah." After a moment, Lucius said thoughtfully, "I really enjoy your crew, Chuck. I know they all think of me as the business guy, but... but I could eat dinner with them once a week or so and be really, really happy."

Chuck let out a sigh. "That would be welcome," he said. "I mean, you and me, we can muddle through and be a thing or not, but I wouldn't ever keep someone from dinner with the Salingers if they were comfortable there."

Lucius's face warmed. "I was thinking more that I'd like to spend the time with them *and* you," he said, not sure how that message had gone awry.

Chuck was silent for a moment.

"What?" Lucius asked.

"I'm not used to that," he confessed, and he sounded upset. "You have to understand—I'm the good-time guy. Nobody wants to have a date with me. I give 'em a good time, and we have a few laughs, and—"

"Why?" Lucius asked. "I'm not, I don't know, judging or anything. But why is Charles only good for a few laughs? You're sort of an action hero, Chuck. You save kids from getting assaulted in dark and dangerous ditches. You stick close to a family that cares about you so you can run errands while their youngest, most vulnerable member is ill. You're handsome as *sin* and fun to talk to, so why would you only be the good-time guy?"

Chuck sighed, and Lucius almost despaired. This wasn't going to work. This could not possibly work if Chuck didn't open up to him. And Chuck was going to deflect again, obviously, because he was being so damned reticent, so damned—

"It's easier," Chuck said, knocking him out of his spiral.

"What?" Lucius had almost forgotten what they were talking about.

"When you're a kid, you trust everything is going to be okay. And then you… you hit a certain age when you realize that some parents talk to each other, and some fathers don't cheat, and some kids can sit down to dinner with their family and not be afraid of what's going to happen next. It's just easier to leave a relationship when it's in that kid stage, you know what I mean? When you can imagine all the good things and you don't have to see the bad ones."

"Good-time Charlie indeed," Lucius murmured. "But don't you want anything deeper?"

"Hey, Scotty, I just started thinking I could deal with a family that's *not* dysfunctional, *and* thinking about having a boyfriend or a lover who would stick around more than a week. Both together are sort of the impossible dream, you know?"

"Try me," Lucius said. Then he rethought that. "I mean, try me, yes. I'm dying to be tried, but try to keep seeing me. Try having a little faith in me. I'm a very good long-term prospect, Charles. Financially and emotionally stable, wild oats sown." He turned toward Chuck and smiled winningly. "I understand I'm quite a catch."

Charles's laughter was boyish and sweet. "You don't have to sell me!" he chortled and then sobered. "I'm sold, Lucius. I really am. But you're vulnerable. I know you think you hide it. You try not to be needy. And I'm sure you could pick up a totally acceptable boring guy at some gala and have a series of meaningless, nonawkward dates with him, even some fun in bed, and your heart would be okay. But you're getting attached to me, and I'm not stupid or blind or entitled. If you're getting attached to me, that's important. I refuse to do anything but right by you, and I am proceeding with caution."

Lucius caught his breath. "That's… that's…." *Gah.* "Very perceptive," he finished finally. Because it was true. After Chuck had left him reeling from the kisses and the lovemaking in the shadows, Lucius had

stared after that long-legged, shoulder-swinging striding body until Chuck had rounded the corner and disappeared. And when he was gone, Lucius had stood for
a few more moments, lost in wonder.

His touch had been exquisite. Amazing. But more
than that, Chuck had taken *care* of him afterward in a
way that couldn't be feigned.

"You're a truly good man," Chuck said, and Lucius had to work hard to keep the car going in a straight
line when he felt Chuck's hand on his knee. "I just want
to make sure I don't hurt you. I mean, last night, Hunter
and I were having a conversation about whether to leave
the bad guy on the side of the road or not, and tonight,
I'm wearing a tux and planning on eating shrimp." He
paused. "Please tell me there will be shrimp. I don't put
on a gig like this without shrimp."

Lucius had to laugh. "There will be definitely be
shrimp, and if their caterer is the one I'm hoping for,
it'll be wrapped in bacon with roasted figs. It's truly
delicious."

"You're killing me!" Chuck laughed. "I'm starving! Anyway, so you can see how I might be worried
that I'm a little rough around the edges for a guy who's
taking me to eat shrimp."

Lucius couldn't stop smiling. He'd gotten a
straight answer—and a hand on the knee. And someone
who saw him for what he was and who wanted to treat
him right. He was calling this a *win*. "Why were you
going to leave him on the side of the road?" he asked
curiously.

Chuck's pause told him that this could be
significant.

"Because Hunter knows where the chain gangs
are working the highways in Illinois. This guy, he'd

assaulted more than just the kid at the shelter, and he had the protection of the police chief in Springfield. We didn't want him going back to being a predator, but, you know. We try to be the good guys."

Lucius frowned, and his mouth moved, repeating, "We try to be the good guys," before it hit him.

"You didn't want to kill him outright," he said, throat dry.

"That's right," Chuck said. "Hunter's done wet work before, but I've only got two bodies in my rearview, and they weren't my bullets. Hunter doesn't do that anymore, and I stay with the Salingers because they'll never ask me to do something like that. But still, it was a conundrum. What do you do with a bad guy who won't get punished?"

"You fly him somewhere he *will* get punished and hope that's enough," Lucius said, getting it.

"Yup," Chuck said. "And I'm glad we could do that. But I'm telling you right now, if it was a choice between sending this guy back to his crooked cop or leaving him in the desert to rot, I would have picked the desert. I wouldn't have killed him outright, but I'm no angel."

Lucius snorted. "I prefer to disagree," he said. Then, "Oh look, there's the hotel."

Chuck gave a low whistle. They'd been driving down Springfield's main drag, and then Lucius had taken a quirky left into an almost-hidden residential section, complete with a mansion big enough to have been converted into a very swanky hotel.

"What's this gig again?" Chuck said, pulling his earpiece out of his pocket and getting ready to pop it in.

"It's sort of a soiree the city council members hold for their local businesses. You know, a 'We appreciate you, please don't leave us, also vote us back in' sort of thing."

Lucius kept his voice neutral and light and tried to hide his discomfort.

"Well, you must be the biggest business in the nearby area," Chuck said, and then, as Lucius slowed the car down over the graveled drive, Lucius sensed Chuck's eyes searching his expression, earbud still at the ready. "You *are* the biggest business in the nearby area," he repeated in wonder. "You're something of a guest of honor here, aren't you!"

"I have to give a speech," Lucius muttered. His hand went automatically to his vest pocket, where his notecards sat.

"And you wanted *me* here?" Chuck asked incredulously.

Lucius gave a sheepish smile, pulling his SUV to an idle behind a line of people waiting for the valet to come get their vehicles. "I was… well, I hate going to these things alone, and you're cute, and you're fun, and I thought I could show you off as someone I was with instead of having everybody go, 'Oh yeah, him, he's one of ten gay men in the business field at your level, of course you're dating him.' And, uhm, I was really looking for an excuse to spend time with you. Is that so bad?"

He peeked over at Chuck from under his lashes and watched as Chuck dramatically clutched his chest.

"You got me!" he cried. "Right in the feels! Jesus, Scotty, I have to be charming and a bag of chips to-night? You could have warned me!"

Lucius snorted but smiled, amused at his foolish-ness. "Something tells me you don't need any warning at all. It comes naturally," he said, keeping his voice prim.

"I'll do my best," Chuck assured him and moved to put the earbud in.

"Wait!" Lucius threw the SUV into Park and leaned over the center console, pulling Chuck delicately by the collar so as not to rumple the starched shirt. "This could be the only time we get a private kiss all night!" he begged.

Chuck's playful expression softened, and his lips on Lucius's were warm and gentle—and private, for the two of them only.

It was a lock. Lucius would officially do or say anything he had to, bare himself to the very skin of his soul, to keep this man for as long as possible.

He opened his mouth, groaned slightly, and pulled away to move the car forward with visible reluctance. "You know," he said, as though Chuck hadn't just kissed him silly, "even with your friends in residence, I have practically the entire top floor of my house all to myself. And with Grace and Hunter at the shelter tonight, I'm thinking... you wouldn't have to go back?"

"Keep thinking that, businessman," Chuck growled. "Let's see if we can make that happen." Then he popped the bud in. "Stirling, man, you got me?"

He *hmm*d for a moment, then turned a startled look to Lucius. "You didn't tell me Felix flew in so he could accompany Julia to this shindig."

Lucius blinked. "I did not know that," he said. "I'm aware that Josh and Stirling are in one of the rooms already so we can keep coms, but that Felix and Julia are here too? That's news to me."

"Wait a sec...." Chuck scowled. "Also, Grace is *not* back at the shelter. He's in the room with Josh, at our disposal should we need a thief. Well, so much for that idea."

"He can go back to the shelter again tonight!" Lucius argued. "Wow, I've never met someone looking so hard for reasons to *not* take me to bed! Jesus, Chuck, it's *sex*, not marriage, adoption, and a china pattern!"

"Uhm," Chuck said apologetically, "you know they can hear you over the com link, don't you?"

Lucius blinked in mortification. "Who can hear me?"

Chuck grimaced as though he'd gotten a chorus in his ear.

"Everybody," he said unhappily.

"Wow," Lucius muttered.

"Well, yeah. Welcome to the game."

Lucius had a sudden thought. "Wait a minute. That night at the gala? When you kissed me. Were people listening then?"

And Lucius heard it—the slight hesitation in Chuck's voice that marked deceit.

"No."

"Are you lying about that?" Lucius asked, testing the waters.

"Maybe."

"How *many* people heard you kiss me?"

"Some of them?"

And now Lucius knew that Chuck knew the jig was up.

"What did they think?" Lucius asked.

Chuck let out a sigh. "Grace told us to stop making babies out on the lawn," he said, with such complete and utter disgust that Lucius realized he had a secret weapon.

He'd actually heard Charles Calder deflect, and he'd heard him lie, and he'd heard Chuck tell the absolute unvarnished truth. For a self-professed criminal, Chuck couldn't have many secrets from Lucius, and that thought gave him hope.

"Well, tell Grace if he doesn't want to see us making babies, he needs to be somewhere we're not naked and in bed," Lucius replied tartly. He moved the vehicle up one more car length and then smiled. "And here's our valet. We can go now!"

"Aces," Chuck muttered. "Let's go dancing."

ONCE THE valet collected their car and took it to the lot behind the hotel, they entered the foyer, and although Lucius was a bit embarrassed to be the guest of honor at the dinner, he really did have a fondness for the place. Old, built with Grecian columns in the front, and dripping crystal chandeliers from the ceiling, the place had a sort of grace and charm that Lucius thought most hotels aspired to but few achieved. The floors were maple hardwood, and the rugs that graced the foyer and grand ballroom stairs were silk/wool, with vibrant roses twining in their design. Lucius and his family had attended functions here many times when he was a child, and he'd expected the charm of the place to fade eventually, but it never did.

He tried to keep that to himself, though, but as they were going up the stairs, Chuck put one hand in the small of Lucius's back and slid the other up the hand-carved, well-waxed, and highly polished maple banister with a low whistle.

"Man, there is probably some reason I should resent this place—Marxist theory, something. But right now, I'm like, 'Oooh, lookit the pretty lights! Sparkly!'"

Lucius chuckled, relaxing into Chuck's heat and his willingness to be impressed. "I've always loved this place," he confessed. "The carpet in the ballroom is damask roses, and the ballroom floor is the same maple as the foyer. I don't know what they have to do to keep it spit-polished, but it's just...." He sighed.

"You, Mr. Broadstone, are a romantic," Chuck said, and the warmth in his voice was unmistakable.

"It's beautiful," Lucius said simply. "My best memories of family were here. My mother in her most gracious gown. Kenny and I wearing suits and trying not to knock over anything with our elbows. My father would go off with his buddies to do business, and the three of us got to sit in the tearoom, and the world would be lovely."

Chuck let out a humorless sound. "I was on the football team," he said. "My older brother had gone to college, which was fine because he's always been an asshole, but my parents would drag our sister to the games, and they'd cheer. And for two, three hours, I'd feel like a hero."

"Good memory," Lucius said. They'd arrived at the landing, and Chuck found his hand and threaded their fingers together for a moment.

"It's nice to have a few," Chuck said cheerfully. "Now let's go make one of our own."

Lucius grinned at him, heartened, and allowed Chuck to pull him through the crowd in search of shrimp.

THEY GOT separated, like couples did when they entered a crowded space such as this one, and if Lucius hadn't been aware that Chuck was on the job, he never would have noticed anything amiss with his behavior.

He certainly wouldn't have noticed that Grace was walking around in black slacks, a vest, and a bow tie, serving canapes, if Grace hadn't kept popping up at Lucius's elbow, murmuring, "I got you some more shrimp, but seriously, the scallops are way better."

But Lucius was so attuned to Chuck that when his date excused himself to go downstairs and then didn't appear in Lucius's view from the balcony, Lucius followed and found Chuck under the stairs, having a pretend conversation on his cell phone, with Grace—hidden even deeper in the shadows—involved in the discussion.

"Yes," he said. "I'm sure."

"I saw them too," Grace muttered. "And they were entitled assholes. 'Boy, get me some champagne that doesn't taste like horse piss.' Jesus. Do they think I pour the stuff? And you know what? I had a sip from one of their glasses. It tasted like champagne. They were just trying to be assholes."

"Yes, Grace," Chuck said patiently, still pretending to talk on the phone. "They were just trying to be assholes. But they're also the three frat boys who beat up on the girls. And Stirling identified one of them as the guy who works at Broadstone Industries."

"Do we have a name?" Lucius asked. "I can fire him right now!"

"No!" Chuck and Grace said at the same time.

"You can't," Chuck continued. "If you let him go, they'll know we're on to him. Right now these three douchebags are the key to nailing the people trying to hack your company. Once we get them, they can roll over on the douchebags who wish to continue to beat up their wives."

"But we can't just *let them be here*!" Lucius growled, because he was trying really hard not to yell and everything was coming out from deep in his throat.

"Well now, Mr. Broadstone, I didn't say we were going to leave those poor misguided souls alone, did I?"

Behind him, almost invisible in the shadows, Grace let out a gremlin's laugh, the kind of sound an evil child in a Stephen King novel would make.

"Please tell me I can help," he begged.

"Grace," Chuck said, "how would you like to run through the kitchen and pick up some raw scallops. And maybe some lettuce leaves to wrap them in. Ooh, and broccoli. Broccoli smells *foul* when it's been left to rot. Three separate packets of it, wrapped in paper."

"Why paper?" Grace asked suspiciously.

"Because when you wrap it in plastic," Chuck explained patiently, "the plastic traps the smell."

"Ooh…," Grace said. "I like the way you think, Mr. Bank Robber man."

"Believe it or not," Chuck said with satisfaction, "I learned this trick from Josh. Speaking of which, Josh? Stirling? If you can tell me the make, model, and license plate of their vehicles, Grace and I can work a little mayhem. In fact, I think we can put a little bit of fear into these assholes. They've been doing this kind of shit to Lucius. Let's see how they like being on the receiving end of some damaging practical jokes."

Lucius was stunned—and a little impressed. Was it illegal? Well, technically, yes. Would it kill anybody? No. Would it inconvenience and mark the people responsible for so much pain and possibly so much damage? Yes. And putting them off balance could lead to their conviction for crimes that the police *did* care about.

"I like it," he said. "I'm in. What can I do?"

Chuck winked. "Why, Mr. Broadstone, all you have to do is go up there in a few moments and give one hell of a speech." He sobered. "And let me know if any of the three douchebags whose pictures I'm about to text you go missing. Stirling is monitoring their hotel rooms. They've booked three. If they end up in their rooms, that's fine. If someone decides to go into town for some alcohol? I'm going to want to know about it."

"I hear you," Lucius said, and he smiled winsomely, feeling ridiculously pleased to be in on the game. "Anything else?"

Chuck winked and brushed Lucius's nose with his knuckle. "Keep your nose clean," he said, and then his eyes widened. "And hurry! This song's winding down, and you're being introduced next!"

Lucius swore and turned and ran fleetly up the stairs and into the ballroom, butterflies in his stomach, but not because he was about to give a speech.

All these weeks of being a victim, and finally, *finally*, he was getting some payback.

Let the Games Begin

"YOU DIDN'T tell him all of it," Grace said, but not in an accusatory way. More in that way he had when he was trying to decide if someone's actions were good or bad, since his own moral compass was somewhat shaky.

"I didn't have time," Chuck murmured hoarsely as he and Grace went striding to the kitchen. Chuck let Grace go a little bit in front of him, so if anyone should ask, Chuck could say Grace was taking him to see Grace's superior.

"Chuck? Grace?" Julia said. "Felix and I are upstairs waiting for the speeches to start. Are you two on your way to the car lot?"

"Making a stop first," Chuck said. "Going to do a little innocent sabotage while we're tagging their cars with bugs."

"Fish?" Felix asked, sounding pleased. "I taught Josh that. That little junior high asshole never saw it coming."

Grace laughed evilly, and Chuck grunted affirmative.

"Yeah, but we need to attach the bugs first. And then Grace and I need to go see what's going down at the shelter. It's not sounding good."

What he hadn't told Lucius was that as Josh and Stirling had looked through Chuck and Grace's bow-tie cameras and into the crowd, running faces and IDs, Stirling had gotten reports of attacks on the security system at the shelter. They'd been waiting for the attack on the company first and then the grounds, so it came as a surprise. But as Julia had pointed out, it shouldn't have. Somebody had sent a thug to terrorize Larry and get information, and the next place the guy had turned up had been in a jail in Chicago. So whoever had been trying to hack the security measures—specifically the motion sensors, cameras, and alarm systems—at the perimeter of the shelter would probably have wanted to talk to their inside person.

Given that Lucius was thirty minutes away, tonight had probably seemed like a good time to try.

So right now, Lucius's job was to be the distraction. Chuck and Grace were going to put trackers on the cars, and some fish inside them, and then hop in the vehicle that Josh, Stirling, and Grace had arrived in. Chuck had no idea how Felix and Julia had gotten there—apparently Danny was coming too—but they could have teleported as far as he was concerned. Their job was to find the muckety-mucks in charge of the sabotage.

His job was to find the hired thugs in charge of the break-ins.

He was a big believer in division of labor, and he could only do one thing at a time.

Watching Grace dodge in and out of the human machinery that was a kitchen in full motion was a thing of beauty. Chuck stuck to the periphery, disabling the alarm on the side door so he and Grace could exit the kitchen without going back into the hotel proper.

As they slid outside into the balmy Illinois night, Grace held up a fat red linen napkin, apparently bundled around other fat napkins.

"No paper," he said. "I went for cloth instead." His footfalls were practically soundless next to Chuck's. But then, Chuck was running in dress shoes, which was never a good idea.

"Good thinking," Chuck praised, and in his ear, Josh was saying the same thing. "Josh, what's Hunter saying?"

"It's not good," Josh told him. "There are at least four bogeys lurking outside the fence. So far, none of them have turned toward Lucius's house, which is good. Cheri was there alone. Mom contacted her and told her to drive out the back way, past the business complex. She just called Mom and said she was on her way to her mother's house for the night, but she wanted to be back in the morning to make sure everything was okay."

"Sweet girl," Chuck murmured. "So it's Hunter, Tara-Lynn, Lisa, and the other two guards inside the house—"

"Hunter, Carl, and Lisa are running the perimeter," Josh said tersely. "The minute you two get those bugs in those cars, you need to get your ass back to the house and help them. Molly is minding the monitors so she can help without breaking her cover, but cover is going to be the least of her worries if four armed assailants get through that fence!"

"Does Stirling have the codes yet?" Chuck asked.

"Sending them to your pocket jammer now," Josh said.

Chuck gave a prayer of thanks and pulled it from his pocket. Stirling had made a lot of modifications since Chuck had met Josh that December. With three double clicks of the green button, three vehicles in the open-air lot behind the hotel chirped in recognition, and Chuck and Grace looked at each other in grim anticipation.

"The green Tesla first," Chuck said, then, "Duck!"

He and Grace crouched behind the nearest vehicle—a Rolls Royce SUV of all things—and waited for a valet to saunter by, tossing his keys as he went. He fetched a car not too far from them, and as soon as he pulled away, they ran toward the first target vehicle. Chuck grabbed the handle and skidded to a halt.

The operation went like butter. Chuck placed and activated the tracker/recorders, which Grace had slipped him at the beginning of the party, underneath the dashboard, by the steering console, the better to pick up voices. While he was doing that, Grace tucked little napkin packets of raw fish and broccoli soaked in milk in the pockets behind the seats. The operation took about thirty seconds, and then they were both out. Chuck locked one car as they ran to the next.

They had just finished the third car, and Chuck had punched his jammer for the second Bentley Bentayga that Lucius had given the family to use, the one he and Grace were going to break into because the keys were upstairs in the hotel room with Josh, when Felix came in over coms.

"Gentlemen, your targets are gathering, looking concerned. I'm not sure if they got a silent alarm on their cars or if they found out about the attempted break-in, but they are headed out your way. Julia is about to pull a femme fatale and hold them up a little, but be advised."

"We hear ya," Chuck muttered. "Tell Lucius I'm sorry I missed his speech."

At that moment, he saw the SUV he was beeping for flashing its lights, and he and Grace tore off for it, sliding in right when Julia spoke clearly.

"They're leaving the hotel now, but they're waiting for the valets. You gentlemen are cleared to go, but Lucius is outside in front of them."

Chuck sucked in a harsh breath.

Dammit. Lucius wasn't supposed to be there. Chuck's first instinct was to leave him at the hotel, blasting by him and letting him be confused but safe. Sure, he could catch a ride with Felix and Julia, who would be driving in hot on Chuck's tail, but by then, hopefully, Chuck and the rest of the security detail would have rounded up the thugs trying to break into the damned women's shelter.

But even as Chuck caught sight of Lucius in front of the hotel, Lucius glanced around—probably looking for Chuck—and Chuck saw his expression. That surprising vulnerability was showing, and Chuck realized how hurt Lucius would be if he was left out of what he was sure was coming next.

"Climb in back," he told Grace, knowing the limber thief would have no problems with the gymnastics that might have stymied someone like Chuck or Hunter.

"The hell?" Grace demanded, but he was unbuckling his seat belt as Chuck swerved in front of the hotel, cutting off the next person handing their vehicle to the valet. With a savage stomp on the brakes that had Grace cursing, he braked to an unceremonious halt in front of the overhang that protected hotel-goers from the elements.

Punching a button on the dash, Chuck swung the front door open just as Grace cleared the front seat. "Lucius!" he barked, and while Lucius may have been startled, he was most definitely not stupid.

Chuck screeched away as soon as Lucius's foot cleared the pavement. The door slammed shut, and Lucius fumbled for his seat belt while Chuck looked for an opening on the main road. There were three vehicles ahead of him trying to make the turn out of the long, rosebush-lined driveway.

"Everyone have their seat belts on?" he asked.

"Yes!" Grace snapped from the back seat. "Get a move on! Hunter is fighting an army!"

"An army?" Lucius asked, alarmed. "You didn't think to tell me about an army?"

"It's four guys," Chuck said. "Everyone hang on."

He stood on the accelerator, reveling in the power of the Bentley Bentayga as he took out some rosebushes and a layer of white rock gravel while swerving around two Porches and a Jaguar as he attempted to hit the hole in traffic he saw up ahead.

"Four guys?" Lucius protested. "And oh my God, we're going to have to pay for that—"

"Did I say hold on?" Chuck demanded, and there, that was his hole. He stomped on the accelerator again and shot into traffic, using the bike lane and the oncoming lane to bob and weave a little so he could hit wide-open road.

"I'm holding on!" Lucius snapped back, and from the corner of his eye, Chuck could see Lucius hanging on to the Praise Jesus bar like a drowning man would cling to a rope.

"Good, because now things are going to get *really* intense!"

"Fan*tas*tic!" Grace said as Chuck pushed the vehicle to 105 in the oncoming lane. "I haven't crapped my pants in at least two minutes. Do your worst!"

"Behind the wheel, Grease Man," Chuck taunted, feeling the thunder of a getaway drive in his veins, "you only get my best."

It had taken them thirty minutes of pleasant, emotionally naked conversation to get from Lucius's property to the hotel, but it only took them nine minutes of public NASCAR driving to get them back.

Chuck had had control of the SUV the entire time, and he did love the way the thing purred under his palms. Lucius was good about closing his eyes and saying his prayers as they sped back to the Broadstone house, and Grace was good about only screaming, "We're all gonna die!" after the danger was truly past.

The last time he did it, about a mile before the turnoff to the long residential drive, Chuck snapped back, "We are not! I've got a straight shot and no one in front of me. We're fine!"

"We are not, Mr. Crazypants!" Grace shouted from the back seat. "We've got po-po on our six!"

Chuck looked into the rearview mirror and snarled, "Fuck me bloody!"

"No blood," Lucius whimpered, eyes still shut. "No blood…."

"Tell me something," Chuck started, all but standing on the accelerator and watching the speedometer peg at the red line.

"Anything," Lucius told him, eyes still squeezed shut.

"If I had to make a choice, which would you rather have me wreck—the car or the fence at the center?"

"What?" Lucius's eyes popped open. "Chuck, we can't crash through the fence!"

"Well now," Chuck said, his best placating voice at work, "that's not entirely true. We *can* crash the fence, but the real question is, can we crash the fence and disappear off cop radar? 'Cause the driveway is that loose gravel, you see? And if we pull off there, we're going to leave a trail of dust. But if we go off the road and through the gap between the gate and the fence, they might zoom right by."

"Is there enough room between the gate and the fence?" Lucius asked, his voice pretty steady for a guy who was looking like he wanted to throw up.

Chuck spied a large flatbed about a quarter of a mile ahead of them and an oncoming sportscar about half a mile up.

"Watch me," Chuck murmured. "Or not. There might be some bumps, but I'm pretty sure we'll survive."

"Reassuring," Lucius said tightly. "This car rates very high on safety. Lots of airbags, even in the back. Grace, I'm sure you'll be fine."

"I'd better be!" Grace snapped. "I finally have a boyfriend, and I think Josh needs me!"

"Josh does need you," Chuck bit out. They'd outstripped the earbud range about two miles back. "I wouldn't do anything to take you away from either of them. Trust me, guys. This is why I'm here."

And with that, he pulled out into the oncoming lane and milked that fine-assed powerful performance engine for every drop of jizz it had.

And that baby blew its load in style, spurting them that quarter of a mile in seconds, giving them a whole eleven and a half inches of clearance as Chuck swerved in front of the flatbed and registered the terrified eyes of the sportscar driver as he stood on his brakes and tried not to spin out.

Then the driveway was, *boom*, right there. Chuck's back and biceps strained as he pulled a ninety-degree turn into the drive, eating up the roadway until the wild-jungle landscaping began. With another brutal yank of the wheel, the car was off the driveway, screeching between the wrought iron of the gate and the chain link of the security fencing, plowing through underbrush and scraping down some of the beech and willow trees as Chuck tried to stay alongside the stream that cut into the edge of the property rather than in it.

"Grace, can you see the cop lights?" Chuck asked over the jouncing. The vehicle had slowed considerably, but he didn't want to jam on the brakes right now.

"Not yet," Grace said. "Ouch! Fuck! They're still a mile back. Can we stop now? I'd love it if we could stop now before we hit that guy!"

Chuck scowled at the guy wearing all black in what was now lowering twilight, hauling ass through the underbrush as the thundering vehicle accidentally pursued him.

"He's a bad guy," Chuck acknowledged. "Tell Hunter to stun him, and we'll find something to do with him later."

"We'll what?" Lucius said, and with one horrible jounce, he ripped the Hail Jesus bar right out of the leather fabric of the roof. "Hail fucking Jesus," he muttered. "We'll what?"

"You are not supposed to be here," Chuck opined. "I should have left you in front of the hotel. You could have said we stole your car, which would have been true, and you would have been fine!"

"So why did you bring him here?" Grace asked.

"Grace, how's the green shit behind us? Has it stopped moving?"

Grace risked a full turn around in his seat. "Yeah, we're pretty hidden. Wait… wait…."

Chuck could see the flashing lights too. Watched them get closer… closer… and—

"Zoom!" Grace crowed. "Watch them fly right by!" He let out a happy sigh. "Well done, Mr. Crazypants Getaway Driver. Let's go save my boyfriend now!"

"Yeah, I'll do that. Everyone stay here," Chuck told them. And then he got out of the vehicle and took off in pursuit of their figure in black, who was still thrashing through the undergrowth, trying to get away.

Chuck flailed through the foliage, wishing with all his heart that Lucius hadn't effectively managed to kill coms for everybody involved with his security measures. Dammit, he needed to know what the others were doing.

But first and foremost, he needed to neutralize this threat.

The guy he was chasing was fit enough, but he'd clearly never trained on a military obstacle course, and he was obviously uncertain of the terrain. The time Chuck hadn't been teaching students or helping fix the security system, he and Hunter had spent trekking through this exact same underbrush and getting to know the ins and outs of the property itself.

It took Chuck two minutes to catch up with the guy, and he launched a flying tackle that would have made an NFL player proud.

"Ouch! Fuck!" the guy yelled from underneath his balaclava. It took Chuck less than a second to strip that thing off his head and stretch it out and yank on it until it ripped enough to tie around his wrists. Yeah, sure, the guy struggled, but Chuck's knee was in the center of his back, so maybe not that hard.

"Ouch!" bad guy cried again, this time as Chuck yanked him to his feet and shoved him against a tree.

"Ouch?" Chuck snapped. "Ouch? Who in the fuck are you, and what are you doing here?"

"I'm here to get my buddy's girlfriend back!" the guy moaned. "He said it would be easy. Said she was being kept in a cult on some rich guy's property. Said he'd paid another rich guy off to help break through the security so we could walk in and get her!"

"Paid a rich guy?" Oh, that didn't sound right. Chuck jacked up his arm again. "Paid a rich guy or *was* the rich guy?" he demanded.

"Does it matter?" his captive whined. "He said the bitch was his, and he needed to get her back!"

Without thinking, Chuck yanked on his shoulder again, finding his howl disturbingly satisfying.

"I told you everything!"

"Yeah, but it still makes you a douchebag!" Chuck snapped. "Your friend? He's an *abuser*, and he's a *bad person*, and *you* are a kidnapper and a criminal. The last guy we found trying to break in got left in front of a police station in Chicago, where he's being arrested for shit he did back in high school. What'll they find on you when we leave *you* in front of the police station?"

"You can't arrest me! My dad's a cop. My friend's a cop. He got his information from *his dad*, who's the chief of cops!"

"Shit," Chuck said, and he reached into his pocket and pulled out the handkerchief that came with the once-snazzy suit he was wearing. He flipped it around itself a couple of times and tied it around the guy's eyes, wishing for a second one to put in his mouth.

This asshole had talked enough. Chuck needed a bigger brain to decide what to do next.

"Charles!" Lucius called, thrashing through the underbrush. "Charles, what are you…?"

Chuck spotted him and held an imperative finger to his lips. When he was sure he had Lucius's attention, he mouthed, "Go. Get. Hunter."

Lucius nodded and headed for the inside of the compound, and Chuck hurled his captive to the ground before kneeling on the small of his back. His grunts of pain were extremely satisfying to hear.

Chasing Down a Plan

HUNTER WAS, thank goodness, running flat out in their direction as Lucius emerged from the brush.

"Get to the house," he ordered. "Find Molly in the viewing room. Use the radio to contact us. Go. *Now!*"

And Lucius, in spite of the fact that this was his bloody property, found himself hauling ass for the house to do exactly what Hunter had ordered.

When he got to the monitor room, Molly was presiding grimly over the proceedings, talking on the radio to what looked to be three other people as they all pursued their own intruder. One of them was Soderburgh, the other was Lisa Sampson, and the third was Kenzy, Lisa's partner for the night.

"Lisa, keep going. He's hiding to your right in the underbrush. He thinks he's got the jump on you."

Lucius looked into the newly repositioned monitor and watched as Lisa caught the unexpected intruder in the jaw with her knee, then kneeled on his back and cuffed him tight. One down.

"Chuck's wrapped your guy, Hunter," she said on another click. "He needs some cuffs to be secure. He's also blindfolded, and you'll have to ask Chuck why he did that. I'll have the others do the same."

Lucius looked to the camera that corresponded to the section of forest he'd just run from and saw Hunter emerging from the same deer path that Lucius had followed to get to the house. He had a conversation with Chuck and then pulled up his radio.

"This asshole's a cop's kid. One of the assholes is a cop and the son of the chief of police. He blindfolded the guy so he couldn't identify who's taking them out."

"Roger that," Molly responded. "I'll pass that on. Lisa's got her quarry, Kenzy's got hers, and Soderburgh—"

"Oh!" Lucius groaned in sympathy. Soderburgh's target was wilier and a better fighter than the targets the others had been pursuing. Molly hissed as they both watched Soderburgh take two solid hits to the kidneys and then—

"Oh my," Lucius said in wonder.

Carl had apparently been a boxer in college. It was hard to spot under the boxy American suits he always wore, but there was considerable power in that build.

"Oh!" Molly groaned. "Wow, I think he broke that guy's jaw!"

"Good," Lucius ground savagely. "Because I was having a *very* good time, and these assholes interrupted my best date in a *year*."

Together, they watched as the four intruders were cuffed and blindfolded and marched to the house. Chuck and Hunter's guy seemed the worst off, because Grace was taking advantage of his sightlessness to run forays from the side, shoving the guy off balance to his left, then to his right, and laughing as he stumbled and fell.

"Vindictive little shit," Lucius muttered, not sure whether he approved or was appalled.

"You're defending that guy?" Molly asked.

"Christ no. I just… you know. Always thought we'd play fair."

"These guys are using the law as a shield, Mr. Broadstone," Molly said, sounding so matter-of-fact that Lucius blinked. "We're not violent, and we don't kill—but we are going to fuck these guys up. You're going to have to decide where your line is and tell us where to draw it, because I'm telling you, I don't see a whole lot of good things happening to these assholes. And I'm pretty sure not much of it is going to be legal."

Lucius nodded thoughtfully and remembered what Chuck's intruder had told him. They were there to "grab a bitch because she was his."

"Legality is overrated," he said. "But you're right, we do need to come up with a plan."

"First," Molly said thoughtfully, "we need to identify our intruders and find out who they're here for. Then we have to get those people out of here."

"That is a very good idea," Lucius murmured. And then, mindful of the suspicion of a mole among the residents, he added, "And we need to do it privately."

Molly gave him a cool once-over and nodded. "Agreed. Where can we send them? I mean, they *really* need to run now!"

Lucius groaned and scrubbed his face with his hands. "I'm going to need some help with that one," he admitted, and it broke something in him to admit it. "I… I wanted this to work so badly."

Molly's cool assessment thawed. "Hey, Mr. Broadstone, don't sweat it. You've been knocking yourself out to keep this place—these people—safe. And everyone's loyal to you: the nurses who make the referrals, the tech people, the security. I mean, half the reason your security was shit was because you couldn't afford professionals when you first started out, and you were trying to make do on a shoestring. You've had your company for, what? Two years? You spent part of that time digging it out of the manure pile your father left it in for you, and once you got it out, did you get a frickin' pony? Shit no. You got a security chief enabling corporate espionage. We help you get rid of that little problem and you've got a cabal of wife- and child-abusers trying to break into one of the most altruistic places I've ever seen, because they're fucking monsters. So you don't get to crap on yourself for this, Mr. Broadstone. We're all here because we think you're worth fighting with."

Lucius scanned the monitors and gave a sigh of relief as he saw everybody emerging with their respective intruders, restrained and resentful, being pushed blindfolded to the back of the house.

"Chuck was going to leave me at the hotel," he said wistfully, watching as Chuck and Hunter, their bad guy between them, got close enough to the porch to shove their prisoner to his knees and then get in position to watch for everybody else.

"Well, he probably didn't want to put you in danger," she consoled. "So…." Her voice took on a mischievous lilt, and he took her in, her mass of naturally orange ringlets replete with little rainbow spirals mixed in, all of it piled on top of her head in a messy bun. She wore old yoga pants, a T-shirt, and a light cardigan against the air-conditioning. And although he'd seen her dressed to the nines, looking stunning and chic and urban, he had the feeling she was dressed like this now because it was after hours and these clothes—thin in places, tatty in others—were things she loved very much to wear. And after running the op like a pro, she was gazing at him with fox light in her eyes, her mobile, lush mouth pursed in anticipation.

"So, what?" he asked, beguiled and charmed by her.

"How was Chuck's driving? Josh said they 'borrowed' a car once and took it for a spin around the city, and it was like being in a Jason Bourne movie. Was he full of bullshit, or…?"

Lucius gave a laugh and recalled those thrilling—and terrifying—nine minutes on the road from the hotel to the middle of the woods. "Not bullshit," he confirmed. "I may very possibly have to change my shorts after all of that, but I'm telling you, not bullshit."

She giggled like a child and clapped her hands. "I want next!" she said, delighted. "I'm due!"

"You are indeed," Lucius had to agree. And as he said it, he felt a pang of jealousy that anybody but him should sit next to Charles Calder, clinging to the chicken-stick and begging for his life.

At that moment, Lisa, Kenzy, and Carl all arrived with their prisoners, and Lucius looked at her. "Are you coming out with us or…."

"I'm staying here," she said. "I'll monitor communications. There's sound from outside, and Julia and Felix and Danny—fuck me, who knew Danny was coming?—are on their way here. I'll keep them briefed."

"Josh and Stirling?"

She shrugged and grimaced. "I think Josh fell asleep once he knew you guys were okay. He… he really shouldn't be here." She breathed out hard through her nose. "He hated to be left behind."

"Well, we'll try to wrap this up quickly," he assured her, "so you all can go back to Chicago where you belong."

"Even Chuck?" she asked, her green eyes intense on his face.

"Well, Chuck is…." He was going to say "his own man" or "welcome here anytime" or something equally noncommittal. But what came out of his mouth was "Very capable of flying here and back to Chicago again, as am I. Chuck and I can most definitely work something out that will let him be a part of both worlds."

She grinned. "Good, because the women here really like his fitness and self-defense classes. If he can keep teaching those three days a week, I think he'll make a lot of people happy."

Lucius lit up a little. "He'd make *me* happy," he said candidly, and she grinned.

Molly's radio crackled at her side. "Little fish." Hunter's voice came through, loud and clear. "Little fish, we need you to send out the shark."

"Can do," she replied cheerfully before looking at Lucius. "You're on, Mr. Broadstone," she said off radio. "I'll set the audio on from the back porch and have Felix and Julia listen from there, then radio Hunter with whatever suggestions they have. Remember, even if you fly these bozos to Antarctica in their underwear and have them hitchhike home, they were going to beat up on helpless women and children, and they deserve whatever you dish out."

He nodded. With a flash of clarity, he remembered being a child, cowering behind his mother as she took his father's backhand, right across her cheek. She'd become very skillful at hiding bruises like that with make-up, but she'd had plans to play cards with her friends that afternoon, and he knew without a doubt she'd have to cancel.

Kenny had been whimpering in his room, fortunate enough to hear the old man storm in unexpectedly right after breakfast because he'd forgotten his briefcase, but Lucius had been looking around the living room for his notebook.

That moment right there, with the realization that everybody's day had been needlessly shattered because his father couldn't forget his briefcase without inflicting pain on somebody, anybody, standing in his way, he'd wished his father dead.

For a moment, he'd been horrified.

Good little boys weren't supposed to have thoughts like that.

But he closed his eyes anyway and prayed that his father would drop dead. He knew without a doubt that if that had happened, he would have laughed without shame.

"I'll show them the mercy they deserve," he said out loud, his voice steely, and she nodded her head.

"Righteous, as Chuck would say. Go do your worst to do your best, Mr. Broadstone. We'll back you, one hundred percent."

WHEN HE strode through Chuck and Hunter's temporary quarters to get to the back porch, he noted that everything there was locked down and organized—boots lined up to perfection, the closet arranged with military precision. He wondered what sorts of booby traps and hidden cameras were in there to spot the intruder who'd rifled through their room, twice, and then dismissed the thought on his way through the laundry room to the porch.

He arrived outside to find all of his security and Chuck, arms folded, staring at the prisoners with a sort of gleeful silence.

Someone had shoved gags in their mouths, and between that and the blindfolds, he wondered how scared they must all be. True dark had fallen in the time it had taken to round everybody up. The house itself was quiet, and nobody had been lingering in the front room when he strode through. The attempted attack and possible kidnapping had happened without the knowledge—and hopefully without the fear—of the women he'd worked so hard to protect.

These men's mission was a failure, he hoped.

It was time to make them feel that keenly.

"So," he said, standing behind them, "one of you may talk. Any ideas who our ringleader is?" He looked at Chuck, who jerked his chin toward the man Carl had brought in. Carl had used strips of his suit jacket to bind the man's eyes and to gag him, and Lucius thought he would happily send the man a fitted suit that actually flattered that remarkable boxer's physique.

Lucius got behind the man—one of those dark-haired men with a complexion that wouldn't stop blotching—and untied his gag, saying softly, "Remember, I can shove this back in again at any time. Be careful what you say to me."

"You fucking asswipe," the man spat. "My old man and I are gonna kill you, and we're gonna gut you, and we're gonna beat our fuckin' bitch wives into the—"

Lucius replaced the gag and resisted the urge to kick the man in the spine.

And then he remembered what Molly had told him and stopped resisting the urge. The guy grunted and squealed, and Lucius took a trembling step backward before he started kicking and never stopped.

"Do we have somebody who can speak civilly, or are we dropping all you bozos off in Antarctica in your underwear, without a parachute, hoping you can hitch-hike home?"

One of the men—the blond man Chuck had tackled and had been managing when he'd told Lucius to find Hunter—started to grunt frantically. Lucius met Chuck's eyes and wasn't surprised when Chuck shrugged.

"So," Lucius murmured as he untied what looked to be a very nice linen handkerchief from behind the guy's neck, "you feel more inclined to talk?"

Their blond friend had a jaw that was a little rounder, a little softer, and enough broken blood vessels in his nose to tell Lucius that his real best friend was probably beer.

Which apparently made it easier to flip on the foul-mouthed asshole that Lucius had kicked.

"Man, I was helping my buddy get his wife back," their snitch said brokenly. "He was like, my dad has been working on getting the women back, and no fag pussy's gonna keep our bitches from being our bitches, right?"

Lucius fought back a wave of nausea. "Charming," he uttered. "Do go on."

"So I thought we'd just, you know, walk up to the house so Chet could go up and get his wife, then shove her in the car. He said his dad was working on a scam to make it easier to get his mom and little brother back, but he was tired of waiting, right? 'Cause she was his bitch—ouch!"

Chuck was the one who stepped forward and smacked him on top of the head with a hard hand.

"Mind your fucking mouth," Lucius said coldly. "These are women, they are human, and if his girl-friend didn't want to be with him, well, I can't blame her. Forcing her to be with him is kidnapping, and that's illegal. Or did you think about that before you hopped in your buddy's car and decided to go on an adventure?"

"Man, you don't know Chet! He's scary! He takes out his service revolver and starts aiming it around the house, and you know, sometimes it's just easier to go with him. The last guy who tried to break off and not hang with him got all his tires shot out and then started getting tickets from every cop in town! So Chet's dad said yeah, fine, he'd been having private investigators looking for weak spots in security, and he could give Chet some pointers for a two-man operation, and Chet said fuck that, he was taking all his boys."

Lucius chuckled, thinking about the improvements Chuck and Hunter had made in the security. "How'd that work out for you?"

Their informant groaned. "*It sucked.* We found some of the fence's weak points, but it was *electri-fied*, and I got fuckin' burns on my hands and I bit my tongue. And I don't know about everyone else, but by the time I was ready to head for the house and meet my buddies and make sure they made it in, some as-shole was driving a *car* at me and I was crapping my pants."

Lucius gave a dry cough and winked at Chuck. "If you think it was scary from the outside, you should have tried being inside the vehicle. You got off easy."

"Yeah, I can believe that," their little Chatty Cathy said glumly. "You people are crazy."

"Yes, we are," Lucius told him, rather enjoying being one of *you people*. "And as such, the sky is the limit in terms of finding a suitable consequence for your behavior. Now, I'm all for the naked-in-Antarctica thing, but I work with some *very* unscrupulous people. Do you know what happened to the last person who tried to break in here?"

"Clive?" their new friend asked, and he put a whole lot of fear into that name. "Did you… did you kill him? Because he worked for Chet's dad, and he was a scary sonofabitch. I… I did not like Clive."

"Good," Lucius told him. "Neither did the Chicago police department. They particularly didn't like that he left his DNA at over a dozen sexual assault crime scenes. So now Clive is making a deal to serve his life sentences concurrently so that he might breathe fresh air while he can still breathe."

"Oh God." Lucius heard the little hiccupping sob. "Chet's dad is going to be pissed."

"Yes," Lucius said. "But then, so am I. And I am the one with the law and a few other people on my side. So you, my friend, we can airlift to a part of the country, any part of the country, and leave you there to start over. You're an asshole, but not too much of an asshole. With some training, you might pass as human. But what would you like us to do with your friends? And Chet? And Chet's father? I'm looking for inspiration here, my friend who likes to make bargains. Do you have any inspiration to give?"

"I got nothing. You... you're just so lucky his dad's not here yet. His dad's a fuckin' nightmare, you hear me? He's even got a fuckin' senator in his pocket!"

Chet, who had been struggling with his bonds and with his gag, finally managed to spit the gag out. "Randy, you fuckin' little cockroach! I'm gonna slit your throat and leave your bones for the goddamned crows. I've done it before. It'll be a fuckin' pleasure!"

Randy, the one who'd been talking, shouted, "Is that what you did to Lara, you fuckin' psycho? 'Cause she was gone, man! One day she was talkin' to us in class, and the next day she was fuckin' gone!"

"Bitch never shoulda looked at you!" Chet snarled. "I showed her, and I'll show you!"

Lucius met horrified gazes with the rest of the team, and Hunter gave a grunt and nodded his head, asking permission.

"Please," Lucius said, at a loss.

A part of him knew—should have known. This attack on him was part organization, part chaos. It was part electronic master-planning and part angry child having a tantrum. They'd already theorized that there were two parties behind the attacks: the people using industrial espionage as a weapon to keep Lucius occupied—and to destroy his company—and the people who were making actual physical attempts on the women's shelter. The temper tantrum was what he was seeing here. The smalltown psychopath with a badge battering his way in was one branch of the attack.

Chet's father, and his father's cronies—including Kyle Miller, the senator—were working the other end of things. Not as physical, no. But the threat to the income stream that made this place run was possibly the more dangerous threat.

Hunter squatted in front of Chet and shoved the gag—not kindly—back into his mouth; then Chuck moved behind the man and yanked on the ties. Hard.

"You're already dead," Hunter said quietly. "Whether it's in prison or by my hands, kid, you're already dead. How bad it is depends on your self-control in the next ten minutes."

They could *all* hear Chet breathe in hard through his nose, but he stopped fighting the gag, so that was something.

"My crew, huddle in," Hunter said, and Lucius, Grace, and Chuck gathered around him behind the four unhappy intruders.

"My take?"

Lucius nodded, willing to hear someone else's perspective. He'd known when he was a child that he couldn't trust law enforcement. Too many of them were "such good friends" with his father. He, his mother, and his brother had been trapped in their violent home, and nobody had extended a hand. Nobody had ever suspected anything because Mr. Jonathan Broadstone was such an important, respectable businessman. Whether Lucius had wanted to articulate it or not, it had been that basic distrust—that bone-deep acknowledgment that the powers that be weren't necessarily there to help the people who needed them the most—that had led him to the Salinger crew's door.

They hadn't let him down yet. In fact, they'd been doing the work of an army, with the dedication one expected of elite special-ops personnel, right down to the girl with the sunset curls and the yoga pants minding coms.

"I say we take this whole group of assholes and drop them on the FBI's doorstep," Hunter said, no bull-shit. "You've got a plane, I've got contacts at Quantico. I land on their airstrip, kick these assholes out on their turf, and let the FBI sort them out. Chet here has at least one murder on his hands. Randy is more than happy to flip on him and win that trip to Antarctica with a fiver in his pocket. We've got enough information now to start sorting out who's behind the cyberattacks and the industrial espionage, but we have this threat off our table. What do you say?"

"I say amen," Lucius told him, his stomach releasing its knots one coil at a time. He'd been afraid, so afraid, that Hunter would flat out suggest assassination. And he'd realized in that moment it took for him to think it and Hunter to come up with a much better plan, that the reason he'd been afraid was because he would have agreed to it.

Chet was a police officer. His friend was a cop's son. Together, they'd used their authority to abuse and terrorize Chet's girlfriends, both past and present, apparently. And all of them had frightened the women who had been herded into the house and told to stay in their rooms with the all-intrusive cameras on.

He was angry; so damned angry. The women in his care had put their faith in him—in the institution he'd tried to create—and these monsters had tried to keep them beaten and afraid.

They had to pay. *Someone* had to pay.

Hunter's way was better, he knew. But he wouldn't have said no to murder. He knew that now. He understood that his father's propensity for violence was in him, and he knew he'd better stick close to good people to help him keep it at bay.

Suddenly Hunter's radio crackled.

"You there?" Molly asked.

"Yeah, urchin, I'm there." It was a pet name, apparently, but it also worked as a code name, and Lucius was very tempted to smile.

"We've got incoming po-po. Whatever you decide to do, do it now. This is the second loop they've done around the property. I'm betting if our intruders are cops, they've got a cruiser with a GPS in it parked here somewhere, and somebody's getting antsy, especially since they know the Bentayga disappeared this way. What's our plan?"

Hunter gaped, and Lucius took a deep breath. But it was Chuck who spoke up next with a plan.

One that called for Lucius to have balls of solid rock.

LUCIUS STOOD on the porch of his own house, wearing a bathrobe with his briefs on underneath it and looking as sheepish as hell. On the one hand, he knew it was what he was supposed to do—look sheepish and disheveled and sexy (Chuck's words)—but on the other?

His pubes were sweating. He wasn't sure why that's where all his freaking-out was concentrated, but he could also feel rivulets of sweat trickling down his back, between the crack of his ass, into his briefs, and down his thighs.

He knew that in a good con, someone had to be a distraction. But he'd never thought he would be that guy.

"So you haven't seen anything unusual?" Newman Damar, chief of the local Springfield police force and apparently the father of Chester Damar, asked with naked suspicion on his face.

"No, Officer. Should I have?"

Lisa had kept the gate closed and instructed Damar, via the intercom, to continue down the long roadway to Lucius's house if he wanted to speak to the owner of the property. She and Carl had been given maybe fifteen minutes to pull cover over the broken plants and wrecked foliage next to the gate that marked the passage of the Bentayga as Chuck had enacted his epic charge through the wooded parts of the shelter's campus. So far Damar hadn't mentioned the mess. Maybe their cleanup efforts had worked, and maybe he was going to bring it up later in an effort to trip Lucius up.

"Well, our GPS showed a police cruiser parked somewhere on the property until right before we arrived. I would have thought you'd have seen it!"

It had, in fact, been parked haphazardly in the middle of the drive, in front of Lucius's garage. Chuck's handy little gizmo had unlocked it, and it had taken him less than a minute of messing with wires under the console to disconnect the GPS. That minute had bought them some more time. As soon as the GPS had disconnected, the sirens that had started screaming down the straightaway toward Lucius's property gave a sad little blip and ceased entirely, and so had the cherry lights. The entire caravan of police cars had gone silent and taken another twenty-mile loop around Lucius's property.

That had been lucky. It had given them time to cover the Bentayga's tracks—and cover the vehicle itself in brush so it didn't so much as glimmer in the moonlight. It had also given them time to shove their prisoners into the back of Chet's abandoned police cruiser, still blindfolded, cuffed, shackled, and gagged.

Well, they'd taken Randy's gag out and given him some water, but had pretty much ignored the other guys. Hunter had the right idea. Drag them all to FBI headquarters and let God sort them out.

So Hunter and Grace were on their way to the airport with the goons, via the road to the industrial complex and with Lucius's key codes that would let them get out of the gated parking lots. Carl had been willing to accompany the two of them, but Chuck rightly pointed out that Molly and Chuck would need Carl there since Hunter was gone.

Chuck had gone to secure the perimeter around the mansion and the grounds, and with Molly, Lisa, and Tara-Lynn's help, to do a wellness check on all of the occupants. Lucius had called up the resident psychiatrist and told her that they'd had a security scare, so she was alert and on call.

And nobody—*nobody*—had forgotten that one of the residents was still a mole for their cabal of bad guys trying to get in.

But the police were coming, and while Hunter was—hopefully—escaping through the back way with their prisoners, someone was needed to distract the police from the giant mansion in the front of the property and the giant wrought iron gate that Lucius's people had refused to open.

And that was why Lucius was standing, barely clothed, on his front porch, hanging his well-ventilated ass out in the breeze.

"Well, yes," Lucius said, keeping his charm and amiability around him like a cast-iron jock. "You would think if there were a police cruiser on the premises, we would have noticed it, wouldn't you? But no, I see no such cruiser, and obviously I didn't see one when I last put a vehicle in the garage."

All of that was perfectly true, because he didn't *put* his last vehicle in the garage. Chuck had parked the battered Bentayga in the middle of the woods on the lower part of the property.

But Damar didn't know that, and there was no reason for him to.

"So, you're saying you haven't noticed anything unusual since you arrived home," Damar said, his thin face and forehead taking on extra grooves.

"Not in the least," Lucius said. He made sure to flash his dimples while suppressing a smile. "Although, as you may have guessed, I wasn't exactly looking around for intruders when I arrived."

And there, that moment of extreme discomfort, as though the esteemed Police Chief Newman Damar had digested some moldy liver and onions, was the moment Lucius had been waiting for.

Damar, who had pulled up to Lucius's house with no fewer than three police cruisers behind him but had gotten out alone and still dressed for the benefit, suddenly could look anywhere but at Lucius standing there suggestively in front of God and everyone, wearing nothing but a satin robe.

"You... you look very comfortable," Damar said, voice strained.

"Well, I was about to be," Lucius told him with an adorable little nose wrinkle.

"You... you...." Suddenly Damar's eyes sharpened. "Weren't you just at a benefit thrown in your honor?" he demanded.

"As were you, Police Chief," Lucius said, hoping his eyes were twinkling. He was *really* trying to get his eyes to twinkle. "I saw you there as I gave my speech." Damar's crisp white shirt and perfect bow tie would actually be a little endearing if the man didn't have an ashen complexion and twisted expression that appeared constantly, as if he'd been sucking lemons.

"You left a little early, didn't you?" The irritation in the man's voice couldn't be missed.

"Well, yes," Lucius said with a shrug. "My companion was quite… diverting. And as I hadn't booked a room in the hotel, we decided to divert ourselves elsewhere. What called you away so precipitously?" Ah yes, the expensive Ivy League education. His father had complained about it bitterly the entire time Lucius was in school, but Lucius knew it would come in handy someday.

Dropping fifty-cent words at the feet of this two-penny tinpot abusive scumbucket was apparently that day.

"Where *is* your companion?" Damar sneered, as much as he *could* sneer when he couldn't look Lucius in the eye.

"Well, inside, probably diverting himself now that I'm not there," Lucius returned. Oh, this was fun. Yes, he was standing on his front porch in his underwear and a bathrobe, but Newman Damar looked like he was going to shit kittens—painfully—at any moment. He was starting to see why the Salinger crew were so addicted to danger.

"Well, it would be great if you could call him out for me, would ya?"

"Sure, Officer Damar, but it may take him a few moments to make himself presentable." Lucius winked. "Given all of the… diversion we were having."

Damar's eyes almost rolled back in his head, and Lucius turned to enter the house, planning to wander from room to room yelling Chuck's name for as long as it took for Charles to climb in through the window Lucius had opened in the back of the house, strip naked, and come outside.

And he'd given Newman Damar the perfect reason why Lucius didn't want to allow him inside without arousing Damar's suspicion, which was fantastic.

Equally fantastic was that all of the officers waiting impatiently, sweltering in their cars in the heat of the night, had forgotten to ask about the elephant in the front of the property—the shelter. The women there were safe as long as Lucius could leave his dignity flapping in the breeze long enough for Newman Damar to give in to the pressure even Lucius felt from those waiting police units and go back to the station, hoping to find his son somewhere else.

As it turned out, he didn't have to wander far at all. He'd taken one step up onto the porch when Chuck blew through the front doors, sopping wet and wearing only a towel wrapped loosely around his waist. Water glistened off his chest and in his hair, pooled in the hollows of his shoulders, traced its way down the front of his pectorals, and raced to hide in the happy place beneath the plain white Egyptian cotton towel.

Lucius had to take a deep breath to remember why they were both standing on his porch mostly naked, and Chuck caught his eyes and winked.

"Lucius," he opined playfully, "I thought you were only going to be a minute. The shower's getting cold!"

Lucius managed a coy look over his shoulder. "Officer Damar? You wanted to meet my date? This is Charles Summers. He's the security expert I've hired to update the systems in my home."

"Was that what you were doing?" Damar sneered. "Updating his security?"

Chuck gave that aw-shucks grin of his. "Well, no, sir. I'd say Lucius's personal security is just fine. But if you'd like me to examine it some more, we'll be happy to go back inside and do that."

"How long have you two fellas been here… diverting?" Damar asked.

"Not long at all," Chuck said, and he gave a coy, flirty look of his own. "We were just showering off the tuxedo sweat, weren't we, Scotty?"

Lucius managed to look abashed. "Well, I was trying to put some champagne on ice when the cruisers pulled up."

"Isn't that sweet." Chuck grinned at the chief of police and gave Lucius a besotted look. "Isn't he just the most gallant man on the planet? I picked me a good one here, Sheriff."

"Officer," Damar corrected icily. "Now could you clarify why we aren't allowed on that part of the property near the front of the drive here?" he demanded.

"You didn't go there, did you, Sher—I mean, Officer?" Chuck asked, suddenly all concern over Damar's safety.

"No, the woman on the intercom said we weren't allowed!" Damar's outrage showed through, but as he got hotter, Chuck's chill just grew more epic.

"Well, good on her," Chuck said. "I've got all sorts of exposed wires and construction sites back there. Lucius here wanted to make a guest house for his out-of-town investors, but he couldn't do it unless the security and facilities were updated, you hear me? So all of my workers are gone for the day, and they cover shit up, but there's no telling what can happen to someone without a hard hat and the proper rubber-soled boots and gloves. Nosirree, that gal's getting a raise for not letting you back beyond that gate. No friend of Lucius gets hurt on my watch, that's for certain."

"So it's a construction site?" Damar asked uncertainly. "Wasn't that your father's mansion?"

"Yes, Officer Damar," Lucius responded. "But it had fallen into disrepair. Not only is Charles here updating the security, but we're doing all sorts of remodeling and reconstruction. Why? What did you think was back there?"

Lucius looked at him with pleasant curiosity and pretended not to see the fury banked in Newman Damar's eyes.

Joanie Damar and her son depended on him looking pleasant and vapid, because the moment Damar knew—knew for certain—Lucius was hiding women in that mansion, they were in danger. Chester Damar's girlfriend was in danger. And that poor kid Larry was in danger too.

While the crushing weight of responsibility for these people's lives pounded inside his chest, Lucius stared incuriously at a man who should have protected them and was, instead, a deadly threat.

"Are you sure there's nothing else back there?" Damar asked, his self-doubt so real that Lucius had a flash of hope. Yes, there was a mole, but obviously their mole didn't know exactly where they were. It was very possible that the person had been driven to that house from the south, not passing through Springfield, Peoria, or even the Broadstone suburb. Somebody could have been brought to the shelter with a vague idea of where in the state they were, but no specifics.

The secret was still safe. Thank God! And the Salinger crew was so much closer to tracking the trail of espionage and hacking to Kyle Miller through the three frat boys who, if Chuck was to be believed, currently had fish in their cars.

Play the idiot philanderer?

Lucius could do it in his sleep.

"Nothing else back there?" Lucius repeated. "Like what? Are we hiding a circus in my father's substandardly constructed mansion? No, Officer Damar, I assure you, there's merely a lot of exposed wiring and some giant holes for sewage and plumbing that I don't want anybody to fall into."

He flashed his dimples again and allowed Chuck to tug gently on his elbow.

"Come on inside, Scotty," he urged. "I bet the water's heated right up again." Chuck grinned at Police Chief Damar. "Now, I get that Lucius left his shindig a little early, but are you here to arrest him for that? 'Cause I can assure you, nothing we're doing in there is illegal. Honest, Sheriff!"

"*Officer!*" Damar snarled, and Chuck held his hands up mockingly.

As he did so, the towel wrapped around his waist plopped to the porch boards under his feet.

"Officer! Of course, you're right. Didn't mean to be disrespectful. Was there anything else you needed to see?"

His voice was guileless and helpful, but that only made the entire… area exposed by the dropped towel all the more… evident.

"See?" Damar asked weakly, and Lucius tried to catch his breath. Outside of "instructional videos" that he watched to "set a mood," he hadn't ever seen anyone with quite Chuck's, uhm, build.

"Well, yes," Chuck drawled, grinning. "Besides, aren't you getting an eyeful already?"

Knowing that bending over would expose his ass in his tight briefs, Lucius took a deep breath and did it anyway to pick up the towel, coming up eye level with Chuck's personal beast and pretending to stumble back in confusion.

"Oh… oh my," he simpered, handing the towel to Chuck while bashfully looking back over at Damar with pleading in his eyes.

"Officer Damar, do you mind telling us what all this is about? I'm sure you can see that we were in the middle of something rather… timely."

Damar was doing everything but clutching his pearls and holding his hand to his forehead.

"You people can go do whatever the fuck you want," he snapped. "I would just like someone to tell me what happened to my son's goddamned cruiser!"

"Oh! That was your son's unit that got misplaced?" Lucius said, giving Chuck a wistful look. "We're so dreadfully sorry. By all means, we'll do anything we can to help. Would you like to come inside and have some…." He put the barest hesitation in his voice, suggesting he had nothing in his home but prophylactics and lubricant. "Tea?" he finished.

Damar let out a noise of disgust and waved his hand at them. "You two go do whatever. Just what-the-fuck ever! But I'm hitting the judge up first thing in the morning for a warrant to check out that property."

Lucius gave him a wide-eyed look. "Well, you could do that, but I'm afraid I'd need to know what crime you think has been committed. Judge Chase is in charge of county matters, and I can have my lawyer down there first thing in the morning. If you give me evidence of a crime, I'll be happy to let you in to check things out."

Fortunately—oh yes, fortunately—Judge Camille Chase was an old friend of his mother's. When he'd first had the idea to build the shelter, he'd gone to Aunt Cammy and asked her about the legalities involved, and she'd given him a lot of tips on how to keep Caraway House a secret from all but the most tenacious of lawmen.

Newman Damar was not a good man—no. But he was also not great at his job. He was too busy hiding the corruption in his precinct to figure out a legal loophole to get onto Lucius's property and discover his secrets. In fact, Lucius was pretty sure that if Damar hadn't been an abusive pusbucket himself, maybe—just maybe—he might have questioned the big chunk of property that nobody seemed to visit, but that was always secure as hell.

Damar didn't have a leg to stand on, and the scream of exasperation he gave as he clambered back into his vehicle—stiffly starched formal jacket and all—told Lucius all he needed to know about having a little more time.

Chuck made a show of tying the towel back around his hips while wrapping a possessive arm around Lucius's waist and pulling him intimately close while they waved goodbye to the chief of police and the four spit-shiny county-marked cruisers that pulled up in front of the house and around the driveway in order to leave.

They waited until the dust of the last vehicle disappeared before turning to go back into the house. And Lucius didn't let his shoulders droop with relief until the door closed behind them.

Who We Are

CHUCK WATCHED most of the starch leach from Lucius's shoulders as he leaned back against the door in relief.

"Oh my God," Lucius breathed. "I can't believe we pulled that off."

Chuck let out a slight laugh, but he kept his eyes on Lucius. "You were amazing," he said, completely sincere. "Felix and Danny couldn't have done better. It was like you were born to the grift!"

Lucius's high cheekbones got a little ruddy, and he looked away. "Thank you," he said with surprising humility. "I've got to admit, you got out there just in time."

Chuck grinned, taking a deep breath in the air-conditioning and wondering if it would be forward to ask if he could jump back in the shower. God knows, watching Lucius parade around in his little bathrobe was certainly driving up his heat.

"Right before I climbed up to the window, Grace told us that Felix and Julia were leaving the hotel in an hour or so," he said seriously. "They want to keep an eye on our three frat boys, but afterward they thought maybe we should go talk to the women who were threatened and see if they wish to be relocated. Julia has a house close to Lansing, along the lake. She says it would only take a little bit of modification and they could have some cameras and security there. That way, if your bad guys got through, they…. Well, they'd still be dangerous but—"

"They wouldn't get who they were coming for," Lucius said. His shoulders slumped a little more, but this time it looked more like defeat than relief.

"Hey, what's wrong?" Chuck took an uncertain step toward him, and then another, looking around the high-ceilinged foyer in belated realization that they were two people in a very big house wearing next to nothing.

"Sorry," Lucius said, looking away. "Just got, you know, carried away. Forgot entirely that we had a job to do, right? Was back to pretending it was a date."

Chuck's heart cracked, tinkled to the ground at his feet, and crumbled into powder.

"Baby," he said softly, closing the gap between them entirely. Lucius's body threw off heat, and Chuck imagined he was probably sweating underneath that little navy-blue satin robe thing, from adrenaline and the humid midwestern night. "It was a date. It was an *amazing* date. Did you think I didn't appreciate seeing you prancing around in that robe thingy? I mean, I got to tell you, I've never owned one of these in my life, but I'm starting to see the appeal."

Lucius turned that vulnerable face to him, the one that was hungry for Chuck's approval, and Chuck….

Every boundary in Chuck's heart evaporated.

What else was he looking for? He had a guy who held on to the chicken-stick as Chuck raised holy hell in a very fine automobile and who played a con like he was born to it. And Lucius wasn't a con man, he wasn't lying to lie, and he wasn't hiding himself in a closet. He was out, open, and his only secrets were the ones that kept people safe as he did his best to honor people in his life that he'd lost. He was a good man, and while his taste in clothes seemed infinitely better than his taste in men, Chuck... Chuck couldn't argue with him anymore. Couldn't try to find reasons to not throw himself at this sweet, canny businessman who knew almost everything Chuck was and didn't object to any of it.

Chuck slid his palm down Lucius's throat, framing Lucius's jaw between his first two fingers and stroking his chin with a roughened thumb.

"Is this what you wanted?" he asked, his stomach knotting. "Is this what you were planning for tonight?"

Lucius looked at him with such hope. "Is that wrong? Am I overreaching? You keep backing away."

"Look at you," Chuck murmured, nuzzling at his temple. "So pretty. So damned fine. I'm backing away 'cause I keep thinking there's got to be some mistake. I've had my share, Lucius. And they've all been a game to me. But not you. You have it in you to be special. You have it in you to break my heart. I just don't want to set my heart out, all ripe for the breaking, and have you suddenly realize who I really am."

Lucius smiled faintly. "You're a man who just did a thirty-minute drive in nine minutes flat. You wrecked my Bentayga and dropped your towel and showed off your *very* impressive manhood in front of the chief of police, and you would do it all over again to protect the same people I'm protecting, because you really are that good of a soul. Do I have it right? Did I leave anything out?"

Chuck closed his eyes and let the words wash over him, Lucius's breath a warm murmur against his lips. "I'm the man who wants you," he said gruffly. "And I still got secrets. I'll spill 'em if you want. But I'll still be the man who wants you."

"Take me," Lucius murmured, and he was the one who closed the last little span between them.

So Chuck did what he did best.

Drove.

He took Lucius's mouth hard and hungry. God, he wanted this. That little show they'd just put on? He wanted that to be real. He wanted the right to be coming out of Lucius's shower for real, putting his hands all over Lucius and telling the world this man was his.

He slid his hands down the satin of the stupid little robe and cupped Lucius's hard thighs, lifting a little so Lucius jumped and wrapped his legs around Chuck's waist.

Chuck kept kissing, thrusting him back against the doorjamb, not minding that Lucius was a bit tall for this. He was slightly built, and Chuck was strong, and Chuck wanted him, all of him, hard and hot and now.

Lucius's briefs slid to the side enough for their cocks to meet, to rub up against each other, and Lucius was undulating desperately in Chuck's arms.

"Want it?" Chuck taunted, nipping on Lucius's earlobe for that bite of pain.

"So much," Lucius begged. "I want it. Want you." And then he surprised Chuck, because Chuck was used to being used. "Inside me," he begged. "Please."

Chuck gulped and moaned, wrapping his arms fiercely around Lucius's shoulders.

"We gotta go upstairs for the kit and caboodle," he warned. "I'm on PReP—"

"Me too," Lucius breathed, doing this thing with his stomach muscles that kept his body gyrating against Chuck's cock. "Forget about the caboodle."

Chuck took a deep breath and pulled back, drawing a line. "I'm not going in without lube," he said sternly. "This… this is going to be good," he added, now showing his own vulnerability, his need for this man to think well of him. He pulled back and smiled tentatively at Lucius, who lowered his feet to the ground so they could stand level.

"Let me make this good," he said.

Lucius's kiss-swollen mouth quirked sideways. "I sincerely doubt that it would be any other way with you."

Chuck grinned, but it still felt wobbly. "No, sir. Let me make it good. Let's shower. Let me give you the bells and whistles. We've got a little time. Let me make it good."

Lucius closed his eyes, and that sweetness, often hidden, seemed to wash over his expression. "Yes."

"Excellent."

And with that Chuck turned toward the stairs, Lucius in tow.

They made it to the third floor, and Chuck kept going to the shower. He'd come in through the window that Lucius had left open, but he'd taken a minute to make their ruse look convincing. Part of that had required water in his hair and dripping down his shoulders. But he'd been hot, sweaty, and disheveled as he stripped for the shower, and he was pretty sure Lucius had been too. Both of them had left their suits in puddles around the bedroom, but Chuck wasn't going to fix that now.

Instead, he pulled Lucius into a newly refurbished marble-tiled shower, one of the super-fancy ones with six shower heads and soap dispensers built into the walls. The tiles themselves were grayish and sort of glimmery, with little sparkles of amber through them, and Chuck could have studied the colors for days.

If he hadn't had Lucius to study instead.

He soaped up the bath sponge hanging from the wall and started running it along Lucius's chest and throat as Chuck plastered himself along Lucius's back.

"Mm…," he said, rubbing the sponge along a fading bump in Lucius's clavicle. "Your father?" he asked, because that was the kind of thing left after a break.

"Snow skiing," Lucius told him, sounding relaxed. He held up his forearm, where Chuck could see surgical scars from long, long ago. "That was my father."

"Twisting break," Chuck murmured, pulling the skin up to kiss.

"It was the last time he hurt me," Lucius told him softly. "Doctors know there's only one way you can do that. Kenny had just passed, and the old man was monstrous with rage. Doctor told him that if I came in with so much as a mosquito bite, he'd file a complaint."

"Mm. So it got better?" Chuck asked, kissing along Lucius's spine as the water sluiced down their bodies. This was the clean he'd wanted, not only the sweat but the fear, the rush, the pain. He wanted those washed away in this moment between them.

"Yeah. He was still a bastard—we still had to duck once in a while—but he mostly stayed out of the house." Lucius shuddered. "God knows who else he took that temper out on. But he died of colon cancer. Perhaps he saved the worst of it for himself."

"Good," Chuck said gently, sliding the sponge down between Lucius's cheeks, parting him, scrubbing, catching Lucius's private bits before going after his own. "You only deserve the best."

Lucius turned in his arms as Chuck was putting the sponge back in its holder and captured Chuck's cheeks in his palms.

"So do you."

Chuck gave him a crooked grin and reached behind him to turn off the water. "Right now, I got you. You're all the best I need." He bent and took Lucius's mouth again and then toweled them both dry and then kissed some more. He kissed Lucius into a practical bedroom, with cotton sheets and a rain-blue comforter that was darn near dryer-fresh, and stretched him out on a bed of mountain ash, sturdy and useful and beautiful at once.

And he kept kissing.

He kissed down Lucius's body, shoving between his thighs so he could lick some more at Lucius's cock.

But he and Lucius's cock were old friends by now, and now that they were all clean and sweet, he wanted closer. He peered over Lucius's body and met those sober hazel eyes. A stranger might think them icy, but Chuck knew better. Lucius was just guarded, and he'd let Chuck in under the gates.

Chuck was going to pillage, of course—but gently.

Lucius was his fortress of safety. Chuck wasn't going to break that.

He parted Lucius's cheeks and started to lick, getting his hole good and wet and savoring the little grunts of need that Lucius tried to keep to himself.

He thrust his finger in and stretched the rim a little, feeling very smug. "You want something?" he goaded.

"Of course!" Lucius burst out, wriggling enough to impale himself on Chuck's finger. "You know I've seen it, and now you're teasing me with its absence!"

Chuck's laughter rolled through the darkened room. "Well, you hand me some lubricant and I might start teasing you with its presence," he goaded.

"Augh! Fine!" Lucius started to reach into the drawer by his head, and Chuck, for the hell of it, kept his finger right where it was, following Lucius's movements, tormenting his nerve endings by never being deep enough but always being there.

Lucius's noises got more and more desperate, until finally Chuck caught a decent-sized bottle of lubricant on the shoulder as Lucius botched the handoff before groaning with a complete lack of repentance.

"Please?" he graveled. "Please? God, Chuck, I want you inside me. I want to keep you inside me forever. Please!"

Chuck couldn't waste any time after that. Just the sound of Lucius's voice made him harder. He slicked himself up quickly, knowing that Lucius was primed and needy. As he lined his cock up to thrust in, he paused.

"I'm sort of an assfull," he apologized. "I'll go as slow as you need me, but don't be afraid to direct traffic here, you understand?"

"I *have* done this before," Lucius told him, looking so earnest Chuck almost called the whole thing off.

"Sure you have," Chuck whispered and began to thrust in.

Lucius begged for more. Pleaded. Screamed for it. And Chuck went as slowly as he could, making sure Lucius was good and stretched before he was seated all the way inside, sweating, aching, afraid his control, which had always been good in this matter, was not going to hold.

"How are you?" he panted before he gulped in a deep breath and nodded.

"I need you," Lucius breathed, "to trust me."

"I trust you," Chuck told him.

"I feel amazing," Lucius confessed, his body quivering under Chuck's like a tuning fork. "I feel like I could fly. But I need you to fuck me. Hard. Like you mean it. I need it so bad, Charles. I need you. Can you do that? Can you...?"

Chuck pulled out, a little, a little, until only his head was inside, clenched hard by Lucius's ring. "Say it," he urged. "Say the words. Scream them. I need them."

Lucius gave a wolfish smile before his eyes went to half-mast and he groaned.

"*Fuck me!*" he screamed, and Chuck—Chuck did what he'd never done with a partner.

Trusted enough to do exactly what he asked.

He thrust, he pounded, he used Lucius Broadstone hard and mercilessly, and Lucius begged for more. Sweat poured down his back, his biceps and stomach ached from use, and his cock? Oh Lord, his cock was being squeezed in a sweet velvet vise.

And still Lucius urged him on.

Finally, when Chuck's heart felt like it would burst, Lucius made a guttural sound, one that Chuck felt in his balls, and his entire body convulsed, rolling Chuck's cock in the ferocity of his grip.

Lucius's come scalded the skin on Chuck's stomach, and Chuck's tenuous hold on his own body fractured, his eyes rolled back in his head, and he came.

And came and came.

His vision went black, and for a moment, his breath stopped in his chest. He came to and found himself collapsed on Lucius's body, his face buried in the hollow of Lucius's shoulder as he dragged air into his lungs, trying to catch his breath.

Lucius was murmuring comfort words into his ear, and Chuck was too far gone to murmur them back.

What an amazing sensation—but one he didn't want to get too used to.

As soon as the spots stopped swimming in front of his eyes, he pushed up a little and tried to pull a blanket over his soul. "I, uhm, don't want to squash you. That would be a helluva way to end up a night."

"Hey," Lucius murmured, his voice saturated in something like wonder. "Hey, don't—what're you doing?" He cupped Chuck's cheek in his palm and pulled Chuck's eyes back to his. "That was wonderful. Don't pull away now."

At that moment, Chuck deflated enough to slide out, and they both gave soft gasps as come rushed over their thighs and onto the sheets.

Chuck gave a playful grin, but Lucius rolled his eyes. "That's not what I meant," he said sternly.

Chuck paused and took a breath. "Let me go get a cloth," he said. "Then I'll come back and cuddle." He gave a fleeting smile but met Lucius's eyes. "Promise. I'll be back. All of me."

Lucius nodded, then grimaced. "A cloth would be… prudent."

Chuck came back with two cloths, one warm and wet and one dry, and initiated a thorough cleanup. At the end, he prodded gently at Lucius's opening, plying his tongue a little, playfully, but mostly checking for soreness.

Lucius gave a soft, happy moan and stroked his cock lazily. "I could do this all night," he murmured. "You could make me come until I dehydrated, just a husk, killed by good sex and happy with it."

Chuck pulled back enough to laugh and was going to go back to doing exactly that when Lucius shook his head.

"We'll do that someday," he said softly. "But not now. C'mon, Charles. Come talk to me. What's to be afraid of?"

Chuck met his eyes squarely. "Being naked."

"Mm." Lucius nodded. "I'll be gentle," he said. "I promise."

Chuck gave a brief smile and wiped his face on his shoulder before scooting up the bed. The air conditioner felt particularly zealous, now that their blood was no longer up, so he tugged the comforter over them while Lucius shoved extra pillows behind. Eventually they were settled, and Chuck sighed, wondering where to begin.

Surprisingly, it wasn't with Car-Car. It was with Kevin.

"Some people don't grow up to fight their abusers," he said thoughtfully. "Some people grow up to be them."

"True," Lucius agreed.

"I was lucky. I didn't just get out. I went into the military and saw… well, a bunch of officers on power trips, really. I put together the puzzle pieces between them and my old man and had my lightbulb moment, and that was great for me."

"It was," Lucius murmured. "Don't make the lightbulb moment small, Chuck. Figuring out who you don't want to be is sometimes more important than thinking you know who you *do* want to be."

Chuck grunted and lowered his lips to drop a kiss on Lucius's crown. How had he remained so sweet? It was a mystery, but one Chuck was content to plumb at another time.

"Well, funny you should say that," he said, thinking this story wasn't funny at all. "Because when I got back from deployment, I was staying at a hotel, sleeping off the ride home, to be honest. And I got word that my folks had died. My sister, Daphne, managed to get hold of me, and she was a mess. 'Cause me and Daphne may have missed out on the asshole gene, but our older brother, Kevin?"

"Not so much?" Lucius filled in.

"Daphne had been staying with Mom and Dad because *her* kid's father was just like our father, and she was trying to get her son away from that fucking cycle. So she told Kevin that I was coming to the house after the funeral, and he… he lost his shit, exactly like Dad would do, and was in the middle of throwing her and her kid out on the street when I got there and broke Kevin's jaw."

Lucius sucked a breath in through his teeth. "Can't say it was a *bad* solution," he temporized.

"Not one I was proud of," Chuck told him honestly. "But it did buy us three days to get enough money to buy the rest of the house from the bank. I left the after-party before the nice neighbors called the cops, and went to a bar to drink and think." He was planning to skip the bartender part there, because the bartender was like pretty much every hookup he'd ever had, besides Car-Car. Sweet, enjoyable, but ultimately as uninterested in strings as Chuck had been. Certainly not as important as the man Chuck was holding right now, listening avidly to how Chuck had ended up here in his bed.

"What did you think about?" Lucius asked.

"Well, I thought about how the bartender had nice eyes," he said, deciding on honesty because lying about this would make it more important than it was. "And he told me to think about waiting for him after his shift. But before that, he pointed me in the direction of four idiots who were trying to get killed robbing a bank in two days."

"And there you had it," Lucius said softly. "Money. Quickly."

"True story." Usually when he used those words, they were facetious or laughing—a way to make light of a life that was not always pretty. But now they had a different ring to them. This was the unvarnished truth, and if Lucius had any regrets after this, Chuck had only himself to blame for bringing his sorry ass to the table.

"So the heist went well?" Lucius asked, and maybe it had been hanging out with the Salinger crew in recent weeks, but Lucius sounded excited about the prospect.

"Like clockwork, thanks to yours truly." Chuck grunted. "I wish I could say I was kidding, but seriously, these yoyos were going to end up dead. When my plan worked—and they all saw that the leader's plan would have gotten them killed—the leader got pissed and took off, but I'd made my nut, see? I could pretty much make the rules when I joined a crew, and one of the first rules was that nobody gets hurt. I made it fucking clear. I'd crack safes, I'd haul loot, I'd drive like a bat out of hell, but the minute a gun got drawn on a civilian and fired, I would not only take off, I'd drive to the local police department and drop the dime on my crew, even if I had to serve twenty-five to life alongside them. I wasn't doing murder. There were so many better ways to rob a bank, you know what I mean?"

"I do," Lucius murmured. "Maybe not my code, but it's a code. Is that how you got recruited into the Salingers?"

Chuck snorted and unconsciously pulled him closer. "Naw. I had my fun doing banks for a while, got pulled from crew to crew. They were puzzles, especially with the nobody-gets-hurt clause, and not a bad way to make money. I lived simple, invested, spent my off hours figuring out how *that* scam worked, and started making more money legally than illegally. And I was seriously thinking about throwing in the towel. Then I got pulled to Texas."

"Why?" Lucius queried, and he turned slightly, aligning their bodies underneath the coverlet, twining their legs together, making sure Chuck wasn't going anywhere.

Chuck was so damned grateful, he almost forgot what the question was about.

"Why was I thinking about quitting or why was I in Texas?"

"Mm." Lucius sounded... well, replete. Satisfied. And at the same time, interested when he spoke next. "Both. Why quit, and why go to Texas?"

"Well, I liked Texas," Chuck said, sounding surprised. "Lived there till I was ten or twelve and the old

man got transferred to Ohio. I wanted to see if the bar-
becue was as good as I remembered, if Austin was as
liberal, if the people were as friendly."

"Then why quit?"

"Because…." Chuck had to chew on this for a moment. "I wasn't doing anybody any good. I had my sister set up for life. Had my*self* getting close to the same.
I was doing something dangerous for no particular reason other than I liked the thrill of it. But I could have
been flying supplies to disaster zones and getting the
same thrill, so I figured it was getting time to quit and
find myself another line of work. But then there was
Texas and—" He swallowed. "—Carmichael Carmody.
The guy I let down."

Lucius's hand came up to stroke his chest, and
Chuck captured it, kissed his palm. Took his silence,
his touch, for permission to go on.

"I was going to say no to the job," he said, remembering that moment with Wilber Forth, Klamath
Jones, and Angus and Scooter Carmichael. "Wilber
and Klamath did not fill me with confidence, and they
were the leaders, and Angus and Scooter were dumb
as a gift box of full diapers. I actually watched Scooter
fall down once because he couldn't watch something in
the sky and keep his mouth closed. I was in *awe* of his
stupidity. And I could see it in their eyes. Wilber and
Klamath would have brought guns to a safe-cracking
and expected to be able to threaten—or kill—anyone
who got in their way. I did not want any part of that."

"But you went," Lucius said, because anyone with
half an ear could hear this was the way the story was
leading.

"Car-Car. Carmichael Carmody, Angus and Scooter's little brother. He was our mechanic, and he was

going to go to be a good little soldier—not because he was a criminal, but because his business, a car repair shop, was about to go under—mostly because his brothers had been stealing from him. He had a wife, he had three kids, and he had—" Chuck swallowed again. "—the loneliest eyes I had ever seen in my life."

Lucius tried to pull his hand away, to unlace their fingers. "Oh," he said softly.

"No, not like that," Chuck said in irritation, reclaiming his hand. "I mean, yeah, we did the thing—"

"Became lovers," Lucius corrected, and Chuck had to take a deep breath in order to name it right.

"Became lovers," he accepted. "And I was telling myself that I was doing it for him. His eyes, man. This was *not* the liberal part of Texas, and he was going to get himself killed if he didn't get rid of some of that energy with someone who wouldn't beat the crap out of him. I told him, flat out, I was not the guy he could leave his family for, and you want to know what he said?"

"What?" Lucius whispered, sounding hurt.

"He said he couldn't leave his family, period. Leave his wife, who never did any harm to anybody, but kept loving him through a failed business and all the shit his brothers gave him? Leave his kids, whom he loved more than life? No. He wasn't going to do it. I mean, never mind that if he'd tried to come out, someone in his pissant town would have killed him. Never mind that his brothers would have been the first in line. He'd married his best friend from high school, and he cared about the girl, and he'd helped make the babies, and he was going to do right by those people. So it was... a couple of nights, really. Doomed before we started. And I was fine with that. We do the bank job, Car-Car keeps his business, I leave him with some beautiful memories, and my conscience is clean, right?"

"Sure it is," Lucius murmured, and Chuck had to take a couple of deep breaths. His throat had closed up and his eyes were burning. This was hard, so much harder than he'd even imagined it being, and he'd been avoiding it in a bad way.

"Except me and Car-Car are back in the office of the garage the night before the heist, and we hear Wilber and Klamath plotting as they disable the vehicle I'm supposed to be driving the next day. They're pretty canny about it. The car will get us to the place, but it's not going anywhere after I keep it in idle for twenty minutes, so we'll be screwed. And while they're doing that, they talk about how they're going to change the plan—guns out, civilians at risk, because how else can they take me and the Carmody brothers out, then get away while the cops are cleaning up the mess, right?"

Lucius gasped. "So did you call off the job?"

Chuck shook his head. "No. We couldn't. There was no reason for me and Car-Car to be in that office other than for what we were doing. And if Car-Car went to his brothers, they wouldn't believe him. They… they really hated him. It was like they knew he was better than they were or something, but that hatred ran deep. And if he outed himself, he'd get killed. And he wouldn't leave. I begged him to, but he knew that if he did, his wife, his kids, they wouldn't just be out on the street, they'd be at the mercy of Wilber and Klamath and his brothers. No, he was right. We didn't have a choice."

"What happened?" Lucius asked. "Is Car-Car…?" He hesitated, the horror and compassion in his eyes eloquent.

"Alive," Chuck said, to put him out of his misery. "He and his brothers are alive. I was supposed to help move the money from the back of the bank to Wilber and Klamath's car, which I did. Then me and the Carmody brothers were supposed to get away in our sabotaged car. Wilber and Klamath went back in the bank, supposedly for that last round. But I'd called the cops—they didn't know that. I had an old army buddy who was a SWAT team member, and I knew he was on the roof. He trusted me. I told him exactly where Wilber and Klamath would be standing in thirty seconds. Then I texted the Carmodys to get the fuck down, and they listened. And I took off when the cops were rushing in."

"You left Carmichael behind?" Lucius asked, and even though there wasn't any recrimination in his voice, there was enough in Chuck's heart to go around.

"I did," Chuck said, voice thick. "I... it was the plan, right? And he and his brothers went to jail, him for two years, his brothers for five apiece. I was in Chicago by the time of the trial, but I did buy them a damned good lawyer. And I put their share of the take into investments, laundered it good, multiplied its value by ten, and sent them the codes to their entire portfolios. I sent Car-Car's to his wife, made sure she had an investment counselor so she could keep the business going and not get ripped off buying the nice house. All the shit I'd done for my sister, I did for Car-Car's family. Swear-ta-god, even his mother got a new house and a new car, and that woman was *not* the reason Car-Car wasn't an asshole, believe me."

"And you haven't forgiven yourself for it," Lucius murmured.

Chuck took a deep, shaky breath and turned his head so he could use the end of a pillowcase to wipe his cheeks. Goddammit. God*dammit.* He liked this man. He *cared* for this man. And here he was, telling the one story that was guaranteed to send Lucius screaming into the night.

Except he wasn't screaming, and Chuck felt like he had to finish, because that was the least Chuck could do.

"I came to Chicago to be someone besides Good Luck Chuck," he confessed. "But I met Josh Salinger, and… and he was so playful, you know? I was moving an asshole's car in the parking garage to fuck with him because he'd been mean to a professor when he should have been respectful. And Josh caught me because Josh was on the way to leave fish in the guy's car."

Lucius gave a surprised snort of laughter against his chest.

"Right? I mean, yeah, it's a little bit of destruction of property, but Josh had needed to get his dad involved to keep the poor professor from quitting. And the guy was so sweet. I mean, I looked at that professor, and I saw a sixty-year-old Carmichael, all good intentions and hard work, and he needed someone to look out for him, right?"

"I get it," Lucius said, and his eyes were shiny as they took in Chuck's face. Chuck didn't know what to make of that, but he raised his thumb to stroke Lucius's cheekbone, then went on.

"So we both set out to screw the guy over in a way that was karmic but not dangerous. And Josh and me—and Grace, because, you know, brothers, the good kind—we went out for pizza. And I met Stirling and Molly and we did a few other jobs. Not big. A little breaking and entering to help a few good causes. Nothing malicious, you know? And then Josh's dad got in trouble, and Josh pulled us all together. And for a little while, I was able to pretend I was a good guy."

Lucius sighed. "You *are* a good guy, Charles," he said softly. "You're one of the best. All of Josh Salinger's people—you've done a lot of good in my life alone, not to mention other people. If I had to hire a real security company to help me, they wouldn't have accomplished what you have, and I wouldn't have been able to trust them as much as I trust you."

Chuck blew out a breath. "Well, I'm sure that makes Car-Car happy in prison," he said bleakly.

Lucius buried his face against Chuck's shoulder and let out a muffled scream of frustration. "Charles, tell me this—this one thing—yes?"

"Shoot."

"Did you mean it? When you told your bank crews you would turn them in and serve your sentence right alongside them if they hurt a civilian?"

"Every word," Chuck said, feeling irritable about it. "You don't make that sort of threat to real criminals and not mean it. They will know, and if you don't mean it, they've got you by the balls."

Lucius nodded. "So you executed your bank jobs with the full knowledge that you could have gone to jail at any time."

"Yeah. So?"

"Do you think Carmichael didn't know that?"

Chuck let out a breath, remembering their last night together, how he'd been almost tearful trying to convince Car-Car not to go to prison.

"He knew," Chuck said softly. "He knew."

"He sounds like a decent man," Lucius said softly. "And you have done as much right as you could. There was a reason you were getting out of the business, Charles, and the potential for collateral damage was obviously it. And you didn't go back to robbing banks, or even breaking the law as a profession. You went back to school, and then you went to something you are...." The almost elfin look of mischief on Lucius's face shot an arrow through Chuck's heart right then and there, killing any thoughts he may have had about running away from this relationship.

"I'm what?" he asked, besotted and charmed.

"Uniquely qualified for," Lucius told him, his eyes crinkling in delight.

"You," Chuck said gruffly. "I am uniquely qualified for you."

"Oh, you are indeed," Lucius said, raising his mouth for a kiss.

They went a little slower this time, were a little more playful, did a little less screaming and a little more sighing.

And in the end, when Chuck shifted his hips just right, hitting Lucius in that place that made his eyes roll back in his head and his entire body stutter, Chuck's body clenched in a release that scalded him from the inside out and made him feel brand new.

This time, when he caught his breath and Lucius kissed his neck, his jaw, his shoulders, comforting him in the aftermath of losing themselves in sex, he allowed the comfort to seep in. As he and Lucius rolled to face each other, to talk about nothing more than kissing and gentle things, he thought, with wonder, that he had finally fallen in love.

Midnight Snacks

CHUCK'S STOMACH woke Lucius up.

They'd been pleasantly dozing, the afterglow almost luminescing off their skin, when Chuck's stomach let out an unholy ruckus, apparently announcing that not only had they missed dinner, but that a couple of bacon-and-fig-wrapped shrimp were not going to cut it after the evening they'd had.

"Sorry," Chuck rumbled, and Lucius slid out of bed, pausing to plant a really excellent kiss on Chuck as he went.

"Not a problem. I'll go down and fix us something."

"No, no. No worries." Chuck struggled to sit up, but the slowness of his movements reminded Lucius that he and Hunter had been basically working eighteen-hour days and spending their few hours in bed with one eye open. "I'll—" Yawn. "—come with you!"

Lucius laughed softly. "Stay right there," he commanded. "Let me tend to you. You can do that, right?"

Chuck yawned hugely again and settled back into the pillows. "I can do that," he said with a crooked smile. "Don't want to impose."

"You're not." Lucius searched his face with troubled eyes, wondering if that urge to back away—to run away—that he'd seen in Chuck before, was going to surface again. It didn't look like it. Not now. So Lucius would take that as a good sign. "I'll be back in a moment," he murmured.

He slid on a pair of underwear, because he was *not* the guy who could wander around his own house naked. His own room, possibly, when he had a lover, but the entire house? No.

He found Chuck's dress shirt on the ground by the bathroom, and he slid that on too, liking it much better than the satin robe, which he'd apparently left downstairs.

Which reminded him... where had he put his cell phone again?

He tried to retrace his steps, ending up in the living room, where he'd stripped down hurriedly and donned the robe because Newman Damar was pounding on his door.

"There you are," he murmured to himself, throwing the clothes haphazardly over the back of the couch and lamenting that his starched, pressed tuxedo was past rumpled. He could look at the phone while he was waiting for leftovers to warm. He snagged the cell phone—and his wallet—and carried them into the kitchen, where he put on coffee and started raiding the fridge for the container of angel-hair pasta that had been left over from lunch. And that's where he was, at the entrance of the kitchen, when the entire world marched into his house.

"Hello?" came a voice, sweetly feminine and yet steely just the same.

"Oh dear Lord!" Lucius whirled, clutching Chuck's shirt around his narrower chest in an embarrassing show of maidenly modesty.

"Oh, Lucius!" Julia said, coming into the kitchen in a swirl of pale blue taffeta and a silk tasseled wrap. "There you are. Is something wrong with your phone? We've been trying to let you know that we were on our way for the past hour."

Lucius's eyes widened enough to dry out. "Phone," he croaked, looking at the offending object on his counter. All it had said was that he'd had texts. He hadn't expected those texts to say that the world was about to end up in his kitchen.

And it really *was* the world.

"Lucius?" Josh said hoarsely behind his mother. Then, "Dad, put me down. This is so embarrassing."

"It's wonderful," Felix said, following Julia as she pushed in through the door that adjoined the dining room and set his son's feet on the tiled floor. "I haven't had you fall asleep on me like that since you were seven."

"Oh God," Josh groaned. "I can't wait to be done with chemo. I'm so sick of this shit!"

"Well, yes, us too."

"Benjamin?" Lucius said in surprise. "You're here too?"

"Now, now," Benjamin Morgan said, "remember, to family I'm Uncle Danny." His tired golden eyes still managed to twinkle. "Stirling? Carl? You're coming in too?"

"I'm starving," Stirling said bluntly. "Is there any more of that pasta stuff in there? Cheri said she'd make extra." He sighed. "I like her. Makes me wish I was straight."

"You could just have her as a friend," Carl pointed out.

"Yes, but I have trouble getting boyfriends. It would be easier if I could just sleep with the people I get along with."

Stirling huffed down on one of the stools that sat around the center marble-topped island, and Josh joined him.

"Yeah," he said, resting his chin on his hands. "I get that. But I wouldn't know what to do with girl parts, so I must hope for boyfriends."

"Are you making a snack?" Julia asked wistfully. "I'm afraid none of us got a chance to eat, either. Where's Chuck? Did he already eat?"

"No," Lucius said weakly. "I was actually getting something together for the two of us, but if someone wants to help me here, I think we've got sandwich fixings and some of the meatloaf from the other night. We can pull together a midnight feast in short order."

It was then he became aware they were all taking him in. The shirt that did not actually fit, the briefs, the coffee brewing, the two plates set up on the counter.

"Or," Danny said delicately, "we could all piss off and leave you and Chuck to finish your evening."

And for a moment, Lucius was tempted to take him up on it, because he'd *had* Chuck to himself, and it had been wonderful.

But in the next breath, he realized that never—not once—since he'd taken a lover, had anybody in his life wanted the details, or even cared who he'd been with. Yes, there'd been friends who'd asked, "How are you doing? Are you seeing anyone?" but that was different.

This entire kitchen full of people seemed to like him—and seemed to be happy for him and Chuck, and he hadn't had that in… well, ever.

"Well, our evening has been wonderful," Lucius said, feeling his cheeks heat, "but we were at the point where a midnight nosh in the kitchen sounded like a good idea. I've got coffee brewing, I can heat all the pasta, and if someone wants to drag the sandwich fixings out and generally raid the fridge, I can go, uhm…."

"Put on some pants?" Carl asked dryly. "I think that sounds like a fabulous idea." He grimaced. "Well, partly because we've got work to discuss, but also because, you know. This group can get into your business, but seeing you in your skivvies in the kitchen is a little too personal, right?"

Lucius smiled, grateful. "Pajamas at the very least," he said, before abandoning the kitchen to whomever felt best suited to cook and running upstairs to dress.

He found Julia accompanying him, shedding her elegant high-heeled dancing slippers as she bounced lightly up the stairs.

"I need to put on comfortable clothes," she confessed. "I suspect Felix will slip out and put on his own pajamas when I'm done. Danny, the rat, has on his thief clothes because they're comfortable, which pisses me off to no end. Felix and I used to come home from functions in clothes and shoes meant to cripple us, and Danny would be home with Josh, wearing basketball shorts and a T-shirt, happy as a clam."

"He does seem very adept at staying out of sight," Lucius told her, and she grimaced.

"Yes, well, that's the flip side to that long con we ran for ten years. The great thing about him and Felix being out is that he's forced to wear the horribly un-comfortable uniform sometimes too. Including the shoes, which, I gather, are slippery as fuck. It drives him nuts when he can't move."

Lucius chuckled, loving the three of them more and more. They reached the landing to the guest bed-rooms, and she paused before peeling off to where she and Josh had been staying.

"Lucius, forgive me for prying, but, about Chuck?"

Lucius nodded, feeling as though this was import-ant. "Yes?"

"We would be very charmed to have you in our family. We understand that you may not be ready to engage in our little hobbies, yes, but it seems Chuck has a place here with your own little hobby, and we're very happy to share time with him."

Lucius's cheeks were on *fire*. "I'll… uhm, propose that to him," he said. "If he's ready when this job is done."

"Do," Julia said, her eyes serious. "Because hap-piness is particularly fleeting, sweetheart. Grab it while you can."

And with that, she went into her room, leaving Lucius wishing he could do something for the love-ly woman whose eyes were incredibly sad. He got to his suite and found Chuck struggling into a T-shirt while looking fruitlessly around for a pair of pants that *weren't* his dress suit. He was sopping with sweat.

"I've got some pajamas that will be fine," Lucius said, coming in and closing the door. "And if you want-ed to keep us a secret from your friends, I'm guessing it's a little late."

Chuck dropped the suit pants and covered his eyes with his hand. "God. No. Tell me."

"They're all downstairs, fixing a midnight snack and getting ready to debrief."

Chuck let out a snort. "I'd say we'd already 'debriefed,' wouldn't you?"

Lucius laughed slightly and walked to his dresser, where he pulled out two pairs of pajama bottoms, both of them cut short. "Here," he said. "They're loose on me, which may hopefully make them not cut off your circulation."

Chuck's body—while impressively muscled—wasn't slender or trim by any means. Still, Chuck slid the pajama bottoms on and then one of Lucius's largest T-shirts, and Lucius did the same. They were about to venture back downstairs again, to the strains of the "Anvil Chorus" emanating from Chuck's increasingly demanding digestive track, when Chuck paused at the door, much like Julia had only moments earlier.

"They're, uhm, okay with us?" he asked hesitantly.

"They are," Lucius said. He kissed Chuck on the cheek. "They're even ready to share custody of you, if you find you have things here you'd like to do."

Chuck looked puzzled. "Like what?"

"Like teach yoga and self-defense to women who really, really love your classes, for one," Lucius said. Then his eyes darkened. "And to be here after work, sometimes, to do some more of what we just did." He saw Chuck's surprise and shook his head. "Think about it, Charles. It's not a ball and chain—merely a relationship. We should be able to make it work just fine."

And with that he led the way downstairs.

Going with the Flowchart

CHUCK SAT at Lucius's dining room table, huddled with the others around Danny's tablet.

Danny had made a bad-guy flowchart, and he seemed very proud of it. Ignoring all that work would have seemed rude.

"So, children," Danny said, sitting at the far end of the table as though he was teaching, "what we have here are three different groups of bad guys, and we need to deal with them in three different kinds of ways."

"And a mole," Stirling blurted, before ducking back into himself and looking at Josh unhappily. "That needs to be said, right? A mole?"

"Yes," Josh told him. "But we need to know which group of bad guys has the mole."

"Okay," Stirling murmured, and then looked back at Danny. "Sorry!"

Chuck noted that Danny appeared to have a true soft spot for Stirling, and it seemed to be working because the boy had really come out of his shell during this adventure.

"No sorrys," Danny said fondly. "You're both right. There is a mole—"

"Is it someone who works there?" Chuck surmised. "I mean, that would make sense, since they seem to have the surveillance worked out."

"The only people who have that access are Lisa and Tara-Lynn," Lucius said. "I mean, we're not suspecting them, are we?"

Chuck had tried to be suspicious of the two of them, but he couldn't wrap his head around it. Tara-Lynn, a survivor of heinous abuse herself, was not going to coldly laser open the fence protecting the people in her care. And Lisa Sampson was tough and seemingly earnest as hell.

"No," he said, after a moment. "Because every fiber in my being says those two women are as straight as they come." He smirked, thinking of their ready acceptance of everybody in the crew. "But not narrow."

"One of the residents, then," Lucius murmured. "That's harder. Unlike poor Larry, who was young and duped, we'd have to look at someone who was only pretending to be scared. We'd have to look at their lives outside the shelter—"

"Which is why we have the flowchart," Danny said, his patience obviously wearing thin. "Once we get this flowchart analyzed, we might be able to figure out who it is."

"Good point," Stirling told him. "Thank you. Keep going."

With anyone else in the crew, that might have gotten a tart response, but Danny's impatience relaxed, and he beamed at the younger man, then did as he'd requested.

"So we have three groups." Danny pointed to a cluster of names in a red blob that was shaped like an arrow, pointed directly at the words "Caraway House."

"See this one? These are the goons that attacked the house tonight, and that Clive person who is going to prison for a very long time because of his visit two nights before. The goons tonight were here for one reason only—to get Chester Damar's girlfriend back. Getting his mother would have been a perk, but as far as we can tell, their entire endeavor this whole time has been to get his poor girlfriend back so he can beat her to death the way he beat to death his high school sweetheart."

The whole table sucked in a harsh breath.

"Did that really happen?" Chuck asked. He'd heard Chet's buddy Randy say it, but it had all been supposition.

Danny and Felix exchanged glances. "Yes," Danny said softly. "Hunter took the goons to the FBI headquarters. It only took about ten minutes of talking to Randy—and then questioning Chester 'Chet' Damar—to discover that Chet had, indeed, killed Lara Flannagan when they were in high school. Randy was so heartbroken, he turned state's evidence. For some reason, he seemed to think he was going to be flown to Antarctica and left in his underwear, but Hunter was assured he'd be taken very good care of in WITSEC. The other goons, also police officers, unlike Randy, who just had the bad luck to be Chet's buddy, are being held on suspicion of breaking and entering a secure facility and aiding an attempted kidnapping. Hunter and Grace are on their way back here."

"Why not Chicago?" Chuck asked, glancing around the table.

"'Cause they're not done yet," Josh told him, rolling his eyes. "Same reason we're all here."

"So we had the boots-on-the-ground bad guys," Lucius redirected. "Who's the next layer?"

"The layer helpfully labeled in blue," Danny said facetiously, and Chuck was not the only person at the table who rolled their eyes.

"Yes, yes, I know," Danny continued, with all the good nature of someone who was holding a strategy meeting at midnight. "But I did that for a reason. These are the middlemen. These are the petty little pissants who are sabotaging Lucius's company and hacking his security. They're getting the goons in, and they're giving the next group access to the money, but they're not the big thinkers. They're the mean children—or I should say, the mean teenagers. We very recently carted the mean *children* off to FBI headquarters to face abduction and murder charges out of state so that Newman Damar isn't tipped off, and neither are any of the people here in the green category. But do you notice anything about this blue group?"

"It's only three names?" Josh hazarded.

"Indeed yes," Danny said. "Chuck, anything else?"

Chuck let out a low laugh and caught Lucius's happy grin over his shoulder.

And Chuck had an epiphany.

Lucius *loved* this.

Chuck had been so worried about Lucius accepting Chuck as a criminal, it hadn't occurred to Chuck that Lucius was *thrilled* to be part of the Salinger crew.

It made sense. Lucius's childhood had been lonely, but more than that, Lucius had nobody—*nobody*—in whom to confide. Not now, not ever. His peers were all businessmen, and of them, he apparently only trusted Linus. Everyone else he knew, every man and woman who ran in his circles, was suspect. Was this an abuser?

Was this person? Was this woman abused? Did Lucius need to watch out for her? Was this man a threat to his operation? None of his peers were really *peers.*

And none of them understood the lengths Lucius would go to in order to keep women like his mother, and children like himself and his brother, safe.

Lucius had been breaking laws all along. He'd been forging false identities, hiding women from their abusive families, lying to his entire peer group about his activities. He was, in essence, a vigilante. And vigilantes didn't get a peer group unless they were in comic books and had to fight aliens.

And *un*like a vigilante, Lucius had never wanted to work alone.

This midnight nosh in his house wasn't just putting up with a bunch of guests he hadn't asked for, it was getting to work with friends who seemed to understand his entire world.

Wobbling a little on his axis, Chuck returned Lucius's grin with his best million-dollar smile and slid a possessive hand along the small of Lucius's back.

Lucius really was one of them. Chuck may need to split his time between *locations* to be with Lucius, but he didn't need to split his *life* in two. As long as he and the Salingers stuck to the same moral code they'd had all along, there didn't need to be any secrets from Lucius. And he'd probably be happy to help.

"Chuck?" Danny prompted, reminding Chuck that his mind was needed on the job at hand.

"These are the three assholes with fish in their cars," Chuck said. "These three fuckers were the ones who beat up their girlfriends as some sort of bet. They graduated, and their girlfriends all ended up trying to do yoga without having PTSD."

"Yes," Danny agreed. "This one right here—in yellow highlighter—his name is Fergus Allen."

"Fergus?" Chuck asked, surprised. "I've never known a Fergus."

"Well, now you've put fish and a tracker in his car," Danny returned pleasantly. "Anyway, Fergus here got a job at Broadstone Industries in June. As you surmised, Lucius, it was very legit. Your company headhunted him in April, offered him the best package, and he took the job. When did he put his girlfriend in the hospital?"

"End of April," Lucius said, which told Chuck he'd been studying up on his residents. "Why?"

"Because it would fit. His friends Ethan Potts and Andrew Keller both got their futures handed to them in the same month. Ethan in law enforcement under…."

"Newman Damar," Lucius breathed.

"Yes, indeed. And Andrew as an investment banker. Anybody have a guess?"

"I've got this one!" Stirling said excitedly. "Fielding Stans. One of the three businesses that keeps buying Lucius's stock every time something bad happens."

"Winner winner chicken dinner!" Danny cried happily. "Yes, folks, there you have it. We have the three middlemen hacking into Lucius's security to A) set it up to be broken into by Ethan's friends in law enforcement, and B) set Lucius up to be bought out by the policemen's, doctors' and teachers' pension, thanks to Kyle Miller, the state senator from Ohio, and Fielding Stans, who probably doesn't know what the hell is going on but is proud of their junior executive for being able to pick a stock that's selling low now but looks like it will bounce back."

"All of which," Felix said, "paves the way for our bad guys in green."

Danny nodded. "Yes indeed. Green for the money people, and green for the power." He came around to the screen to wave his finger at the green section of the arrow, the one furthest removed from Caraway House, but the one that carried the most force against it.

"Kyle Miller and Newman Damar are the only two names here, but there should be a third."

"We did notice the big gold question marks, Danny," Julia said dryly. She was dressed in yoga pants and one of Felix's old shirts, and her hair was pulled away from her face in a messy gold ponytail. Chuck thought wistfully that he would so have hit on her if he'd been straight, because damn, what a stunning human being.

But then Lucius shifted under his hand and Chuck was no longer wistful. Julia was loved. She seemed content. She would find a lover—or not—but nobody could say she didn't live her life on her own terms.

"Yes," Danny said. "And I can't tell you why. All I can tell you is that my grifter sense is tingling. We've got somebody at Caraway House giving information—someone who carved a hole in the fence to make it easier to give out information and left that poor Larry kid a phone. And we know that none of our identified assholes are beloved by any of their victims. Somebody in Caraway House has an attachment to somebody here." Danny waved his finger around the green section again. "It has to be here. The blue section is being directed, and none of the guys telling them what to do are goons. I suspect when Hunter gets back, we'll discover that Chet and Randy were in charge of the other attempts on the fence, and Chet pulled in reinforcements tonight because…."

There was a moment of silence while they all thought. "Because somebody told him that Lucius and one of the new security people would be gone!" Felix said excitedly.

"Yes!" Danny grinned at him, the game giving them both a sort of glow. "And Newman Damar may have been claiming to be chasing his son's police cruiser, but it's not like they were on broadband saying 'Breaking into Lucius Broadstone's private property. Wish me luck getting my battered girlfriend back'! Somebody *told them* things were going cattywampus. So Kyle Miller and Newman Damar are being given information by somebody they don't have a connection to."

"Odds are good it's a woman," Julia murmured, deep into the game as well. "Why would a woman report to her abuser?"

"Maybe he promised her something?" Josh said, and both Danny and Julia shook their heads.

"Those promises are useless," Julia said. "If these people—this woman—had a safe place and a chance for a new life, she was beyond promises. Promises are for the time when there's hope for reform. By the time you crash a car through a gate because you're passing out from blood loss, it's too late for that sort of hope."

She was talking about the police chief's wife, Chuck knew, but it sparked an idea in him. In all his classes, only one woman had taken his corrections for granted, even asking him to fix her form.

"Wait a minute," Chuck said, as something that had been niggling at the back of his mind suddenly started wiggling to the forefront. "What kind of pensions does that one investment firm manage?"

"Doctors, policemen, teachers—"

"Doctors," Chuck said grimly. "Doctors."

"What?" Lucius asked, turning toward him in surprise.

"Well," Chuck muttered, "namas-fucking-te."

"What?" Lucius repeated, and Chuck fumbled for words that would make sense.

"First of all, answer me this. Why isn't Molly in on this conversation?"

"Because she had to remain at the shelter so she didn't blow her cover," Julia answered, frowning.

"Yes. But why isn't she on a tablet or a computer or something?"

"Because those devices are strictly monitored," Lucius replied. "And cell phone usage is restricted. It's essentially a dead zone, except for certain hot spots so people can do internet searches with supervision."

Chuck nodded. "That's why Clive had to intimidate poor Larry when Larry came out of the hole in the fence. Larry was escaping to tell his shitty boyfriend that he was okay, and it turns out that his shitty boyfriend really just wanted to pound his face in." Chuck paused. "And I know who his shitty boyfriend is. You know, right, Lucius?"

Lucius looked away. "Yes."

"It's Kyle Miller, right? He put his wife in the hospital, and his boyfriend said, 'Well good, we can be together,' and...."

"And he put Larry in the hospital too," Lucius said softly. "Larry knows she's there. I had to have that conversation before he was admitted. He... he seemed very content to let her and her children find their own way back out into the world, and he would find his."

"Fair enough," Chuck said. It wasn't—it seemed as though the wife should have the full story—but then,

Larry needed Lucius's help too. "So they were smart about it. Kyle and Newman Damar end up in some sort of soiree—I mean, they were both in the same room tonight, and I'll bet they end up in the same room a lot of times. Lucius? Felix? The odds on that?"

"No bet," Felix said flatly. "There are people I loathe that I have ended up drinking with for hours, because dammit, we're stuck there and somebody provided scotch."

"Lucius?"

Lucius's cheeks grew pink. "I've, uhm—"

"Slept with guys like that." Josh laughed softly. "Look at his face. He totally has."

Chuck grinned at him. "Lucius, I forgive you. But you illustrated my point. Social functions make strange bedfellows. So there's Kyle Miller and Newman Damar, knocking back a few. Hell, their fathers probably knew each other, because that's the way money runs. And they're assholes. They're gonna start bitching about the wives. Damar's probably lamenting his son's girlfriend, his other kid, who just needs a boot to knock the straight into him, and the ungrateful wife. Kyle's like, uhm-hm. Preach. Anyway, so there they are, shooting the shit, and this is the fuzzy part—sort of. Kyle and I went to Ohio State, and our three frat boys with their cute little bet did too. I don't know about you guys, but I didn't even graduate from Ohio State, and I had their fliers follow me until I got out of the military."

"And that nice Senator Miller would most certainly speak to his alma mater," Lucius said. "Scumbags seem to have no problem finding their own, do they?"

"No, they don't," Danny said thoughtfully. "So, I see what you're saying. At some point, our third contact was in on one of these conversations. And he said, 'Wait, it can't be a coincidence that we can't find these women. I'll bet we can send somebody under-cover.' And they do, just like we sent Molly in. Lu-cius, you've spoken several times about nurses. That's probably their point of entry, and...." Danny looked at Chuck and his fox-shaped features lit up. "And *doctors*. That's what you meant, isn't it, Chuck? A prominent doctor who would be at these functions, and who also might intersect with the nurses who have been helping women find Lucius!"

"*Exactly*!" Chuck punctuated his excitement with a fist pump. "Exactly. And that third investor, he's with the pension fund. Funds law enforcement and medical professionals."

"That's it," Lucius murmured. "That's our three-pronged attack. That's where everyone is coming from. *That's who we're dealing with*!"

"Oh yes, it is," Danny agreed, and Chuck could feel it—the collective electricity as the crew took its breath, and the hope rising like the hair on the back of their arms as they realized that now that they knew who they were dealing with, they could formulate a plan.

"Okay," Felix murmured, stalking like a lion back and forth behind the table. "O*kay*. So now we're get-ting somewhere. But we've got three different groups of people and three different crimes. How are we going to pull this all together?"

"In three different ways, of course," Julia said thoughtfully, leaning forward and tapping her lower lip with her finger. She glanced sideways at Carl, who was polishing off the last of the pasta. "What do you think?"

Carl grunted. "I think we got the red group by ship-ping them off to Quantico," he said, swallowing the last bit. "And I think the blue group is going to be making a big move soon. As in, Lucius, I'd have your security guards run extra laps tomorrow—"

"Tomorrow's Saturday!" Lucius said, surprised.

"Yes, exactly. And I know you've got a lot of people coming in on Saturday, but it's still no more than a quarter full. Once Damar realizes his son has disappeared, he's going to put pressure on Fergus, his inside man, to do something. And he and Miller and our doctor friend are going to be in position to clean up on Monday because something has gone horribly wrong."

"Wow," Lucius muttered. "Has anyone told you you're a buzzkill?"

"Only every human I've ever dated," Carl returned dourly.

"That's not true!" Danny protested, and Chuck felt compelled to add, "I totally never said that."

Carl glared at them both. "You both suck. And no, that's not a double entendre because obviously you're with other people. But I'm telling you, I don't know what shape the next attack is coming in, but it'll likely be soon, on-site, at Broadstone Industries."

"I'll alert Linus and the security company after we're done," Lucius said, nodding. "Stirling, if you can tell Linus how to track Fergus's vehicle?"

Stirling nodded, but there was so much more to do.

"Okay," Chuck said, "so that means we need to hurry. I know Stirling's got alarms in place, but Carl's right. It may not be late tonight because those guys were already hitting the bar before we hit their cars, but yeah. It's coming soon. Anyway—there is a woman at Caraway House who was supposedly hit once by her husband, who's a doctor, and she put pressure on a nurse to help her get out of there. Her version of the story is that she's waiting until he comes back from a vacation with the current girlfriend before she hits him up for divorce, but…." Chuck breathed out. "I wasn't buying her brand of defensiveness. And it's not that I don't think a woman who's been beaten up wouldn't harass the shit out of the hired help as a way to restore power over her life. But this was different. This wasn't a woman who was waiting for the next blow to land."

"Marla Crandall," Lucius said, again not consulting his notes. "I know her. Her husband is Barker Crandall, and yes, he's a topflight plastic surgeon, and he does have a girlfriend that he likes to take to the Bahamas. What makes you think she's involved?"

"Well, for one thing, I don't like her," Chuck said baldly. "When we were looking for a husband who was going to try to batter down the doors to get her out, she wasn't a suspect. But with something like this, where her husband is trying to fatten his portfolio and she's trying to fatten her divorce settlement…."

The others were nodding.

"I say we talk to her tonight," Carl said. He'd finally finished eating, and Chuck was a little jealous. He'd gotten a few bites in, but he'd been so busy talking, he'd never made up for missing dinner.

"Groovy," Chuck said. "Let me go put on some real pants."

"But wait!" Lucius held up a hand. "What… how are we going to get these guys? I don't want to make the women testify, and if they did, there's no guarantee they'd ever be safe again. We know how the law works in this country. The whole reason Caraway House exists still stands."

Danny chuckled, and it was a terrible sound. "No, dear boy, you're right. We certainly want to keep your endeavor here secret and safe. But it doesn't matter if the women come forward at this point, because everyone, from our frat boys to our power brokers, has violated a fantastic number of laws here. Felix, do tell me you still have friends at the Securities and Trade Commission?"

"Oh yes," Felix said, his tone as evil as Danny's. "I do. They love me. All my tax forms are on the up-and-up. I report every source of income, and all of it is legal. Nothing to see here, folks. Now our frat boys, on the other hand...."

"Insider trading at the very least," Danny said.

"But is that enough to get the top three?" Lucius asked, and Chuck rubbed his back gently. The stress, the worry, the need for justice—it was all apparent in his voice.

"Well...," Josh said, obviously thinking in spite of the fact that he was pillowing his head on his arms and nearing the end of his rope. "How about we put Torrance Grayson on their asses."

"Oooh...." The collective opinion seemed impressed, and Lucius clarified, "Grayson the reporter?"

"You've seen him at our house," Josh said through a yawn.

"He *was* a little miffed to be left out of this job," Felix said thoughtfully. "I think that's a good idea. Gray will leave the women out of it, and we've got enough illegal doings that I bet he could have a pretty good piece ready to run by Monday. Industrial sabotage, insider trading, police corruption. It would be fantastic if beating up actual human beings would get him this kind of justice, but usually…." He sighed, and so did the rest of the table. Victim shaming was so common in the press that simply to speak about it would open up a can of worms they didn't have time to scream about right now.

"They don't get what they've done wrong anyway," Julia said, her voice steely. "No, we need to hit them where they *really* hurt. Not with the people in their lives but with their image, their power and their prestige. You were right, Josh. Let's ask Grayson to keep the women out of it, but instead point to the *many* illegal things we know they've done. Maybe Gray's exposé can beat the trap your father was going to set in the stock market."

"How did you know I planned to set a trap in the stock market?" Felix asked gently.

"Does she look like an amateur?" Josh asked, and his parents laughed softly.

"I know you, my darling," Julia said fondly. "Tell me you don't have one planned."

"Oh, I do," Felix said, surprising none of them. "In fact, Lucius, I hope you don't mind, but I put it in motion when we first met you, two months ago."

Lucius frowned. "But how could you even…?"

"Oh! I didn't know what had been going on. You've been very good at keeping your sabotage a secret, which shows that you know about perception and marketing, and I'm very impressed. But I've been quietly putting a bug in the ear of my more affluent friends, and they've been picking up your stock on the regular. The next time it goes up, they'll be ready to buy even more and sell to anyone *but* those other three markets. That will do two things. One is that it will keep our three powerhouses from being able to take control of your company. We'll keep the stock nice and spread out throughout the market and not concentrated in the pockets of your enemies, thank you very much."

"What else will it do?" Chuck asked, curious.

"Probably drive it up," Felix said happily. "I know I set a very high bar for my broker to sell it, and I think my friends have too. So while there might be an initial drop, there will also be scarcity and a scramble for it." He looked at Lucius and smiled happily. "I think you might come out on top of this, my boy."

"Is that even legal?" Stirling asked, sounding confused.

"Probably not," Josh replied. "But it's a lot more ethical than wrecking the company so they can buy Lucius out when the stock tanks. I'm pretty sure Dad's conscience is just fine."

Chuck looked at Lucius soberly. "What about you, Lucius? Is that good for you?"

"Well, my conscience would be clear about it also, if that's what you mean," Lucius replied, but his expression was still sober. "But what if they decide to sell? I hate to think those guys in the green group will make money off of me."

"Well, they won't," Felix said. "Not really. They may make some cash in the short sale of your stock, but remember, they were planning a coup. And I'm pretty sure, with Torrance Grayson's research, their actions will expose them for insider trading, so I don't know how much of that money they'll get to spend."

"Their reputations will be ruined," Danny said. "They'll probably go to prison, since American justice seems to get more upset at the abuse of its money than its citizens. Still, it will be prison all the same. And we'll keep their victims safe. Can we live with that?"

Lucius nodded. "Speaking of keeping the women safe—we should probably meet with Joanie Damar, Heather Miller, and the three girls from Ohio State first thing tomorrow. I'd like to offer them an alternative place to stay...." He trailed off and sighed, scrubbing his hand through his hair, and Chuck realized that this was it. He didn't have a place to offer him.

Chuck caught Julia's eyes, and she stepped in flawlessly.

"And we have the perfect place. I've got a little summer house in Michigan, right off the lake. It's got six or so rooms, which is enough for the girls, and some really topflight security."

"I had to study it for at least a day before I showed up there," Danny said, nodding encouragingly.

Lucius gave him a tired smile. "I assume that's high praise indeed."

"You have no idea," Felix murmured, and he and Danny shared a heated glance that might have made Chuck blush.

"But before that," Chuck said grimly, "Carl and I need to get back to the ranch and have a chat with the namaste lady. That is, if she's not skulking outside the perimeter as we speak, looking for her gap in the fence."

Carl growled. "Gah! You're right. Oh my God, this night will never end!"

"What will we do with her once we get her?" Lucius asked.

"Oh, I'll think of something," Julia said grimly. "A doctor's wife, you say?"

"Yes," Lucius murmured. "Marla Crandall."

"I remember. Wife of Barker Crandall." Julia breathed softly out her nose. "Let me listen in on the interview, but out of sight. There are ways women can punish each other that are incredibly cruel. What she's done may not be classified as illegal, and I don't think she'd do any jail time, but handled the right way, with the right society, I think we can make Marla Crandall wish she'd stayed in her uptown apartment with her personal trainer."

Felix looked at her curiously. "Do I want to know?" he asked.

Julia's smile was as predatory and ruthless as anything Chuck had ever seen. "Let's just say I'm going to hit her where she lives."

Lucius nodded, and in his eyes, Chuck saw the same faith that he himself placed in the Salingers.

"My lady, I look forward to seeing what you can do."

THEY WRAPPED it up after that, with Chuck asking Carl if he could hitch a ride back to Caraway House. Sure, he *could* walk the distance, but frankly he was bushed, and a little depressed. He'd had visions of sleeping in Lucius's bed that night, but the logistics didn't track, and they were doing something more important than the two of them right now.

That didn't stop Lucius from having to try *very* hard not to look hurt when they went upstairs for Chuck to gather his tux and borrow a pair of flip-flops.

"I'd stay if I could," Chuck said, taking an offered hooded sweatshirt to put over the T-shirt he was wearing. "This is huge. Is there another man living here I don't know about?"

Lucius rolled his eyes. "Linus and his mother tried to give me Christmas gifts this year. Linus is gay. We never clicked, but his mother has wanted to adopt me since college. Anyway, she's five-foot-one, and apparently all men over five six look alike to her."

Chuck snorted, charmed. "What did you give Linus and his mother?"

Lucius smiled sheepishly. "Well, Linus got stock options and a watch, because he's pretty awesome. His mother got a three-day spa weekend and some sort of purse that Linus assures me she's been looking at but was too expensive for her to ask for."

"Even from Linus?" Chuck asked, bemused.

"Well, Linus would have gotten it for her, but she keeps putting five-dollar bills in his holiday cards. He's sort of stuck. He keeps trying to tell her how much he makes, but...."

Chuck was laughing outright at this point. "Now I'm jealous of Linus. I haven't even met him, but his mother sounds like possibly the most adorable person on the planet."

Lucius nodded. "Right? Anyway, I put the sweatshirt she gave me on and said I loved it, and she came to kiss my cheek and left lipstick on the collar, so...." He shrugged.

"No returning it for one that fit," Chuck said. His smile softened. "And you couldn't give it away after that, could you."

Lucius shook his head no. "Having that sort of affection... I mean, some people take it for granted, but you know."

"Not us," Chuck said softly, drawing close enough to put his hands on Lucius's hips. "It's like the suits Julia buys me. I don't need more than a standard tuxedo, you know? Until I met Josh, I didn't know anybody who'd ever worn one except to prom. But I saved her baby boy doing what I know how to do, and I will keep every suit she sends me because she's not just being grateful—she's showing me she cares."

Lucius's smile was very young, very shining, and Chuck's heart twisted. He'd wondered a little, after they'd made love. Had he really fallen? How could he fall so hard for a guy he'd only slept with once?

But that smile twisted his heart into pieces and put it back together, a better, sounder, more inclusive organ. Chuck would do anything for that smile.

"I really love your family," Lucius said shyly. "They... they've let me be a part of them. A part of this. I want them. Is that okay? Can we both want them?"

Chuck's eyes burned. "Yeah. Yeah, Scotty. We can both want them. I promise."

Lucius nodded and kissed him, hard, and Chuck wrapped tight arms around his shoulders and held on.

"Chuck!" Carl's yell from the landing below had them both yanking apart. "Chuck, dammit, it's one in the morning!"

They both let out a breath on a growl.

"He's a friend," Chuck said in defense. Then, in all honesty, "I mean, we did the thing a couple of times back in the day, but it was like sticking my dick in a mattress full of dessert. I got off, it was cream-filled in the end, and we both fell asleep."

Lucius's mouth fell open in stunned surprise, and Chuck realized he might have to do better than that if he didn't want Lucius to start looking at Carl with green eyes.

"And I never cared about him the way I care about you," he said, capturing Lucius's chin between his thumb and forefinger.

"Chuck!" Soderburgh called again.

"Radio us if anything changes," Chuck said, going in for a quick, hard kiss. "Love you. Bye."

As he was flip-flopping his way across the bedroom, reaching for the doorknob, he heard Lucius say weakly, "Love you too."

Chuck flashed a grin over his shoulder and winked before heading down the stairs.

"Sorry," Carl said as he and Chuck headed outside to get into what looked like Felix's SUV.

"Not the one Lucius gave you?" Chuck asked.

"Well, Felix figured Lucius would need that one tomorrow. Felix and Julia are going to spend some time getting rid of the Bentayga parked in the middle of the woods so the cops can't trace it."

"Well, I appreciate you coming out to help with security tonight," Chuck said, meaning it. "Hunter and Grace are going to need their sleep."

Chuck smothered a yawn. "We are *all* going to need our sleep, brother," he said soberly. "We've been working three jobs for the last week!"

"Yeah," Chuck said, thinking about what was probably waiting for them back at the house. "But not yet." He popped Carl a grin. "And isn't it more interesting than insurance claims?"

Carl didn't laugh. "At least the people I'm working for don't suck."

Chuck frowned. "What do you mean?"

"Just… when you work for rich people, their whole focus, usually, is staying rich. I have seen companies steal from themselves more times than I can count, trying to get the insurance money. And the insurance companies deserve it. The shit they try to get out of paying! And not just insuring houses or art. I'm talking about health insurance. I mean, that's their *job* to give money to help people get better. But some of them build loopholes in loopholes, giving them every excuse not to pay people's doctor bills. That last person I busted for stealing from an insurance company was doing it to pay off the medical bills of their entire neighborhood who *bought their insurance*. And I met these people. They were good, hardworking people. But another shitty company built their homes in a cancer node, and someone else comes along hawking shitty insurance, and…."

He let out a sigh and rubbed his stomach.

"And you'd suddenly rather work for the criminals, who are at least trying to do what's right," Chuck said, getting his friend a little better.

"Can yagimmehallelujia!" Carl said it with passion, so Chuck answered.

"A-fuckin'-men."

They laughed a little, and Carl slowed to pull the U-turn at the end of the drive that would put them on the shelter property, both of them freezing as the gate opened, without a car behind it, to let a slim, shadowy figure slip out.

"Is that Marla Crandall?" Carl asked, but Chuck was already out of the SUV and running her down.

"Stop!" he shouted as the figure froze. After a moment of indecision, caught in the amber of Carl's headlights, the shadow—and it was the platinum-blond namaste lady—turned and began racing for the mansion.

"Where does she think she's going?" Chuck asked, and as he ran after Marla Crandall, he pulled the radio from his belt and hollered, "Security, Marla Crandall is heading back to the mansion. Get her! She's our mole and a danger to Caraway House. Repeat, capture and detain."

But he didn't really want anybody else to capture and detain her. *He* wanted to capture and detain her, because he was that fucking mad about it.

Chuck had put his dress shoes back on, and they were slippery and unwieldy on the gravel, and dammit, his feet were not doing him any favors. He didn't know where this lady thought she was going. Alerted by the opening of the gate, the lights had come up all over the front yard. Everybody could see her. She couldn't run inside and pretend nothing had happened. If she went behind the mansion, did she think she could hop a fence and get to Lucius's place? Was she planning to hide?

Was she planning to hurt someone or force someone to help her?

The thought chilled him to the bone. And when he saw a slim, fleet figure burst out of the mansion's front doors and leap over the stairs onto the drive, all the air in his lungs froze, along with his blood.

"Molly!" he screamed, forgetting her code name, forgetting his *own* name, in a panic for what Marla Crandall might do to her.

He needn't have worried. Molly ran like a gazelle, and Marla didn't bother to change her course, probably thinking she could dodge or weave out of the way.

Molly barreled into her without hesitation, taking Marla out on the front lawn and leaving her gasping on her back, while Molly scrambled up, rolled her to her stomach, and was busy pulling a thick elastic band from her hair to bind Marla's wrists with.

As Chuck pulled up, still slipping in his dress shoes, he had to laugh, because he could hear Molly swearing to herself as she bound Marla's wrists extra, extra tight.

"Get off me!" Marla snarled, struggling, but Molly just stood—putting her weight on the knee on Marla's back as she did so—and then bent down to haul the traitor in their midst to her feet.

"You fucking bitch," Molly snapped, giving the woman a hard shake. "What in the fuck was your end-game here, huh?"

"You don't understand!" Marla howled. "I don't know what they're going to do if they don't hear from me! The men who broke onto the grounds today weren't mere thugs! They were *cops*. They're backed by really powerful people, and if they want in here, they're going to get in!"

"And what are they going to do?" Chuck asked.

Marla tried to shake Molly's grip, but Molly was apparently like Chuck—a Jill of all trades, including muscle when it was needed. She kept a tight hold on the woman, her body language hard and ready for action.

"I don't know!" Marla cried. "But they didn't get who they were coming for, and if I don't get word to my husband about what happened, the shit is going to hit the fan!"

Chuck gave an ugly laugh. "Oh, lady, pull the other one. We know who they were coming for, and we know who was here. Those guys who broke in? They're in the hands of the FBI now, and those powerful people you were so worried about? Well, we've got plans for them too."

"You monster!" she sobbed. "What are you going to do to—"

Molly slapped her. Not overly hard, just enough to make her stop talking.

"You bitch!" Marla hissed, all tears, all over-wrought emotion gone. Simple hatred shone in her eyes then, and she lunged to get out of Molly's grip.

It occurred to Chuck that nobody had ever raised a hand to this woman in her life. There was too much entitlement here, and not enough fear.

"Mol—I mean, Maisy my dear," Chuck said, grimacing, "how about we bring Miss Crandall into the sleeping quarters, and we can find out where she put the bugs this time." She had to have bugged them. The attack that night had been too well orches-trated not to have been fueled with some inside in-formation. "We have some questions to ask her, and then we have to find some place to stash her for the night."

"Why?" Marla asked. "What's going to happen tomorrow?"

"It's more what's going to happen Monday," Chuck said. "But we're not going to let you in on the secret. Don't you know, Marla? The wife is always the last to know."

Carl had pulled up while they were talking, and he helped Molly escort Marla Crandall into the house while Chuck radioed Lucius—he thought—but got Danny instead.

"We sent your young man to bed, like a good toddler," Danny said over the radio. "He was beat, and he's going to have a lot to do tomorrow. We can handle this, I think, until he's had a few winks. Which is more than you'll get, I'm afraid."

Chuck yawned and explained the situation. "We don't know where she thought she was going. We left the hole in the fence open for a reason, though, and it worked—it caught her. Maybe she was trying to get a signal on her cell phone."

"Mm," Danny said thoughtfully. "Look, when you go back in to talk to her, record her on your cell. I'll be by in half an hour to pick her up. I think, with what Julia has in mind for this woman, Chicago is probably the safest place for her, don't you?"

"But what if she recognizes you, or Julia for that matter?"

Danny didn't sound ruffled. "Felix's SUV has the driver option for the barrier between the back seat and the front. And I'm pretty sure Julia's plan called for them to speak face-to-face anyway. But get her to talk to you, and get it on video. Julia and I will drive back to Chicago, leave Felix here with Josh, and get back to you sometime tomorrow. Hopefully our sabotage-the-company people will give us until then to regroup."

Chuck yawned again. "God, Danny, I'm so tired of chasing our tails."

"I understand, my boy," Danny said, all the kindness in the world suffusing his voice. "Hold on a little longer and we can start chasing theirs."

Chuck closed his eyes for a moment and remembered that as soon as Marla "namaste" Crandall was on the way to Chicago, he, Molly, and Carl could actually catch some real sleep.

"I'll be ready," he said staunchly.

"Good boy. We may have Torrance Grayson with us when we return, so that'll be reinforcements. Hold tight—help is coming."

"Can do."

And with that, Chuck signed off of the radio and stalked into the house for a "come to Jesus" talk with a woman who very obviously was not an abused wife.

Code Red

DANNY SENT Lucius the interview as Lucius was sleeping, and he was able to view it as he was eating breakfast. He almost threw up his eggs.

Josh hung out on one side and Stirling on the other, with Felix hovering behind him, and Lucius didn't mind the crowd because it felt almost like being surrounded by his pack. Felix's avuncular hand on his shoulder helped with that emotion, and Lucius, confidence bolstered by the last week of being included in the meetings and made to feel like his plan and Caraway House were important and worth fighting for, wasn't going to shake it off.

These people were his friends, and he needed all the friends he could get.

Particularly now.

"God, she's really revolting, isn't she," Felix said rhetorically. He got a quiet chorus of head bobs and yeses anyway, because it was cathartic to have company when confronted with a monster.

Or at least a monster's helper.

Marla was seated on a wooden stool in Chuck and Hunter's quarters, and Chuck had already told Lucius that he and Hunter were living bare bones, so Lucius was prepared. With the exception of their bags—both zipped and locked shut now—nothing personal was in sight. Not even a shaving kit through the open door of the tiny bathroom gave a hint to the two human beings who lived there, and Lucius felt a pang that Chuck and Hunter knew how to live like this.

But that thought was quickly replaced by his reaction to the events on screen.

Chuck was standing a little behind Marla, close enough to her side to be captured in profile, but far enough behind her for her to forget he was there. She was seated near the back wall, and Molly was leaning against the door. There was nowhere else for Marla to look but at Molly.

Molly's hair was loose down her shoulders and back, and her clothes—a T-shirt and yoga pants—looked casually worn. She looked quick and fit and a little bit rough-and-tumble, but by no means discomfited.

Marla Crandall, on the other hand, was in considerable dishabille. Her usually coiffed hair straggled over her brow, and the very pricey millennial pink leisure suit she was wearing had rips and grass stains all down the front. Her hands were secured behind her, and her feet were tied to the chair—apparently Chuck had broken into Hunter's stash of zip ties, because they looked specially made. But besides being bound to the chair in dirty clothes, Marla's face looked as though Molly had landed a couple of hard rights and a cross to her in their tussle. Lucius appreciated the fact that Felix let him know that Molly had delivered the blows. It wasn't that he ever thought Chuck capable of beating a woman, but it was reassuring somehow that everybody else had the same sort of sensitivity.

"If you don't let me out of here, I'll scream," Marla snarled, and Molly gave a brutal laugh.

"Scream and I'll tell everyone that you told your husband when and where people could come kidnap Sabrina—and Joanie and her son. You put their lives in danger, Marla. You're our leak, right?"

"You're being overdramatic," Marla snapped. She looked sideways, but apparently caught Chuck there with the camera and turned her attention back to Molly. "The men just wanted to know where their women are."

"So they could beat them," Molly said, not moved in the least. "You were willing to turn them over to their abusers because…. See, that's the piece still missing here. We know you called Barker, and he and his buddies sent all sorts of wheels spinning once he got the information, but we—" She moved close enough to Marla to poke her in the chest with an accusing finger. "—don't." Poke. "Know." Poke. "Why."

Marla hawked back in her throat as though to spit in Molly's face, but Molly stepped smoothly aside.

The spit landed on the floor, and Molly looked from the glop on the tile to Marla and then back.

"Typical," she said, catching Chuck's eye.

"White trash is white trash," Chuck drawled.

"My husband makes two mil a year," Marla retorted, and seemed genuinely discombobulated when they broke into raucous laughter.

"Yeah," Molly murmured. "This one doesn't know what class is. In fact…." She pursed her lips. "Let's make a bet. You and me, we try to guess why she was trying to turn women—women who'd never done a thing to her—over to men who might very well beat them to death someday."

"Hmm… accessory to murder." Chuck adjusted his stance, and Lucius imagined him with his arms crossed, one hand holding the camera, the other tapping his lower lip, much like Julia did so often. "What would it take to make a person of such low character an accessory to murder? I got it! Her trailer was about to be repossessed!"

"Aw, that's not fair," Molly said. "In fact, that's classist. I'm thinking that's a legit complaint there. That's someone's home."

"Yup. Sorry about that, Maisy girl, you're right. We mustn't confuse being poor with being a shitty person with zero morality. Let me try again."

"You're both so fucking smug," Marla said, sulking.

"Wait, no, give us a chance," Chuck said, his voice dripping with contempt. "I think I got it! That line about the ex in the Bahamas with his sweet young thing wasn't a line after all, was it?"

"Ooh," Molly murmured. "Yes, I like this! Roll with it, Charles."

"You were getting dumped, trophy wife, for a younger, shinier trophy, and dollars to donuts the only screwing *you* were in for was going to come when your husband took most of his two mil a year in divorce court."

"I'd take that bet," Molly said, nodding. "But only because I like donuts."

"God, me too," Chuck told her, sounding serious for the first time since the interview began. "I swear to God, next time we're in town, you and me are gonna split a dozen, 'cause I could really use some damned pastry right now."

"You're killing me!" Molly complained. "Killing. Me! Let's finish with this bitch so we can get some donuts."

"Deal." Chuck paced a little, but he was, Lucius noticed, very careful to keep the camera on Marla's face. "I'm betting her husband came to her one day and said, 'Marla, baby, I still want to screw this sweet young thing, but I tell you what....'"

"Yes!" Molly pumped her fist. "Marla, sweetie baby honey face, you sneak into a facility where battered women go to recover from abuse and get the fuck away from the assholes who have broken their bones and robbed them of their lives and safety, and then report back to me. And when you're done, if you've done a good job, I might not—*might*, mind you—leave you a shattered husk after the divorce. Whaddya say, sweetie pants? Pretend I hit you, just a little. I've got a nurse who will sneak you in to save her job, right?"

"Ooh," Chuck said, nodding. "Nurse is a nice touch. You're right. I bet he threatened her job—probably her family and career too—to get the nurse to sneak ol' Marla in."

"So what do you say, Marla?" Molly was leaning on her thighs, face level with Marla's now, but Marla wasn't looking at her. "Did we get that right?"

"I'm not talking to you," Marla muttered.

At that moment, the door behind Molly opened, and Carl strode in. He must have done some freshening up, because he was wearing his suit coat over his carefully buttoned sleeves. He'd been decidedly more casual over Lucius's dinner table less than an hour before this had been filmed.

"She doesn't have to," Carl said. "Because we've got a source who has pretty much confirmed all of this."

Julia, obviously, but Marla didn't know that.

"You can't do anything to me," she told them, trying to pull the tattered remains of her superiority around her. "I haven't done anything illegal."

"Well, yes, you have," Carl said. He looked at Molly and Chuck and nodded, as though they might doubt him. "No, seriously. She's totally in the wrong here, legally. The foundation that runs this place filed restraining orders against the abusers. The address listed for the victims was the legal office that issued them to make it harder to track. Helping the abusers invade their sanctuary is very illegal. You're an accessory to a crime."

Chuck let out a very evil, very angry laugh. "Did you hear that, Marla? We could put you in jail." And he must have known the dam was going to break, because the camera subtly shifted. Marla's face was now in three-quarter profile, and anybody could recognize her.

Until she opened her mouth and turned into a snake before their eyes.

"For what?" Marla asked, incredulous. "For telling my husband I met friends here? These women—they're so pathetic. They have money, they have social standing, and all you hear is, 'Wah wah wah, he hit me!' If they don't like it with the guy, they should just *leave*, not go through all this cloak-and-dagger shit!" Her face twisted with hatred and contempt. "They *deserve* to be beaten if they can't take the money, put out, and get whatever they can. Do you think my life is a picnic? I work my body to *death* so I can stay fit and fuck-ing perky and get pawed once a week as a Friday night special. And still he throws me over for another woman. These whores are the same. If they could get their fucking mani-pedis and not catch a fat lip, they'd put out and shut up like I've been doing for *years*!"

There was a beat of silence after she finished speaking, and Lucius heard indrawn breaths around him.

"That's it, isn't it?" Josh asked.

"That's the money shot," Felix breathed, but then Molly started speaking, and they quieted down.

"Not everybody's a whore like you," Molly snapped. Her green eyes were sparking with honest anger, and Lucius's chest gave a big throb. Oh, this was real for all of them, wasn't it? "And they weren't hurting *you*. They were trying to get the fuck away from you and your husband who makes two mil a year. This place was a sanctuary, and you've tried to shit in it. But I've got news for you, lady. You're the one who's going to end up floating around like a turd in a pool."

And something about Molly's demeanor actually got through to Marla. For a moment, her hauteur dissolved and she looked afraid—genuinely afraid.

"What… what do you plan to do with me?"

Molly glanced over at Chuck, and the fury that had possessed her drained away. "Oh, Marla. It's going to be absolutely terrible. Your husband is gonna go to jail, you're not going to have any money, and none of your high-class friends are going to talk to you. Not one. You are going to go back to your high-rise apartment and pack up your shit and move back to whatever hole you came out of, because not a soul in Chicago is going to want to speak to you." She shrugged. "I mean, I wouldn't want to after I saw that footage, would you?"

"What footage?" Marla asked. And then, as though noticing Chuck's camera for the first time, she began to scream, "What footage? What are you going to do with that? *What*?"

And then the screen went dim.

The breakfast table went silent, and Lucius set the camera down before looking over his shoulder at Felix.

"What *are* we going to do with it?" Lucius asked.

"Send it to all of Julia's friends, I imagine," Felix replied thoughtfully. "Edited, of course."

"Oh yeah," Josh said. "I mostly pulled out the bit with Marla losing her shit. It's great. I mean, not as awful as she is in context, but even out of context, you know. Nobody's gonna wanna invite her to any parties."

"So Molly and Chuck and Carl?" Lucius asked, to be sure.

"Nobody will ever know," Felix said complacently.

"So what did they do to her?" Lucius knew that, once upon a time, he'd have been a little fearful when he asked this. But not now. Now he trusted these people. They weren't going to leave Marla Crandall's body in a dumpster, no matter how tempting it might be.

"Well, mostly they just packed her up and tucked her in the back of the SUV and blindfolded her. Danny and Julia took her home and deposited her in front of her condo with all her luggage, safe as a kitten."

Lucius frowned. "But that doesn't mean Barker Crandall doesn't already know—"

"Oh, he does," Felix said, nodding. "I'm sure of it. Marla Crandall's social life is about to go kaboom, but Barker Crandall, Kyle Miller, and Newman Damar are still very potent threats. That's why this morning,

Chuck and Molly packed up Joanie Damar and her son, Sabrina Hardy—Chet Damar's girlfriend—Heather Miller, and poor Larry, the side piece, and took them to our property in Lansing. We've already hired independent security for them, but they are safely removed from the premises."

Lucius frowned, and then shivered. "What about the girls from Ohio State?" he asked.

"Carl is going to be taking them as soon as Chuck and Molly get back." Felix grimaced. "We're a bit spread thin, my boy. I hope that's a fair solution."

Hunter and Grace had arrived at around five that morning. As far as Lucius knew, they were going to sleep for another five hours, and they had certainly earned it.

"No, that's good," Lucius said, letting out a breath. "In fact—" He managed to summon a smile. "—it's more than good. That's way better than I could have done by myself. Thank you."

"Don't thank us yet." Felix had grown very sober. "Because now that the victims of the abuse are safe, that leaves only one target, Lucius. You know what that is, right?"

Lucius grimaced. "Me and my company," he said softly.

"Indeed." Felix nodded. "I know it's Saturday, but I think you and I should make a tour of the premises as soon as Grace is awake. Too much is riding on that place to have it go under now."

"Josh and I will go now," Stirling said. "The tracker doesn't have Fergus Allen's car moving from the hotel yet, but if he's about to head for the business complex, we don't have much time." He paused and gave Josh an uncertain glance. "If you're feeling up to it."

Josh nodded, tired but composed. "Yeah. The barfing has cleared up. I may need to nap in the staff room while we're running reports, but I think it would be best if I was there."

"What are you doing?" Lucius asked, cognizant that nobody had been idle.

"Well, now that we know who the players are," Josh said, "we figure there should be a record of all of their non-face-to-face interaction. Texts, phone numbers, payouts—that sort of thing. Even Barker Crandall's divorce settlement and any changes to it. And of course, any calls or texts Marla made to her husband. We got her phone last night and made her unlock it. It's just a little bit of light hacking after that. Anyway, we're funneling the information to Torrance Grayson. He pinged me this morning and said he could run with the story tonight possibly, tomorrow afternoon at the latest. It would be great to see what the endgame is— what they're planning to do to your company. But until Fergus tries his key card and his back door to get in, we won't have any ideas."

Which would mean odds were good that whatever "accident" they'd planned as a final act of revenge would happen that day.

Lucius's stomach tightened. There would be people there today, and he was worried.

"Are you sure you don't want to wait for me and Felix?" he asked, his sense of responsibility for these young people suddenly overwhelming.

Josh rolled his eyes, and Stirling managed to look bored.

"Gee, mister," Josh said in his best Beaver Cleaver voice, "We're just two boys alone in the world. Whatever will we do without you to protect us."

Stirling made an ungraceful snorting noise, and both Lucius *and* Felix glared at them.

"Do I need to remind you," Felix said archly, "that the last time you were 'just doing tech things' Chuck had to disassemble a bomb under your van?"

"Was that us?" Josh asked Stirling.

"I don't think so," Stirling replied flatly. "Couldn't be us."

"Besides," Grace muttered, padding into the kitchen dining area wearing only a pair of briefs, "I'm going with them."

Everybody at the kitchen table stopped and stared at him.

"What?" Grace glared back. "Josh, you're the one who told me Lucius was down here in his briefs and a shirt. I just forgot the shirt."

"It's his house, you freak," Josh replied, looking surprised but obviously not shocked. "And he thought it was empty! Aren't you supposed to be asleep anyway?"

Grace shrugged, the movement as fluid as flame. "Flying is boring. I slept to Quantico, and once I got there, it was all 'Stay in the plane, Grace, these people aren't ready for you,' so I slept in the plane, and then Hunter flew us back, and I slept then too. He said my muttering in my sleep was almost like I was keeping him company. It's fine."

Lucius glanced at the other people at the table, and their faces were perfectly accepting of this.

"But Hunter needs his sleep," Josh said, making sure.

"God yes. He's beat. Let me eat and put on some clothes, maybe. We can go pretend we're breaking into Lucius's big butt-plug building." He gave Lucius a

patently false smile and two thumbs up. "Way to design that, Mr. Zillionaire Businessman. Well done." He
turned for a moment, shouting over his shoulder, "Stirling, did you eat all the fucking yogurt?"

"Yes," Stirling replied deadpan, although Lucius
was pretty sure there was half a case left in the fridge.

"You suck at lying," Grace called as he strolled
into the kitchen. "Oh, hi, Cheri. Did you get the peach
yogurt like you said?"

"Don't listen to him," Josh murmured. "I totally
believed you."

Stirling grunted. "Asshole."

"Glad he's going with us?" And there was a plain-
tive note in Josh's voice. *He* was glad Grace was going with them, and he obviously wanted Stirling to be
glad too.

"'Course." Stirling nodded. "Don't tell him,
though. If he thinks he's pissing me off, he's happy."

Josh made a pleased little hum in his throat.
"'Course. Let's go get our shit together. We can take off
when Grace gets dressed."

They wandered off, and Felix let out half a laugh
and sank down in the seat next to Lucius. "Oh, that's
nice. The boys haven't had much of a chance to play
since the diagnosis. They miss each other."

Lucius blinked, and Felix laughed, the crinkles
at his eyes revealing kindness. "You didn't have close
friends through school?" he asked.

"Linus," Lucius confessed. "But…." He bit his lip.

Felix's kind blue eyes seemed to bore into his soul.
"When we met Julia," he said softly, "Danny and I were
there to steal her father's things."

Lucius actually yelped. Julia had said *con*. "You
were there to *what*?"

"We were con men, my boy. And Julia saw through us—in a heartbeat she saw through us—but she approached us for help anyway, because she was pregnant and because she was desperate and because her father was a monster."

Lucius swallowed. He'd known this, but hearing Felix tell it made it hurt all over again. "I don't—"

"The worst thing about being the victim of domestic abuse is that it isolates you. Makes you feel like you are all alone. Julia and I have lived in the same house for twenty years as brother and sister, and besides Danny—and Josh, of course—sometimes I think the proudest moments of my life are when she comes to sit and watch TV with us in her pajamas. She curls up and leans her head on my shoulder or Danny's and just… just trusts us, I guess."

Lucius couldn't find enough spit to swallow again. "Oh," he managed.

"You *are* going to come by the house for Sunday dinners when this is done, aren't you?" Felix asked, seemingly out of the blue.

"Chuck—"

"Besides to see Chuck. Or even to bring him to visit. Danny and I were split up for ten years, and he still managed to sneak in to see Josh. You and I can still be friends—you and this family can *still* be friends— even if things don't work out at their best. I thought you should know."

Lucius nodded, his eyes burning and his throat thick and all of his words gone.

"Thank you," he rasped finally.

"I'm so proud that you trusted us to help with this," Felix said modestly. "I want you to know how much it means to the entire lot of us that we get to help you do something good."

Lucius wiped a palm across his eyes, and then again, and dammit, again. Felix's arm came around his shoulder, and he pressed his face into Felix's bicep and cried silently, not even sure what had set him off besides this promise—the second one he'd received from this family—that he was no longer in this endeavor, or even in this *world*, alone.

He pulled himself together eventually, and Felix excused himself, charmingly enough, to go change his shirt. In less than half an hour, they'd all gathered into the remaining Bentayga so he could transport them to the business campus.

Lucius let them into the center building, the one where most of the sabotage had occurred. It held their clean rooms and their research and development rooms, heating and cooling units, and essentially all of the elements needed to create chaos and mayhem and destruction.

And it contained two floors of computers too, the kind that needed big servers and cooling towers because they were designed to run models of what the products being researched and developed would do after being assembled.

Fergus Allen, abusive frat boy and general scumbag, worked with the modeling computers. It shouldn't have given him access to the R and D rooms, but it was close enough that one little back door into security would make it not unlikely for him to show up.

The bottom two floors, though, housed software engineers, and that had been a perfect place to establish Carl and Stirling. Lucius guided them across the tiled corridors through open-air cubicles with colorful walls and ergonomic chairs and computer designs, many decorated with pictures of family and sports trophies. He'd opened up as much of the floor as possible to natural light but had carpeted the cubicles so the echoes in the open air didn't become too distracting. There was a quiet "meditation" staff room, with couches and vending machines and a strict no-talking policy, and a "play" staff room down the hall, which featured beanbags, colorful couches, two foosball tables, and a video-game screen. The cantina was in the larger building, but Lucius had put covered picnic tables between the buildings to make eating outside as easy as possible.

There was even an employee gym in a smaller outbuilding across the quad, complete with locker rooms and an indoor pool, and he knew quite a few employees had signed on so they could work out during lunch or before or after work.

No, the business had not been his primary concern, but he had tried very hard not to neglect it and to make working there as pleasant and creatively engaging as possible.

As he led Felix, Josh, Stirling, and Grace through the halls and to the lushly appointed elevators, he heard the hum of the employees working there on a sunny Saturday and felt a pang of real worry. Until this moment, it hadn't occurred to him how much he'd enjoyed making this a good place to work, how much he'd hoped to foster a healthy work environment. He showed up every day so Linus could brief him on day-to-day operations, but until now, as their footsteps rang in the barely occupied space, it hadn't really hit him that part of him lived here too.

He'd always taken his role here seriously. He'd been responsible for the redesigned buildings when he was fresh out of college, and although his father had openly scoffed at his "liberal bullshit designer fuck-off office," the improved productivity—and vastly reduced turnover rate—had spoken for itself. His and Linus's frequent, valiant attempts to improve the work culture had been acts of love.

He'd convinced himself that the purpose of the company had been strictly to fund the charity, but he realized that there was more to it than that. He loved this place—truly. It may have been an arranged marriage of sorts, but time, patience, and dedication had been their own rewards.

His grandfather had loved the place, and while Lucius's memories of him were few, they were considerably warmer than his memories of his father. His grandfather had been so proud of his business. Thinking of that, Lucius couldn't help but want to see the old girl thrive, remember her beauty and her heyday, and be the vital part of this community she deserved to be.

And the abused spouse's shelters didn't have to be the hidden mistresses, really. They could, instead, be the nurtured offspring, children of his and the business's attempts to build a better world.

Nice sentiment, but it was helped along by Felix's long whistle of appreciation as the elevator doors closed in front of them.

"Pretty," he said, nodding with sincerity.

"It's *very* cool, Dad," Josh said. "I mean, I took a nap in the meditation room, and it was seriously peaceful. Nobody bothered me. I'm sold."

"You have this incredible playground at your fingertips and you're excited because we let you sleep?" Grace asked in disgust. "Do you have any idea how much fun this place would be to *burgle*?"

"I thought the idea was to keep someone else from doing that," Stirling said, straight-faced.

"Well, sure, if you want to go about it *that* way." Grace gave them a serene smile, and Josh shook his head.

"No hanging from the skylights or trying to scale the outside," he said sternly. "Hunter made that a caveat, right? No unnecessary risk."

Grace examined his nails. "Yeah. Sure. Whatever. Where's the ventilation shafts, and do any of them drop into a furnace?"

"Not as far as I know," Lucius replied diplomatically. "I'll try to pull up some schematics while Josh and Stirling work."

Grace gave him a happy smile. "You're okay, Mr. Zillionaire Businessman. We'll keep you."

"A pleasure," Lucius said, bowing slightly. As the elevator door opened and they all moved out into the fifth floor, he had to admit, it truly was.

LATER HE would reflect on things like "kismet," "timing," and "serendipity"—or, as Chuck would say, "What are the fucking *odds*!" And on the one hand, the way the whole thing played out seemed entirely coincidental. But on the other, well, while opportunity's knock can be sort of a random force of nature, it helps if you're prepared to answer the door.

Lucius and the entire Salinger crew had been preparing for this *opportunity* for most of their lives. They just didn't know what it would look like.

At first, it looked like an average white guy with sandy blond hair, hazel eyes, a broad forehead, and a somewhat flat nose.

Lucius saw him pass behind their group as he was directing everybody into an open-use center near the clean rooms. The developmental engineers divided their time between the clean rooms, where many of their experiments and developing products lay in various stages of suspension, and the computer rooms, where they worked up models and did their projections. There were computers in the clean rooms, yes, but since there were layers of decontamination to get into the clean room, some days it was easier for the engineers to spend their time working on the computer without working on the substances in the lab.

The open-use centers were more user-friendly, with circular shared towers so they could power their laptops and work in a group while sitting on padded stools, almost like an internet café. For those who liked an even more casual air, there was a leather couch and some stuffed chairs facing the window, which looked out at the quad. There were even beanbag chairs and Pilates balls, so nobody had to feel like they were trapped in a cubicle. Lucius and Linus had always felt that the staff's greatest strength lay in collaboration.

And of course there were vending machines with snacks—both healthy and unhealthy—and drinks in both varieties as well.

But as Lucius steered everybody in and pulled up the all-access pass to the internet and facilities on his phone so Stirling didn't have to hack it, he felt a little niggle in the back of his brain that had nothing to do with his company setup.

What had that guy been doing there? Working on computers, yes—that's what people did on the weekends—but very few people came in to use the labs, particularly alone. There were some dangerous substances in those freezers. This particular lab dealt with chemical electronics cleaners, as well as pesticides for toxic molds that could eat through wire. He and Linus had put together a clearance and background check procedure for employees who could enter there that would rival NASA. He'd seen the dossier on every chemist they'd employed.

And that kid who'd passed them, walking quickly and avoiding eye contact, hadn't been on that list.

But he *had* looked familiar.

"Stirling," he said thoughtfully, "could you check to see—"

At that moment, Stirling's phone started to emit a faint beeping sound, like an alarm.

"Wait," Josh said. "Stirling, is that your—"

"Tracker alarm for Fergus Allen and the alarm for the sabotage guy," Stirling said, and Lucius made that helpless sound people make when they have something direly important to say but their brains have outstripped their tongues.

Felix spun on his heel and bolted from the room, with Grace hot on his tail.

Lucius took a deep breath and managed to sputter, "That was *him*! The guy in the hallway. That was the *guy*!"

He expected Josh and Stirling to leap out of their seats too, but they were made of more practical stuff.

"Did you find the breach?" Josh murmured, pulling up a schematic of the building that must have been already open.

"Four doors down, at the end of the hallway," Stirling replied.

"I'm sending you the room specs. Tell me what's in it."

Lucius closed his eyes and tried to remember. "Pesticides," he said. "We're trying to develop a retardant for toxic mold that's not just safe for electronics but also for people, plants, and pets."

"Oh, that's bad," Josh muttered. "But we don't know how bad. That's chemical bad. Lucius, get Chuck on the phone."

"Chuck?" Lucius asked, brain shorting out. "Why Chuck?"

"Because he's got the equivalent of a degree in chemical engineering," Josh said, staring at him. "Didn't he tell you?"

"He said he didn't finish school," Lucius said. "And he accidentally blew up the frat-house toilets."

Josh paused in his frantic clicking. "What he did with the frat-house toilets? That wasn't like a cherry bomb, Lucius, that was *fucking genius*. Ninety-five bank jobs in three years with no casualties, when he's the one cracking the safes? That's not an accident. Man, call your boyfriend, because we're going to need his help!"

As Lucius was staring at him, gaping in complete surprise, Felix burst into the room holding a struggling Fergus Allen by an arm wrenched behind his back and a hand twisting his ear.

"Ouch!" the young man yelped. "Mr. Broadstone, this man *assaulted* me as I was heading for the elevator. And some other guy tripped me. I need to *go*, man! I have a lunch date. My ex-girlfriend is *waiting* for me."

Lucius turned his head slowly, everything they knew about this guy trickling down. "You mean the girl from Ohio State?" he asked pleasantly.

Fergus flushed hotly, so hot his face broke into a red sweat and dark stains appeared in the pits of his casual dark blue henley shirt.

"Yeah. Sheryl. She's the one."

"How's she going to do that, Fergus? She has a restraining order against you."

"Oh, she's going to drop that," Fergus said, sweat beading from under his hair. "I was going to talk to her as soon as... you know... in a couple of hours—"

"As soon as you destroyed my company so I'd be too busy to know you'd gotten your cop friends to break into the women's shelter and kidnap her?" Lucius continued mildly, which was hard, because a three-ton elephant was sitting on his chest and he was having trouble breathing.

"It's not kidnapping if she wants to come!" Fergus protested. "She just doesn't have her head on, you know? I told her it was a joke, but she ghosted me, and that's not right! I... me and the guys were complaining, and Mr. Miller, he said he had a plan, and, well, you know. You're the one who's keeping us from seeing our girls."

"*You broke her jaw!*" Lucius roared, and he wasn't aware of lunging, but before he knew it, he had his hands around Fergus's throat and Felix was yelling at him.

"Lucius! *Lucius!*"

That last yell was punctuated by a smack to the back of his head, the kind a loving parent would give to a wayward teenager. Not meant to hurt, just meant to stop. And while Lucius had suffered worse—much worse—at the hands of his own father, maybe it was that very lack of force that made Lucius back down.

"Felix, he broke her jaw! He terrorized her! He... he—"

"He did something we need to fix," Felix said grimly. "And we need to know exactly what it was."

"Wait, Dad, look! I think we know. See? Mr. Broadstone, come here. Come look. Is this right?"

"You tapped into my cameras," Lucius said, his voice far away and tinny in his own ears. It was like channeling himself through a tin can with a string.

"And?" Josh demanded. "Look. See this production line? It's starting up. And that's a bad thing."

Lucius stared at the uniform bank of test tubes set on a roller cart in an assembly line and tried to remember what the tubes contained. "Okay, that machine injects distilled water into the test tubes, and then air," he murmured. "Compressed air. The rubber seal on top makes each tube a little aerosol bomb. Usually we use it for scent—for cleaners and such. To see how many parts of scent per part water we'll need. But that fluid isn't scent. There's too much of it." He stared as the bank of test tubes made its way along the conveyor belt. The belt paused for a good fifteen seconds as the aerosol infuser clicked down on what would be a flat of test tubes if the conveyor belt was full, and then the belt moved things smoothly to the next flat. The flat at the end of the conveyor belt probably had, at best, fifteen minutes before it went under the machine. If they hadn't caught Fergus, hadn't known where to look, it would have been the perfect fuse.

Slowly, swimming under water, he turned his head and stared at Fergus Allen, who was staring at the bank of test tubes in Josh's laptop and sweating profusely.

"What did you put in there?" he asked.

Fergus Allen gaped like a fish, and as Josh worked on the computer, the image changed, grew larger, and magnified, and they could all see the tiny crumbled bit of soft mineral in the test tubes, the faint sheen of baby oil giving it a gray rainbow as it shielded the mineral from air so it didn't react.

"Fergus, you fucker," Josh breathed, "even I know what that is. That's *potassium*."

Potassium, which reacted *very badly* when exposed to air and even worse when exposed to water. The blast of air would be hard enough to remove the layer of neutralizing baby oil, and the blast of water would make each test tube into a tiny bomb. One test tube may not have done much damage, but all of them together, reacting under the pressure of the heavy shell of the aerosol infuser, would do a lot more.

"Evacuate the building," Lucius said, surfacing into reality. "We need to evacuate the building, *now!*"

And as though the building were listening, they heard the kerchunk and thud as a timer closed every door lock on their floor.

And an alarm began to sound.

Fergus began to weep. "You don't understand. I… I gotta go. I got people waiting for me to help me see Sheryl. I gotta go. I—"

"We shipped all your cop friends to the FBI last night," Lucius said, his brain screaming *bomb* but his mouth fixated on this. "Who is going to help you kidnap your battered girlfriend?"

"I paid people," Fergus choked. "We… once Chet told us for sure that was the place, we were responsible for getting our own women out of there."

Charming. Lucius took a deep breath, then another, but it was Felix who spoke.

"Stirling?"

"Yessir?"

"We need you to call your sister and tell her and Soderburgh to be on the lookout. Ask her to put the coeds from Ohio State under guard. There will be people attempting another breach, and they need to be ready."

"Yessir," Stirling said.

"Josh?"

"On it, Dad," Josh muttered.

"What is he on?" Lucius asked, trying to keep his teeth from chattering.

"I'm unlocking the doors so your employees can get out. When Stirling's off the phone with Molly, he's going to be working on stopping that conveyor belt from here." Suddenly Josh stopped tapping and looked away from his computer screen. "Wait a minute. Dad, where's Grace?"

"He was right behind me when I came in with this baggage," Felix muttered. Fergus gave a weak struggle, and Felix turned to Lucius, who had dropped his hands from Fergus's throat but was still standing uncomfortably close.

"Lucius, could you do something about this?" he said delicately. "Don't kill him, just—"

"*Augh*!" Lucius snarled and let loose with the best punch of his life, right into Fergus Allen's jaw.

Fergus gave a moan and collapsed to the floor, and Felix bent and searched his pockets, coming up with a wallet, phone, and keys, which he pocketed. When he was done, he kicked Fergus Allen in the balls without compunction as he lay unconscious and sniffed in distaste as the creature moaned a little and tried to curl into a ball.

"Nice punch," Felix muttered. "He's well and truly out."

"Dad," Josh said urgently. "Where's Grace?"

"I imagine he's in the ventilation shaft," Felix replied. "Probably thinking he can go in there and turn the machine off manually. Can he, Lucius?"

"No," Lucius said shortly. "You need a passkey. Fergus Allen used the one with the old password. That's how he's been committing the sabotage all along."

"Well, he doesn't have his earbud in," Josh said, his voice pitching with worry. "And I don't have any way to tell him this won't work!"

Lucius shook out his aching wrist and knuckles and saw the answer very, very clearly. With a sigh he began to strip off his shoes and socks, and then his slacks and polo shirt.

"Not that the view isn't nice," Felix said, "but what are you doing?"

"Josh?" Lucius asked, heading for the telltale grill on the wall by the utility closet door. "Please tell me this goes where Grace is going?"

Lucius could see the look shared by father and son, and Josh said, "Yeah. That one there. Hold on, Mr. Broadstone. I have earbuds here, and they should work. Are you ready?"

"I am," Lucius said. He paused for a moment and took stock. Stirling had hung up with his sister and was working on unlocking the building so the other employees could escape, and Josh was looking at schematics to help him find his way. Felix had blown past him and was checking the bolts at the corners of the vent cover, which were, strangely enough, already unscrewed. He had a moment—just a moment—to wish Chuck was there.

Chuck apparently lived and breathed this kind of danger all the time.

"Uhm, tell Chuck—"

"You tell him," Josh snapped. "We're not doing death here. You're going in that vent to save Grace because I'm too fucking sick. Now go!"

Oh. Suddenly he understood. *This* was how people were heroes.

What Heroes Do

CHUCK HAD picked up passengers on the way back from Lansing.

The trip there hadn't been bad. The women had been afraid—but also grateful. When Molly had made it clear that Lucius was moving them as a preemptive measure and that the danger had probably passed, there was a quiet sort of acceptance about them. Joanie Damar had sat in the passenger seat on the way there, rambling quietly about how her husband had changed. How he had gone from an earnest young lawman to a stressed-out detective to the cold-blooded monster that had put her in the hospital when he learned his son was not what he'd planned.

"The changes were so small at first," she murmured. "At first he was late, but he always apologized. Then he just didn't show. Then he'd start yelling if I so much as asked him where he'd been. And then he…."

"Stopped yelling?" Chuck asked delicately.

"Yeah."

The house in Lansing—apparently Julia and Felix's summer vacation house anyway—was as big as Lucius's "smaller" mansion, and was situated over-looking the lake, with its own private, gated beach and three of Hunter's most trusted mercenary friends, armed and in constant communication, to watch out for Chet Damar's girlfriend, Newman Damar's wife and son, and Kyle Miller's wife and rent boy.

As Chuck, Larry, and Joanie's son, Trevor, had been unloading the luggage, Heather Miller had come up to Larry quietly and said, "I know who you are, you know. You don't have to avoid me."

Larry had begun to cry, and Heather and her two children had hugged and comforted him. It left Chuck and Trevor Damar alone with the luggage, but it was a small price to pay. Chuck was leaving people who could take care of each other.

On the way through Chicago, he stopped and picked up Danny, Julia, and Torrance Grayson.

And an entire thermos of expresso.

Julia and Danny were content to doze in the back, but Torrance sat up front, his handsome matinee-idol features disgustingly perky and his dark hair perfectly coiffed. Chuck guzzled expresso and tried not to feel like warmed death while he kept the car on the far north edge of the acceptable speed of traffic.

"You know," Torrance said delicately after Chuck swerved around two big-rig trucks, both going fast enough to blow a virgin's socks off, "you *could* let me drive."

Chuck grunted and shook his head. He couldn't explain the itch between his shoulders, the bone-deep grifter's twitch that told him something was up.

"They were expecting an attack on the business today," Chuck said. "They weren't sure where it was coming from, but Lucius and Felix and God knows who else were going there. I don't like it. We are spread too thin."

Torrance looked at him worriedly. "You think they'd do something besides petty espionage?"

Chuck blew out a breath. "You've got to understand," he said. "This… this has gotten more and more personal toward Lucius. I think it started out as a way to get the women back, which is pretty sick as it is. But Lucius is someone in their social strata, and he's standing in their way. These people are powerful, and they're abusive, and they're going to be pissed. I…." He let out his next breath on a growl.

And edged the accelerator to ninety.

"You can go faster if you want," Torrance said, pulling out his phone and looking at it dispassionately. "I've got a police scanner here that tells me where the roads are being monitored. You're clear most of the way to Peoria."

Chuck gave a relieved smile. "Excellent. I left mine back at the shelter. You keep an eye out there, and I'll tell you where to track Kyle Miller's financials so his wife and side piece can go live their own fucking lives."

"Speaking of him," Torrance murmured, "how about now that his wife is somewhere he can't guess, we call him to our little party. I mean, I was pretty much going to get in Newman Damar's face, but do you think I should call a press conference and invite him too?"

Chuck frowned. "Do you think he'd come? I mean, he lives in Ohio."

Torrance gave a snort. "Yeah, but he *parties* in Chicago. And my sources say he's been drinking and whoring in his South Loop pied-à-terre for the last month."

"Doesn't he, like, have a *job*?"

"State congress isn't in session in the summer, so I'm going to take that as a yes," Torrance laughed. He spent a few moments apparently practicing world domination on his cell phone before looking up. "How do you not know politicians get a vacation?"

"Because I dropped out of college," Chuck told him honestly, and then added, "and I was getting my degree in chemical engineering anyway."

Torrance arched a plucked and styled eyebrow at him. "You are a man of hidden depths, my friend."

Chuck shrugged. "I yam what I yam," he said, thinking about those quiet moments last night in Lucius's arms. Lucius hadn't let him shrug it off. Lucius had forced him to, for better or worse, own up to the best and worst parts of his past, of his own heart.

He'd been in love with Carmichael Carmody. Not a lot—not deeply. It wasn't what he felt for Lucius by any stretch of the imagination.

But that man had been important to him, and Chuck had walked away. Carmichael had insisted on it, and Carmichael had been the one with everything to lose. But Chuck had lost *him* and had been unconsciously grieving that relationship for a year and a half. He'd been so focused on feeling guilty for walking away from Carmichael that he'd never acknowledged, not once, how much it had hurt to do that.

Until the night before, when he'd realized that he hadn't wanted to leave Lucius's bed, or his home, or the safety of his arms. When he realized that if he had to walk away from Lucius to protect Lucius's reputation, to protect his business or his good work with Caraway House, to protect Lucius's so very vulnerable heart, taking those steps would kill him.

Carmichael Carmody had been an ache in his heart, like a cavity in his tooth.

Lucius would be an ache in his heart like he was *missing his heart*.

And now that he knew what love was—now that he knew he was *in* love—he didn't have it in him to treat it lightly, to blow off the things he'd been given, the things he was good at.

He could admit he'd been going to be a damned good engineer before he'd thrown it away to exact revenge on Kyle Miller's ass. And he couldn't regret it now, especially knowing what Kyle Miller had become, but he could most definitely work to not throw away the blessings he had, now that he knew how hard they were to come by.

And now, he felt for the first time in his life how very much he had to lose if things went wrong.

"And what are you?" Torrance Grayson asked thoughtfully as Chuck pushed the edge of every speed limit between Chicago and Springfield.

"I'm a guy who is very worried about the people we left behind," he said honestly. "I'm sort of in love with one of them."

Torrance didn't laugh, and Chuck was grateful. "How's Josh doing?" he asked softly, and the ache in his voice told Chuck everything he wanted to know about unrequited love.

"He's thin and tired," Chuck said, because he was always honest. "But thrilled he could keep his hair."

Torrance let out a pained little grunt. "Well, it looks good on him."

"He, uh, isn't really looking for—"

"I know." Torrance held up a hand and looked determinedly at the phone in his other one. "He was obviously in love with that one cop he couldn't have and probably getting over that. It's…. Even when you know it's useless and over, sometimes it takes a while to fade, you know?"

"Yeah," Chuck said. Two days ago, he would have tried to jolly Torrance out of it, but not now. "I've been there."

"Did it go away?" And even though he and Torrance Grayson didn't know each other that well, there was a hope in his voice, an ache, that somehow Chuck could give him reassurance in this matter.

"Yeah," Chuck said, feeling the reality of the night before in his bones. "When I fell in love harder with someone else."

"Harder?" Torrance was trying to laugh, but Chuck couldn't.

"Losing the one guy hurt, but I was able to pretend it didn't. But this guy? There'd be no pretending."

"Ouch," Torrance whispered. "I'm a little afraid of loving someone that much."

Chuck looked at the speedometer for the thousandth time, and then at the clock, and then at the road sign that said they had another twenty miles to go before they drove through Broadstone, Illinois.

"You should be," he said grimly. "But brother, I don't know how I could have stopped it from happening. God knows I tried."

The call from Felix came ten minutes later.

Danny—who had received it—put the call on speaker right as Chuck exited the freeway and pulled onto the main drag of Broadstone, and Chuck's breath caught as they all heard Felix explain the situation.

"Are you still locked in?" he asked, heart in his throat.

"The outer doors are open," Felix said composedly. "Everyone in the main floors was able to get down and evacuate. Unfortunately, all the doors to *this* floor are still locked."

"And Lucius and Grace are *in* the ventilation shafts."

"Yes."

"Sounds calm, doesn't he, Julia," Danny asked, voice strained.

"The boys and I are hunkered behind a couch in a corner of the room while they try to work their electronic magic, Danny. We're not calm."

Danny emitted a sound of pure frustration that Chuck could identify with in the extreme.

"What's in the test tubes again?" he asked.

"Potassium covered in mineral oil," Felix told him. "The machine is meant to shoot compressed air into the tubes and then infuse it with water."

"Why was there potassium in the test tubes?" Torrance asked. "I mean, that would take a lot of preparation. What were they making?"

"Focus!" Chuck snarled. He'd pulled up to a stoplight by necessity because there were other cars crossing and the hard and fast rule of doing no harm still held. "Look, everybody in the car, if I promise not to mow anybody over, is it okay if I break several or all of the traffic laws?"

"Yes!" they all snapped, and Chuck took a deep breath. He could drive and think at the same time, but not if people were yelling at him.

"Good. Hold on to your asses, because when this light goes green, we're vapor. Now, Felix?"

"Yes?"

"Potassium reacts badly to the hydrogen in both air and water, but the mineral oil protects it from that right now. Odds are good that if it was one or the other—air or water—there wouldn't be a big enough reaction to do more than shatter a couple of tubes. But with both of them shooting in there, well, yeah. Especially in a contained space like something with a lid and a bunch of little needles. It could be bad. So barring computer magic, you *can* stop the explosion manually without disrupting the conveyor belt. But you're gonna need Josh and Stirling to call up some schematics again, you hear?"

"I hear," Felix said grimly. "Can you walk us through it?"

"Sure," Chuck said. "How much time before the bank of test tubes hits the infuser?"

Felix paused, and over the phone they could hear Josh say, "Nine minutes, Dad."

Chuck watched as the light turned green. "We'll be there in five."

LUCIUS WAS halfway down the ventilation shaft when he saw a wisp of black shoe disappear around the corner.

"Grace! Grace, goddammit! Grace, we've got to get out of here. That's a clean room—there's a whole nest of filters and shit between the regular ventilation and the rest of the build... oh."

As he continued to clamber through the shaft, wishing he was five foot seven and whisper thin instead of five foot ten and average, he came up against Grace, lying on his stomach with a series of displaced air filters collapsing in front of him as he wielded a tiny power tool less than half the size of his palm.

"Grace," Lucius said, trying hard to keep his voice from pitching hysterically. "There's nothing we can do. I don't even know if the manual shutoff will work. When this explodes, it's going to produce gas—poisonous gas. We can wait out the explosion in the other room, but not here."

Grace gave a grunt as the last rectangular filter fell forward, and then he started to push his way through, shoving the filters ahead of them.

"Not the manual shutoff. Even that moron would have jammed it," he said, and Lucius followed him as the shaft took a vaguely downward slant and some sort of fan kicked on behind them.

"Then what are you doing?" Lucius asked, fear roiling in his stomach.

"Waiting for your boyfriend to call," Grace said amicably. "He'll know what to do."

Lucius stared at him, irritated. "Oddly enough, I was going to do that, but then we thought we should warn *you*! And according to him, all he's got is three-quarters of a degree."

"He worked munitions in the military and has a chemical engineering degree," Grace argued, working deftly on a screen that was apparently the last obstacle in the shaft before they hit the clean room. "Felix is probably on the phone right—"

The scuffling behind them spoke for itself. Lucius half turned his head and saw Felix, broad shoulders not doing nearly as well in the shaft as Lucius and Grace.

"Lucius!" Felix barked hoarsely. "Duck your head. I'm throwing to Grace and then backing out. Chuck's got a solution for you."

"Wha—"

"*Duck!*"

Lucius ducked, and the pass was made over his head. The scuffling of Felix backing out of the shaft didn't cover Grace's quickfire conversation over the phone.

"No, I'm not crazy!" he said. "I knew you'd call. Because this is your shit. If we waited for you on the phone, we'd be too late. Well then, don't let us die. Hunter can't have another dead boyfriend. The last dead boyfriend fucked him right up. Yeah, won't be a picnic for you, either. So wait."

Grace slid out of sight down the dusty aluminum vent and neatly onto his feet in the white-tiled, no-longer-clean lab. Lucius clambered after him, and Grace handed Lucius the phone.

"Howyadoin', Scotty?" Chuck said. His Texas drawl was pronounced and even, and Lucius wondered if that was because he was making an effort not to panic. Lucius knew that *he* had a much worse time hiding the stress in his voice.

"Fucking peachy," he snapped. "Fantastic. Walking on the beach. You?"

"Well—shit, hold on."

Lucius examined the clean white lab space as he waited for Chuck's reply. The room itself was long and narrow, designed almost exclusively for the conveyor belt and aerosolizer that was currently functioning, making a *whirrrrrrrrrrrrr… kachunk…* rhythmic clacking as the induction part of the machine pulled the racks of empty test tubes into its giant steel cavern, injected air and water onto nothing, where it drained down into the depths of the machine, and then spat out an empty rack. The one full rack—the one loaded with tiny little silver pebbles of death—was about midway through the zig-zag of the full induction, and Lucius glared at it, wishing he could *will* the rack of test tubes stuck into the grooves of the belt back to wherever Fergus had gotten it.

In the background, Lucius heard what sounded to be a series of low moans and then a squeal of metal and Julia's distinctly feminine voice saying, "Oh dear."

"What was that?"

"That was the sound of your car insurance jumping for the stars, Scotty. Hope you don't mind," Chuck said.

"Not at all," Lucius breathed. "Don't hurry on my account."

"Well, you know. Looking forward to seeing you again. We didn't get our morning snuggle, now did we?"

Lucius closed his eyes tightly so they wouldn't sting. It didn't work. "No."

"Maybe next time. Right now, I need you and Grace to do something for me."

And like that, Lucius calmed down. Maybe it was the ease in Chuck's voice, or maybe it was the hope that he'd see Chuck again. Maybe it was Grace's irritation at the thought of being a dead boyfriend. He had to admit he shared the sentiment.

"Okay," Chuck said, not allowing him to think too deeply, not when time mattered. "According to Josh, the water and air tubes run into the back of the machine from a port in the wall. The water runs east and the air runs west. Can you see them?"

"I don't know which one's which," Lucius muttered.

"Doesn't matter. Break them. Spill the water, cut the air hose—do whatever you have to do to make sure that element isn't getting to that machine. As soon as you're done, get the hell out of there, you understand? There's electronics all over the place, and the water's going to be dangerous. Grace!"

"Here, Chuck!"

"You guys got four minutes. Take two minutes to cut the tubes and then get in the ventilation shaft and scoot. Do you need a timer?"

Grace shook his head. "It's all up here," he said confidently.

"Good. Give Lucius the tools he needs, and you guys talk out loud while I…. I gotta do a thing, you hear?"

"Got it!"

While they spoke, Lucius stared wildly around the room before starting toward the aerosolizer like Chuck told him. He and Grace sprinted around the still-clunking conveyor belt, but not before Grace paused at the bank of potassium in test tubes and gave the rack an experimental yank.

Nothing happened.

"It's on tracks, Grace," Lucius explained impatiently. "And the tubes are held in place with wire clips around the rims. We can't just lift them out!"

"Worth a try!" Grace defended, but he was already on his way to the back of the machine, pulling a series of small cases out of the sleeves of his long-sleeved, lightweight mesh T-shirt. "Here," he said as he and Lucius studied the nest of wires and tubes coming through the back of the machine. "I've got three small blades that can cut through steel. You take the bigger one and hit the water tube, I'll take the smaller ones and hit everything else. You do yours closer to the machine so you can control the hose better."

Lucius set the phone on top of the machine that might kill them right when Chuck said, "You doing okay, Scotty?"

"Chuck, dammit!" Whoever was speaking sounded mildly upset.

"It's fine!" he hollered back to whomever. "Lucius! Answer me!"

"Can't answer. Busy cutting a hose with a gerbil's steak knife."

"Okay, then I'll just drive."

The next thirty seconds were the longest ten years of Lucius's life. He took the tiny blade Grace had given him and sawed, cursing the thick silicone outer tubing and the slippery, tough inner coating simultaneously.

Across from him, separated by the bundle of tubes and wires coming out of the wall, Grace was working contentedly and quietly, apparently not disturbed in the least by the pressure. After about two thousand years, Lucius felt the first spurt of water under his fingers and then a slightly thicker flow—but the tube was by no means severed.

"Done!" Grace called. "C'mon, Zillionaire, let's go!"

"But I'm not—"

Grace ducked under the bundle of tubes and wires as lithely as a cat and grabbed Lucius's hand, yanking him away from the conveyor belt with such speed, Lucius barely had time to grab the squawking phone as they hauled ass for the ventilation shaft.

"Scotty!" Chuck barked. "Scotty! You okay?"

"Crawling to safety, Chuck. Let you know when we're there!"

"Roger that. How long until detonation?" His voice fractured at the last note, quivering just enough to tell Lucius that Chuck had been terrified.

For him.

"Fifteen seconds," Grace muttered. "If it was going to detonate. Ten. Don't stop."

But Lucius heard it. Chuck heard it. The entire world heard the countdown in the pits of their stomach as the conveyor belt thunked behind them with a *whirr… kachunk. Whirr… kachunk. Whirr….*

Was that a *pffft*? A clatter? A thunder? Would they hear an explosion, or would the world just go silent?

Or—

"Keep going!" Grace urged. "Don't stop! I don't care if it went boom or not. I'm done with this shit!"

"Yes, of course," Lucius muttered, wondering if he was sweating enough to be shoved along the bottom of the shaft, riding it like a one-man bobsled team.

"You okay, Scotty?" Chuck asked weakly.

"Yeah. It—uhm, something must have worked because—"

A weak clatter came from behind them, the sound of breaking glass and the twisting of metal, and Lucius found he *could* go faster in the ventilation shaft.

The smoke didn't get down the shaft until about six feet before they spilled out, but what did follow them was noxious and awful.

Felix and Stirling rushed in with couch cushions and a small beanbag from the meditation corner of the room and shoved them into the shaft, blocking the smoke temporarily while Lucius struggled into his pants and tried to clear the crap out of his lungs. God, he'd only gotten a breath of it, but everything burned: eyes, lungs, skin, everything.

Felix grabbed him roughly by the shoulder and hauled him to the corner with the sink, ran the water and shoved Lucius's face underneath the cool stream of it without ceremony. The water felt good, soothing, and Lucius pulled out of the stream long enough to splash some on his face and saw that Grace was doing the same at the sink next to him.

"What's our status?" he managed when he could talk.

"Stirling's almost got the outside locks taken care of," Josh said weakly. "One switch to flip and we're out of here."

Lucius looked up and saw that he and Stirling were sitting on the floor in the shelter made by the couch, tilted forward so that the back touched the window. "And Fergus?" he called to the young man still lying in the middle of the tile portion of the floor, clutching his balls.

Fergus moaned. "You brk mm sjjjaw!"

"Good," Josh snapped back. "I'm glad he broke your jaw. You want to know what else happened while you were out? The two goons you sent to kidnap your girlfriend are now bound and gagged and sitting in a car that's currently being towed to Chicago, where we're pretty sure they have outstanding records. Grace, Hunter says hi, and Carl may need stitches."

"They got to beat up people?" Grace said through a coughing fit. "Damn, I love watching that happen."

"Wait," Lucius muttered. "Which car?"

"A Bentley Bentayga that was suspiciously parked on private property," Josh muttered, staring at Lucius like he was stupid.

Lucius made a little "Oh" shape with his lips and remembered that the night before—Was it only the night before?—Chuck had driven his SUV into the middle of the heavily overgrown part of his property and left it there. Julia and Felix had been going to have it moved earlier, he knew, but then, everybody's day had not gone to plan.

"So," Josh continued on, "if you want to lay claim to them, Fergus, I'm sure they'll be willing to spill their guts about who hired them. Hell, I'm pretty sure they're ready to do that already. Also, in case you're wondering? Since there was no big explosion tonight? All those plans to 'buy low, sell high' that your buddies were making in their investment corporations are gonna fall through. They'll probably lose their jobs."

"You're also fired," Lucius coughed, and Fergus gave another little moan and folded up even tighter, trying to protect his balls.

Good for him.

Lucius's back pocket squawked, and Lucius pulled his phone out and gulped air. "We're fine," he rasped. "Sorry. There was no big boom—just a small *poof*."

"You sound a little rough there," Chuck said gently. "You sure you're going to be okay?"

"Yeah," Lucius told him. "Yeah. You're coming here to get us?"

Chuck made a noise. "Mm... I'm going to be there in time to get *some* of you. Lucius? Torrance Grayson called Kyle Miller and pretty much dared him to meet us in front of your building. From what we can see, half the police force of the county is there too. You can play this one of two ways, Scotty. You can sneak out the back with Josh, Stirling, and Grace, or you and Felix can go face the cameras and the music and put a stop to this right now. I got to tell you, I talked to Kyle Miller's wife and his boyfriend, and they are *fine* if you tell the world what he did. They'll get new ID's if they need to, but they don't want him to get away with shit. Joanie Damar and Trevor feel the same way. Joanie's heartbroken about her older son, Chet, but she is all about not letting another asshole run free. And Julia has shown Marla Crandall's video to half the socialites in Chicago. So you can let Torrance Grayson make a meal of Damar and Miller there on your own turf, or you can go out and face them and tell the world who they are, and add

Marla Crandall's husband to the mix. You make it clear that an attack on Caraway House, wherever it may be, is an attack on the victims of domestic abuse, and you make these assholes look like the wife-beaters they are. It's up to you."

Lucius wiped his face on his shoulder again and glared at the piece of garbage on the floor. Then he met Felix Salinger's eyes.

"You'd really stand with me?" he asked Felix.

"Oh, I would," Felix said softly. He looked at his son over Lucius's shoulder. "Josh's mother didn't have anyone to turn to but a couple of grifters. The world deserves better."

Lucius swallowed and then spoke into the phone again. "Sure, but I need…." He closed his eyes. He was going to make it a condition or a caveat or something, but he found he couldn't do that.

He could only ask.

"Need what, Scotty?" Chuck asked quietly.

"I *want* you to stand with me," Lucius said. "Please, Charles? I'll call you my head of security or my boyfriend. It's up to you. But I… I would just—"

"Yeah, baby," Chuck said. "Yeah. I'll be there. You and Felix come to the front and meet me and Torrance. I'll be whatever you need me to be, Scotty. I'm down with that."

Lucius smiled weakly and then nodded and looked around the room. "Stirling, can we get out of here now?"

The *thunk* of the released locks was the best answer he could have received.

Crossroads and Road Trips

Two Weeks Later

CHUCK'S PHONE was going off next to the bed in Glencoe, and he moaned and rolled over, missing Lucius's body as he did so.

He'd spent two more weeks on Lucius's property, sometimes spelling the security guards with Hunter and Soderburgh in the aftermath of Lucius's interview that day, sometimes teaching yoga and self-defense like his cover had promised, except for real. He found something wholly rewarding in running those classes, in coaxing frightened, battered people into feeling confidence in their bodies again, into feeling as though they had some power over their lives.

He liked doing that. He could do that for quite a while, he thought, and Lucius had not once suggested he find another place to go.

But the nights he wasn't working security, he'd spent in Lucius's house, doing the same things he did when he was in the Salinger house or even the apartment in Chicago.

Reading, working out, and enjoying the company of the people around him.

More particularly, enjoying Lucius's company. Enjoying Lucius's bed.

He kept expecting the wonder of the two of them together to fade somehow, to dissipate. He would reach for Lucius in the morning to kiss him, expecting *this* touch of their lips, their tongues, to be not as wonderful as the last touch. He was always surprised when it was as good—or, more often, better. He expected falling asleep while spooning around that delightfully strong male body to pall somehow, to become less marvelous, like a memory of Christmas as a kid versus what Christmas often had been as an adult.

It was always better. *Always* better than he remembered. How was that possible?

He didn't understand.

Julia had told him to stay at Lucius's as long as he needed to. She would happily take care of his cat, but since she had co-opted Cary Grant the cat at first glance and the sneaky thing had taken to sleeping with her even when Chuck was home, he felt like that was mostly a formality anyway. And he'd continued to stay, figuring he could always bug out when things faded, or when he got too close, or when Lucius's long hours—and he did work long hours—got too arduous.

It hadn't happened yet. In fact, Chuck had offered his services as Lucius's Guy Friday when Lucius had to work, doing random data entry and contacts, signing email as Lucius's chief of security, which is how Lucius had introduced him when on camera, that terrible, fateful day Chuck had almost lost him.

Chuck had parked the battered Bentayga around the back of the parking lot, allowing Josh, Stirling, and Grace to exit unremarked upon so Danny and Julia could drive them quietly back to Lucius's house without anybody the wiser.

Then he, Lucius, and Felix had marched around the front of the building to face the music.

Torrance had been in fine form that day. He'd called a friend in Springfield to come assist, and by the time Chuck, Felix, and Lucius got to the front, the two of them were set up with a camera on a tripod and a handheld in Phillip, his photographer's, hand. Newman Damar got out of his cruiser, and Torrance was in his face within three footsteps with "How long have you been beating your wife?"

While Damar's men tried to hold him back, Phillip began editing the clip. He sent it out on the internet as a teaser, and by the time Kyle Miller arrived, less than fifteen minutes later, they had a streaming audience in the hundreds of thousands.

Torrance Grayson was magnetic to watch—Chuck could admit it. Slick, sharp, lightning quick on the comeback or follow-up question, he would have made a fantastic litigator. But then all that pretty might have gone to waste. He had Newman Damar on the ropes for fifteen minutes while Lucius quietly directed the paramedics, first responders, and hazmat team that had been summoned by the alarm system. The employees who had been in the building had streamed out, and Lucius spoke to them in all honesty, explaining what had happened and telling them who was responsible for it and why.

"I have a foundation that assists battered women," he said, as Torrance was literally pinning Damar to the wall. "I assisted Fergus Allen's ex-girlfriend, Kyle Miller's and Newman Damar's wives, and Damar's son's girlfriend, as well as a few other women whose husbands are powerful and rich and think they are above reproach. This accident, as well as the others in the past weeks, are a result of Fergus Allen's direct tampering. For those of you worried about your stock options, the larger plan was to step in, buy up all your stock, and take over the company. I hope you will stick with Broadstone Industries. I have it on good authority"—and he glanced at Felix, who winked—"that we're about to get a cash infusion and a lucrative merger with the Dormer-Salinger Corporation, and our stock will be ironclad."

The group of employees—men, women, young, older—all stared at him with a little bit of hero worship in their eyes.

Chuck, who knew nothing about business and less about stock options, had a feeling that Broadstone Industries was going to be just fine.

But that didn't mean he left Lucius's side, not through the long series of interviews and phone calls to the state attorney's office and the ensuing twelve hours of bureaucracy that left them all exhausted and wrung out. It had been worth it.

Kyle Miller—who still walked with a limp, after sitting on an exploding toilet all those years ago—hadn't been arrested on scene, but that was only because the charges were filed by the state attorney. A week after that terrible day at Broadstone Industries, warrants for everything from insider trading to conspiracy to commit murder were issued for Miller, Damar, and Marla Crandall's husband, Barker Crandall, who was greeted by federal marshals the moment he exited the plane. As exhausting as that day had been, seeing the three of them endure scandal, backlash, and finally a perp walk had been very worth it.

Chuck had wondered why Josh and Stirling hadn't volunteered to help Grayson, but after that circus, he understood. A year ago, yes, Josh would have eaten that shit up with a spoon, but on this day, Chuck was told he'd gone back to Lucius's and crashed for a full twelve hours.

And the next day, he'd been back in the hospital, suffering from dehydration and promising upon his honor that until he was at 70 percent at least, he would confine the thief-work to stuff he could accomplish from his parents' couch.

Hunter and Soderburgh had stayed on for another week, making sure security would never be vulnerable again. Carl Soderburgh, Chuck suspected, proved himself invaluable when the official insurance inspector arrived. Carl was proof that Lucius had taken threats to his property and his employees seriously and that he was still an excellent risk.

After those two weeks in Lucius's bed, Chuck had to agree.

He'd only left, really, because he'd gotten called to another job—a fun one, in fact. A used car dealership in Wyoming was using their cars to transport drugs, and the casualties were the people who got busted for possession and transpo without having any idea what was in their vehicles. Chuck had driven a classic Dodge Charger 130 miles an hour through the wilds of Wyoming, Hunter by his side, with half the state's deputies on their tail, stopping only when they hit a sheriff's office in Montana, where Hunter called an old contact to come search the Dodge.

Given that he had the Wyoming police force to vouch for the fact that he drove the car off the lot with all those drugs inside, Chuck was in the free and clear, and the dealer was *dealt.*

And Chuck and Hunter quietly melted into the background and caught a plane home, high-fiving all the way.

It had been a good job. Fun in Chuck's favorite way. Foot to the gas pedal, wind through their hair, and it had cemented Hunter as one of his favorite coworkers ever, because they made a *dynamite* team.

But they had gotten back to Chicago the night before, and Hunter had wanted nothing more than to crawl into bed next to Grace.

And Chuck? Chuck realized that he felt the same way about Lucius. Seeing him, telling him the high-points of the job—that mattered. Lucius wouldn't judge. He'd worry the appropriate amount, but he wouldn't judge. And given that he'd seen what the *second* brand-new Bentayga had looked like after he'd gotten home that horrible night, Chuck knew that Lucius understood that for Chuck, collateral damage was strictly cosmetic and not very pricey.

Humans were never part of that equation.

That was, he had to admit, a really wonderful foundation for what the two of them loved to do.

Chuck may not be able to crawl into bed next to Lucius *every* night, but he'd certainly love to look forward to it as often as possible.

And he most definitely missed Lucius's tight, warm body as he rolled over to answer the phone.

The voice on the other end made him sit up straight, eyes popped wide open, in the sleek, graciously styled bedroom Julia had outfitted exclusively for Chuck when he'd asked if he could move in, not so many months ago.

"Chuckie?"

"Car-Car?" Oh my God, Car-Car? "Where are you calling from?" He paused. "Where did you get my cell number? You're not due to be out on parole for a while, are you?"

"Not parole," Carmichael Carmody said, sounding proud. "Good behavior." His voice fell. "Also, I kept getting the shit beat out of me. The guards actually spoke up and said if I didn't get out of there, I wasn't going to survive. And that seemed a shame after all you did to help me out."

Chuck closed his eyes. "Carmichael, I turned you in to the cops." God. He would never forgive himself. Ever.

"You saved my life!" Car-Car protested. "You have no idea!" Somewhere outside wherever he was calling from, a horn honked, and he swore. "Look, I'm in some tiny little suburb called Broadstone. I went to talk to that Lucius guy who lives here, the guy you were on the news with, and he gave me your number. Is there any way I can come see you?"

"Yeah," Chuck said hurriedly, smoothing his hand over the fawn-colored coverlet Julia had picked out for him. She seemed to think he should wear green and rust a lot, and he sure did love to make that woman happy. "Yeah, Car-Car. Here, let me text you the address of where I'm staying right now, and we can meet." He had a vague idea of making Car-Car let him take the wheel and maybe showing him what real pizza tasted like in the city, but beyond that, he had nothing.

"Sure! That would be… that would be great!" And then Carmichael Carmody proved he was not a fool. "But, uhm, you're taken, right?"

Chuck swallowed, so relieved that he didn't have to break that news himself, he could have cried. "Yeah. Yeah, Car, I am."

"That Lucius guy—he seemed really nice and all, but he... he was real firm about letting me know that you and he were a thing. I told him I wanted to visit an old friend, that's all."

Chuck squeezed his eyes tight and realized that he really *could* cry, because his eyes were burning hot right now. "A visit from an old friend would be great," he said softly. "Lucius would have no problem with that."

"Good, see you in a few."

"See you in a few *hours*, Car. It's not close."

"Well, that too." And then he hung up.

And Chuck spent the next twenty minutes showering and getting dressed and trying not to stress out.

According to Julia, he failed badly.

"Charles," she said gently, sipping a cup of tea in the kitchen with him as he ate eggs and bacon at the counter. "This shouldn't be a big deal. You don't still have feelings for this man, do you?"

Chuck shook his head vehemently. "No," he said, closing his eyes and trying not to gulp his coffee.

Phyllis forked the last two pieces of bacon from the pan onto his plate.

"Bless you, sweetheart," he said throatily. "You know, you didn't have to cook for me today."

She grinned and wrinkled her nose. "After you and Hunter bailed my nephew out yesterday? Are you kidding? He was looking at twenty years for drug smuggling when all he did was buy a car. He's home with his wife this morning. Chuck, I'll cook you anything you want!"

Chuck grinned at her, delighted. "You know, I have been gay all my life, but I keep meeting women who make me want to change my mind."

Phyllis giggled, and although he'd never seen that expression on her, he had to admit, he liked it. Then she added a beignet, which he gathered she'd made a lot of the day before and had saved a few for him and Hunter.

He really did like his life right now, he had to admit. While it wasn't waking up with Lucius, waking up in the Salinger house sure placed a close second.

"Charles," Julia prompted softly, and he sighed.

"I never admitted I had feelings for him in the first place," he said, taking a bite of the beignet. Mm. Still good. "Still, it... it was sort of fucking me up, ma'am. I don't know how else to say it. I left him behind, and while it felt like the only option at the time, it didn't feel like the right one. I wouldn't do something like that to Lucius, and I feel like I shouldn't have done it to Carmichael."

"Mm." The touch of her hand on his arm was warm and gracious, and he turned toward her because this was obviously something important.

"What?"

"I get the feeling you've spent a lot of your life trying to pretend like nothing gets to you, Charles. That you're only in it for a good time."

He flushed but couldn't find any words.

"There are a bunch of people in our house in Lansing who tell me you went out of your way to make them feel better during a really frightening time in their lives. And I know that you don't spend your time at Lucius's lying out in the sun and working on your tan. You spend it teaching and working security and generally taking Lucius's good idea and making it better. So ask yourself something. Are you a better person because Carmichael Carmody made you take your own feelings seriously?"

He had to swallow—more than once. "Yeah," he rasped.

"And taking your own feelings seriously has made you a better partner for Lucius, hasn't it?"

He nodded. "Yeah."

"Then think about this meeting as a chance to thank your old boyfriend for making you see that admitting your feelings is important. And tell him he was important to you. And that way, you can move into this next stage of your life with Lucius with a whole heart."

Chuck found himself blinking rapidly. "I'm supposed to tell him that over pizza?" he asked, and his attempt at being funny was ruined by the way his voice cracked.

She stood and kissed his cheek. "No, my boy. You're supposed to tell him that in our sitting room, as Phyllis bakes cookies. I'll be downstairs playing video games with Josh and Grace should you need me."

Chuck paused to take her hand and kiss her knuckles. "Thank you, ma'am. I think that would be a great place to talk."

She patted his cheek. "You told me he was a mechanic. Is he any good?"

"He's great," Chuck said with sincerity. "He could work magic with cars. He sucked as a businessman, but he could soup up a minivan until it topped 150 on a straightaway." And it had. "Why?"

"Because meeting Lucius's mechanic, Saoirse, at the airfield made Felix and I rather… covetous. I think that's the word. We would like to deal with our own mechanic." She waved her hand with an insouciance that might have fooled anybody else but family. "You know, mechanical things. The timing couldn't be better. If your friend is looking to settle down in this area, ask him if he'd like the job."

And then, before he could protest or argue—or even call her on a blatant lie that she and Felix coveted *anything* of Lucius's—she popped up from her place at the counter and strolled out of the breakfast room, waving a little "ta-ta" over her shoulder as she went.

"Wow," he said in admiration.

"She's really good," Phyllis agreed. "Now, is your friend staying for lunch?"

"I guess so, why?"

"Because Patty, that student who comes to cook sometimes, keeps me looking for new recipes, and I think I want to try deep-dish pizza. How long until your friend arrives?"

Chuck checked his watch. "About two hours, why?"

Phyllis pulled her Nietzsche was Nuts apron over her head of iron-gray spiral curls. "Because that gives us an hour and a half to go shopping and come back with enough pepperoni and tomato sauce to feed the entire family. You game?"

Well, it would beat the hell out of sitting there and waiting.

CHUCK WAS helping Phyllis unload the Navigator when a perfectly practical Honda C-RV pulled up the long driveway through the parklike environs of the Salinger mansion in Glencoe. If Chuck hadn't been expecting Carmichael Carmody, he never would have guessed he'd be driving that vehicle.

But the young man—dark-haired, slightly built, with big brown eyes and a narrow, vulnerable face that would always make him look like a Boy Scout—who hopped out and smiled rather diffidently at Chuck as Phyllis stacked his arms with grocery boxes was definitely a leaner, less baby-faced version of the man Chuck had left inside a bank nearly two years before.

Chuck smiled at him casually. "Don't just stand there, Car-Car. Help us get this stuff inside! She's making pizza for lunch, man. It's worth it!"

Carmichael laughed and came up the walkway for his own stack of boxes, and together they went through the garage to the kitchen, where they set down their burdens before Phyllis shooed them into the sitting room.

"I'll be in there with drinks and snacks as soon as I'm done putting things away," she said. "Carmichael, do you prefer pop, water, what?"

"Pop is fine, ma'am," he said gratefully, the Texas even stronger in his voice than Chuck's. "I'd be so appreciative."

"Give me twenty and I'll be right on it," she said, and then it was Chuck and Carmichael, alone.

Which turned out to not be a bad thing, really.

They sank onto the couch and the love seat, kitty-corner to each other, and Carmichael looked around nervously. "This is a real nice place. Is it yours?"

Chuck laughed. "This? God no. This size of house is a responsibility, and I'm still not great with that. No, you might say I'm working for a new crew now. This is the crew chiefs' place, and they let us stay here."

"Is that the Broadstone guy?" Carmichael asked in confusion, and Chuck laughed again and spent the next half hour explaining the Salingers and what they did and how they helped people because they could, and how they were very good at it indeed.

"But Lucius…?" Car asked eventually, and Chuck shrugged.

And decided that this was a good time for the hard part.

"I split my time," he said, "between Lucius's shelter for battered women and here. It's good. I think this might work out perfectly. I hope so. Lucius is the best thing to happen to me since…." He grimaced. "Leaving you behind really fucked me up, Car-Car. I knew we could never be together, but leaving you to go to jail? I didn't want to be with anyone else after that. What kind of lowlife was I, that I let you get picked up by the cops?"

And unexpectedly, Carmichael's eyes filled with tears. "You were the best fuckin' thing to ever happen to me, that was what you were," he said, voice thick. "Dammit, Chuckie, don't you see? I was trapped. I was so trapped I did the gods of stupid a favor and tried to rob a bank. And you—you saved my life. And then, instead of just taking off with the money, you *saved my life*. I got out of prison, and my wife had a house somewhere besides Texas, and the kids and she'd built this life. Such a good life. And because we weren't so desperate, so hurting for cash, so stuck in the same shitty place, I could tell her the truth, Chuck. Do you get that? I could *tell her the truth*. And she cried. She cried a lot. But then she asked why I'd held on for so long, and I told her that I couldn't leave her in the cold, where she'd get shit on in our old neighborhood, where the kids would have to live with the 'their dad's a faggot' crap. And she cried some more, and she said, 'You must have felt so trapped.' And then *I* cried, and… and we're still friends. I mean, the divorce is gonna go through, but that frees her up too. She'll get a man who will love her like she should be loved, and I'll get a chance to know my kids, to visit them and let them visit me when I get set up. And I'll still have her in my life, which is good."

He paused, wiping his eyes on his shoulder.

"I love her," he said, voice thick. "Just, you know, not the way I loved you."

Chuck closed his eyes against his own tears.

"I loved you too," he whispered. "But not… not as much as you needed. Not like you deserved. But you weren't alone, Carmichael. That was the worst part of leaving you. Letting you think you were all alone."

Carmichael wiped his face on his shoulder again. "You didn't leave me alone, Chuckie. You left me with hope. And now that I'm out of prison and I've got some hope, I am looking forward to a whole new life. Don't you worry none about doing me wrong. You were the first damned person in my life besides Beth who did me right. You go on with Mr. Broadstone and you feel good about that. You did Carmichael Carmody right, and you can do right by him too."

Chuck nodded. "I can do that," he said. "I can do right by him."

"Well, you sure did right by me."

CARMICHAEL STAYED for lunch and then left, but he didn't go far. Danny offered him the use of the Chicago apartment, since Carmichael decided to take the job and Chuck really wasn't using it anymore. Chuck liked that—liked the idea that they might be friends—but not nearly as much as he liked seeing the brand-new navy-blue Bentley Bentayga that pulled up the drive about an hour after Carmichael Carmody left.

He was out the door and down the driveway before Lucius had even stopped the car, and after Lucius hopped out, Chuck took him in for a hard, mauling, breathless kiss that left them both moaning and sweaty in the fading August light.

"God!" Lucius muttered. "That was awesome. Why did we do that?"

"Because I'm so glad to see my boyfriend," Chuck said, smiling.

Lucius smiled back, that hint of shyness Chuck's perpetual undoing. "We're boyfriends, right? I mean, your crew keeps using that word—"

"Oh yeah," Chuck said. "We're boyfriends. It doesn't matter where I sleep, I'll always want to come home to you."

Lucius bit his lip. "Even after… you know, Car-Car?"

Chuck knew he was in love with this man, but damn. Every day he fell a little harder.

"Yeah, Lucius. I had to admit I was in love with Car-Car. I had to. Because that way, I could understand that I'd fallen so much more in love with you. I am so in love with you. That okay?"

Lucius nodded. "I missed you," he said, burying his face against Chuck's shoulder. "I missed you so much."

Chuck laughed a little. "You're not gonna say it?" he teased.

Lucius shook his head. "It might make me cry," he admitted hoarsely. "I don't want to go in to your family and have dinner with my eyes all red and—"

"I love you," Chuck sang in his ear. "I love you more than going 130 miles an hour in a souped-up Dodge Charger. I love you more that trashing two Bentley Bentaygas in the span of two days. I love you more than the chase and more than the catch and more than the game—"

Lucius caught his mouth, kissing him so hard Chuck felt compelled to reach under that silk-suit-clad bottom and lift him up, making Lucius wrap his legs around Chuck's waist and hold on for dear life.

"I love you," Lucius said breathlessly. "I've never loved anybody like I love you. Now put me down so I don't have to be embarrassed in front of your fam—"

Chuck kissed him again.

Sure, Lucius Broadstone might be a little mussed, but that was okay. They were talking forever now, and if that didn't blow back their hair, they were doing forever wrong.

Tensile Strength
—a Long Con Fic

By Amy Lane

THE SOLUTION had occurred to Julia before, in a peripheral sort of way. She was just so used to thinking of Josh's father as out of bounds, that was all. But something Lucius Broadstone had said when he'd come to the hospital to speak with her, Danny, and Josh… it had made her ponder.

After Chuck had escorted her and Danny home, she'd gone up to her room to rest for a bit and then called Danny and Felix in right before dinner.

She'd changed after a few hours of working up in her suite. Leggings or sweats and voluminous T-shirts, comfortable clothing was such a wonderful innovation. Sometimes she'd steal Felix's shirts, because he smelled familiar and comforting, and sometimes, when she wanted something a little more fitted, she'd take Danny's. She supposed she really ought to find a long-term lover of her own so she could wear *his* shirts, but at this juncture, she couldn't see the point. Sex was lovely, but it had never caught her imagination, made her yearn and burn for a man, particularly not in a way that would preempt her family as it stood. Danny and Felix made her feel safe and treasured, valued in a way a lover had yet to achieve, and that was without all the awkwardness that came from actually stripping down to bare skin and meshing private parts together.

If she could find a man who could take at least as equal a place in her life as the two people who were kindest to her when she needed it most, she might think of getting married again, this time for real.

But right now she was worried to death for her son and holding on to her composure by a thread while in public. Here, in private, she was going to wear Danny's sweats and Felix's shirt and ask Danny and Felix to do what they did best—come up with a plan.

"Julia?" Felix knocked tentatively on the door to her suite, and she called him in from her place on the couch. The suite itself took up the top floor of a wing in the house. Felix had even installed a small elevator accessible from the outside so she could have her privacy. She rarely used it, but the fact that he'd given it to her as a birthday present one of the years after Danny had left and they'd divorced, only reinforced her passionate platonic love for the man. They'd both needed comfort and distraction that year. The elevator was as close as they could get.

"Come in," she said softly. "Is Danny with—"

"*Oolf*!" Felix stumbled inside as Danny apparently plowed into him from behind. "Dammit, Danny—"

"Well, what were you doing, lurking in her doorway? We wake up all the time with her sitting on our bed like Snow White singing to the bloody birds. Go sit next to her and give her a hug, for God's sake!"

Julia laughed softly, even more so when Felix sank next to her on the couch and extended his arm. He was wearing a dress shirt and slacks—dinner clothes—although he took off his shiny hard-soled shoes and wore slippers inside.

Danny had put on "thieves clothes"—black leggings and a black knit shirt—pretty much as soon as he cleared the doorway, and he'd wear that to dinner as well. Danny knew he should probably dress, but like Grace, he would break that rule unless somebody really enforced it. And nobody was going to enforce it for him because, well, he was Danny.

And then he sank down on the couch on her other side, and she tilted her head to rest on his shoulder.

"How are you doing?" Danny asked softly.

"I will be doing absolutely terribly," she said softly, "until our son is doing better."

"Yeah." Felix sighed, squeezing her tightly around the middle as they huddled. They all gave a collective shudder, and then Felix relaxed his hold on her, and she straightened where she sat and pulled her knees to her chest.

"Boys," she said, "it's time we talk about Josh's birth father. It's important." Her son had leukemia, and it was a terrible, terrible disease. The chemotherapy would probably kill it, but whether or not it killed Josh at the same time was the question. A bone marrow transplant would be his most hopeful bet for recovery, but Julia's blood type wasn't a match. Someone from Josh's immediate genetic family was the best chance he had, but since Felix and Danny were his fathers in love only, that left one option.

The man—boy, really—who had spent a week dancing with Julia at the local community events while their fathers plotted illegal and dangerous business deals.

Oh, he'd been so pretty—and so kind. And when he'd tugged on her hand, spiriting her away to a quiet picnic in the olive trees during the heat of the summer, she knew what would happen under the stars. But it had been lovely, and it had been tender. And it had been hers.

When she'd realized she was pregnant, he was long gone, pulled away by his father, who had the same sort of plans for him that her father had for her, and she hadn't resented him for a moment. They'd carved some time out of the night to be themselves, to have some joy. She couldn't begrudge him that.

Danny and Felix exchanged a pained glance over her head, which told her this wasn't the first time they'd thought of it, and her heart constricted in her chest.

"What?" she asked thickly. "What do you know that I don't?"

"Dearest," Felix said softly, "we never asked you about a name—"

"Matteo di Rossi," she said flatly. "What do you know about him?"

Felix grimaced. "How did you know?"

Her eyes burned, and she chewed her lower lip. "Because you and Danny love me, and Danny lived in Rome around the time Matteo was in town," she said. "Danny could have figured it out."

Danny let out a breath. "Pretty much from the moment we met," he said. "It was your secret, Julia. We all had so very little back then. You had the secret of Josh's father, and you had Josh. We wouldn't take any of that away from you."

"You looked him up?" she asked. Felix's arms were back around her shoulders, and she was glad.

"He was killed," Danny said, dropping a kiss in her hair. "About a year after his father was killed, actually, which was five or so years ago. We looked into it right after learning Josh's diagnosis."

"Oh." Oh Lord. For a moment—a bare moment—she'd been so very happy, sure she had an answer, something they could do to help her son, who looked so goddamned sick!

"His brother," Felix said, his voice coming from far away. "Leon di Rossi. He is still very much alive."

Julia caught her breath. "His brother—"

"We need to find out his blood type," Danny said. "We… we were going to ask Stirling for his help, given that Leon is based in Europe and it's not quite so simple to find things out. Soderburgh—"

"Carl?" she asked, a faint smile on her lips. She was starting to become really fond of the big, handsome, taciturn man who seemed to show up and do things for them out of sheer competency and—she suspected—kindness.

"Yes," Felix said, which meant that, possibly, his rude name for Carl Cox had been left in the dust where it belonged. "Carl has started drawing up contractual agreements already. He's going to be here tonight to help with Lucius Broadstone's project, but he'll be working on this as soon as he can." Lucius's needs were very immediate—people were depending on him for their safety, and that meant that the Salinger crew, with their specific skill set, was going to be busy for the next week or so.

She took a quick gulp of air, sudden grief for Matteo di Rossi assailing her, as well as relief that they had one more option and hope was not yet lost.

"And Liam Craig has asked to help," Danny said, surprising her.

"How?" she asked, because it would keep her from falling apart from sheer relief.

"A couple of ways," Danny told her. "He has access to medical records for one, as well as the medical records for Leon's teenaged children, in case they're willing to assist. And...." He shrugged. "Their father was a famous womanizer. It's possible there are a few uncles or aunts out there who may be as in the dark as Leon di Rossi that they have a blood relative they could help. Liam has offered to track down as many leads as he can." Danny smiled sweetly, and Julia knew he had a soft spot for the young Interpol officer who had helped him out of the gutter when he'd been at his lowest. "Liam's a nice young man. I think he's got something of a sweet spot for Josh."

Josh had swooned into Liam's arms, actually, but Julia would convince the man it was a confession of undying love if it would get Liam to bend some rules for them.

She opened her mouth to say exactly that, but what came out was a little bit of a hiccup.

"Julia?" Felix asked, concerned.

"I just thought of it," she managed to gasp. "It's been three weeks, and I only just...." She sobbed again. "Only just...."

Danny reached out to take one of her hands and threaded their fingers together. "Dearest," he said softly. "He's your heart. Your world. It's possible that you could get up, dress, look fabulous, and do your job, then visit him, and deal with all the other people in this mansion right now, and seem as though you have your collective shit together. But…." His voice caught a little, wrinkled, broke. "None of us—*none* of us— have our collective shit together. You were keeping your son happy and loved on a minute-by-minute basis. Your brain can only do so much with all the internal screaming you're doing. I've got to tell you, having to ask Stirling to do the hack for us was Felix's job, because I couldn't make that leap when I ran up against a wall. I was not thinking straight either, so you're in good company."

Felix gave a humorless laugh. "And Danny was the one who suggested Leon or illegitimate siblings, because, like you, I despaired when we found out Matteo had passed." He grimaced and held out his knuckles to Julia, and she only now saw they were bruised. "I hit a wall," he said. "Quite literally."

And that broke her. She leaned her head on Felix's chest this time, while Danny rested his head in her lap, and they cried, soundlessly, like grownups were supposed to, out of stress and fear.

Danny was the one who sat up first and grabbed the Kleenex box from the end table by the couch. "Come on, my loves," he said, voice rusty. "We need to get cleaned up. Julia, you probably wish to dress. We need to go pretend that we're adults and we have everything in hand."

Julia hiccupped again, but it was softer than it had been before, and eventually she was able to mop her face and shoo them both out of her sanctuary while she changed and redid her makeup.

As she was putting on her lipstick, she recalled her thoughts about taking a lover, and while she felt maybe a twinge of regret, she took that possibility and threw it over her shoulder and out an imaginary window.

In a perfect world, everybody would be matched up two by two, like animals on Noah's Ark.

Or maybe not.

In her perfect world, her son would be healthy, and they would get to work together with the two men who had loved him like a father and treated her like someone precious and valuable. Men who had never, ever deserted her and her son, not even when it would have been in their best interests to do so.

With a final adjustment to her makeup, Julia straightened her hair and the pantsuit she was wearing to dinner before she turned around and left her room.

It really had been sweet of Felix to install that elevator, but the truth was, she was ever so much happier knowing that the two men in her life could break into her sanctuary at any time.

Exclusive Excerpt

A LONG CON ADVENTURE

The Suit

AMY LANE

A Long Con Adventure
Sequel to *The Driver*

Two and a half years ago, Michael Carmody made the biggest mistake of his life. Thanks to the Salinger crew, he has a second chance. Now he's working as their mechanic and nursing a starry-eyed crush on the crew's stoic suit, insurance investigator and spin doctor Carl Cox.

Carl has always been an almost-ran, so Michael's crush baffles him. When it comes to the Salingers, he's the designated wet blanket. But watching Michael forge the life he wants instead of the one he fell into inspires him. In Michael's eyes, he isn't an almost-ran—he just hasn't found the right person to run with. And while the mechanic and the suit shouldn't have much to talk about, suddenly they're seeking out each other's company.

Then the Salingers take a case from their past, and it's all hands on deck. For once, behind-the-scenes guys Michael and Carl find themselves front and center. Between monster trucks, missing women, and murder birds, the case is a jigsaw puzzle with a lot of missing pieces—but confronting the unknown is a hell of a lot easier when they're side by side.

Coming Soon to
www.dreamspinnerpress.com

Humble Beginnings

CARL COX was nine when he realized his last name was going to get him teased on the playground. That didn't stop him from doing his duty as a class monitor though.

"Put that back," he said, looking levelly at Johnny Clemson, who, apparently, had a name so unremarkable that he would never get teased about it ever. It didn't hurt that Johnny had been held back twice and stood head and shoulders above the other kids in the fourth grade—and unlike Topher Garrity, who was just naturally genetically huge but had no skill or coordination, Johnny used *his* advantage to beat up the little kids and steal their lunch money.

Or, in this case, take books from the library without checking them out and break their spines and rip out their pages. Carl—who really loved reading—was not just the monitor from his class this week, he was also really irritated because Johnny had a book in his hand that Carl had been waiting to read.

"What're ya gonna do about it, Cox-sucker!" Johnny sneered.

Carl blinked. He knew the swearwords, yes, because he could listen to the big kids use them just like Johnny, but he'd never put two and two together.

He did now, and made the sad realization that suck was going to be the operative word in this matter, and then continued with his mission.

"Put that back," he insisted.

"No!" Johnny retorted. "Who cares about a stupid book!"

Carl scowled at him. "I do. It's about birds. Birds are cool."

Johnny scoffed, apparently out of words and held the hard-bound cover open like wings, letting the beautiful illustrations flap about in the New England autumn wind. "Then let's see if this book will fly!" he cackled, and Carl took the only option open to him.

He punched Johnny in the nose and caught the book as it fell. Johnny howled and doubled over, clutching at the blood spurting from his nose and Carl trotted to the library to inform the librarian that Johnny Clemson had tried to steal the book, but Carl was returning it, and he'd like to check it out after school if that wasn't too much trouble.

The surprised librarian—a sweet-faced, older man who had never had children of his own and was often surprised to find other people's children responding so excitedly to reading—had reclaimed the book and was holding it to his chest when the vice principal strode in, looking baffled.

"Carl!" she said in exasperation. "Did you really hit Johnny Clemson in the nose in the play yard?"

Carl turned to her and tried a smile. She was a handsome, buxom woman in her thirties, sort of mommish to the max, but with very stylish suits, and he'd noted that mom-ish women *liked* his smile. Blond, green-eyed, with a choirboy's face, he could get away with everything from extra cookies at lunch time to extra time on his math test by giving a pretty smile.

"He was going to tear the book, Mrs. Stewart. I couldn't let him tear the book! It's on birds!" The next thing he said was totally sincere. "Birds are cool."

Mrs. Stewart stared at him, dismayed because this was not a problem with an obvious solution, and Mr. Patrick, the librarian, held out the book in question.

"He, uhm, just returned it," Mr. Patrick said hesitantly. "The Clemson boy was in here eating and I made him leave the library. The book was in the display of science books by the door. I didn't see him take it on his way out."

Mrs. Steward scrubbed at her face with her hand. "Oh Carl," she muttered. "What are we going to do with you? Johnny Clemson's father is furious—you punched his kid in the nose!"

Well, Carl *did* know the penalty for fighting. "Two day's suspension," he said glumly. "And you're going to have to call my parents."

She let out a laugh. "Well, maybe not *that* severe," she said. She met eyes with Mr. Patrick. "So, uhm, you like that book?"

"Yeah. I didn't want him to tear it up," Carl said.

"Well, how about Mr. Patrick checks that out to you, and you can read it in my office this afternoon. It will count as one day's suspension, and we can skip tomorrow's. How's that?"

"You mean I get out of PE?" Carl asked excitedly. Johnny and his friends would be there, and he was pretty sure his new nickname was going to make the rounds.

"Don't sound so excited, Carl," Mrs. Stewart said dryly. "People might believe this isn't a punishment."

Carl nodded soberly, but inside, he was beginning to see the benefits of this law-and-order thing.

And spending the afternoon with the book still left him thinking that birds were cool.

ALAS, BIRDS were *not* cool enough to let him get a degree in ornithology, although part of that was his college didn't have a good program. He *did* get to indulge his other fascination, spawned in part by looking at big picture books with antique illustrations, and that was art history.

"Carl, baby, it's a very nice BA and all, but what are you going to do with it?"

"Get a law degree!" Carl said.

"Like your Uncle Roger?" his mother asked. "He makes good money."

"Like international law," Carl told her. "So I can be an art dealer." He had, in fact, completed his first semester of law school at Georgetown. He had grants, loans, and letters of recommendation—it seemed prestigious to *him*.

She shook her head, unimpressed. "Uncle Roger sues people. This other stuff, I don't know about."

"Ma, it's a good degree—and I got lots of grants and stuff."

"So you got a degree in something useless and you're going to get a bigger degree in more useless?" his mother asked him, absolutely baffled. "Why don't you get your business degree? Then you can be like your cousin Jed! He got a degree in English and then a degree in business, and now he makes six figures."

Carl stared at her helplessly. Born in New Jersey, she had a wig of gold and brown hair, piled high, a tight-fitting shirt around her bust with a fitted jacket over it in leopard skin print, and matching tight pants. A lifelong smoker, she had lines in her lips that could be seen on her lipstick prints on her highball glasses. She'd moved with his father to Maine but had refused to leave the accent behind her.

Or the New Jersey.

"Because I don't *want* a degree in business," he said helplessly.

"Well you need to get a degree in something that pays the rent," she said, pulling hard on her cigarette. He really hated that she smoked, but like so much about his mother, it was something he'd been powerless against. "I'm moving to Florida, Carl—it's not like you can stay here."

"But I *don't* stay here," he argued. "I live in off-campus student housing!"

"I don't give a shit, Carl. You need to do something I can tell your Aunt Bessie about, because this, 'My son's gonna die a student' bullshit is not gonna cut it. Do you want me to commit murder in Florida, Carl? Do you want me to? Because I'll kill that bitch, not to watch her bleed, but to please you, because you wouldn't get a goddamned job to make your mother happy!"

"You're not gonna kill Aunt Bessie!" he told her.

"Well you're gonna kill me," his mother retorted. They were sitting in the kitchen of the house he'd grown up in, and the yellow tile on the floors may have been cracked and the laminate on the table may have been peeling, but his mother, it seemed, was still as relentless as she'd been when he was a little kid. ("You got into a fight? Are you trying to kill me? Is this any way to repay me for cooking your dinner and buying your clothes?" Oh, he remembered it well.)

"I'm not gonna kill you, Ma," he said, trying to calm her down.

"Well if you don't get a real job for *me*, could you do it for your sainted father who's dead, God rest his soul? He wanted you to have a life, Carl—he wanted you to *live*!"

Augh! There was no arguing with that, because who *knew* what his father had wanted him to have? His father had been a quiet guy who managed a shoe store until it went out of business, and then managed a Wal-Mart until he retired, and then spent most of Carl's recollection reading his newspaper in the middle of the living room, looking up very rarely to grace Carl with an absent smile. But for a guy who had been so very, very absent as Carl had grown up, he was very very *there* when it came to throwing his weight in with whatever his mother wanted Carl to do.

In this case, it was apparently drop out of law school before he began and find a real job.

"Fine, Ma. I'll look for a job in my field," he placated her, thinking that no, the only job he could get with a BA in Art History was as a masters candidate so he could get a masters degree and then go on to get a PhD and teach—or get that law degree and be an art dealer.

Wasn't *he* surprised to see an ad posted at the student union for insurance investigators—a background in Art History needed, and a willingness to take a course in investigation and law enforcement required.

Most of those courses doubled with his law school prerequisites.

For one of the first times in his life, he realized that his mother had been right. Getting a job *was* a good idea.

Three years, one short marriage, and one law degree later…

"CARL, YOU'RE leaving for Europe again?"

Mandy Jessup, the secretary in charge of investigator assignments, smiled prettily at him over her desk. Carl had been flirting with her in a desultory fashion over the past few months and she'd returned the attention. He'd needed the ego boost.

It turned out, Serpentus Inc had been more than happy to put Carl through the rest of law school as long as he worked for them for at least five years after he graduated. Once trained in some criminal justice classes with an emphasis on international relations, he'd been their perfect weapon: the polyglottal investigator with a background in international law and a degree in Art History. He hadn't known it when he'd been going through school, but he had the credentials to be James frickin' Bond!

Sort of.

The fact was, the more he did this job, the more he wasn't sure he hadn't sold his soul to the devil at a bargain price.

Take the case he'd solved the month before, for example.

Yes, it was true—the client *had* stolen their own painting, but they'd done to *pay the insurance company* so their other paintings would be safe as well. And they'd known they were in trouble—they'd offered to sell off the painting to pay the premiums, only to be told that there was a hidden clause prohibiting breaking up any part of the collection, and to do so would be to forfeit the entire thing to the bank. They'd offered to cancel their premiums and *then* sell the collection only to be told that the collection was protected by their government as a historical find. They'd offered to abdicate the historical albatross that threatened to bankrupt their family only to be threatened with prosecution and imprisonment.

In truth, a bit of discreet thievery hadn't been a bad option.

But Carl hadn't realized that when he'd seen that the security system was such that it could only be breached from the inside, and the look on the family patriarch's face when he'd asked, kindly, if perhaps one of the grandson's might have done it had… well, it had ripped Carl's heart out.

Unfortunately, by the time he learned the entire story, the damage had been done. The claims department had been alerted by Interpol, who had been there to assist in the investigation, and the company had impounded the tiny museum, the family livelihood, and three centuries of tradition to hide in their warehouse and hoard like the unscrupulous dragon they were.

As he'd boarded the plane back to America, his Interpol liaison, a *very* young policeman by the name of Liam Craig, had told him that the patriarch, Signore Marco Bianchi, had suffered a heart attack and been rushed to the hospital, but the prognosis wasn't good.

Carl had boarded the plane feeling like the angel of death.

When he'd gotten to his small DC apartment, he'd found the divorce papers from his fleeting marriage to a girl he'd met in law school just waiting to be signed. She'd been *so* excited—two lawyers in the family! Mr.

and Mrs. Esquire! She hadn't realized that he'd signed his soul away to Serpentus, and he'd be expected to be on a plane three weeks out of the month as he put his knowledge to work.

So, given the depression that had begun to set in, flirting with Mandy had proved to be good medicine. She was cute, didn't know any of his flaws, and knew he traveled. Win/win, right?

Besides, since she knew the score, maybe it would only be flirting on the table—flirting was free and fun, and it didn't lead to signing a ream of paper and then hearing your mother tell you that your Aunt Bessie always knew you'd take the one good thing in your life and fuck it up.

"So where are you going to this time?" Mandy asked, giving him that adorable side-eye. She had dark, curly hair and big brown eyes with apple cheeks. Everything about her was adorable.

"France, I think," Carl said through a yawn. His usual nightly scotch had turned into two or three the night before. Part of him was a little worried—that had been happening a lot--but part of him was thinking at least he'd be able to sleep on the plane. "But it's a weird one. Apparently the museum suddenly had a priceless statue they'd never had before. Set up on display, no less. And since the statue had been insured by us, and then had disappeared, they're wondering what to do with it."

"Uhm… thank their lucky stars?" Mandy asked, as baffled as he was.

"You'd think. But there was also a claim of theft," Carl told her. "From a private collector. When the museum said, 'Well, it turned up, but our provenance is the last to be notarized,' the private collector stopped talking. Anyway, it's a mess and they need someone who can look at stuff and sign things, and that's me." He gave a playful wave. "The stuff-looker and thing-signer."

Mandy giggled and waved him on his way.

When he got to France, his first stop had been the private collector, who had been pouting his way through trying to make a claim. He'd filled out the paperwork—and even paid his premium—but the collector, a dour old man with no hair and a lip pulled up in a permanent sneer—could not be pinned down for a straight answer about where the piece had come from, or even who the artist was.

"So you don't have provenance?" Carl had asked finally, out of patience.

"I didn't say that!" the old man barked, in French. "Here!" Stumping on his cane, he made his way to a giant, dusty monstrosity of a desk and pulled a file from one of the drawers. "Here! Here is my provenance! See? It is signed by someone from your own company! Mr. Thomakins."

He practically threw the file at Carl who leafed through it, eyebrows raised. "It looks in order," he said weakly—and it did. Every "I" dotted, every "t" crossed, right down to the watermark his company used to document provenance.

But Carl worked in a specialized field, with relatively few players, and Carl had never seen the name Thomakins before.

Besides—it sounded like something from a Puss'n'Boots story.

"I told you—"

"Wait," Carl muttered. "Wait—it says here the piece was a twenty-inch terracotta model of a John Flaxman memorial piece—the Virgin Ascends. But you weren't keeping it anywhere heat and humidity controlled. What, were you trying to age it like a pot?" He knew that keeping terracotta pots somewhere warm and damp was a great way to get the clay to change colors and appear vintage—but who wanted to do that to an expensive piece of art?

"That Thomakins guy complained about it too," the old man sneered. "But it sat in my solarium just like it sat in my father's—I don't see the problem. He signed it, didn't he?"

Yeah, Carl thought resentfully. *Right before he stole it and took it to the museum.*

He didn't say that, though. He just smiled politely and went about getting as many details about "Thomakins" as he possibly could.

Then he looked at the set up and wondered why this man hadn't just put a "steal me" sign on his property. The pedestal looked great—marble, with a cushion of black velvet on which to display the statue. It had some mild security—motion detectors on the glass bell jar that protected the thing from dust, and standard break-in security to the man's villa in general, but other than that? A reasonably competent thief with steady hands could lift the bell jar without setting off the alarm.

And a man who had been inside to assess the security would have been in a prime position to insert a piece of tinfoil over a couple of window breakers to fool the basic system.

The only real wrinkle would have been the pressure point under the statue, but apparently their light-fingered thief had replaced the statue with a counterweight without even a hiccup.

Carl frowned, remembering that. "Can I see what they used as a counterweight?" he asked. There was almost always a clue to that—something in the soil, if it was rocks in a bag, something in the fabric itself. Even carefully eked out lead balls held secrets of origins that could lead Carl to the perpetrator—

"That?" Carl's voice squeaked. It was so undignified.

"Bastard was *laughing* at me," the old man snarled, and Carl couldn't argue.

The counterweight was terracotta as well—but obviously a more recent work, done by an immature if not juvenile hand.

"Some sort of cartoon character," the owner snapped, and Carl nodded. He didn't have nephews or nieces, but the cartoon was everywhere. Even he recognized the Squidward character from *SpongeBob Squarepants*.

"That will be very helpful," he said dryly. "May I keep it?"

"Oui."

Carl took the thing, noting it's weight, it's texture— it really had been formed from terracotta, no matter how inexpertly, and it was almost perfect in dimension.

This Thomakins or whomever, was a very clever, very *unusual* thief.

CARL'S NEXT stop was the museum in which the original statue had appeared—or *re*appeared as it were. The Musee' du Quai Branly in Paris was a creative mix of the traditional and contemporary, right down to the architecture. Half of the building was ivy-grown brick and glass, with wide curving windows, and the other half was a colorful hodge-podge of various room-sized "boxes" rising from a wooden-shingled wall. There was a small strip of gardened walk-ways on one side, but the face that lined the street was the dramatic contrast of new and old, chaotic and ordered.

Carl was more of a sucker for the Louvre, himself, but that was because he was never there on business. Quai Branly was not a small venue—but that's what made it so perfect for breaking into.

Which was where Carl's mind was *supposed* to be as he walked up the steps, only to fall in line behind two uncles—he assumed—helping a small boy up the wide steps.

They were singing together, in French.

It was the theme song to *SpongeBob Squarepants*.

Carl's heart thundered in his ears for a moment, that adrenaline fueled thrill that meant he'd just cracked a case, but he had to make himself sit on that. That was stupid—these two perfectly nice men and the little boy between them were singing a song that literally millions of children around the world knew. It would be like accusing someone of theft because they knew the theme song to *Friends*. Even people who *hated* that show knew the song. It was a supremely dumb way to make a connection.

Then they started singing it in Italian.

And English.

And Spanish.

Hopping sideways on the steps as they did so, as though this was a game they played all the time. As Carl neared the front door, the boy began speaking in a patois of all three languages, and Carl felt a secret resentment—he'd studied languages since he'd hit high school and he'd never be that good.

"Your mother will be out in a moment," the smaller of the men replied in flawless French. He was... arresting looking, with curly brown hair, vulpine features and teeth that were slightly crooked in the front. Carl thought, "European!" because Americans, it seemed, were the ones who stressed so badly about slight imperfections in the smile.

"Where would you like to go for lunch?" the taller man asked. Bold and blond, with a radiant handsomeness and perfectly straight teeth, he spoke English with an American accent.

The boy began to babble—a series of cafes bubbled out of his mouth, until the smaller man told him laughingly that they would eat at the first place that served peanut butter and jelly and the boy would like it.

"Yes, Uncle Danny, I *would* like it! Make sure the bread is crusty—and there is butter too."

The two men exchanged glances—not of worry, so much, but of planning.

"Go," the taller one told him. "Get food. I'll see what's taking so long."

"Oui," the shorter one said, and then they shared a touch—brief as it was—of hands.

And Carl rethought everything he knew about them again.

He had no excuse to linger on the steps, so he breached the door and stood for a moment, orienting himself and wondering how to speak to the head docent. As he was scanning the various corridors and displays, looking for the standard, "Offices" or something similar, he saw an exquisite woman rushing by, dressed in a pencil thin black skirt and a red sweater, with her blond hair swept up almost like Grace Kelly by design, she turned a brilliant smile over her shoulder and spoke a brilliant patter of French, thanking the docent manager for being so very, very kind.

The man in turn called out, "Mrs. Thomakins, you and your husband may return any day—we are always so pleased to meet a donor."

She cast a brilliant smile at him and, as Carl watched, blew outside to snag the taller man by the hand. Together they rushed after the other man and the boy, off to find a peanut butter and jelly sandwich in a Parisian café, and Carl turned to the docent manager in a dream.

"Did you say Thomakins?" he asked the little man with the incredibly earnest face who was swishing his handkerchief after the exquisite blond woman with something like worship.

"Oui! Their family is so very gracious—they found a lost Renoir, can you imagine that? They donated it to our museum—it will be ready for display in a matter of weeks!"

"That's, uhm, generous," Carl said, his mind racing. "I'm, uhm, Carl Soderburgh—from Serpentus?" They'd given him a cover name and he used it in Europe. He wasn't sure exactly what it did to keep him safe, but, well, company policy. "I'm here to look at your John Flaxwood statue, but you wouldn't mind if I looked at this as well?"

Both the statue and the Renoir were 100% authentic—although only the statue's right to be there was contested. Carl wasn't able to pay the client who'd contested, though—as he'd thought, nobody named "Thomakins" existed at Serpentus.

Carl was able to interest the company enough to give him some investigative leeway, where his obsession with the "Thomakins" family was allowed to take root and flourish.

Even after the trip to rehab and the sad, doomed affair with Danny Mitchell, fox-featured master thief who could sing the theme to Spongebob in four languages to occupy a little boy, he would forever be grateful to the four thieves he'd seen at Quai Branly that day.

They helped make his life extraordinary.

Award winning author AMY LANE lives in a crumbling crapmansion with a couple of teenagers, a passel of furbabies, and a bemused spouse. She has too damned much yarn, a penchant for action-adventure movies, and a need to know that somewhere in all the pain is a story of Wuv, Twu Wuv, which she continues to believe in to this day! She writes contemporary romance, paranormal romance, urban fantasy, and romantic suspense, teaches the occasional writing class, and likes to pretend her very simple life is as exciting as the lives of the people who live in her head. She'll also tell you that sacrifices, large and small, are worth the urge to write.

Website: www.greenshill.com
Blog:www.writerslane.blogspot.com
Email: amylane@greenshill.com
Facebook:www.facebook.com/amy.lane.167
Twitter: @amymaclane

A LONG CON ADVENTURE

The Mastermind

AMY LANE

"Delicious fun." — *Booklist*

A Long Con Adventure

Once upon a time in Rome, Felix Salinger got caught picking his first pocket and Danny Mitchell saved his bacon. The two of them were inseparable… until they weren't.

Twenty years after that first meeting, Danny returns to Chicago, the city he shared with Felix and their perfect, secret family, to save him again. Felix's news network—the business that broke them apart—is under fire from an unscrupulous employee pointing the finger at Felix. An official investigation could topple their house of cards. The only way to prove Felix is innocent is to pull off their biggest con yet.

But though Felix still has the gift of grift, his reunion with Danny is bittersweet. Their ten-year separation left holes in their hearts that no amount of stolen property can fill. A green crew of young thieves looks to them for guidance as they negotiate old jewels and new threats to pull off the perfect heist—but the hardest job is proving that love is the only thing of value they've ever had.

www.dreamspinnerpress.com

The Muscle

AMY LANE

A Long Con Adventure

A true protector will guard your heart before his own.

Hunter Rutledge saw one too many people die in his life as mercenary muscle to go back to the job, so he was conveniently at loose ends when Josh Salinger offered him a place in his altruistic den of thieves.

Hunter is almost content having found a home with a group of people who want justice badly enough to steal it. If only one of them didn't keep stealing his attention from the task at hand….

Superlative dancer and transcendent thief Dylan "Grace" Li lives in the moment. But when mobsters blackmail the people who gave him dance—and the means to save his own soul—Grace turns to Josh for help.

Unfortunately, working with Josh's crew means working with Hunter Rutledge, and for Grace, that's more dangerous than any heist.

Grace's childhood left him thinking he was too difficult to love—so he's better off not risking his love on anyone else. Avoiding commitment keeps him safe. But somehow Hunter's solid, grounding presence makes him feel safer. Can Grace trust that letting down his guard to a former mercenary doesn't mean he'll get shot in the heart?

www.dreamspinnerpress.com

AMY LANE

Late for Christmas

Cassidy Hancock hates being late—he's pathological about it. Until the crisp fall morning when he pauses to watch his neighbor's handsome son chase his dog down the sidewalk… and gets hit by a tree.

Mark Taylor sees the whole thing, and as a second-year medical resident, he gets Cassidy top-notch care. In spite of himself, he's fascinated by his mother's stodgy neighbor, and as he strives to help Cassidy recover from a broken leg, he begins to realize that behind Cassidy's obsession with punctuality is the story of a lonely boy who thought he had to be perfect to be loved.

Mark and his family are far from perfect—but they might be perfect for Cassidy. As the two of them get to know each other, Cassidy fantasizes about the family and happy-ever-after he never thought he'd have, and Mark starts to yearn for Cassidy's wide-eyed kindness and surprising creativity. But first they have to overcome Cassidy's fears, because there is so much more fun to be had during Christmas than just being on time.

www.dreamspinnerpress.com

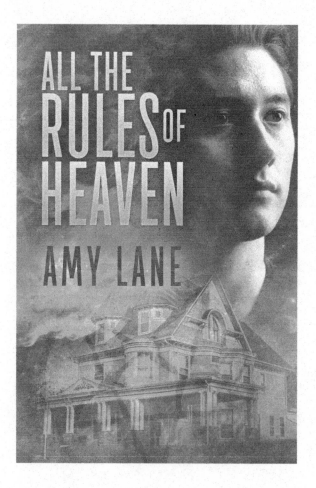

All That Heaven Will Allow: Book One

When Tucker Henderson inherits Daisy Place, he's pretty sure it's not a windfall—everything in his life has come with strings attached. He's prepared to do his bit to satisfy the supernatural forces in the old house, but he refuses to be all sweetness and light about it.

Angel was sort of hoping for sweetness and light.

Trapped at Daisy Place for over fifty years, Angel hasn't always been kind to the humans who have helped him in his duty of guiding spirits to the beyond. When Tucker shows up, Angel vows to be more accommodating, but Tucker's layers of cynicism and apparent selfishness don't make it easy.

Can Tucker work with a gender-bending, shape-shifting irritant, and can Angel retain his divine intentions when his heart proves all too human?

www.dreamspinnerpress.com

DREAMSPUN
BEYOND

Hedge Witches
Lonely Hearts
Club

Book One

SHORTBREAD
AND SHADOWS

Amy Lane

The recipe was supposed to be for
cookies—he got disaster instead.

Hedge Witches Lonely Hearts Club: Book One

When a coven of hedge witches casts a spell for their hearts' desires, the world turns upside down.

Bartholomew Baker is afraid to hope for his heart's true desire—the gregarious woodworker who sells his wares next to Bartholomew at the local craft fairs—so he writes the spell for his baking business to thrive and allow him to quit his office job. He'd rather pour his energy into emotionally gratifying pastry! But the magic won't allow him to lie, even to himself, and the spellcasting has unexpected consequences.

For two years Lachlan has been flirting with Bartholomew, but the shy baker with the beautiful gray eyes runs away whenever their conversation turns personal. He's about to give up hope… and then Bartholomew rushes into a convention in the midst of a spellcasting disaster of epic proportions.

Suddenly everybody wants a taste of Bartholomew's baked goods—and Bartholomew himself. Lachlan gladly jumps on for the ride, enduring rioting crowds and supernatural birds for a chance with Bartholomew. Can Bartholomew overcome the shyness that has kept him from giving his heart to Lachlan?

www.dreamspinnerpress.com